After The Chimes Are Silent

BERNARD BLESTEL

Publisher: Firsttime Publishing
                    Frankston, Victoria, 3199
                    Ph. 03 9789 5496, 0413 469 702
                    joancalaitzis41@dodo.com.au

Published: September 2017

A catalogue record for this book is available from The Australian
Library, Canberra and The State Library, Victoria.

ISBN   978 0 9942894 4 5

Typeset: Charmaine Calaitzis
Copy Editing: Charmaine Calaitzis
Proof Reading :   Charmaine, Bernard Blestel
Printing: BookPOD www.bookpod.com.au
Images: Courtesy of Pixabay and private collections

Dedicated to

Marjorie Darling Ward

Member of Frankston Writers Block
who is an inspiration to us all with her dedication to writing and
generosity of comment to budding writers.

Acknowledgement

Thank you to Charmaine Calaitzis for bringing the manuscript to a print-ready book.

Foreword

On many occasions the author has been asked, 'Where is Guernsey?' A surprising query in this day and age when the world is open for travel. Those who have read the history of the Second World War will understand the Channel Islands incorporate the islands of Guernsey, Jersey, Alderney and a jewel of an island, Sark. These and small adjacent Isles were the only British soil occupied by German forces from 1940 until May 1945, remaining steadfastly loyal to the British crown under duress. These Isles became part of Hitler's dream to create an Atlantic sea wall, coast lines that were absorbed as fortifications, instigated to take control of shipping seaways, a so-called wall incorporating miles of European coast. The concrete monoliths housed tools of war to impede those who came their way, built by slave workers working in terrible conditions.

After The Chimes Are Silent tells the story of Rachel Sarre's forbidden love during Guernsey's turbulent years. A chronicle to warm your heart when starving Islanders only survived after receiving much-wanted food by the ship Vega, a vessel under the auspices of the Red Cross delivering food parcels during the final year of the Occupation. If these parcels had not arrived, then many an Islander would not have seen the joy in May 1945 of the liberating forces after five long years of captivity.

After The Chimes Are Silent is a narrative of romance, humour and tears, a must-have for the book-lover's shelf and a suggested present for relatives and friends.

Part 1

Chapter 1
Sofia

Many years of dramatic change have passed since Guernsey was finally released from the Occupation of German domination, so it is fitting that a celebration will be held in thanksgiving of its being liberated. At last the air was free to those who lived and starved on *The Pearls of the Sea* as quoted by Victor Hugo who was exiled in Guernsey for seventeen years writing some of his most famous works including the unforgettable *Les Miserable's* and the lesser known work *Toilers of the Sea*, a tragic love story set in Guernsey.

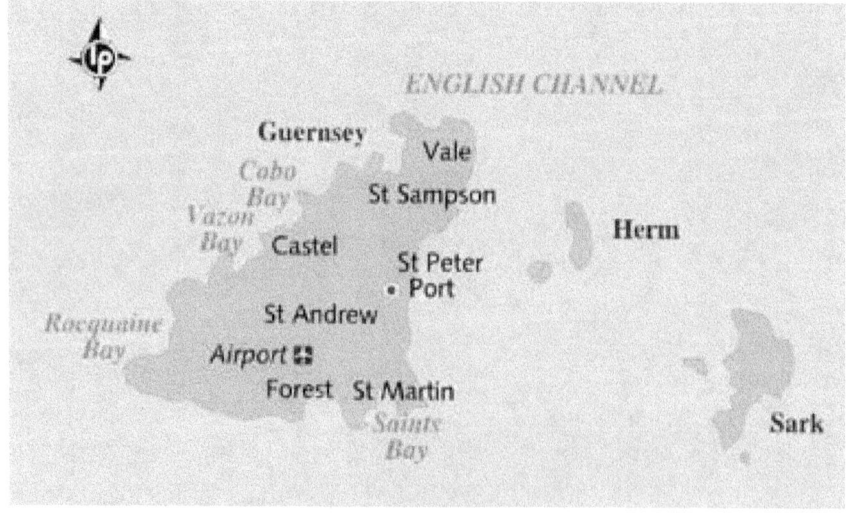

Guernsey

Today, the sun shone brightly on the faces of those who made the journey from the ten parishes to the hub of the celebrations in St Peter Port, a parish where the government of the Island decide the commerce and laws of this ancient isle. The custom in past celebrations of this kind was begun with a church service at the age-old church of St Peter, commonly known to Islanders as the Town Church, whose very roots go back a thousand years. If one's eyes took the trouble to look upwards when walking in the street to the south side of the steeple, one would see engraved on the tiles the facsimile keys of St Peter, whom we are lead to believe is the keeper of the keys of the Kingdom of Heaven.

The highlight of the day is the cavalcade, a procession of decorated floats depicting scenes from past and present. This colourful event draws the crowd from all walks life, including children who enjoy this Island holiday and a day off from school. Many would perhaps not fully understand why this date, May 9th, was so important in the history of the Channel Islands. Historians state in their wisdom in the chronicles of times past that it is essential to pass on the account of what took place during the years 1940-1945 of the Occupation by Germany and of those who lived in exile.

A youthful sixteen-year-old teenager, Sofia Tostivin, is among the crowd and is accompanied her aged grandmother Rachel Sarre. Sofia was ever eager to ask questions of her grandmother on her heritage knowledge, including the rest of the family of the Sarres and the Lihous. She was a most attractive fair-headed girl who was hopeful of entering a university in England, perhaps in Bristol or Bath, the city Jane Austin grew to love. After studying, Sofia is hopeful of becoming a teacher or a writer. She was always a romantic at heart. She was an enthusiastic follower of the classic authors. Jane Austin, the Bronte sisters, Thackeray and Charles Dickens were among a vast selection of favourites, but her hero was Victor Hugo after she read his *Compensations* and *Toilers of the Sea* three times while at university. It was her aim to incorporate a degree in languages, enabling her to travel to countries of her interest. This would happen if she passed the entrance exams. Grandmother Rachel had similar intentions at the same age, but unfortunately, war changed the course of her life, which it did to so many other lives. Sofia was at the moment enjoying her return to Island life after living overseas with father,

John Tostivin, a widower, having lost his wife in tragic circumstances -a drowning off the coast of Alderney when the boat foundered on treacherous, submerged, lethal rocks, causing death to two other people including Elizabeth Tostivin, Sofia's beloved mother. Sofia was approaching three years, not yet school age. It had been intimated the drowning of Elizabeth in such circumstances pointed a tragic finger to another chapter in the ill-fated curse of the Sarres and Lihous, a curse that had invaded these families over generations. This indelible blight stained every age group for generations till it was laid to rest.

John is Rachel's only child, truly an apple of his mother's eye. Facing the fact of grieving for the loss of Elizabeth, he made a big decision in life to leave the home of his birth La Petitt Close. John's personal history was withheld regarding his birthright; an ever-looming fear in her mind on this subject for it is based on a lie that grew in proportion. John had the option to live in Switzerland, a lifestyle made possible when in receipt of an unexpected inheritance bequeathed a few years earlier, a surprise to the recipient, but not to Rachel as she secretly knew her son's undisclosed background. Due to certain circumstances, Rachel retained her maiden name Sarre. Only in the recesses of her heart she knew the truthful reason why this well-kept secret in her life was not divulged to others.

Chapter 2
White Rock Harbour

White Rock Harbour, a port whose livelihood depended on full-time activity, saw many comings and goings of cargo ships. These carriers of trade were berthed, awaiting continual loading alongside the concrete harbour pier. In years past this port was built in a vicinity of rocks covered by nesting white seagulls, so for want of a better name the harbour became known as the White Rock. However, the harbour was extended over the years to accommodate the increasing shipping container traffic. Some Islanders found the transformation incompatible, preferring the less hustle and bustle of this well-suited sanctuary of a past era.

Yachts of all sizes were flag-decked with assorted nationalities, for this was a joyous remembrance of a truly memorable occasion for an island that is now classed as offshore for the advantage of business investment, bringing revenue to the fast-changing economic situation. Truly a joyous occasion when, at the end of the day, the harbour would be aglow with the wonder of pyrotechnics, mesmerising over-excited young, bringing tears and emotions to the old, cementing together those who had experienced the trauma of the German Occupation, now long since passed, leaving good and bad memories. These patriotic islands were the only British soil captured during the 1939-1945 Second World War

Ocean liners made the Islands a port of call during their world cruises, the liner classed as 'A giant escape to happiness in a relaxing playground!' Launches hooted and tooted as they transported tourists from ship to shore for those who wished to view the scene from shore, or shop at this port of call, an isle which is predominately English with a fervently distinctive French background. Owing to the displacement of water, the harbour does not allow such huge ships of this size an entrance to this natural harbour. However, liners berthed outside the harbour in a strip of the English Channel nautically known as The Roads, hence the launches.

Recently a memorial was erected in memory of men and women who, on that fateful day in June 1940, were killed or injured when German aircraft swooped down bombing the undefended Channel Isles. True to character, Sofia eyed the commemorative plaque on which is engraved the names of those who succumbed to a tragic oversight blunder, an unforgivable error when at the time the British government failed to inform Germany that the Islands were demilitarised. Sofia's eyes quickly caught the sight of the name Sarre, being one of her grandfather's relatives. As she read the list of those either killed or injured, sadness sparked a volley of distressing questions to which Rachel had no wish answer on this particular day.

"Please Sofia, let us enjoy our time together. Maybe at some other reasonable occasion we can talk about it when back at La Petit Close, maybe darling. Let us make it a special explanation time, a time when snuggled together roasting chestnuts by the old fire grate which your great grandfather fitted when I was a baby. Perhaps on a cold winter's night, I'll maybe recount the stories of everything you wish to know. Sometimes some things are best left unsaid or unknown in the history of the Sarres and the Lihous. Unfortunately, at this moment my poor feet have overdone the spring of youth. Sofia darling, I must rest these feet. Today has been a fun time with a glimmer of history, but when you are over ninety, ancient legs desire a rest, feet included. Let us rest for a few minutes on this very inviting seat which seems to be placed just for an old relic like myself. Have patience darling, later I'll be able to answer the story you wish to know. The Sarres have a long recounting of the past, too long to relate on this beautiful sunny day sitting on this very convenient seat near the marked bullet holes."

Chapter 3
Please, No More Questions

Rachel sat as Sofia walked up to the granite sea wall inspecting indented holes caused by stray bullets on that fateful day in June.

Rachel continued, "Those machine gunners flying low over the unsuspecting lorry drivers, aimlessly shooting at them, regrettably left evidence of their bloodied visit on these scarred walls, a memento for all to see. These were left during an exercise which shot at human targets, including poor defenseless animals awaiting shipment. Death came for man and beast as they stood waiting on that sunny afternoon in June with the sun overcast by lingering indented shadows. Dear Sofia, all this seems so long ago, please no more questions at the moment. On this day of celebration, shadows are meant to be lifted not dwelt upon. Sometimes as I often repeat, some things are best unsaid or unknown in the history of the Sarres and their relatives the Lihous. Guernsey has also had its share of tragedy, what with shipwrecks and occupation by an enemy force. Sofia darling, look at the beautiful blue sky." Words hurriedly said by Rachel to overcome any further conversation on the subject of Sarres and Lihous.

Undefeated by Rachel's reply, Sofia ignored her grandmother's remarks, saying as Grandma sat to relieve her tired feet. "Is it true that the Sarres and Lihous are cursed with awful and terrible things happening?"

Rachel said, "I've been told that long ago in the sad past, one of our ancestors hanged from the yardarm of the king's ship, accused of piracy and smuggling which included brutal murders, at the time leaving his poor wife pregnant, who was then arrested, charged, and sentenced by the law, all for stealing a loaf of bread, done in desperation to save her from near starvation. Consequently, the law with no mercy, sentenced the poor wretched person to prison to be treated cruelly. Jail was not the end of the story. In addition, this woman who had so little in life was sentenced to Australia on one of those terrible convict ships. As if this was not enough, the poor half-starved, tormented, pregnant woman, during a terrible voyage, gave birth to baby boy.

"Oh Gran," said Sofia as tears welled in her eyes.

"You now see why I wanted this story unsaid on this day, so please, that is enough. No more," demanded Rachel.

The words 'no more' went unheard in Sofia's ears but not out of disrespect. Young Sofia was always in search of facts regarding Sarres and Lihous for she was an explorer for truth. "Oh, grandma, I heard that the captain wanted to throw the baby overboard. How awful. Is that true grandma?"

Rachel replied, "He believed that the wretch was a witch, demanding in his ignorance all babies born to a witch on the journey brought bad luck to the ship and crew, therefore it had to be thrown overboard, either alive or dead.

"Oh, how horrible. What a cruel terrible man to do this, surely it is not true grandma?"

"Sofia dear, you are so young, you have yet to be emotionally touched and know the brutal deeds of this world. Sofia again, please, no more, this is supposed to be a happy afternoon not with grim tales." Rachel's words continued to be ignored as Sofia in excited mood repeated what she had gleaned earlier as Rachel attempted to quieten her. "Please, Sofia."

"Grandma, let me tell you what I know."

Rachel sighed, nodded, saying, "Darling Sofia, you are impossible."

Sofia, unflustered in her exuberance, retold what she had gathered. "In despondency, the mother wrapped up a parcel which was masquerading as the baby, threw the bundle into the ocean to be absorbed by the predators of the sea. Mercifully with the help of others, she hid the infant Jonah for the rest of the journey. I think grandma, his mother gave him that name Jonah, saying he was saved from drowning like Jonah of old who was saved from a sea death. It must have been an appalling time for the mother on that horrendous passage to Australia. Grandma, in some ways it's a beautiful but sad story, don't you think? Luckily Jonah was not swallowed by a whale or we might not be here today," said Sofia laughing. "Grandma, it was an appalling time for this mother on that long horrendous passage, just imagine how she must have felt, Oh, the poor woman, all for a loaf of bread." Tears issued from Sofia's eyes that had never seen such cruelty.

Rachel passed a lace handkerchief to her upset granddaughter saying, "No more tears darling, you will redden those lovely blue eyes!"

"Oh Gran, I can feel the rolling of the waves, flashing blinding lightning as the ship plows on, I see that frightened mother making a cot out of her stained ragged clothes, no fineries for that precious baby. Oh, that poor cold baby. Grandma, close your eyes, listen to the roar of the wind, ceaseless waves pounding, pouncing on the ship with sails damaged ripped to shreds, a crew member falls from the mast into the cold, cruel, relentless cauldron of sea. No one cares, for that is the way of things on that devil vessel. Vomiting prisoners below in rat-infested quarters, chained without dignity as the ship struggles to a non-existing Shangri-La. On and on the desolate ship travelled, its contents braving its misery." Sofia, with a stubborn will of her own, and caught up in the past, suggested for Rachel to resume the rest of the story.

"Stop it, Sofia. Both of us will have will have nightmares."

Sofia egged Rachel to continue.

With the details that Rachel had heard so many times as a child, it was easy to continue where Sofia stopped.

"Here goes, you inquisitive child, giving your grandmother a hard time," smiling as she said so. "Thankfully, or providentially, the boy Jonah survived growing to manhood, living in the inadequate conditions which prevailed. He subsequently worked relentlessly, becoming rich in that sunburnt land, a cruel country demanding backbreaking work for sustenance."

Sofia, still in a fact-finding mood said, "Grandma, my father once told me, although his knowledge of the family was limited, he said I should ask you what happened, saying you know everything."

"Sofia darling, contrary to your father's words, I still have a lot to learn. I shall continue then. Jonah slaved to save enough to undergo a marriage with lovable Bridget O'Hara, a fair Irish colleen from county Cork, who also bore the scars of Port Arthur. Eventually, they produced three girls and two sons. The youngest boy died at an early age as so many did in those days, cause unknown. Childbirth and diseases, with only meagre nourishment to fight against infection and food that was prepared in unhygienic conditions, brought about untreated sickness. All sorts of setbacks did not fare well for the poor working class. Yes, Sofia, life was certainly hard for the poor who lived with the shortage of everyday things we take for granted. I missed so many things during the Occupation, so I know how they felt. I shall not talk about it now. It was through the line of the eldest daughter of Jacob, that the Corbins became related to the Sarres and Lihous. One of his great-great-grandsons, James Corbin, decided to return to Guernsey, hopefully to track down his ancestors, the Lihous and Sarres. This is the nice part of the story.

"Oh, so exciting, tell me more Gran."

"Please Sofia, no more questions. I've already told you enough. Perhaps at some other time, I shall answer all the information you want. Let us leave the sad part until some other time. I can see you will not take any notice of your poor old grandmother but we must be on our way."

Chapter 4
James Corbin

"I think it is time for coffee at Frank Stroobant's old cafe in the Pollet, providing it is still open," said Rachel. "Frank started this life-saving café way back, during the Occupation, thus helping Islanders when the Islands suffered food shortage. He produced tasty homemade soups on meagre rations. Your great grandfather often supplied vegetables grown at La Petit Close. Frank's soup was truly a godsend to the weak and hungry. Poor Frank was caught having an illegal wireless set which was not allowed during certain times in the Occupation, found guilty, then, as a prisoner sent to Lafaune, an internment camp far away from the Island."

This suggestion of afternoon tea quelled Sofia's questions for the moment with the thought of Guernsey Gache and Jersey Wonders. In the years when Rachel was a young girl, she had similar tastes to Sofia regarding the choice of cakes, a taste that still lingered. Both viewed the engaging scene around them; for Rachel so very different from the days when Guernsey had lost its freedom. They arose from their restful seat with Sofia's mind full of yet unsaid questions, a last look at the hustle and bustle, smiling as they made their way to a café with past memories.

Rachel had no desire to travel into a past situation on this specific day of all days. Festering wounds that would never heal unless cauterised are best left untouched; burning them from her brain was just too much ache during this particular time. Perhaps Sofia would never fully understand what had happened ages ago. Deep in her heart Rachel knew the truth which, over time would be truly told. "Not yet please God," was the constant prayer in her concerned mind, having no desire for awkward questions as they walked arm in arm towards the Pollet. Over time, the street had retained its old-world French charm with granite cobble pavements under foot, its surface slowly worn by friend and foe, a street where the atmosphere of the past survived and lingered. Rachel drew a deep breath drawing in the crisp, invigorating sea breeze, eyeing the quaintness of the street around her with perception, proud of her Island heritage. Inward reflection on that day told a story, her story, which must be soon told.

She did on that day return to inner thoughts: to a cherished spell before the war, a period prior to the mists and shadows clouding, disquieting her life, which never seem to clear. Only to her at this instant, she was without hesitation back in the carefree spring of 1938. Her eyes mysteriously projected to her brain unknown people in this street enjoying the newfound yo-yo craze, in memory seeing the open-top Guernsey trams passing old St George's dance hall, now long since updated with change, at that time strutting out new songs and dances and introducing roller-skating for all to learn and tumble. Oh, carefree 1938. In her mind, she perceived all this in moments. Hollywood was at its height, producing musicals setting the tempo in romance; the rich and poor set apart in the fantasies created on the silver screen - anyone could become a Ginger Rogers or a Fred Astaire. Life was for living, the beat of the music leaving behind the tired and weary. Time for the big bands to broadcast over the newborn radio wavelengths, injecting jazz and sexual rhythms to the fore. The hunger marches and the depression lifted, art deco turned drab rooms into the mood of the masses searching for Shangri-La. An era when King Edward gave up the throne for the love of an American lover, Wallis Simpson, a divorcee seductress who seduced him from the crown of England, annexed him from his royal family along with the illustrious realm of Great Britain. A time when young and old put caution to the wind oblivious of what lay ahead, a sweeping wind, no, a storm of change in this area, blowing, raging bitterly, thus engulfing the whole deafened earth, a world that missed the forecast. All this flowed through Rachel's aged mind returning her to her youth, for a few seconds. She sighed when autumn took its place.

They approached Frank's Cafe, and she peered through the windows in memory, glancing from side to side through the

14

swirling mist of yesteryear, seeing Frank Stroobant, smiling as he served the Occupation soup, a few cheerful words on his lips, his face denoting satisfaction for those who received generous portions of steaming soup made perhaps with vegetables supplied from La Pettit Close. At a glimpse he was gone, the mist faded as tears welled, for these times are revered, causing her to close her smarting eyelids and when reopened, gone was yesterday. Frank's Cafe, with the trimmings of a past era, was replaced by clinical modernization; precious moments of humanity that have passed to another domain out of our reach till we are ourselves caught in the inexplicable change of life. Oh, the heartlessness of time!

The youthful voice of Sofia brought her to the threshold of the Stroobant café, in the knowledge that Sofia too will have her yesterdays. Rachel Sarre will, in time, obtain another domain, joining Frank and loved ones. All will experience a swirling miasma that each of us has to pass through from mortal to spiritual, each culture finding its own way to immortality.

The Pollet

Sitting in the café Stroobant, the enterprise as remembered in the Occupation had long since disappeared, replaced over the years by an updated market establishment. Modification at times hard to accept if one becomes insular to adjustment.

"Gran please tell me about James Corbin, our distant relative from Australia. Was he good-looking, because the ones I met are?

On that day James Corbin reached down from immortality for Rachel Sarre, the mist cleared and he was but a touch away, smiling as Sofia spoke.

"How old were you, did you fall in love with this tall Australian? Did you?"

"Sofia you are impossible, it was so long ago nearly seventy years. How can you expect me to remember?"

But Rachel did remember: who could not forget at sixteen-year's old, this tall, handsome fair-headed, blue-eyed Australian, recounting his adventures in a vast world beyond her furthest dreams. James had decided at the ripe old age of twenty-two years to spread his wings, visiting the birthplace of his dubious ancestors. Quoting his words to relatives on leaving Australia, the land of his birth, he said, "This will be an adventure of a lifetime finding my family roots." And so it was.

"Darling Sofia you are taking advantage of your old grandmother pushing me on, to tell you more. You may remember I said you will hear the rest later and here I am spilling the beans." Smiling, she remarked, "You young people are so full of life; you expect us to catch up with you having no patience to wait so here goes.

James's great-grandfather made a fortune in the Yackandandah goldfields, reinvested it in cattle and sheep and its by-product wool, amassing further wealth. Over time, James's father inherited the labours of his father plus the house *Golden Yackandandah*. This outstanding homestead was built on a hill which surveyed the ever-changing superlative landscape, complete with a newly-growing interesting mining township. The original owner, a moneyed merchant, had sold the house before moving to Sydney. This mansion was far removed from the terror of the new owner's humble beginnings, so now he lived to enjoy the fruits of his forebear's grueling labour. This abode was situated on the outskirts of a small town known as Yak to those around. It started life as a community settlement in the Victorian Alpine ranges, where the original owners of this sunburned country walked in The Dreamtime, their dreams shattered by man's intractable progression. I reckon Sofia this house will have many tales to tell. The property consisted of thousands of hectares of pastureland; mountains glistened in winter snow, but in summer the blazing, ruthless sun turned the green verdant grass into an astronomical burnt carpet.

"Hmm," interrupted Sofia as Rachel continued, "I shall visit *Golden Yackandandah*, of course only when I've saved some money."

"Yes my darling Sofia, but at first you must finish your studies. Then you will be able to work and save. You will find in life that things you have worked and saved for are special!"

"Please Gran, carry on."

Rachel continued. "The blue skies were devoid of cloud or promise of rain to quench the soil or revitalise the cattle who sheltered under sparse trees, scattered not by man but birds entwined with nature's scurrying wind in the ages past, who dropped seeds from their beaks in transit to their woven nests. Phantom sentinels kept watch, arms outstretched, on broken limbs devoid of greenery struck by Thor's companion. Stark, but not alone, to commune only with those who succumbed to the deadly vicious lightning flash, then gnarled, contorted in nature's cosmic playground, an unjust reward from this uncontrollable transit of energy. In doing so, turning their green mantles a smoky grey tinged with black, static as if in mourning. These trees were surrounded by jaundiced undulating meadows, a warning of nature's omnipotent power. Upon the pinnacle of these so-called honorary sentinels sits a crow, or is it a vulture? Watching, waiting for nature's clock to chime, for them an uncompromising wait. A cockatoo is in flight screeching, demanding ground space when invaded by other creatures of flight. Birds of many mixed types, seek for the diminished water and drying foliage in their act to survive in this cruel clock of nature as the sun ticks and heats to a midday high. Cuddly kolas seek eucalyptus trees and in so doing attract casual tourists wishing to cuddle them, reminders of teddy bears of childhood. These koalas climb the leafy branches for the juice that will give them succour for another season if not traumatised by man."

Sofia listened in awe. "Please continue Grandma."

Rachel drew a breath, now lost in the past. To continue she must, for here, on this day James Corbin was in her presence, for communion with loved ones are but a breath away. Smiling she replied, "Darling Sofia, of course I shall.

The telling stories of drought or bushfire in this Dorothea Mackellar sunburnt country, the farmer's dread or death, a country where only the fittest survive, and yet a country that fills men's heart with pride as witnessed with heroic deeds in Gallipoli's soldiers and nurses dying for the love of their country.

> *An open-hearted country*
> *A willful lavish land*
> *All of you who have not loved her*
> *You will not understand*
> *Though earth holds much splendour*
> *Wherever I may die*
> *I know to what brown country*
> *My homing thoughts will fly.*

Yes darling Sofia, James made his country vibrant through the effective telling of his stories. His arduous forbearers who came as piteous prisoners worked to make the country what it is today. Sofia, you are forcing me against my stubborn will to continue. Through me, the voice of James Corbin must be heard.

Wombats, the trampling hooves of wild brumby horses seeking to escape from those who will ordain them as prisoners in servitude forever, culling all those who impede the grabbing wealth of men. Dingoes, a dog-like predator of bush and plain. Venomous snakes, whose bite forecast certain death. Toxic spiders, whose lethal injection sends one to an early grave. Who are the conquerors? Man or creature, great or small, is the question? Oh, Sofia, you have put this Guernsey girl under James's Australian spell," she said as she continued. "Stories and ballads of Banjo Paterson, Henry Lawson, Dorothy McKellar whose writings and poems seduce me and lure the listener to Australia. Oh, Sofia, why did I start?

The lucky country, as portrayed by James whose ancestors suffered in Tasmania's Port Arthur, a malicious prison where human dignity was raped away and replaced only by a desire to survive, regardless of whose quality of life was taken through unjust law-givers. Yes, lucky to those whose purse swelled with coins of gold and printed notes earned by fair means or foul - for others the bitter taste of aloes upon the lips of those who failed.

Oh my precious Sofia, I, Rachel Sarre, your grandmother, living on the small Guernsey farm listened to the expanse of knowledge that James related pertaining to his beloved Australia, of its history, its beauty in flowers and trees, loving the full bloom of the beautiful wattle tree, an emblem that became a symbol of the fast growth in cultural Australia fair. Memories, of so many years past now relayed to you, my ever inquiring Sofia. Yes, I loved him as a brother, not as a lover. Yes, I loved him, not romantic as such, but a warm loving friendship as a sister to a brother, a fun time, uncomplicated. I see you are disappointed darling." Rachel noticed a look of regret on Sofia's inquiring countenance, the youngster expecting a storybook romance. "No darling, we did not go to bed and make love, our love for each other had to be of a very special quality before that happened."

Rachel's eyes looked intently at Sofia. "Yes very special," she uttered as if caught in a whirlpool of questions that might come to the surface, questions she wished drowned at this particular time.

Chapter 5
The Café

Further conversation then abruptly halted. A middle-aged waitress came for the order, not a born Islander, but one who had migrated from London with an accent that did not belie where she was born. She was pleasant enough in her service, but obviously tired, yawning as she took the order.

Rachel placed the request, for Sofia's favourite cakes, Guernsey Gache and Jersey Wonders.

Of course, it was with disappointment she received the reply, "Sorry dearie, sold out, only caraway cake left." Then the waitress went into a monologue regarding the selling wares of the café, cakes included. "I like the taste of caraways but it's the little seeds gets under my teeth, can't abide them. My mother made a lovely seed cake which I used to eat, spitting out the seeds. Can't do that now, they find a way under my falsies. My teeth dearie pointing to her mouth." She turned to Sofia saying, "You will be all right dearie. I expect you do not have falsies at your age, but mind dearie, too much sugar in fizzy drinks rots our teeth it does, so they say. My Ernie can't abide caraway seed cake it gives him you know what!"

Then in low tones almost a whisper, "The runs dearie. Rather naughty to say so because we sell a lot of Coke. Maybe I am out of a job if I say too much."

Covering her mouth with her left hand it showed a gold marriage ring underneath with a jeweled engagement ring. "My hubby, Ernie, always says your mouth will lead you into trouble Liz. I guess he may be right after twenty-three years of married bliss, and it only seems like yesterday! Sorry dearie, mother said I was born talking! You can't alter your nature can you dearie? Ernie is ever so nice really! Sort of refined but gets his moods at times when I least expect them. I am not one for moods myself but then dearie, we are all different, thank God. Sulkers I can't abide, unreliable people, you don't know what going on upstairs, if you know what I mean. My Ernie never uses a bad word. Only once did I hear the forbidden words from his lips. I forgave him; after all, he had to climb up our chimney because the so-and-so cat had kittens half way up. You never saw such a sight as Ernie, God bless him. That's when he uttered I'll kill that cat yet. I suppose it was a slip of the tongue. He's a good man, says his prayers every night when he don't forget. I suppose that why he doesn't win the lottery. Still dearie, money's not everything in life. I'd rather have Ernie to keep me warm on a chilly night than a fur coat – still, a fur coat would be nice! When he came down the chimney he just looked like a Zulu man, black as the Ace of Spades he was. Even Monty, the cat, took fright, not going near him for days, which I thought was ungrateful after Ernie rescued her. Monty was named after Montgomery whom Ernie served in the war. Very fond of the general. I don't think the general will hold it against Ernie for calling our cat Monty. I can just see Ernie now, ha ha, a Zulu man."

Sofia enjoyed the conversation, giving a chuckle as the story progressed.

Rachel was about to interrupt the conversation regarding the benefits or not of caraway seed cake when the talkative waitress got on with the business of serving.

"Now as I was saying, sorry no Jersey Wonders or Guernsey Gache. I've been run off my feet dearie; some customers get a bit rude if we are sold out. They would improve their manners if they had lived during the Occupation starving under old Hitler's boys in beautiful Guernsey. We had his bombs in dear old London town. Oh, those were the days, people more friendly; it was the war you see, you didn't know if old Adolf was going to run up your alley. Thank God you were too young to know what we all suffered."

Rachel interrupted the conversation and the benefits or not of caraway seed cake, taking the opportunity at this point of ordering two slices of it and a cup of coffee plus a malted milk for Sofia, intimating to Sofia, that James had introduced her to a chocolate-flavored malted milk, which at the time was unknown in Guernsey, however, a great favorite in Australian milk bars. "So dear Sofia, it's fitting you should have one today since you insist the conversation is around James Corbin, our dear distant cousin."

"Thank you, grandma, I feel I shall get to know him with the exciting time he had on our Island. Perhaps, you will tell all about your secret lover during the time when women were women and men were men who swept any beautiful girl off her feet. Please tell all the romantic details," asked Sofia, her eyes closed in anticipation to hear grandmother's romantic dream story.

"Sofia, please stop this nonsense, you seem to have a silly romantic notion we were lovers which we were certainly not, young lady. Girls in 1938 were not swept off their feet. Hopefully, they were sensible; marrying the man they chose and loved." Giving a little laugh she turned to Sofia saying, "I think that's what they did."

The talkative waitress placed the much-celebrated caraway cakes on the table as Sofia drew the malted milk through a multi-colored straw.

Sofia received a little pat on the back of her hand as Rachel asked, "What do you think of the malted milk?"

"Hmm, I love the malty flavour. With every sip I am going to hear about the wide open spaces of Australia." She was in a dreamy, closed-eye state replying, "Of its lofty snow-capped mountains, the deep blue oceans sending lacy white waves upon the golden sands and pebbled beaches as if in perpetual motion." These enlivening thoughts caused Sofia to open wide her blue eyes, turning to Rachel in excitement, hesitating. James Corbin, your wonderful boyfriend!"

"Sofia, you are making something out of something that is not true. Yes, I loved him as a dear friend or brother. I loved him because on this tiny Island he introduced me to a new vast world, to places I would never visit. We had fun in the meadows. He plaited daisies and buttercups to make me a crown to wear as if I were a May queen. I never had such attention, bringing joy and fun to a Guernsey farm girl who had never been out of the Channel Islands. Yes Sofia, he had the gift to make love in conversation after which I then received his love in the warmth of his words. You see darling, I learned over the years you do not have to go to bed to find fulfilment, you can find it in a marriage of troth of mind. A solemn pledge of friendship that would not be divorced or broken thus giving you fulfilment. Do you understand my darling? Please Sofia, no more," she said as she fought unseen tears.

"Oh, that was beautiful grandma." She noticed tears wetting her aged grandmother's striking face. "Why are you crying, he gave you happiness?"

"Yes, but he also brought me sadness. You will see my dear darling, happiness comes at a price."

"James stayed at the farm for over six months, and then travelled back to Australia after visiting Europe, but not before making me promise to visit his wonderful land. Yes, I would go, but unfortunately, I never did because the war was declared a year or so later. He did as so many young men, joined the Air Force. Both our worlds then changed. On a mission over Germany near the end of the war, this handsome fun-loving Australian relative was blown to bits, his disintegrated body never recovered from the watery grave. His only memorial was in his family's heart. In that same war, my life also altered never to recover as such."

The malted milk so loved by James was accidently knocked over by Sofia, spilling onto the fresh white tablecloth as she was trying to comfort grandmother's distress. Sofia's love for theatrics declared to ease the situation. "These are James's tears upon the cloth, a sure sign he was listening from the wide open spaces."

Rachel smiled, her hand reached out to touch Sofia's soft blond hair, thinking how beautiful and un-spoilt this young teenager looked; noticing a close resemblance to one that was ever with her, a love secretly within her mind and body.

Sofia uttered an apology for the upsetting conversation, which she had inflicted in her exuberance to her beloved Gran.

"Darling, it's not your fault; I am a silly old woman. It was also so long ago. Memories can bring happiness as well as tears! Come, finish your malted milk, James wouldn't want it wasted and we must get back.

"Oh Gran, I am so sorry I made you cry, it was selfish asking so many questions, but I did so want to hear part of our history, and the Corbins are part of the Sarre family. I know so little of our past."

"Now please Sofia drink up, we must get back to the farm. Holidays are okay, but farm work has to go on, rain or shine, holidays are no exception. I must be there to help if needed; these old hands can still milk a cow when called upon. Electric milking machines may go on strike, then your old Gran will have to sit on the old stool as she did when I first met........" She ceased the conversation in fear she would disclose her secret

"Yes, Gran, who did you meet? Was it your boyfriend?" asked Sofia excitedly.

"No more Sofia, one day when we are by the warm winter fire at La Petit Close, then it will be as the magician said - all will be revealed!"

Sofia insisted on paying, thanking the caraway cake serving lady. Both visitors departed to their home in the Forest parish after which Sofia exclaimed to grandma, "This is the most exciting day of my life."

Rachel smiled, her inner thoughts returned to past celebrations of today, then reflected on a time all those years ago during the troubled days of Occupation when a youthful Island girl met a young handsome man from overseas, not from the land of wide open spaces, but a man who influenced the rest of her life. Perhaps maybe, like Sofia, in his thoughts he declared, "This is the most important day of my life."

Chapter 6
Poor Edie

As far as Rachel was concerned it was one of those days when the generation gap was firmly bridged; each understood another's differences, agreeing that the young and old, though poles apart at times, had something useful to offer providing they respected each other's point of view.

They enjoyed a delicious meal prepared by Rachel's spinster cousin, who regrettably was somewhat intellectually backwards, but gifted in the running of the La Petit Close household creating a spotless domain. Not a speck of dust escaped the weld of her duster and according to Sofia, "Edie is a cook fit for the Queen of England in Buckingham's Place's kitchen."

Edith came to be known as Poor Edie due to a transformation in her personality which occurred when, as a child, she claimed she witnessed a ghost near the entrance of the smuggler's tunnel at La Gree. Those familiar with this passageway that leads to the beach, knew that in the past it had a claim to evil deeds. This poor demented child was never quite the same again. Schoolwork was certainly an impossibility. Brain damage stayed with her for the rest of her life. Strangely, housework and cooking came as second nature to Poor Edie who would never venture to divulge what she had actually witnessed at the threshold of the tunnel. The elders of the family who knew the strangeness of Poor Edie insisted it was the curse of the Sarres and Lihous, a curse that had caused mischief and sorrow over time. Others jested saying, "The child had bad blood in her veins due to intermarriage, or worst still incest!" Poor Edie was to be branded forever with such unkind remarks from insensitive people.

No sooner had this ill-fated woman cleared away the dishes, tidied and brushed the crumbs from the table surveying if these duties were to her liking, she made post-haste to the kitchen to complete the tasks that lay in the kitchen sink.

Sofia, yet again, could not refrain asking in a whispered voice, "Do you know what Edie saw at La Gree? The poor soul must have seen something horrible and terrible."

Rachel replied, saying to an ever-inquisitive granddaughter, "No more questions," impressing on her never to mention this subject in front of Edie. The very thought sends her to bed distraught and weeping, requiring patience on our part to calm her. The only thing I will say, I felt a presence when I ventured into the dark, uninviting, damp, cold tunnel. A deep foreboding, as if something mysterious and tragic was about to happen, a cold shiver invaded my body as I rushed breathlessly from that claustrophobic place. I later bucked up courage, daring to return into that uninviting space where evil lurked from the past. Sofia darling, one thing I experienced after my adventure was the knowledge that the ghosts of long ago live in that tunnel at La Gree. I have seen them as I walked along the passageway."

As far as Sofia was concerned this was going to be a thrilling first-hand information session; in no way was she going to let her grandmother off the hook. "Oh, you have seen a ghost! Oh, exciting. Please put me in the picture and tell me all, I cannot wait. You've seen a ghost, tell me please!"

"Sorry darling, I am afraid you will have to wait. No more for this evening we have both had a busy day. Do not forget my age; tiredness is suggesting we both go to bed. I promise to tell you on another night then you will quake with fear hearing of the ghosts that lay in wait in La Gree, but not tonight. Goodnight, my sweetest darling. May God's blessing rest upon you. Thanks for a lovely day," she said placing a gentle kiss on her cheek. Turning as she departed towards Sofia, she could not shut her eyes to a family resemblance of one that was ever with her, whom she had loved and still loved though he was long ago. That love lay buried in her silent voice but was still alive within her heart. Tears came to her eyes, eyes that had witnessed good and bad times, sad and happy times in this house La Petit Close, a sanctuary within its walls.

Speaking as she left, "To live in the past, youth has to accept what the future holds, the past affects the present and it holds the key to unlocking the potential." With these words, she closed the ornate glass panel doors upon which was painted two coloured peacocks. Peacocks were supposedly unlucky. She glanced at the ornate birds, stopped, wondering at the reason behind the saying that they bring unhappiness. When the war was on did they bring sadness to La Petit Close or is it just superstitious nonsense?

Sofia pondered the words her grandmother had spoken as she closed the door. "Youth has to accept what the future holds."

Chapter 7
Thoughts in the Night

Rachel mounted the stairs leading to the landing on which her bedroom was situated. Turning the highly-polished door handle, which efficient Poor Edie always kept shining, she noticed Poor Edie had switched on the bed light, giving the room a warm glow that suited Rachel tired eyes. Poor Edie, also with love for her kind mistress, had taken the trouble to heat the bed, for although it was the month of May there was still a chill in the air during eventide. Earlier, when adjusting the comforts of the room, Poor Edie mumbled as she outstretched her arm under a bed of plain Victorian design to locate an almost in assessable switch, "Why don't she get the bloody thing moved?" Yes, Poor Edie knew how to use the vernacular and more when required. During her unsighted search, she grazed her hand on the chipped, flowered, china chamber pot. This private concealed receptacle was unused for many years and simply left snuggly under the bed since Rachel's childhood. It now obtained the state of an heirloom, first used in the days of the French Revolution - or so they say! Receiving what Robespierre had to offer?

Rachel mused at the kindness shown by Poor Edie.

Poor Edie decided, while still in grief after the untimely death of her consumptive mother, to devote her life to the Sarres and Lihous, she was unwed and remained so, but like in a state of marriage in service to others. Surely a kindly soul, gifted with a will of her own which, many say, perhaps unkindly, she is difficult! Domestic duties had to be strictly accepted her way; this pronouncement was usually accepted, for to upset Poor Edie led to a flowing of tears.

Through the half-drawn curtains, the stars of the universe twinkled with the silvery moon casting its light over the now emergent meadow. This quiet serenity reminded her of Debussy's Clair du Laune music she had played many times on the second-hand upright piano her father had purchased at Fuzzey's, a well-known shop in the High Street many years ago which seemed like only yesterday. Oh, there had been so many yesterdays, when, as a young girl, she started lessons with one of the Islands finest music teachers, Muriel Luckie, who also at times gave recitals with another Islander, Dominic Santangelo, a renowned master teacher of the violin. These special concerts were given in the glass-roofed auditorium in Candie gardens, now long since gone to make room for the Guernsey Museum. Her trip from home in the parish of the Forest was undertaken on summer evenings in the family's second-hand Citron car. Rachel loved hearing classical masterpiece and from an early age attended ballet classes at the Connie Cumber School, and after Miss Cumber retired transferred to the newly-formed Dorothy Hurrell School of Dancing. Oh, what fun days.

Looking up at the twinkling sky, taking in the wonder of the stars she began humming a carol that had a special place in her childhood memories, way back when she first started Sunday school. 'Away in a manger.....' As the words came into her reflective mind she began humming the tune, 'the stars in the bright sky looked down where he lay........' Tears welled because of its beauty, and then thoughts of yesteryear brought emotional feelings for long-departed Hans. Yes, those same stars are shining where he lay; at this very second sharing its beauty together as one. Suddenly she knew she must put the lie that changed the essence of her life to rest: the family deserved to know the truth whatever the consequences. The moments of negative reflection of her life would become positive if she returned to the legitimacy of her journey at La Petit Close. Drawing open the half-drawn curtains letting nature's light consume the room as the shadows diminished; she knew what path to travel to rid herself of the so-called curse of the Lihous and Sarres. The story will tell exactly as it happened. I shall not spare myself.

As she lay there in the comfort of a warm bed she watched the stars twinkling reminding her of dear Sofia, whose blue eyes twinkled at times in the joy of living. Dear, un-spoilt, Sofia, you're such a comfort. Yes, Sofia shall be the one I choose to write to, telling my story in truth so she will perhaps understand why I withheld the reality of my life. I shall ask Sofia saying, "Will you travel back in time reliving the exciting years of when I was young, a time of sadness and joy. In those days I was, and still am, unbelievably quite naive of life, as most youngsters were on the tiny Island of Guernsey, not like you young people of today who have seen so many horizons in the world. Oh, how I envy you in many ways, forfeiting tradition, slipping on a knapsack then up and away to find adventure across the sea, in some cases only returning for holidays, perhaps still calling Guernsey home even though living far away. Sofia darling, I am going to ask a special request. If you don't wish to do what I ask, I shall understand.

With these, thoughts Rachel drifted into sleep.

'…..And the bright stars looked down where they lay.'

Rachel awoke as the morning sun shone gently into the bedroom, the blinds still left opened wide, due to the excitement of the previous day. Sleep had overcome her swiftly, but not before the decision to ask Sofia to write her life narrative. In doing so she completely forgot to close the new floral curtains to lock out the twinkling stars. Laying in the comfort of her bed with her thoughts engrossed on the day ahead, her eyes focused to the crystal vase given as a wedding gift by her intended bridesmaid Mollie Gaudion; dear Mollie long since gone. Poor Mollie never got to be a bridesmaid. That is the trouble with old age; you sometimes outlive most of your friends and relatives!

The sun's rays cast their light, filtering through the silver birch tree planted by her father when a young man. The gentle morning breeze caused rainbow imprints via the cut crystal vase to materialise on the cream-coloured walls. Over the years, Rachel had watched this apparition of dancing colours, naming them her spiritual fairies. For each time as she lay the fairies appeared, the vibrant colors reminding her of aspects of her life. Those animated hues are impalpable worlds suggesting good times as well as the unhappy periods. Such is her imagination. Oh, how she waited for the dancing fairies, for some days the sun of life never showed; the fairies slept, at these times causing Rachel to feel the negative side of life knowing its sadness. However, today the colours glowed telling her what she had to do - get out of bed early - the freshness of the dawn convincing her that her decision was right. This will be the time to approach Sofia, regarding writing the long overdue truth memories. Rachel knew that Sofia should be capable of such a task, yet Sofia may feel, on hearing her grandmother's personal issues, embarrassed by the truth.

These notions went through Rachel's over-active and excited mind in the early hours of the dawn. Before embarking on such a task, she herself will be subjected to a lingering search of the taunting scar left within her soul, irritating her unsettled mind. Naturally, this will bring to the surface execrating pain, loathsome with the passage of time. Releasing this hurt restricted all aspects of her daily living and submitting herself to, as they say in the movies, 'the third degree.' Whatever it takes, the defamation of old must be laid to rest, oblivious of all painful costs; this undertaking cannot be postponed.

Rachel waited for beloved Sofia's appearance to the well-laid breakfast table, which only Poor Edie could achieve to personal satisfaction. Set on the round, highly-polished, inlaid walnut table exquisitely crafted over a long time, constructed from the wood of an aged tree grown and matured on this homestead of her ancestors, La Petit Close. Entering the dining room, one cannot but notice this family heirloom, lovingly set for the serving of food, complete with a snow-white, starched, damask tablecloth, upon which rests matched napkins inserted in a silver serviette ring, the cutlery laid in correct positions pending each course. In addition, there is a silver gleaming cruet holding the usual condiments, which if desired add flavour to the cuisine. The cruet, by hearsay conveyed through the ancestral grapevine, has a disreputable but interesting history, its origins talked of in subdued whispers. This much-discussed cruet accompanied the white china, gold-rimmed breakfast set, as well as a cut-glass water jug filled with freshly-squeezed orange juice.

Yes. Poor Edie is a perfectionist in her service to the Sarres, a service poor Edie holds dearly and extends to their relatives, the esteemed Lihous, when occasional help is required at beloved La Gree. However, to Poor Edie, La Petit Close is her domain with Rachel her mistress, so be it. If others think otherwise they will have to think again!

Rachel's thoughts turn to Sofia, inwardly suggesting that when she asked her granddaughter to take on such a task, she herself must have a delicate approach, not forcing the topic. Sofia must feel confident inwardly and trusting to do justice to the sensitive undertaking revealing sensitive secrets, probably with tearful emotions, for this is not a usual narrative. Varied thoughts and questions invade Rachel's mind only banished with Sofia's appearance.

"Good morning, grandma," she says as she placed an affectionate kiss on grandma's cheek. Grandma Rachel is a very special person in Sofia's eyes. "Sorry, I over slept. Yesterday was such an exciting celebration, not forgetting the highlight, hearing of the far-off shores of Australia. And dare I say it, James Corbin, your boyfriend."

Sofia's conversation came to a halt when Rachel interrupted her granddaughter, ignoring the mention of James Corbin. "Sofia, please, I have something to ask of you. If you do not think it appropriate you may wish to refuse."

"Oh Grandma, I would never refuse you anything you asked."

"Well darling, you may when you hear. I shall put aside all my forethoughts going straight to the point; no use delaying the agony. I wish you to write my life story with all my precious memories. The love and sadness, joy, and dare I say it, the dark phase that lingered through my life. Yes, Sofia, dark selfish times when I only considered myself. I was fearsome of the future. I suppressed the truth at the expense of others, sadly not willing to pay the price for my sin; I took a lie as my companion. This story will be my nemesis, a retribution and punishment for all that happened at La Petit Close and La Gree. So dear Sofia, this will be a mammoth task if you accept. One chapter I fear may disgust you!"

"Oh Grandma, have no fears, we live in the liberal age. We must start at once. How exciting, a thrilling tale of love and adventure."

"Darling, are you sure? I am surprised at your acceptance so quickly."

"Oh, Grandma, a big thank you. Do you think I am capable?"

"Sofia dear, I will not be hurt if you have second thoughts. Darling, you are the only person I trust to do it. Others will, or may not understand why I chose the road I travelled. You will see when you glean the details of my extraordinary life. I am so glad if you accept, thus giving you an opportunity to learn the family history, perhaps accepting or rejecting the chronicle of the so-called curse of the Sarres and Lihous, intertwined as one with the secrets of my heart. Sofia, there is only one condition, what you write must be the truth and at times the truth can hurt, not only to oneself but also to others! This risk I will have to take."

"Yes, nothing but the truth," answered Sofia with a mischievous glint in her eyes, noticing tears trickling down the lines on Rachel's characteristic face. Over the years her face had kept a shaded beauty not blemished by the inward secret she concealed. "With a little romance, eh grandma!"

"Sofia please, James from Australia was not my lover."

Sofia laughed. "Remember grandma, nothing but the truth.

Through the half-opened French window, the soft morning breeze entered the room, cheerfully warmed by the rising sunbeams, its warmth bringing the fragrance of the white perfumed rose. A special rose, so loving planted by Eunice, her mother, on her wedding day long ago, to be cosseted in the rich soil at the break of dawn, to Eunice a symbol of a new life ahead. Rachel remembered the beautiful words her mother often remarked over the years when these flowers were in bloom. "May God grant happiness to all who smell their fragrance, let its fragrance be a balm when the thorns of life pierce our heart."

Rachel took hold of Sofia's delicate hands, placed a gentle kiss on her cheek, recalling her mother's words regarding the fragrance of the rose as she drew Sofia closer. "May those hands bring you happiness with love in all you will undertake. God gave us hands to work lovingly and to heal; use them wisely. Darling Sofia, I know on this very day, through you, my story shall be borne by a pen held in these very hands.

Chapter 8
All will be Revealed

The weeks and months that followed were full of writing for Sofia, questioning Rachel with the details of her long life, which features turned out to be a consuming and interesting time for young Sofia. Luckily, over the years, Rachel had kept a semblance of a diary, which up to now remained a reserved secret from preying eyes.

Nowadays, the young are not as easily shocked in what they see and hear. Sofia took it all in her stride, typing away on an old Remington typewriter resurrected from the local charity shop. Tears often clouded her beautiful blue eyes as she realised what mendacity grandmother had lived through. With Sofia's natural perception and positive thinking, she understood why Rachel chose the path she trod. Sofia typed, reflecting she was certainly never subjected to the rigours of five years of war or the temptations which had waylaid her grandmother during the Nazi Occupation. Sofia's upbringing, in some ways, had sheltered her in this fast-changing planet. Sadly, it was now a world where principles are set aside and integrity and veracity of biblical teaching made redundant. Thankfully, the laws of the Good Book were never relinquished at La Petit Close or La Gree. After her mother died, her father in Switzerland gave Sofia stability in her formative years. Sofia, never critical of others misdeeds, frequently remembered one expression her great-grandma repeated after hearing or seeing the downfall of others, 'By the grace of God so go I.'

Rachel, though keen to see the progress of what she called the cleansing of her soul, left Sofia to work on the commission without too many interruptions or interference, interested to see how the story developed through the eyes of another person without being biased. Sofia, a vibrant, related teenager, should have an unbiased interpretation of the very complex life set down in rough drafts by Rachel.

One particular episode the young romantic, Sofia, wished to explore, the visit of James Corbin, the far-removed cousin from the distant shores of Australia. To date, she had not yet seen any specific draft from grandma. In anticipation, together with much disappointment, she awaited the sequence of events for him to make an appearance on her Edwardian-style polished desk, a domain kept shining through the undaunted efforts of Poor Edie. This endeavour added frustration to young Sofia when, after the faithful servant religiously straightened the notes muttering, "Can't abide untidiness."

Sofia, with her head-in-the-clouds imagination, felt this was a passionate love story deserving narrative to the fore. Oh, romantic youth. In the meantime, the adventurous Sofia firmly cast a travel log in her mind's eye, with a zeal to visit the soil where the Guernsey family roots are permanently grafted to those ancestors of James Corbin, all united in the land of wide open spaces - Australia the brave. She realised this adventure would only happen after her exams for acceptance to a university, together with the workload of grandma's book finished and subsequently located on bookshop shelves, for in starry-eyed Sofia's mind this was a best seller. Only after these achievements, would she purchase a ticket to board a Qantas plane in London fulfilling a romantic notion in old London town for visiting Yackandandah in Australia, hopefully discovering long-lost relatives with Sarre and Lihou connections. Needless to say, this idea was much to Rachel's amusement, for intuition told her why her granddaughter decided to go hunting a romance that Sofia imagined had taken place.

Before this idea came to a realisation, numerous bridges needed to be confronted, overcome and crossed. Months of typing and re-writing passed, with changes suggested by Rachel, when those inevitable bridges were finally surmounted, producing what was, Sofia suggested, an epic of caring and love. Eventually a successful book launch took place in the colorful grounds of La Petit Close, decorated with nature's spring flowers blossoming in the well-kept, landscaped garden of delight which Rachel named

Eunice's paradise, remembering it was her mother who first planted the seeds, starting what it is today a sweet bower of diverse flowers in due season surrounding the house and home. This venue throughout past ages dwelt in happiness and love, followed by inevitable sadness, morally distasteful and sorrowful in all aspects. Life sometimes has a habit of changing with the blink of an eye. La Petit Close, a locality where Rachel Sarre cleansed her troubled soul, putting to rest a deception of untruths, which had transpired at two places her beloved La Petit Close and La Gree.

La Petit Close, a spot on the Isle of Guernsey, causing you, the reader, to take interest and time, to travel on an astral journey, in the spirit of an open mind, feeling the mesmeric Island magic of these two somewhat intriguing houses, La Petit Close and La Gree. For they exist for all to enter within, captivating, and then seducing you to cross the threshold, gaining an inexplicable insight of those past and present who dwelled and lived within that granite preservation. Perhaps at exodus, you an excited voyager, will discover a verdict, announcing what you gleaned either in truth or fiction; whether Rachel Sarre justified a lie covering a loving, forbidden relationship, or to accept the consequence of guilt for associating with a foe. Then, paying the penalty, when after the chimes of happiness are silent, in a situation while two souls were then caught up, strangled, choked in self-reproach throughout a war not of their making or choosing. Conflicts do turn everyday folk, from vastly different lands and cultures into enemies. Great wars fought to suppress greed and tyranny. Wars where no one is a direct winner. Materialism with domination still lives. Will man ever learn? We cannot change the past, those who refuse to take into account the past, are condemned to repetition, whatever colour, race, creed or culture they belong to. Each one must find an answer, starting with the universal keystone, love.

Here before you is Rachel Sarre's story set in an Island engulfed in war.

For without love everything withers and dies. Let us connectively win the real peace that passes all understanding, initially within ourselves, for it is only then we can be of use to others.

Part 2

Chapter 9
War Breaks Out

Life in the Channel Isles prior to 1940 was a haven for holidaymakers. In 1940 Sir Kingsley Wood had the honour of declaring the newly-built Guernsey airport open. This venue would bring tourists who otherwise ventured on a Channel sea-crossing with the risk of mal de mere if Neptune decided to stir the waves. The English Channel can prove a rough journey.

Adjacent to the airport is the hotel Happy Landings, a structure built with a flavour suggesting art deco, a style that took hold in the 1920s-1930s. For those who took the flight from England, this hotel provided near at hand accommodation. It also served the parishioners of the Forest, to sup a local beer or cider while puffing a cigarette, fortunately now banned in public places.

The Forest was one of ten parishes making up the Island. This bailiwick was presided over by the Bailiff of the time, Victor Carey. The other nine consisted of St Peter Port, St Martin's, St Andrews, St Sampson's, St Saviors, The Vale, Torteval, Castel, and St Peters in the Wood. Needless to say, the folk of the Forest were certainly not in favour of having land commandeered for the new airport; many forecasted how the famous Guernsey-bred cows would react in nearby meadows due to the comings and goings of aircraft. Many predicted the milk yield would be affected, or the cream would turn sour.

War was declared on September 3rd 1939.

In 1940 a different type of plane would be touching down, so what caused the good folk of the Forest distress in '39 would be minute compared to the future advents in June and July 1940 when the tranquility of the Channel Isle was banished for five long years,

To those given to superstition, Friday 13th is considered unlucky, and in this case, on a pleasant summer's evening, Friday,

June 28, 1940, evil rained from the clear blue skies on an Island declared an open town. Unfortunately, this declaration did not reach the Nazi rulers in Berlin, owing to the blundering of the British government.

Lined up at St Peter Port harbour, alongside the jetty were parked lorries laden with boxes of tomatoes awaiting shipping to England. Trading at this time was extremely unsettled.

The earlier rush of people to exit from the Island to the safety of England had quelled. Out of 43,000 population, 19,000 sought refuge in different parts of Britain, including Yorkshire, Lancashire and even Scotland. Included in this total were 5,000 children, some of which went en-block with their school and later billeted out in private homes, This was an agonising, soul-searching period for parents. Should they let their children go or risk the consequences of staying? Seeing French refugees arriving at the Island did not help matters. To go or stay? For those who made the exodus from the sunny Isle, the journey to Weymouth was long and arduous. For those seeking refuge in England, they had to wait twenty-four hours for permission to land at the port, due to the congestion caused by ships bringing refugees from Bordeaux, France and other areas.

European battlefields would soon be aggressively dominated by a dangerous psycho, mad, conqueror, which reduced life to cinders. A scorched earth policy. To make matters worse, what little food there was on board or in their possession, dwindled to non-existence. Hunger for those who risked the dangerous sea crossing from the Isles.

This was certainly not a happy period. Abandoning their homes and livelihoods through no fault of their own, uncertain what the future held, perhaps at any given moment-machine-gunned or blown sky-high by unseen mines.

Another worry for many having to survive with little clothing in the suitcase, together with modest or no money, starting a new life in an unknown destination, not knowing if the English people would welcome them as many Englishmen had not heard of the Islands. Cold and hungry, this unpromising time in their lives needed courage and perseverance to survive. This sad part of history will certainly will be remembered, in the glorious chronicle of the Channel Isles in years to come.

With the departure of Lieutenant Governor Major General Minshall Ford on 21st June, the seventy- year-old Bailiff, Victor Carey, was sworn in as the Lieutenant Governor of the Island and on the same day the States of Deliberation, (the government of the Island) swore in a new Controlling Committee. This Committee was given the power to make swift decisions in the event of occupation. Attorney General Major Ambrose Sherwill was elected President.

The exile of Islanders brought problems., With the abandonment of farm stock, animals proved a worry having to be re-directed to existing farms; 2000 cats or dogs had to be dejectedly euthanised - busy times for the vets. Unlocked business premises and houses left by owners were made secure for fear of looting. The remains of a last meal left on the table or in a saucepan in unoccupied houses, required clearing. Such was the rush of householders to get away. Distant gunfire and smoke-laden air hurried their departure; this was no time to be house-proud. Canned and non-perishable foods were put in storage, awaiting collection by owners on their unlikely return to the Island.

Chapter 10
Bombardment

On the brighter side, in London, the Channel Islands Refugees Committee raised £25,000 to help those in need. In due course the Stockport & District Channel Islands Society maintained a link between the refugees, enabling a way to trace friends and loved ones and published the Channel Islands Monthly Review.

School children were billeted in foster homes. Brothers and sisters were at times separated due to homes unable to take more than one child. The Islands had their problems, so did those who had escaped. Their heartache reigned for five years. Guernsey started sending tomatoes to the mainland again during a lull in the war.

Life gradually returned to some sort of normal living. Those on the Islands never suspected the full impact that was to follow. Fishing boats with refugees from France were still arriving at the White Rock harbour, some of those poor souls injured but still venturing the hazards of the Channel to seek help with food and medication. The injured needed hospitalisation, many relating the horrors they had escaped from due to the advancement of the German army to the coast of Brittany and Normandy. At this point in time, the Islands were in turmoil. All were dazed, by the situation, though the union jack was still fluttering over Castle Cornet. Islanders in their hearts still singing with sincere gusto and courage sang, *There always is an England, God save the King*. For how long depended on when the jackboot trod the cobblestones of this independent Isle.

There is one song the Germans will never silence, *Sarnia Cherie*, the words and music which had unintentionally been written, became Guernsey's National Anthem, a love song to the beauty of the Island.

Sarnia dear homeland gem of the sea

Lorry drivers relaxed with cigarette in hand waiting to load tomatoes on a cargo ship,

"No cause for alarm, those bloody Germans won't land here; the Island's too small and unimportant. The British Tommie's fighting spirit and determination kept them at bay during the 1914 - 18 conflict. The armed forces of today will rise to the occasion, No, they won't land here."

These fatal words uttered on the lips of the drivers relaxing on a calm summer's evening in June.

One of the drivers called to his mate, "What's the time? Left the bloody watch at home. With my missus and the kids going off to England the house is a bloody mess. The old girl is certainly missed bless her heart. Can't find a thing. Still, with a bit of luck, she'll be back soon. I told her to keep her pussy warm, the war will not last long, and those Tommie's and our Guernsey boys together will soon have old Adolf on the run."

Bombed town

No sooner, the driver's words had left his lips, suddenly out of nowhere there came the spatter rat-tat-tats of machine guns riddling walls and lorries, bullets aimlessly focused to kill or maim, followed by the screeching of falling bombs thus creating havoc.

Crates of tomatoes scattered unevenly on the boardwalk, the hideous lethal exploding German bombs producing mayhem previously unexpected on this peaceful terrain. Mashed tomato pulp was mingling with red human blood, initiating a macabre flowing rivulet, all united with ruptured veins, the flesh of horses and cows, ill-fated creatures innocently waiting to be shipped to a place of safety. All this deplorable horror over in a few minutes, terminated as quickly as it started, claiming the lives of twenty-nine people killed in Guernsey on that pleasant summer's evening.

Bombed lorries

Regrettably, the ticking of the lorry-driver's forgotten watch will never reach his ears; the missing watch will remain where he left it, resting ticking, still unwound lying on the bedside table in the safety of his home. Regrettably for him, never again to hear the laughter of his children, or feel the warmth of his wife, instead, eternal silence. A terrible needless episode earned a place in history. Apart from the dead, it left many serious wounded casualties on indifferent roadsides. A sorrowful unanticipated incident, its bloodshed left a bad taste towards the British government allowing such a thing to happen.

Among those machine-gunned was Harold Hobbs, a valued crewmember of the Guernsey lifeboat, *The Alfred and Clara Heath*. In the attempt to save the boat, Harold Hobbs died a brave man of the sea. This gallant man was shot at sea while helping to bring the lifeboat back to Guernsey, a brave operation to protect the vessel from falling into enemy hands. This family heartbreak occurred near the Jersey coast within St Aubin's Bay. Jersey did not escape the killing of the innocent.

Many islanders asked who took the blame for the delay in not informing the Berlin government of its status prior to the incidents taking place, stating that the Channel Isles were undefended. This remains a mystery with no satisfactory answers. After the raid the Home Office ordered the BBC to announce the Islands has been demilitarised. Later, the announcement came that the Islands had been brutally desecrated. This news was held over until the following day. Even then, it was not until June 30th when the Foreign Office asked the U.S Embassy to pass a message to the German government in Berlin that these independent Islands were undefended. If Berlin had been informed earlier it may have saved lives. Bureaucratic blundering; those in charge did not feel the wounds and pain or grief for loved ones. A voice in Whitehall, "It's unfortunate decisions are sometimes delayed, very sad. There is a war going on." End of story. The delay will be filed away as a tragedy of war.

The Channel Islands now tasting war, the flavour to last five long years.

Bombed weighbridge

Chapter 11
The Enemy Arrives

On Sunday, June 30th, 1940, between six and seven on a summer evening, four German transport planes landed after scaring away cows which had been rescued from Alderney and left on the airport landing strip to wander and graze, possibly with the dual purpose of making landing of reconnaissance aircraft more difficult. The enemy had arrived. After 900 years, the ties with England severed in the space of four days. Another important phase of history about to be written for these Isles de la Mancha.

Six ships arrived in Alderney, which is situated only eight miles from the coast of France. They evacuated the population of the Isle leaving only one family to take care of the lighthouse. This Isle earned notoriety later when it housed a concentration camp. Operation Todt brought slave prisoners to the Island. It was a nightmare; they worked in appalling conditions according to reports written after the war when this Island period was documented. They discovered over a thousand deaths were caused through atrocities and neglect to the unfortunates who had slaved, then perished, building fortifications apparently buried in the concrete. A premature death with no last rites. Relatives denied the location of their loved one's unmarked graves.

Alderney was not alone. These conditions happened wherever the slave workers built fortifications. This slave population was captured all over Europe, including Russia. After the war, those who survived were classed as displaced persons and many countries would not accept them. They were declared stateless, all papers of identification destroyed or lost by the enemy - a tragic time in the aftermath of war. Alderney was known at that period as the island of silence, where nightmare and terror reigned.

Fritz Todt instigated Operation Todt in 1938 and oversaw it until his death in a plane crash in 1942. His successor was Albert Speer. Both were high-ranking Nazi engineers.

A total of 1.4 million slave labourers were in the organisation up to the end of the 1939--1945 war.

On the tiny Isle of Sark, which lies approximately 11 kilometers east of Guernsey, was a different story. The Isle was under the rule of Dame Sybil Hathaway since 1926 and had instigated changes for the better in many ways. Four hundred and seventy-one Islanders remained on the Isle.

The Dame stood up to the Germans, making sure the Islanders were not subjected to ill-treatment, her efforts leaving this 'Pearl of the Sea' in a peaceful understanding with the occupation force. Sybil Hathaway is classed as a remarkable woman who gained the support of her American husband Bob.

Sark is unique, attracting people from all over the world feasting on its beauty and its way of life. Victor Hugo, the French novelist and poet, first visited Sark in 1859 which he described in his writing and poems, staying two weeks enjoying its beauty. He once remarked, "I feel heaven throbbing through things of the earth." Such was his love of nature.

Chapter 12
Rachel

If Germany had decided, not to invade the Channel Islands in 1940, then the basis of the Rachel Sarre story, *After the Chimes are Silent* would probably not been written as such.

The German occupation changed her life to a direction she or her parents would have never dreamed in peacetime. In the pre-war year, young Rachel was keen to seek a higher education, then leave the island and attend university, which by all accounts Rachel was capable of attaining. Young people in those far-off days found entry to a training college or university on the mainland a difficulty. One of the main factors depended on the financial circumstances of parents; further education of this nature could only be undertaken by a select few. Things have changed today when young students have the opportunity to do so regardless of their parent's financial position. Rachel remained a scholar during her lifetime, ever seeking knowledge; her interests took her to the arts, music, painting museums. In her enthusiasm, she often paid a visit to the Guille Alles library with its vast collection of books, searching Island history. She also a visited beautiful Candie Gardens with its adjoined neighbour, Priaulx Library plying her time gaining knowledge of the Island's past.

Sarnia, the Roman name for Guernsey, sounded romantic to Rachel visualising the old Sarnian farmers ploughing the fields with a hand-plough; tractors in those far away days would become a helpmate of the future. Perhaps her ancestors lived in Roman times ploughing the very fields of her home La Petit Close? One of the joys for her was to ruminate in the past, searching for the history of the Channel Islands. Her grandmother, Mary, nicknamed her 'Guernsey's little bookworm.'

Such was her love of books, the interest of which took her to Hauteville house, a home like no other. Hauteville, a street in the parish of St Peter Port, would invariably lead her to the grand, mysterious Hauteville House in which Victor Hugo lived for seventeen years while in exile, writing such masterpieces as *Les Miserable's, Les Travallieurs de la Mer. (Toilers of the sea)* that he dedicated to Guernsey. "I dedicate this book to the rock of hospitality and freedom, to this corner of old Norman-land where the ordinary people of the sea live, to the Island of Guernsey, severe and gentle, my present refuge, and my probable grave."

An English pirate built Hauteville House, and then over sixty years elapsed before Hugo acquired his house of sanctuary, having purchased this sea view house with land from Dr Ozanne. Victor immediately set about creating a residence which became only one of its kind in the world. Rachel loved this unique house, its coloured tapestry hung for all to see, a task that needle workers spent many hours to create the masterpiece. Her grandma, Priaulx, taught Rachel, an intelligent grandchild who sat contently, the art of cross-stitching. Grandma treasured the embroidery tapestry stitched during her courtship with Grandpa depicting two lovebirds holding a wedding ring in their beaks.

"Oh Gran, it looks so beautiful. I shall do attractive embroidery before marriage. It will remain a treasure for my grandchildren."

Grandma smiled saying, "Well you have to find a husband. You may have to wait a little while, but I am sure when you are older a handsome farmer will become your boyfriend. In the meantime, you have a good friend Eustace, so enjoy his companionship. Little did she know where that friendship would lead!

Hugo lined his walls with wooden carvings carefully stripped from furniture bought from auction sales to create sophisticated workmanship, after which he would cover the plaster in various rooms of this distinctive Hauteville house with these alterations - a unique tribute to one of the world's greatest writers.

Delft china plates with irreplaceable dinner sets were housed in a cabinet or displayed on a wooden dresser. Upon the walls hung paintings and photographs taken early in the art of photography, of Victor's relatives and friends in France.

To Rachel, this place was a storehouse of history. When entering its portals she sensed Hugo's presence. A spiritual charisma or magnetism drew her into the house as if she knew and lived in the company of the great writer. She was thus affected through vaporous happenings of the past. Rachel loved this Island that Hugo wrote about in praise of its many features, including the town of St Peter Port with its winding cobbled streets, it's lanes with French names, and the steep steps leading up to the higher part of the town overlooking the harbour and bay. On the right from the seafront stood the age-old Castel Cornet, a fortress set on solid rocks, and a bastion of old guarding the Island from would-be foes. When young, Rachel, with childlike curiosity, explored the aged citadel venturing into the clamminess of the dark cold dungeons she sensed the wretchedness of bygone prisoners. In her imagination, sitting listening to the ever-changing kaleidoscopic sea lapping against its solid rock walls, she never ceased to wonder about its power, a force to be reckoned with, bringing its turbulence to destroy, or a gentle caress upon multicoloured shells and coloured pebbles, repetitive since time began.

Rachel could often be found sitting on the sloping cliff rocks, which overlooked the bay at Le Gouffe, listening to the tunes created by nature, the whistling of the wind rustling through bushes and long grass, intermittent songs of the birds as they tweet a love call. She loved the rippling tunes of the waves, the warm breeze hustling through the yellow gorse projecting its malty perfume in spring and summer.

Soldiers of the castle dressed in uniforms of a past era, pending midday endeavoured to mount the hewn, knarled, steps to the ramparts of the castle upon which stood a well-used, long-standing, cannon ready to be loaded, this age-old canon having stood the test of time awaiting the stroke of midday, when the roar of the fired explosives would inform Islanders all is well. Upon the horizon with the mail boat in sight to the Islanders, hoping the mailbags would bring much-anticipated news, either good or sad, from across the seas.

Guernsey Castle

Firing the Cannon at Guernsey Castle

On one visit to St Peter Port with Grandma Mary, both sitting in the pew of the town church, St Peters, Grandma remarked this was the Island's cathedral built hundreds of years ago. Rachel loved the quietness of the church when sitting in one of the oak pews. Eyes glimpse around this stone edifice; so much to see. White marble plaques upon which engraved gold-and-black lettering denote past deeds of important people of the Island, recording his or hers birth or death; many such gifts in memory of loved ones or past ancestors.

Grandma would point out the color-leaded stained glass biblical windows, which the magic of the sun's rays projected to create a kaleidoscope of colour upon interior walls. This, to young Rachel, an exciting moment together, when at times hearing the pealing of the bells inviting all to worship. Sometimes on very special occasions, lingering to hear the bells welcoming bride and groom. Rachel always felt happy when the bells chimed, a little sad, when they ceased, saying she wanted the sounds of happiness to continue.

On certain occasions, the organist would practice on the pipe organ. Rachel appreciated the beautiful music which he performed with such ease. At a young age, she started piano lessons, which she found useful when singing in the church choir at the Forest Methodist Church. Many remarked on her beautiful voice.

The sightseeing day ended but not before either lunch or afternoon tea at Le Noury's, situated in the quaint cobblestoned arcade, one of best eating houses in St Peter Port. This long-established bakery produced mouth-watering cream cakes, Guernsey Gache and Jersey Wonders, these favourites even though cream cakes held an attraction. Oh, the warm enticing lingering smell of freshly-baked bread when entering its portals. The family, Le Noury's, had served the public for many a year in this establishment.

Chapter 13
Witches and Wizards

Grandma knew everything. or so it seemed to Rachel when in her delightful presence. As a child, she loved to sit with her Grandmother as she did with elderly Great Grandmother to listen to folklore tales of witches and ghosts that haunted some of the old Guernsey houses.

The builders of old would set a Corbel, a large stone jutting out from the gable of the house, on which witches could rest while in flight if a house offered, a resting place for one who cast spells. These Corbel stones guaranteed safety for those within the abode, from the wrath of one who took flight on a broomstick. The house without a stone took a chance of bad luck.

Corbel – a witch's seat

Rachel listened intently as grandmother recounted tales of Guernsey Folklore. On a Friday night, the witches and wizards would meet after dark in places such as Les Eturs or the Longfrie to cast their spells, holding a lighted tallow candle illuminating the darkness. The saying goes 'A Witch's tallow candle is as good as a devil's torch.' So say those in the know of such things.

Pope Innocent VIII declared witchcraft illegal, persecuting all who practised the craft with those found guilty burnt alive at the stake.

On many a Friday night, Rachel looked out of her bedroom window to catch a glimpse of a witch in flight. She was very disappointed if one did not appear. This vision is only granted to individuals who follow the ancient laws.' "Witches only appear to those whom they choose to watch their flight' So say it! Another reason given by a knowledgeable Guernsey historian is,' Those who receive this gift must have the bloodline of a martyred witch flowing in their veins.' During an eighty-year period between 1560-1640, a total of forty-four persons were convicted, suffering death after being burnt at the stake situated at the bottom of Tower Hill in St Peter Port plus another thirty-five were banished from the Island.

Grandmother went on to say, much to young Rachel's amusement and enchantment, that fairies existed and still do on Guernsey Island. There is a fairy circle at Torteval at Les Creux. Fairies, at certain times, would dance around the ring, a remarkable enchanting sight, or so say those who have witnessed their performance. Not all fairies were of a good disposition and when upset they at times turned to anger.

Two well-known fairies by the name of Le Grand Colin, the other, La Petit Colin, are both respected according to those who are addicted to folklore.

Rachel's Grandmother, Mary, was well versed in Guernsey and Sark folklore, having spent childhood holidays on the charming Isle of Sark. Folklore is still accepted to this day.

In times gone past, women knitting the traditional Guernsey jumpers would gather in cottages to pass on the happenings of folklore, the clicking of the needles accelerating with the excitement of the story.

Chapter 14
Christmas Joy

Rachel, a simple farmer's daughter with a determined spirit, tried to escape from the insular mind of Island thinking, extending her education when possible. The usual farmer's offspring lives centered on the farm with regular visits to church where their social life consisted of fêtes. Sales of works leaving little time for the finer things of life, Rachel desired more. During ensuing years the whole structure of education changed. One of the joys of Christmas for any parish child was to visit St Peter Port. This parish came alive during the Christmas season. Rachel's expectation of this joyful season filled her with agitation as the days seemed to linger before it happened.

In pre-war days, when as a child, part of the annual trip highlight for Rachel was posting a letter to Father Christmas in his red-and-white mailbox situated at the entrance of Creasy and its magical toy shop with make-believe snow complete with sparkling snow dust. Reindeers pulled the heavy-laden sledge piled high with an assortment of colourful books and toys to suit the taste of a boy or girl. Oh, the excitement of seeing that benevolent person sitting on a chair covered in cotton snow, him ringing his hand bell to summon the excited children, with memories of that bearded red-clad legend as he lifted her on his knee whispering, "If a good girl, her stocking will be filled with presents." The joy of those spoken words never left her throughout life, reminding her of happier times before the occupation when sitting in that make-believe snow land listening to the jingle-jangle of the merry tunes of Christmas with shops aglow, decked with holly intermingled with mistletoe and ivy. This was no make-believe it was real for the moment in every child's mind. Rachel dismissed the farm, replaced with a yearning to loiter here forever in this never-never-land so she chose to delay leaving the hustle and bustle which was so exciting after the quietness of the farm.

Time was precious to the farming Sarres. Leave she must, to accompany her parents visiting various hops, all incandescent for the festive season. Everyone greeted you with a smile together with good wishes. If only the spirit of Christmas would last forever!

To have thoughts of a war in the 1930s - rubbish. Wars were outdated; had not a politician predicted in this in a 1918 armistice, which the war-torn world foolishly believed.

The thirties went through the depression. Everyone suffered in some way, although it was easier for the farmers who grew the fruits of the land to supply their family needs. Vegetables made a nourishing soup to feed a hungry belly, fresh cream and milk nourished young bones.

In spite of growing up and raised on the farm, Rachel remained naive to the true facts of life, as often children did in many cases when they faced puberty, no one explained to them the birds and the bees. Sex between humans, male and female a No, No. Animals were different that is nature. What happened between men and women and its outcome was never discussed in the Sarre household. Many couples relied on instinct to find out more or in some cases by trial and error which could lead to unfortunate circumstances. Sex an unspeakable subject, or so we were lead to believe. Private parts were private parts! Only to be used for the call of nature. Years later, television, plus the gyrations on the cinema screen, left no doubt that the storks did not bring the baby. Or did they?

Chapter 15
Occupation

The occupation of Guernsey wrought change in many lives. Laws and rules set down by the German Commandant had to be obeyed or face the consequences.

In October 1940 registration forms had to be completed for the issue of identity cards and had to be filled in by every resident except children under fourteen years, but details of their birth etc. had to be included on the reverse side of the form.

Only few motor cars were allowed to remain with their owners and not to be used for pleasure. It became necessary to issue driving permits only for essential services. Use of petrol had to be curtailed. In the autumn of 1940, a purchasing commission was set up by the Germans to requisition cars that were to be sent to France. The States appointed a person to value the cars under the supervision of German valuers, who paid for the cars which had been sent to St Milo. Shortage of petrol brought in horse-drawn vans, bicycles old and new became part of everyday life.

New bicycle tires were the thing of the past; a piece of garden hose served the purpose - uncomfortable but serviceable, always knowing when a bike was approaching by the humpty-hump over a cobblestoned roadway. One Guernsey man was heard to remark in broken patois, 'Core Damee, my bum is black and blue after the ride from Torteval to St Peter Port. The wife had to rub it with Mr Cumber's liniment. (Mr Cumber a long established chemist in the Island renowned for his potions to cure all ills.) Core Damee, it's as hot as cinders. Rub some on those Germans and they will jump in the sea. I think I keep my sore bum, no offence Mr Cumber."

Those who had found refuge in England and elsewhere can relate many tales of life during those five long years of separation from loved ones and freedom; some relationships never achieved a bond after the war.

The five long war years changed the life of Rachel Sarre, this young eighteen-year-old daughter of Nickolas and Eunice Sarre, a respected Methodist family residing at Petit Close in the Forest Parish. Nickolas had fought in the 1914-18 'war to end all wars.' Nickolas, who like so many ex-soldiers, never talked about the horrors of the battlefield blood baths. His family understood he had seen things he wished to forget, or at least put the memory in the recesses of his mind, dwelling in shadows, too painful to recall what he and his comrades endured.

The Sarre family consisted of himself, his wife and his only child Rachel, and Mary, his mother. A son was born two years after Rachel, but tragedy struck when the young, apparently healthy child, succumbed to diphtheria. This disease had taken many lives of children during an outbreak in the 1930s. Nickolas dearly wanted a son to carry on the family name but unfortunately, this was not to be. He had hopes that one day Rachel would marry a boy of the land and run Petit Close. Included in the household, Mary Sarre, his elderly mother, still helping with the farm chores at the age of seventy-six, showed the true grit of the Guernsey folk. During haymaking season she pitched a fork with the best of them. The early morning chills did not stop this innovative Guernsey lady sitting on a milking stool in the field extracting the warm rich milk from which rich yellow Guernsey butter and curds were produced. Regularly the Sarres butter and curds were often displayed on fresh crisp green cabbage leaves in St Peter Port market. Cabbage leaves are the traditional way of keeping perishables fresh. Individual stalls in St Peter Port fruit market did not have refrigeration; they relied on communal storage cool rooms which kept fruit, meat, fish and flowers overnight ensuring a saleable condition the following day. Its produce much sought after by the town locals, it took a war to introduce modernization in refrigeration and other aspects.

The famous Guernsey market was known the world over for its unique structure. In the pre-war years, the market consisted of four sections: Meat, Fish, Vegetables, and Flowers. Stall holders often heard conversing in Guernsey/French patios intermingled with English. A curiosity to visitors. Guernsey market proved a great attraction to tourists wandering through each section admiring the fresh produce, inquiring of the local stall holders the name of the various fish displayed on ice, and seeing the fish kettle filled with boiling water ready to receive an unsuspecting crab or crayfish into its depth to create meat for a tasty sandwich or salad.

The lure of flowers brings you to stalls with a mass of colour, flowers as only Guernsey can grow them. Displayed when in season: daffodils, chrysanthemums, roses, freesias iris, gladiolas, hyacinths, and if lucky the Guernsey lily. (Jersey has Lily Langtry of historic fame) but Guernsey has its own special flower, the famous lily. Also on the stalls, there was the sweet perfume of violets and lily of the valley; such an array of beauty to feast the eyes.

The market held another attraction being one of the places folk went to meet and chat and gossip with friends while purchasing the market's produce.

Mary at times made the journey into St Peter Port but was quite content to remain on the farm milking the Guernsey breed of cattle or enjoying the peace of the meadows. It was Rachel who often enticed her beloved Gran into St Peter Port, each enjoying the others company.

Many a time the unperturbed cow whom Mary milked, switched her tail to combat the flies. Unfortunately, this happened at unannounced intervals and the tail covered in dung sent a spray over the unsuspecting person. Guernsey dairy cows with their distinctive brown and white markings are renowned the world over. Local farmers from Guernsey and her sister Isles Jersey and Alderney dispatched their Island breed to all parts of the world. Due to the lush green grass on the Island, this breed produced rich creamy milk.

It is no wonder Guernsey attracted tourism with its sandy beaches, a carpet of coloured shells in many shapes and sizes, the smell of seaweed and Vraic washed from the clear blue sea. In the background, tall cliffs covered in yellow gorse intermingle with bluebells, primroses, violets, white and yellow daisies, tall foxgloves, vetch, dog-roses, blackthorn, golden sapphires, pennywort, wild garlic and many others. It is said flowers are God's way of smiling at us. What a lovely thought!

To those whose partiality is gin, then the Sloe bush is a must. The partakers in season collect its fruit, combine the ripe fruit with gin, leave it to mature for three months and the end product is aptly named Sloe Gin.

Enjoying a walk along the cliff paths, you stop to cosset your eyes on the magnificent panorama as you walk in the direction of Fermain Bay or to St Peter Port. On the edge of the cliff overlooking the sea, below is a sandy stone lookout built in Napoleonic times which first acquired the name Pepper Pot as its shape resembles the vessel that graced the table.

On your leisurely walk here and there, you may come across a crabapple tree. These apples are at times gathered by locals who wish to make a conserve. They boil the apples in the traditional Guernsey Bashan; the mixture will then be strained through muslin, a process in the making of delicious crabapple jelly. Mixed varieties of jams made by Islanders are sold at Le Viaer Marchi, the old market, under the auspices of the National Trust. When the market is in progress, the stallholders encourage dress in traditional Guernsey costumes, selling locally-designed art e.g. the traditional Guernsey - a jumper knitted with oiled wool making the garment waterproof as used by fishermen to keep them dry when the sea gives an unwelcome shower. Another interesting item from a bygone era, a locally-made Guernsey copper milk can, a replica of the original used on farms in yesteryear. There are shell brooches, necklaces, pressed flowers, or perhaps you will be tempted to buy the famous Guernsey Gache or sample the tasty bean jar, cooked on a slow heat overnight. Guernsey Bean Jar is a traditional Sunday breakfast in many homes. In St Peter Port the bean jar is taken to a nearby bakery, cooked overnight in the bread oven and the maker is charged a small fee for this service. In the country parishes, it is cooked in a furze-fueled oven, the furze gathered from the cliffs or nearby fields during the course of the day.

At Le Viaer Marchi, dancers, complete with traditional Guernsey costumes, will dance and sing songs in the Island patois. In July, this venue is one of the highlights of the Castel parish portraying Guernsey way of life traditions.

Petit Close Farm built in traditional Guernsey style in 1710, was run for generations by the Sarre ancestors to this present day in the various parishes throughout the Island. Guernsey patois is passed on from one generation to the next; they say this particular language is understood by the Welsh.

Copper milk can

Chapter 16
Eustace

Eustace Tostivin was drawn into Rachel's life from school days, sharing each other's secrets away from the adult world as youngsters do. Eustace, blighted by a speech impediment, proved a true friend in what he offered later in Rachel's life. He had a shy nature due to his difficulty with speech. Nevertheless this did not impede him from joining in games, especially if Rachel was in the group.

Rachel at times became a tomboy after dressing in a shirt and jeans. When the local lads climbed trees she followed suit. The fun times included trips to the beaches, diving off the high rocks into the cool blue waters of Petit Bay, or scaling the cliffs with the boys together with some of the adventurous girls. Life in the Forest parish at that time for the youngsters was carefree. From an early age she lent a hand in the daily running of the farm which she loved, over the years learning the ropes of running it. Nickolas, her father, appreciated the help given and often remarked Rachel was as good as any male. Farming entails hard work, long hours, sometimes with small remuneration. The work was not a hardship to her as she loved the farm of her ancestors.

Nickolas Sarre was small in stature as most true Island people were, judging by the low beams in the Guernsey farmhouses. Visitors of average height unsuspectingly met offending low beams in various parts of the house, an experience they had no wish to repeat. According to folklore, Guernsey males were small in stature because they had fairy blood in their veins, or so the story goes.

Nick, a hard worker, together with Eunice and Rachel, spoke the Guernsey patois at home reverting to English on occasions when needed for those who did not understand the Guernsey French. Soon after Nick's marriage he built a 100ft greenhouse in which he started to grow the famous Guernsey tomatoes (love

64

apples as they are named) as well as white and black sweet juicy grapes which were exported to England by cargo boat. During the season local women were gainfully employed, sorting and packing the produce into woodchip baskets, which agents collected then transported by motor carrier to the White Rock for shipment to England, so life at La Petit Close was far from boring.

Eunice and Rachel formed a close relationship when they worked in the dairy at Petit Close chattering away as they churned the rich yellow Guernsey butter and curds later to be sold at various shops and taken to St Peter Port to be sold in the market together with the fresh vegetables grown at Petit Close.

Not having a brother who would have eventually owned Petit Close, Rachel knew that one day she would inherit the properties which included two Guernsey cottages which were an inheritance left to her mother Eunice by great aunt Salena, who in her later years became a recluse, neglecting the cottages and herself. Eventually, on a sad visit by her great niece, Eunice found the poor soul lying dead in the somewhat unhygienic kitchen. Nestled in her arms an overlarge cat who answered to Cat. Aunt Salena never bothered to give the affectionate animal a name so the cherished feline remained 'Cat.'

Eunice felt a tinge of guilt that she had not given this sour-faced, ill-fated, bitter, unmarried woman more time to her welfare. Alas, when she did visit Salena's aged granite house that over the years became partly covered by green and red ivy which grew dejectedly over time at La Fontanel, poor Eunice received a string of caustic abuse from her aunt's tongue that never gave praise, leaving Eunice often departing in tears, vowing never to return. But Eunice, a forgiving person, remembered Salena's life had a few hard knocks, including her intended husband being killed on the way to his wedding. The saying, 'Happy the bride the sun shines on', unfortunately, on that sad day, was overcast by a shadow which never left her. Guernsey suffered a violent storm on that ill-fated day; the thunder roared, the lightning flashed, and the horse and buggy on its way to the church bolted, overturning in a slush of mud, killing the frightened horse and her beloved bridegroom.

When the news reached the poor bride waiting in the porch of Torteval church, the shock was too much. Her father and family tried their best to control her sobbing and grief to no avail. Salena from then on, somewhat mentally unbalanced at times, was never quite the same.

Torteval Church

The sadness of this catastrophe progressed to an unhealthy hatred concerning any connection with the outside world, thus leading to an insalubrious lavishing of affection towards one of the many cats in the household, which, in due course, became her close companions even until her sudden death! It was on that fateful wedding day, Selena renounced her God and never again set a foot inside of what was once the family's place of worship. Selena, when passing the church on occasions during her lifetime, took it upon herself never to open her eyes keeping her vision closed in reverence, consequently not having to look at the place where she received words that pierced her heart and mind. Sadly no other suitor entered her life to eradicate the fatality. Did Charles Dickens draw upon her plight creating that wonderful exocentric character Miss Haversham?

Strangely, and mysteriously to her family, she left a large sum in her will to be used in the furtherance of God's work in the parish, stipulating brides married in that church be given a bible on their wedding day to sustain them in trouble. Maybe she did hold on to her faith, who knows?

Rachel, of gentle nature, was shocked at the sad story of Aunt Salena. If only Rachel could foresee the future she would understand why Salena acted so in leaving the church to wipe its memory from her mind. Both Rachel and her mother, gifted with true soprano voices, used to singing during Sunday's services, delighted those within the Forest Methodist Church when hearing mother and daughter giving praise to the Lord with the rest of the choir.

Chapter 17
Hans Gruber

The winds of war brought change to a twenty four-year-old German soldier, Hans Gruber. Conscripted into the army after training, followed by a short stay in France, he became part of the occupation force in Guernsey. This fair-headed, blue-eyed, good-looking soldier was brought up in the Lutheran faith at a time when Christianity was not in vogue in the so-called glorious Fatherland. A clean-living lad, not brow-beaten by Hitler's youth policy.

His German-born grandmother lived in England for many years. Her first husband died after four years of marriage, leaving two children, a boy Otto the father of Hans, and a baby girl Olga. Grandmother re-married, an Englishman of means, to sustain a comfortable lifestyle at an address in Craven Street near the abode of the late 18th-century German poet, Heinrich Heine. On seeing the house she was reminded her of the beloved Berlin she once knew. Although she corresponded with friends and relatives, she never returned to unsettled Germany due to the rise of the Hitler regime.

Hans spent many happy holidays with her in London, the English way of life familiar to him. During this time his grandmother encouraged him to learn the language.

Hans's sister, Martha, though loving her grandmother, never enjoyed her holidays in London, claiming the English were capitalist snobs. During her visits she, a gifted artist, painted scenes of the English countryside, her works shown and purchased over the world. One watercolor of London found its way into Hitler's Bavarian household, where he often boasted he would tramp England's soil in victory. Martha's personality was totally different from Hans who considered her an enigma, at the age of eighteen marrying a high Nazi official and bearing him twin girls. Her husband was a fervent follower of the policy of Adolf Hitler and her life was not without incident. She was invited on occasions as a guest at Berchtesgaden. Apparently, during her first visit, Hitler's roving eye requested the attractive Martha to sit in a place of honour next to him. Fortunately, little did he know that there was a line of Jewish blood which flowed through her veins, or did he choose to ignore the heritage? Either way, lucky for her, or she may have ended in a not so comfortable seat joining others doomed to die in a concentration camp. Hitler's request for her to sit at his right-hand side was in Martha's mind considered an honour for she desired his company and her husband Kurt encouraged it to further his rise in the Reich.

Hans's lifestyle and his sister's were very different in many ways; he was conscripted into the army, certainly not by choice and the uncertain German politics at that time caused him anguish.

Otto Gruber, her father, who had seen the horrors of the 1914-18 war, had no wish to follow the newfound Hitler policy. This meant keeping low key with Hitler's fervent doctrine catching the unstable youth to build a new Germany. During this unsettled time in German history, Otto Gruber, a professional lawyer, used caution at all times. Martha did not take her father's views lightly, which at times ended in a strained relationship between them.

Did destiny or fate allow Hans Gruber to be billeted near La Petit Close in a cottage near La Gree? It enabled him to see Rachel often milking the cows or riding her horse along the Grande Marche on the way to her uncle's farm.

Chapter 18
Lihou Family

The Lihou family were certainly glad of her helping with daily chores. Harold, her larrikin cousin, prior to the occupation, together with his mates, decided to join the forces in England. Hal, as he was known to friends and family, was a daredevil who took life as a challenge. He chose the army; the last news from him before the telephone cable to England was disconnected informed his parents he was in the Intelligence Corp much to the surprise of his father. Educated at the Intermediate school, considered not one of the brightest, The Headmaster, Mr Fulford, often administered corporal punishment to him due to some misdemeanour. Harold simply did not put his mind to study, but as so many do, improved his education after he left the seat of learning. On hearing the news of Harold's posting to the Intelligence Corp his father remarked, "God Save England."

His sister Madeline was evacuated with the Forest school. Rachel felt she should lend a hand as one of the farm hands had also left for England, which meant that there was only Uncle Ernie and Auntie Rita to manage the farm La Gree, a heritage going back many years in the Lihou family.

La Gree fascinated Rachel. According to legend, the Lihous were privateers and smugglers. What interested Rachel, one day on entering the stone-flagged hallway, noticed a straw mat covering a trapdoor concealing a flight of steps which lead to an empty cellar, empty except for cobwebs brushing your face if you dared to trespass in their domain, acting as self-imposed guardians hanging from the ceiling, a perfect home for spiders and creepy-crawlies. Around the cellar a series of stone shelves that in the past housed stacked contraband, were now long-since empty. Later, this musty-smelling room would serve a different purpose. Painstaking labour, drilling a tunnel through the hard granite cliff rock, connected this secret storeroom to a cave, its beach entrance cleverly hidden by nature's formation of rocks, its entrance unseen by swimmers, sunbathers, or unconcerned children busy building sandcastles. Through this cave, the smugglers, who had lured unsuspected boats to their doom, carried the booty from the ill-fated ships, now anchored and sinking helplessly in the bay, brought the ill-gotten gains of their escapades to be stored in the cellar of La Gree and sold later for a profit.

The treacherous rocks around Guernsey's coast claimed many wrecks and lives; resulting in an assortment of vessels meeting their misfortune through unscrupulous Islanders engineering a perilous unsafe course through the reef. Treachery done by misplaced braziers, whose flames guided, then floundered the boats on jagged rocks. Once this murderous deed was accomplished the smugglers rowed in peril through the ferocious, wailing, turbulent, sea to risk their lives to collect cargo from the sinking wreck. If hampered by crew members they were quickly disposed of by the flick of a sharpened knife. If a knife was not available, then they were held under the freezing water until drowned, their gurgling blood flowing with the salty ebbing tide.

No time for niceties, their livelihood depended on the cargo. Mouths had to be fed.

Rachel knew of the cellar tunnel, its entrance covered long ago with a heavy granite bolder, leaving only minimum space for a body to squeeze and enter. In her mind's eye, wondering what lay beyond those citadel stones, what part did her great, great, great grandfather, and other ancestors play in this house? Often when the moon was full, a foggy mist swirled around the mossed granite walls, portraying an air of vaporous mystery. It was here in this house Rachel felt a bonding connecting with the past, an experience never felt at Petit Close. In a drama that followed later, she would see beyond those huge granite stones with its ethereal presence as she travelled along the same tunnel her ancestor carried their ill-gotten prizes. She will crunch underfoot the same pebbles as did her past relatives when advancing back and forth towards the sea and become conscious of their existence. Was imagination playing unsettling tricks while in this house? Her eyes gazed at forms of people dressed in costumes of centuries past.

On one occasion which Rachel tried to forget, she saw a young girl dressed as a bride, upon her face the bloom of youth, her eyes shining with love mingled with happiness, such pretty hair. Suddenly her whole countenance changed; no longer the bride, hair tangled unkempt, deep anguish on her face. Gone the flowing white bridal gown replaced by a torn black dress of uncertain material, clutched in her hand remnants of the white veil that adorned the pretty hair. Dejection and tears completed the scene before Rachel's eyes. In her other hand, this girl held a length of twisted rope dragging snake-like along the stone, cold, damp floor, her glassy staring eyes focused to a rafter above. Is this the poor wretch who ended her life at La Gree, whose beautiful neck was severed by a twisted rope? Rachel had no wish to see a repeat performance. The poor girl's mind bereft of sanity, out of touch with reality. This Rachel will remember as part of her heritage, an indelible legacy passed from one generation to another, this destiny ordained!

Chapter 19
Resistance

The German occupation forces treated the islanders with respect providing they abided by the rules of their treatment of Operation Todd slave workers brought in from many countries These workers were forced to build what Hitler named The Atlantic Sea Wall, concrete fortifications overlooking the English Channel, thus impeding the British and Allied shipping. Islanders would often see these souls without shoes, sacking wrapped around their blistered feet, bodies denied of hygiene. If death overtook them while building a maniac's dream, then the wet grey mixture that held walls together received their mortal remains sealed in an unmarked grave, devoid of the last Sacraments, lost, unfound forever to those who grieve.

As time went by, life became more settled. Islanders passed the time of day with their captors, yet they still remembered these unwelcome visitors were their enemy. Islanders developed a devious cunning to beat rules laid down by unsuspecting jailors. Guernsey Underground News Service (G.U.N.S.) a resistance newssheet was started. This publication, a form of passive resistance, was the brainchild of Charles Machon, a 51-year-old linotype operator at The Star newspaper, in league with Cecil Duquemin, Ernest Legg, Frank Falla, and Joseph Gillingham. Together, in May 1942, they started G.U.N.S. They listened to the BBC wireless news in secret then typed it up on thin tomato wrapping paper. It had a circulation of three hundred throughout the Island, which continued until 11 February 1944 when it was betrayed by an Irishman. Some Irish seasonal workers were on the Island when the German's took over. These workers belonged to The Republic of Ireland which was neutral during the 1939-45 war and many did not have allegiance to England. Sark received three copies of G.U.N.S. Herbert Lanyon, a baker by trade, with a friend

Mr Wakley, a carrier, decided that the Sarkees must know what was going on during the conflict. They took it upon themselves to read the news items to more than seventy people as well as to a few trusted Germans who did not believe the German radio broadcast. It was through this newssheet the islanders knew the truth of how the war was progressing. News sheets were distributed secretly throughout the island. Rachel played a part acting as a deliverer.

Hidden radio sets and homemade crystal sets were one of the means that Islanders gained information of the whereabouts of the Allied forces. By law, punishable if caught by jail or deported to Germany as the occupation forces forbade owning or listening to one of these sets. An enterprising Guernsey man who had wireless knowledge as part of his trade, Harry Capper by name, made and fixed hundreds of crystal sets in the cellar of his house which was also occupied by the Feldgendarmerie. Radio sets were allowed up to the end of 1940 when they were withdrawn as a punishment for help given by several Islanders to British agents landing secretly on the Island. After a short while, they were returned to the owners, only to be confiscated again in June 1942. The reason was the BBC was encouraging listeners in France and other occupied countries to take part in a general resistance campaign. Berlin feared this would lead to unofficial military training and in turn an uprising against German forces in the Islands. Banning the sets silenced the BBC news in loyal Islanders' ears, and even though eight thousand sets were unwillingly returned, a few were kept in secret.

The Guernsey people are determined like a donkey; stubborn, overcoming all odds; they say there are more ways than one in killing a pig. The Islanders were devious in their methods of resistance. Having crystal sets was one of them.

Chapter 20
Romance

One sunny afternoon when Rachel was visiting her Aunt Rita, she was surprised to find a German motorcycle in the attractive front garden. There were daisies, bluebells, primroses and buttercups, all blending a picture of charm with the age old Granite farmhouse. Aunt Rita loved her garden, saying, "God's grace is found in a garden." As the seasons went by, other flowers changed places with spring enchantments. Rachel loved the perfume of roses, lavender, honeysuckle and the Guernsey lily with a red semi-orchid flower. Legend has it that the bulbs were found washed up on the seashore from their homeland Japan. A miniature Eden in these young girl's eyes.

Seeing a German motorcycle surprised her with concern. What has happened? Hurrying into the house she passed a black cat sitting by the oak-grained doorway, the animal mewing to seek attention. "What is the matter Tibbles?" asked Rachel, as she bent to stroke his shiny black coat. Its cry became more intense as if in pain, then, as she gently stroked his fur Tibbles began purring. Once he gained her attention he returned to mewing as if he was trying to say something.

On entering the hallway she found Aunt Rita smiling, listening to a tall handsome Hans Gruber whom Rachel recognised, having seen him when he passed Petit Close, Why is he here? The thought was soon answered by her aunt.

"This is my niece Rachel, the daughter of my brother Nick. Hans has been billeted with us. Due to the influx of German soldiers, any unoccupied bedrooms or rooms can be requisitioned by the Commandant. Hans will live in the little cottage next to the barn."

Hans, smiling, offered his hand to Rachel, who timidly placed her hand in his, whereupon he kissed it gently, clicked his heels and with a nod spoke in English with a slight accent that Rachel found disturbingly attractive. Is it wrong to feel attraction to your enemy? Hans broke the silence of her thoughts. "You have a charming niece Madam. I trust we will meet again. I must admit this is not the first time I've seen you. My wish was to sketch you milking the cows, such a pretty picture." Then shyly, "It would do me a great honour if at some time you would allow me. During happier times in Berlin, I enjoyed sketching beautiful buildings, perhaps now painting a beautiful milk maiden?"

Though people had remarked she was a nice looking girl, beautiful had never reached Rachel's ears before so this remark brought a flush of colour to her cheeks. Embarrassed to the point of not wishing to stay, she must go. There was something about this handsome man whose blue eyes reflected the clear water of Sark's Venus pool. The reflection frightened her. His words may spell unhappiness. Within, an emotion she never felt before rose into a desire to know this person. An attraction for this man, her so-called enemy could never be.

Had not her aunt relayed a story of a young bride of long ago rejected by her lover dying in this house broken-hearted? She may have cast a spell. Rachel recalled that in the past, the Islanders believed in spells and witches, part of Guernsey folklore. Great-grandmother, who died at ninety-seven years, often sat Rachel on her knee, telling the tales of how the witch of Longfrie cast a spell on the fields of the Forest parish, claiming that all cabbages would become miniatures growing on a stalk, re-naming them Brussels sprouts. Why she chose that name it will never be known. Remembering witches do not part with information, the curse was the reward for not allowing the Longfrie witch to take part in the Viaer Marchi. Legends say; 'When sprouts taste bitter, the cause is due to her spittle upon the stalks,' a curse to remind all that a witches wishes and desires cannot be refused or tampered with.

Rachel half-believed what her great-grandmother related, thus making the folklore stories so convincing, sometimes terrifying to a young child. Today of all days brought back the childhood memory of the tale of the black cat's strange power. It is said, 'When a black cat is seen sitting at the entrance of a house, an uninvited stranger will be inside. If this is so be warned, as trouble will descend within its portals before the moon is up.' Yes, this German soldier is a stranger. Rachel knew nothing of his background. Perhaps the young girl of ages past did cast a spell forbidding happiness for any girl of the blood line of the Lihou and Sarre family. When young men suggested she was beautiful, was this part of the bonding she often felt in this house?

Hans stretched out his hand to say goodbye and a coldness came over her. Why is she having such thoughts? She had never been in romantic love, not even with her long-time school friend, Eustace. Yet, she loved Eustace as one who shared all her secrets. How strange to feel like this. These new emotions went further; she seemed drawn to him in a special way. Why! Is this love at first sight? Does it happen in real life, or is it the fancy of one who pens a romantic novel, a tale written to inject romance in humdrum lives? Poor Rachel, little did she know or understand what lies before her. Therefore, with a hasty goodbye, she vanished to the safety of Petit Close as fast as she could. This was no time to stay and help. The chores remained untouched at La Gree farm. Her actions unexplained to Aunt Rita.

During the days that followed, Rachel avoided meeting Hans making sure he was not on her aunt's property.

Love finds a way, so it was with Hans. Rachel, the first girl he felt attracted to and this attraction different for any of the females in he had met in Germany. Naturally, he had sought their company; invitations to dinner or a night at the cinema; at times enjoying a tennis set. Reading travel books was an interest that caught his eye. As a young man, he attended social get-togethers, but this was as far as it went. Sexually, on occasions he had the opportunity to go further. His male friends boasted of their conquest with females; drinking, getting the girls under their control, making sure the end product was a good night in bed which usually meant to quote the three F's: Find them, Feel them then F*** them. Whatever! This was not Hans's direction in life. Sex at times was certainly tempting, but he restrained from going further, due perhaps to his Lutheran teaching. However brief their meeting, to him Rachel was special. He had never made conversation with her until the meeting at the farm, yet deep inside he desired to know her as the beautiful person she is.

One fine morning, as Rachel sat on her milking stool in the meadow where the daisy and buttercups grew, Hans slowly approached her carrying a mixed bunch of flowers. Included in the colourful bouquet was a red rose which gave out a captivating delicate perfume. Back in Germany, a florist had once told him, "Red roses for love." Touching this enchanting milkmaid's shoulder suddenly caused her to jump in fright as she held the cow's teat, which unfortunately took the improbable course of squirting milk over Hans's lower trouser leg. Poor Rachel blushed with embarrassment at the antics of this mischievous cow.

"Oh, I am sorry."

"There is no need to apologise, it's entirely my fault Miss Sarre catching you unaware."

By this time both had seen the funny side of the situation. Both had a laugh as Hans handed her the flowers, "For the most beautiful milk maiden in the world. Miss Sarre, may I call you Rachel, and I will be delighted if you can find this is possible without shame, to call me Hans."

So on that bright summer's day Rachel's life took a different direction; out of the seeds of friendship grew love. Though Rachel deeply loved Hans, she had a misgiving that hers was a forbidden love because he came from a country that was her enemy. The thought of Hal, her cousin, fighting against Hans's fellow citizens filled her with a fear that could never be quelled. Each side killing the other for a peace that will never last. Man's greed will destroy the fantasy of peace. Greed holds the trump card which he has played throughout generations.

Hans assured her that he loved her as no other and when this wretched war is over they will marry. The plans of mice and men! He said, "My darling Rachel, it is not the everyday people who are enemies on our own accord; we are programmed by government. Those in the street are against bloodshed. I do not wish to kill; it's the fanatics who desire blood for selfish gains. I love you with all my heart my darling."

Rachel lifted her face to his, kissing his lips that returned her passion. Apart from embracing, this was as far as their lovemaking went; both had control of their passions.

Rachel confided in Eustace of her love for Hans and their secret meetings. Eustace was a good friend; he would tell no one. So the months passed by and their love grew stronger, both vowing they would remain true to each other whatever the circumstances. True love never runs smooth or so the saying goes.

Chapter 21
Curfews

Life on the Island took on a different pattern. Curfews had been introduced; all inhabitants had to be indoors by 11 p.m. and not permitted to leave their homes before 6 a.m. These were the new rules set down by the German occupiers: We will respect the population in Guernsey, but for anyone attempting to cause the least trouble, serious measures will be taken and the town will be bombed.

All orders given by the military authority are to be strictly obeyed.

All spirits must be locked up immediately; no spirits may be supplied and obtained or consumed henceforth. This prohibition does not apply to stocks in private houses.

No person shall enter the aerodrome.

All dangerous weapons, which include rifles, air guns, pistols, revolvers, daggers, sporting guns and all other weapons whatsoever, except souvenirs, must, together with all ammunition, be delivered at the Royal Hotel by 12 noon today, July 1st.

All British sailors, aviators and soldiers on leave must report to the police station.

No boat or vessel of any description, including any fishing boat, shall leave the harbours without an order from the military authority.

The sale of motor spirit is prohibited except for essential services. The use of cars for private purposes is forbidden.

All blackout regulations already in force must be observed as before.

Banks and shops will open as usual.

The Islanders now knew where they stood; the rules were what they expected. Guns were handed in with some humorists presenting toy pistols bought from Woolworths.

More German troops arrived, and then the occupation continued for five years after the ill-fated air raid at the White Rock Harbor. Among those troops, little did the aforementioned Hans Gruber realise how his stay on the sunny Isle would affect his life.

Chapter 22

Consummation

One rainy winter's day news came that Hans's stay in Guernsey had come to an end; he was to be transferred and posted overseas, the whereabouts undisclosed. This news came as a shock to Rachel. Hans, while in Guernsey, was safe on the Island - no battlefield where one has to fight for one's life. Fortunately, he lived on a peaceful Isle with only the occasional Allied plane on reconnaissance sorting out ships that held German supplies on their way to the islands, destroying them when possible, but never releasing bombs over the Island population. St Peter Port Harbor was one of the selected targets. Hans leaving the Island would be a different story, he would probably be sent to a war zone where bullets and bombs spell death.

So, on the final day of his stay, as they said a secret goodbye laying in the loft among the sweet-smelling hay, the inevitable happened. As tears of grief trickled down each face, a fear came over Hans and his beloved Rachel. This moment in time may be their last together to consummate their love. Fear for the future drew them closer in this moment of time; nothing else mattered, only love. He gently guided his passion into her excited cove, a domain where no other man had entered. Maintaining a rhythm he gently forged forward into the sanctity of his beloved Rachel enclosing him in her legs.

Oh, the pure joy of love found in the arms of this man whom she now loved from the depth of her soul. Rachel's lips tingled as Hans sealed her mouth with kisses that sent a message throughout his being, an uncontrollable desire to abandon self-control. His heart beat faster sending blood surging through his veins, his brain receiving an urge to satisfy his passion. Rightly or wrongly there could be no turning back. The hunter had sorted out his prey to be devoured, not in lust but in pure undiluted love that knew no bounds. Hans had found his Goddess of Love, she, her Adonis. Each had feelings within that had to be satisfied or left to die. Rachel felt the warmth and hardness of Hans's now naked body drawing her close. Removing her arm from around his neck, then placing her hand on his hardened instrument of life, sent a quiver of excitement. His fate was now sealed. Nature had ordained man's desire; you do not reject the passion within. Continue he must, or bear the guilt of self-gratification if the trophy is not claimed in love. Otherwise, the partnership is lust.

Oh, the reassuring comfort of his arms. Mingled thoughts played upon her mind; she had entered the threshold of a woman. So, leaving behind girlish innocence, she gave the sanctity of her body in what she understood to be love, or was this new experience self-satisfaction quelling the desires within? Was this a means to satisfy a lustful sexual experience? No, she gave in love to be shared by no other, a union of two people, consummated by an action obtaining fulfilment. Yes, to this defrocked virgin this was love! Rachel found her body tingling warm with excitement. Hans softly whispered in her sensitive ear as both traveled through the pathway of their lost virginity, assuring this woman that he wished these precious moments of bliss would last forever; not withholding the final moment of ejaculation knowing with his instinctive understanding this was no rape of enemy soil but the yearning of two lovers proclaiming allegiance to each other, not to the country of birth, race or political cravings, entering in their minds to destroy a sublime moment. The fanatical ravings of Hitler were gone forever in the ears of Hans. He now belonged to Rachel and she to him, the seeds of his forefathers planted within her womb to bear fruit in its season. Not the fruit of forbidden love, this was a fruit to be cherished for the rest of their lives, its seeds growing in future generations.

Both lay on that afternoon in a hayloft, not in the elegance of the bridal chamber. Beneath them, age-old planks of wood served them as a hard mattress. No springs to help the movement in transit of desire. No fine quilts covering naked bodies, only sweet smelling hay, the same hay as of long ago that gave warmth to a babe wrapped in swaddling clothes. The conqueror and his so-called enemy, together on the brink of heaven, both fearing this paradise will be lost, never regained. Nay, this was no brink; they had entered the portals of heavenly fulfillments. Can man be deceived thus forgetting the consequences? On that cold winter's day to Rachel, it was Spring, the season of love.

Was it imagination in her eyes, or did a coloured rainbow circle the barn, birds flutter by with hay in beak thus building a nest to nurture its young protected under wing from predators? Hans would also take his beloved under his wing. Darling Rachel, how I love you!

Winter returned on that cold day, a robin alighted on a beam above Rachel's head, her eyes seeing the red-breasted bird. Legends say it is the blood of Christ spilt on the robin's breast. On Golgotha's hill, amid the darkening of the world, left one caring robin to pluck a cruel agonising thorn from the King of King's brow. From that day the king vowed, as legend proclaims, every robin shall display a red breast in remembrance of that act of love. A sudden chill passed quickly through Rachel at the thought of blood. Would she and Hans suffer for their love? Happiness, unfortunately, does not last forever. Will tainted blood be spilt on the scorched earth of a battlefield?

Chapter 23
Eustace

A few days later Hans Gruber left the island that had become his adopted home. Yes, he would miss the charm of the Isle and its law-abiding people. He dreaded the wrench of leaving behind Rachel, the girl whom he loved above all others. When lovers part each gives a gift, a token of their love. Upon a finger of her left hand, he placed a plain gold ring, the special band given by his grandmother on his twenty-first birthday, engraved with the initials H G 1937, and a dove of peace. He gently kissed her lips saying, "Wear this symbol binding our hearts in love, a recollection of how we spent my last hours on your beautiful Island my darling." Rachel kissed the ring holding it close to her face.

"Thank you, darling Hans. I shall never part with this emblem of our love. May God keep you safe wherever you go. Slowly she drew him near placing a silver locket around his neck which enclosed a miniature photo of herself saying, "This also is a token of my love."

It was no surprise to Rachel she became pregnant, a secret she told only to Eustace when her pregnancy was in the second month. Rachel later received the tragic news through a friend of Hans who was in the occupation forces that Hans was killed in action, how or when the friend did not know. For days Rachel grieved, fearing to seek further information which would class her as a collaborator. Hans's baby was now more precious.

She was embarrassed to reveal her condition to her parents, such thoughts sending nausea through her body. In this situation, she would be classed as an unmarried mother, a shameful condition in those far-off days. Rachel had no wish for an abortion, a situation too dangerous to consider. Besides, she wanted Hans's baby. It must not be harmed in thought or deed. How can she explain who fathered the baby? If the truth got out she would be classed as a Jerry Bag! This ugly name was given to women who fraternised and succumbed to the desires of fair-headed, attractive soldiers of the Whermeach, whose sexual desire could be terminated through slaughter on a battlefield, their seed entombed within their corpse. The gratification or deprivation of the flesh - who can blame male or female grabbing the opportunity regardless of consequences? Each must have a mate whether friend or foe. Moral issues relinquished the predator's sexual requirements which human nature fulfilled.

To Eustace, her speech impediment friend who shared all her secrets, Rachel was special. Other girls made fun of his stammer saying unkind remarks, losing patience when the words did not issue from his lips. Deep within him, an awareness caused further concern, plaguing him that somewhere in the recesses of a tormented insecure psyche, he was not like other men, having no physical desire to court a women or lay united in body as other men did. Rachel, sweet Rachel, never taunted him. Oh, how he loved her. Oh, how he wished she loved him as a lover. Perhaps one day she would. His heart knew she would never love him as she did Hans-theirs a special love; she had told him so. This was his cross to bear in silence. Only he knew the depth of her grief and the shame she would have to face regarding her bastard baby. A child born out of wedlock conceived through her enemy; that word 'enemy' would brand her as a traitor forever in the minds of the world, a collaborator who must be punished by death or assassinated by lethal gossip. Whatever faults Eustace had, he was a good man. He would not let Rachel travel alone. He would not let her bear these troubles alone. There is a path he must take whatever the consequences. He must take it.

Early one morning as Rachel sat milking, he nervously approached her with a plan that would solve her problems, daring not to think of the outcome of what he was about to ask. Oh how beautiful she looked sitting there in the meadow on the little milking stool, her soft brown hair flowing in the warm breeze, tints of gold intermingled. Enhanced by the sunlight, her face bore the expression of sadness. Eustace gazed as she milked. The animal's tail swished back and forth to disturb the flies whose aim was to annoy the poor beast's doleful eyes. The look on her face told him everything. Here was his friend whom he loved without reservation, sat on a stool dwelling with painful thoughts of yesteryear. A glimpse of the past captured a strange loveliness upon a face whose mind was dwelling on thoughts only known to her. Strange as it may seem, it is a picture he wished to keep in his memory forever for he could not bear for her to be unhappy. He knew at this moment his life and hers will never be the same if she accepted the proposal he was about to unfold. He prayed a silent prayer for courage, He did not want her get angry or laugh at the step he was about to undertake. Whatever thoughts he had in mind were put on hold. As Rachel hailed him the look of sadness vanished as she spoke to her friend.

He stammered, "Good morning." Yes, she is so beautiful!

Rachel rose from the stool. Stepping closer, her arms outstretched, she embraced him, not as a lover, for she knew this could never be, it was with a sisterly hug. At that moment her fears felt the warmth of his body and the strength of his enfolded arms spelt security. Rightly or wrongly she must accept his love and escape from the well of disgrace and loneliness. She combined frigidness as a wife together with an overwhelming love as his sister. A lifesaver from a bogus marriage built on a lie. Yes, he would be the brother she never had.

For the want of something better to say due to his nervousness, he embarked, "Is the dress new? You look beautiful."

Tears rolled down her face. She had heard those words before by one who now lay in a foreign grave and far from the sweet-smelling hayloft where she had become a woman.

Eustace gently kissed her cheek, tears brimming in his eyes to mingle with hers. On his cheeks, the freshness of her body mixed with her perfume intensified his love. He spoke softly, trying his uppermost to overcome his stammer.

"Dear Rachel, what I am about to say…… You have always been my friend, never making fun of me and long ago my friendship turned to love." These words were too much for Eustace.

Tears rolled down his face as he sobbed uttering his love, his stammer uncontrolled.

Rachel pulled him closer to her. In her thoughts he was a man yet immature in ways of life; she must help him in any way she can. "Dear Eustace don't cry. I know you love me. I love you too."

At those words, the sobbing ceased. He gathered his thoughts. This was the chance to unburden the feelings within. Yes, within her arms, he received strength to ask the question concerning her feelings towards him. His uncertainties left as he gently kissed her soft cheek, "If you love me as I do you, will you marry me? Finally, he had found the courage to ask what had been on his mind for some time.

"Yes my dear friend I do love you, but please understand, not in the same way as I loved Hans. Our love was special as if I am his wife, he, my husband." Our love for each other Eustace is also special, ours is a love of true friendship. What is so wonderful Eustace, love has many aspects whether it be for mother, father, sister, brother, wife, husband, boy or girlfriend, your dog, cat, etc. It is still love if your love is true. Then it is special. Love cannot be halved, there are no half measures. Eustace, my darling friend. Do not cry there is a special place in my heart for you and always will be. Accepting your offer of marriage, please understand my love for you cannot match the love Hans and I had for each other. Hans's love cannot be replaced by another. Understand it will never replace the love I have for you."

"Darling Rachel, I have loved you from the depths of my heart ever since schooldays. What I am about to say may alter our love and friendship. In my life, I've a secret which I've not dared to divulge to any, not even to you." Nervousness overtook him, his stammer became more pronounced, his body shook at the thoughts within. "I cannot continue please forgive me."

"Darling Eustace, there is nothing to forgive. Please tell me what is wrong. You know I will understand." Rachel had never seen him this way, his whole body trembling. She placed her arms tightly around his waist. This contact, feeling the coolness against the hot perspiration of his torso, reduced the rigour of his mind and body. A body contact with the opposite sex, an experience foreign to him. He quickly released his hold. At that moment he never knew why, perhaps a feeling of guilt. Knowing this domain was not a place to linger, he inwardly could not betray his secret feelings that perhaps nature designed. If nurtured, he then would break the law and be punished within by trial and judgment. "Oh Rachel I do so love you. Understand I am not capable of offering the love a man should give his wife satisfying her emotions and desires for a family. I am different in a manner I don't understand. Please help me, Rachel."

A thousand and one thoughts passed her mind. As his sobs continued she, his mentor, was at a loss how to calm him. Her hand reached for his brow gently massaging. Maybe this will help to restore a tormented mind. She searched for the words to inquire of his dilemma. "Tell me, what is so terrible that makes you afraid. We never had secrets, so why can't you say?"

"Please, Rachel, let me finish, however painful. You have to listen before you give an answer. I have prayed to God to change me but to no avail."

He was fighting and defending a secret that had caused him so much anxiety over the years, not given to understand the bitter truth at that period, why his emotions had the desire to seek in mind and body one of his own sex, an inordinate yearning for one of his own gender? This unnatural longing to search for and hold a male in his arms. This ache went even further, frightening thoughts to consume those he embraced. Then, to share his emotional hardness that took over a part that is deemed sacred flesh you never exposed to the world, a private sanctuary these terrifying longings that men of his breed have. This fragment of desire shall in no way be exhibited to a woman. "Oh God help me," he cried in a wilderness, crying with a silent voice with fear of his secret being heard. But help never came. For what Eustace suffered is a part of congenital nature within himself and others likewise in the world, regardless of race, creed or colour. Eustace was not alone. When inquiring why, many times asking, "Am I sick or mad....mad people do stammer and have strange thoughts. "Why am I cursed? Do others feel the same, or is this a quirk in my soul." These questions remained

89

unanswered, only enlightened when people in the course of time had the courage to speak disclosing their sexuality. Only then would the so-called afflicted be allowed to exit from the closet that had held them prisoner until change arrived. In addition, a revision of jail punishment for those who come under the same category as Eustace helped the situation. However, until then, Eustace and others would have to survive in their puzzlement, waiting in exile when each man and woman had the grace to understand each other's individuality with courageousness to accept the difference regardless of religious belief.

Rachel continued to caress his brow trusting hopefully, that she was giving him momentary peace with courage to continue. "I will make you happy as a brother. I can never love you as a husband."

He replied, "Regrettably there is something wrong within, a numbness for physical attraction towards women. I enjoy their company. A relationship as a husband is impossible. I cannot love you as a husband, the desire I should have for a girl is redirected to a man. What is wrong with me Rachel? (Little did he know that question was asked the world over). Amidst sobs, he wrestled with his conscience that he had divulged his innermost secret

After much mind-searching, Eustace found courage on that day to ask Rachel Sarre to become his wife. If we marry, we will take each other as we are a companionship of love. This sacrifice that would save her from the gossip of disgrace, redeeming her in the eyes of other people. If she accepts the offer of marriage, no one will ever suspect that he is not the baby's father. The two had been friends since schooldays, so it was only natural it would be assumed that they would fall in love. Marriage is necessary to give the child a name, even if the baby is premature, saving the poor mite being branded as a bastard born out of wedlock. In the position that faced Rachel was there was only one door open not branded with disgrace and that was to accept what Eustace unselfishly offered.

On that sunny morning, Rachel sealed her fate. There was no other way she could go. Hans lay in a grave far from Guernsey shores, sadly never to return. Their baby would need a father. Her parents would not feel the derogation of disgrace that certainly would have been thrust upon them through their daughter's indiscretion, never knowing just how much hurt and regret surrounds Rachel's heart and mind in guarding her secret. The course of her life had changed; she must go with the flow, the wedding must be arranged as soon as possible before visible signs appear. In retrospect, she felt a sense of betrayal. Days of remorse and guilt, when in her mind she believed she should have faced the consequences for loving the enemy. No, she must not think him as an enemy, he was the man whom she loved, not one ordained by governments to hate and suppress in war, killing for the price of victory. Hans pledging his love in the hayloft, not in lust, but in the desire to hold in his arms forever a woman who stirred his emotions to the point of fulfilment. A person whom he wished to share his life with knowing there would be no other woman but Rachel. After this insane war ceased they would receive the blessing of a church wedding, their dream would be a reality. That hope was now shattered. Information says Hans lies dead by a sniper's bullet. Rachel, tortured by the thought that the death bullet may have been fired by cousin Hal! War is a game of Russian Roulette fired to a nameless target. "God, take these thoughts from me."

Rachel, smiling, took Eustace's hand, drew it to her cheek, then gently kissed the finger that will hold a ring of troth declaring a symbol of love on their wedding day. Eustace, in reality, placed a gold band on her third left-hand finger pledging his love. Both knew this facet of love for each other was superficial only, not as husband and wife; this a marriage of convenience, yet sincere in all other issues bonding them, hopefully, that in the course of time love would blossom from a marriage of expediency and perhaps in time heal the hurt of loss . On this day Eustace found courage, sealing their fate to pursue a course whether right or wrong.

Chapter 24
A Wedding

Announcements in the form of wedding invitations were sent, the date hurriedly set for three weeks hence. Happily, parents on both sides agreed it was a love match, thankful that the loving duo had grown up together at the same school, had the same interests and went to the same church. Yes, this had the basics of a good marriage; may they be blest with children. Yes, it's a good match even with the uncertainty of war.

Friends rallied with ingredients for the wedding cake, even though it meant sacrificing the cupboards of precious stores which were now unattainable in the shops; war brings shortages in many quarters. This wedding deserved the best, war or no war, a real traditional Guernsey reception for the uniting of two respected Island families, the Sarres and Tostivins, whose heritage went back for generations.

Eunice's excitement led her to the dusty attic delving into stored boxes which gave pleasure as she retrieved her white wedding dress laid packed away in tissue paper. The faint smell of mothballs reached her nostrils from the long unopened trunk, bringing tears to her eyes, possibly from a mixture of dust irritation and joy when recalling the memory of her wedding day as she sat sitting on a chair in a cherished garret. Its contents, like so many other things, outlived its everyday usefulness in the home but were too precious to discard. Perhaps this made the owners hoarders. Eunice gathered the gown, caressing the disused article with love as her eyes caught sight of the orange blossom headdress upon which was stitched a netted lily of the valley veil. Is it imagination that the freshness of yesteryear still remained? She remembered the fragrant essence of the flowers decorating the Methodist church on that God-sent sunny day years ago. This, in some way, felt like the recent past, when your happy time never seems over too quick. She pictured the bridesmaids dressed in mauve with pink capes waiting in the arched porch, the young flower boy in velvet trousers and a Persil-white frilled blouse. Eunice sighed, remembering he now has children of his own. She saw excited guests waiting in expectancy for the bride to appear. There, standing in nervous anticipation at the front of the communion rail with his chosen best man, stood Nick, her husband-to-be. How handsome he looked! Turning his head slightly he viewed his beautiful bride clinging to the arm of her father, nervous but resplendent and glowing in a white virginal gown. Yes, a virgin. She caught the look in his eyes which spoke, 'I love you.' Can she ever forget that moment or the honeymoon night when they first slept together making love?

Hmm! How nervous she was before the day. Nickolas banished her fears as she cuddled alongside the man whose life she would share. She enjoyed the touch of his sensuous hands caressing her naked body and his gently kissing her, she who was now his 'To Have and To Hold' forever in eternity. He fought to restrain the passion that he felt within; unrushed movements to assure her of his love, not of the lust of a would-be rapist satisfying primitive desires. This for her a moment of fulfilment she will never forget. Gone were her fears. She was now a woman consummated in love not the sin of Eden. Their life had its ups and downs; a caring love which survived the sadness of losing a young son, then joy regained when receiving a blessing with Rachel's birth.

Rising from the dusty, creaking chair, the effort reminded her that her bones sometimes reacted in the same way. Farming was not easy on the back; digging the good earth, lifting hay, then making stacks, ensuring food for the animals in the cold winter. Yes, farm work is not for the lazy. Descending the ladder her mind reflected that this is not the time to recapture the past. There is a wedding to arrange. Rachel shall have the best, Germans or no Germans. Hitler is not going to spoil her day.

Poor Rachel awoke on her wedding day with a feeling of nausea, uncertainty and guilt, last minute thoughts that would invade her mind for the rest of her life. Is it wrong to have accepted Eustace's proposal? Did she not pledge her love to Hans and he to her? But Hans lay dead, where she did not know. At this very thought of him, tears streamed down her face. No, she must not upset herself, it's his live baby snuggled in her now cherished womb, she must save the treasure that dwelt within. Yes, protect from harm the unborn babe. None must have the slightest inkling that the child is not Eustace's. A lie must survive at all costs. Eustace Tostivin is the baby's father.

Oh, how easy it was to dwell on memories wishing for a replay, to ignore the present things you want to eliminate from a negative mind. Oh, bitter truth, the past is past it cannot be regained. Selfish grieving based on self-pity must go. She must now concentrate on the positive to give her future husband as much love that she incapable of. Eustace is a good and trusted friend. Without his understanding and love, she could not face the future. Yes, she loved him but not the same. "Oh, Hans, please forgive me." Illogical thinking took over, "You are dead and I am alive. Oh, how I wish I was with you on that foreign soil. No, I must live for our baby." In the silence of her bedroom, she uttered a prayer asking forgiveness for entering into a sexual relationship before marriage leading to deceit. God give me the courage to face the future. May Eustace have patience with my shortcomings as his wife and give me the understanding of his needs.

Rachel never finished the prayer as her bedroom door opened and the voice of her mother fell upon her ears.

"Time to get up, this is your wedding day, the most wonderful day of your life." Eunice advanced to the bed on which Rachel still lay, and kissed her daughter. "I cannot believe that time has gone so quickly; it seems only yesterday, that I arose as excited as you must be when it was my wedding day. Your father and I pray for you to be happy as we are. May this day always hold treasured memories. I often wish I could relive that wonderful time in my life, however, I must admit I was a little nervous entering the church, but as soon as I heard the music and saw your father then the fears went. He was so handsome! Darling, marriage is not an easy road. Eustace is a good man and he loves you. Your father and I are pleased and grateful you have happiness and love."

Rachel knew that her love could not stretch to Eustace in the capacity as a wife but she would extend her love in sisterly companionship. The union of heart and soul would remain with Hans even though now he is buried in a foreign soil, and his unborn child will receive his love and hers as if he is living - a posthumous marriage. Eustace the proxy. Dear Eustace, a good supportive man. She must endeavour to love and uphold him whatever he may choose to do. As the chimes ticked away in silence on this her wedding day, in the quiet of her room she vowed to make Eustace her intended husband happy even though she would hold cherished memories of Hans forever.

A slight knocking on the bedroom door transferred her thoughts to wondering who wished to gain entry. Mollie Gaudion, a long time school friend and bridesmaid-to-be entered, on her face a look of surprise at seeing Rachel still in her night attire. "Good morning, Mrs Sarre, what a lovely day for a wedding!" My grandma says, 'Happy the bride, the sun shines on,' so what more can you wish for?" she said, hugging her friend. "Dear Rachel you will be the loveliest bride in Guernsey, thanks to you Mrs Sarre for making her dress.

"Mollie dear, you will be the most beautiful bridesmaid this side of the Casquets," Eunice smiled as she spoke. "Both of you will look belles of the ball. Come on Rachel; put a smile on your face."

Poor Rachel was not in the land of smiles. As she gazed out the window, the sun's rays glistened on the morning dew, sparkling as diamonds upon the trees. Could this picture be a representation forecasting happiness? Within her womb lay a bastard child only to be purified by an untruthful vow to banish the shame. Tears welled in her eyes and then she bit her lip to avoid an outburst of sobbing.

Her mother quickly noticed she was distressed and drew her close saying, "A good cry sometimes does us good." Rachel released her pent up emotions and tears streamed down her pale face, tears only she knew the reason why they flowed on this her wedding day, tears not of joy, but remorse tinged with secret guilt that will never abscond on this earth and beyond. Oh Hans, what have I done? Forgive me my darling. The silent words within her heart only induced never-ending sobbing. Eunice and Mollie both held Rachel close to console her, not suspecting the true cause of this emotional outburst on her wedding day, both never suspecting this well of emotion within destroyed the happiness that a bride should experience on her wedding day.

The tearful, silent communion of three souls ceased. Eunice spoke sincerely trusting what she was about to say would stem any uncertainty within her daughter's mind or heart. "Wipe away your tears; replace joy in their place. It is only natural that you should give vent to your feelings on this most important day of your life. We all feel doubtful when embarking on a new phase of our journey; it is part of human nature. I did, and you will too Molly, if and when the day arrives. Have no fears Rachel; God will be with you helping you over the intimate side of marriage. Eustace is a good man. He will be gentle in his love-making so hush now. Darling Rachel, the intimate side of marriage takes time to adjust to. I was fearful on my wedding night, not of the man I married, but of the pain that I might experience during our love-making which is private and sacred. Darling, understand my words are spoken in Christian love. Dear Rachel, I went to the altar on my wedding day a virgin, having never let a man touch or feel the part of my body that is revered as a gift to be given and received only to your husband on the day you became his wife. Its act should bring satisfaction and fulfilment to you both. Sealing your love any other way is sinful in the eyes of God."

These sympathetic words delivered with fondness by Eunice to hopefully bring comfort to her daughter should have remained silent, as they had the reverse effect of bringing back the pangs of guilt that Rachel had endured over time, and they now loomed greater than ever as the very word sinful etched in her brain. God will withhold his blessing on her, bringing a curse on the newborn infant. This furthering the curse of Sarre and Lihou.

Chapter 25
There will be no Wedding

If Rachel had any further thoughts regarding the position in which she found herself in it was suddenly brought to a halt with a loud repetitive banging on the farmhouse oak door, causing the occupants of the bedroom to wonder who would knock in such haste? Eunice made an attempt to open the bedroom window which had recently received a coat of paint to freshen the appearance of the farmhouse for the wedding. In fact, the whole house had succumbed to the paint brush ready for the bridal reception, but the window remained closed to her efforts. "Oh, why can't they be checked after painting? They all be the same! What if there was a fire?" muttered an exasperated Eunice as the knocking increased.

"It's Eustace's father," said Eunice, replying to the voice that betrayed urgency. "Alright Sid, hold your horses. I am coming. If you continue hammering the door there will be no paint left." On reaching the unlocked door she greeted Sid Tostivin, whose face was as red as the rose that grew near the front door and his breathing was now in puffs and pants due to express delivery of what he was about to say. Mollie, at the sight of Sid in such a condition guided him to a chair, a carved oak family heirloom placed on the granite stone floor in the recently-painted hallway, a location it had held for many years. Petit Close housed many such treasures from a bygone era.

"Whatever the rush, only the declaration of peace requires such haste. These Germans are here for some time yet worse luck. Just sit and get your breath or it is a heart attack? You'll not make it to the wedding and we cannot do without the father of the groom. So what's the hurry?"

At the word wedding, sobs and tears flowed from already red eyes. His speech became irregular as he fought to breathe. "Eunice, there will be no wedding," he said in a voice cracked with emotion

"Whatever are you saying? Of course, there will be a wedding." Before Eunice could say more, Sid found the breath to utter the fatal words, "Eustace is wounded and near death. He is now in the Castel emergency hospital. "Rachel, poor Rachel," he said, as he took his intended daughter-in-law into his arms.

The occupants of the bedroom descended the winding stairs to witness the commotion. All stood bewildered as they gathered in the entrance hallway, each person looking at one another in dismay. Willing not to ask why or how Eustace had met his injuries as all were in a state of numbness pending Sid to resume.

He continued then, with his hands that had seen the rigours of hard work clutched tightly around Rachel's thin waist as if she might escape after he had spoken. Body language showed an assurance that the young couple would be upheld in whatever the future held. The Tostivin family had known Rachel all her life, considered her a good match as a wife and she understood Eustace had a speech problem and he was a good son helping to run the farm. Yes, they make a fine pair and hopefully will have a family to carry on the name of Tostivin. In the twinkling of an eye, the words that he was about to utter would bring untold heartache on this her wedding day. "A bloody German shot him. It seemed that Eustace was helping a slave worker to escape, guiding the poor starving wretch down the mined cliffs. On seeing a flashing light out at sea, the sentry shouted, then raised his gun and fired, killing the slave worker, then fired another shot in the uncertainty that Eustace was a second escapee. His action seriously wounded Eustace."

Eunice turned to Rachel who stood throughout the conversation as if turned to marble, the colour drained from a once happy face, incapable of uttering any voice or signs of emotion; shock had taken over.

Sid released his grip as her mother took her daughter's arm suggesting she should sit in a nearby old-fashioned settle which Nick had purchased from Mr Honey's antique shop in the Bordage in St Peter Port. Nick, ever a romantic, said the story goes Shakespeare had proposed to Ann Hathaway on a settle. In jest, he asked Eunice the same question. Yes was her answer. Rachel disregarded her mother's words and remained as if glued to the spot, her thoughts confused by the present and perplexed by the past. A mind reader would have read the depth of Rachel's anguish. Others only saw the surface.

"Oh, Hans, what have we done? Is this a nemesis of our forbidden love? Fornicators in the sight of God, his retribution, or is this the curse uttered by the young bride dressed in a torn bridal gown haunting La Gree tunnel - a curse passed on to the family brides; or is this a re-enactment of Aunt Salinas's tragic wedding day at La Fontanel's?" Rachel's mind, numbed by what she heard, was incapable of inquiring of the fate of Eustace. Guilt overtook her, suffocating any rational thought in mind and body.

Somewhere in the distance she heard her name uttered in urgency. Replying was beyond her capability. Words failed to make or enter into conversation; it was if she was tongue-tied, stuck in the dryness of the mouth. Then she was transported into oblivion, into a world devoid of light and sound, a probationary state before re-admission into the unavoidable anguish of living. Slowly her limp body slumped towards the cold granite floor. Eunice prevented the impact as Sid guided a chair on which he had been sitting under Rachel's body. Molly, who had remained motionless and silent throughout the tragic news, was now in a state of shock. Suddenly, through the mist of the unspoken words which were now scrambling in her mind, she let out a scream as she rushed to Rachel's rescue. Rachel, now in her mother arms, slowly re-entered the real world. Molly, kneeling down, grasped her friend's hands; her one desire to alleviate the anguish.

"I am sure Eustace is only injured." To what degree, no one in that room of despair knew the extent of the damage which could prove severe and life-threatening which, if he survived, he would live for the rest of his days in a vegetable condition. This frightening prognosis was later diagnosed by the specialist in that field of medicine.

The warmth of her mother's body intermingled with the smell of a familiar fragrance. Rachel had accustomed herself since childhood to this safety zone from woes, when she alone faced an escape from hurt and fear, a pattern since childhood to seek those encircled arms, the cushion of breasts, the smell of a refreshed body, a safe haven for a crying child and now a safety zone for a bereft adult with a subconscious wish that time would stand still until strength flowed as an avenger. She faced the onslaught of the uncertainty of living without awareness or desire as she lay encircled with a want to escape to know the worse, however painful. What untold knowledge regarding Eustace had been withheld, denying her a carnival of blessings and the dishonest consummation of a marriage from one whose pretense guaranteed her atonement? In the twinkling of an eye, the swiftness of an aimed bullet changed the potential of one who sought to cover an act of love, a forbidden love with one who is classed as your enemy in war. Will what she seeks to heal, subject her to unresolved penance for life? In a voice that was strange to her ears, she fought to know the truth. An answer came from her mother who tried to shroud the density of the tragedy.

"Darling, by what I gather from Sid, Eustace had been injured through helping a poor escaping slave worker. The unfortunate man received fatal wounds from gunfire by a German soldier. Eustace also received wounds and is now in the Castel hospital, how serious we do not know. God has placed him thankfully safe. We must pray for his recovery. My darling, I am so sorry, your wedding has to be postponed until Eustace is recovered. In my heart, I know all will be well. Eunice spoke with misgiving, uncertain of the full extent of the injuries. On this happy day at dawn, her eyes had surveyed a picture of life in glowing colours, replaced now in sepia. In a few seconds, life can change its course, either in war and peace; dreams are shattered in knowledge to the brutality of life. Man's first cry from the womb prefaces joy from the months of the bondage now severed, only to be united with spasmodic happiness intermingled with sadness and suffering, till the final curtain returns us to the bondage of the grave, or to the consummation of fire of the believer to eternal life.

Chapter 26
Herr Lang

All thoughts and words were suddenly erased from those in the room by the sound of a vehicle drawing up outside on the sunlit gravel path, the crunch of heavy army boots left no one in doubt whom the wearer was, a member of the occupation forces.

Eunice's arm tightened around Rachel's waist for comfort and protection not knowing if the knocking on the door of this age-old farmhouse brought even more tragic news. Eunice walked slowly to the heavy oak door, her arm still around her daughter in an unspoken bond that will remain forged throughout time. Turning the heavy iron handle that for generations had opened or locked the entrance or exit to family and friends, today it will be neither family nor friend that enters its portal.

As the door swung on its creaking hinges it revealed Herr Commandant Lang, a member of the occupation forces who had served in the 1914-1918 War. Here stood a man who knew the anguish that war brings, a soldier who long since disbelieved the ideologies of the Nazis. To the onlooker, his appearance displayed the face of a man who, in his late fifties, still bore the handsome looks that attracted females seeking a sexual liaison with a viral soldier in the German army. When a younger man, Herr Lang certainly did not have to seek female company for those who desired what he had to offer between or on top of ruffled bed clothes. According to those whom he sampled, he fulfilled their desires. In view of that, Herr Lang had more than enough to offer.

His dalliances for the lust of the flesh ceased when he fell in love with fair Lottie, the daughter of a Lutheran Pastor whom he married while she was still a virgin strong to her belief in the scriptures. The interim period between the two wars brought much happiness in the Lang household, cementing their love when Lottie gave birth to a daughter, and two years later a son. They prayed that their children would not be embroiled in the teaching of the Hitler Youth, and if a war eventuated in the thirties, please God, not be old enough to take up arms. Herr Lang stood at the front door in friendship, not as an enemy to those within but in the requirement of his duty. The information he gave would shatter them beyond belief; a tragic event that would change the direction of those waiting to hear what news Herr Lang would offer to minds already scarred.

Eunice stood aside as Herr Lang stepped inside remaining silent. His face showed the gravity of his mission as did the occupants. The silence was interrupted only as Rachel wept in the safety of her mother's arms. A cue came for Herr Lang to communicate in the language that was understood. Lifting his head, his eyes met the tear-filled eyes of Eunice, who through the haze of distress noticed a deep-seated scar on his left temple, an unwarranted trophy of war.

"It is with deep sorrow that brings me to your house on a day that should be full of joy and expectancy. What has happened was an act of foolishness on the part of the foreign worker to involve your future husband in a scheme doomed to failure. However, on the other hand, your loved one showed compassion to one less fortunate. The guard who fired the shot has shown remorse for the injury caused to your fiancé, for this, I ask your understanding. War is a brutal devastation of life. We await the bells of victory proclaiming peace. After the chimes are silent there are no victors; each has paid a price far beyond the cost of triumph. No side ever wins, the collateral damage consumed and spent in sacrificed human life to await another, is an unjust cause to spill blood. Will man ever learn?"

A thousand thoughts passed through Herr Lang's mind as he stood before the waiting group. If anyone could have tuned into his horrifying memories over two decades, which now surfaced in the blink of an eye, they would understand what changed his understanding of warfare. Standing silently amid the sobs of Rachel, he raised his ringed left hand and caressed the temple scar, now a memory, a memento received by the thrusting of a much-blooded bayonet from a person, an enemy, who remained a nameless British soldier. Hopefully, this wound would heal over time. At that time blood freely gushed down to soak an already stained uniform tainted with the blood of others. Herr Lang pulled the trigger, click-click, a sound only heard by those who released the trigger of an instrument of death, its counterpart bullet that would extinguish the light of life embedded into the heart of a soldier, who would remain anonymous throughout Herr Lang's life on that unforgettable historic day in 1916 when fifty thousand died. Herr Lang, the said victor, watched the cascading arterial blood, its spectacle oozing from his assailants chest, the young Englishman whose information tag would later reveal the name of some mother's son or husband, who would grieve for one who sank into the cold unmerciful ground, to be warmed by blood of the Somme.

Two scars would remain in Herr Lang's twenty-three-year-old body. The temple wound, that in time would heal leaving a keepsake of his brush with death. His other memento would live in his mind and heart kept alive forever by the disturbing knowledge that war meant killing unknown people, men and women whose only crime are views alien to your own government. He was oblivious in mind and body on that day as Herr Lang awaited a stretcher-bearer to carry him far from this procession of blood, away from the close proximity of death that his German bullets had annihilated people on the fatal day.

"They shall not grow old." As he reflected in silence words of an English hymn came to his mind. His brain attuned to ask, 'Oh, God, wherever are you?' In the confusion of the day, unspoken words echoed in his mind.

I am in a still voice to those who cry my name
I am a power above all others
You can attain me in the warmth of the sun
obtain me in the cold winters chill
discover me in a rushing wind
or in the calm and turbulence of the sea.
Locate me in the depth of a soul.
You will witness my handiwork
at the first breath of a newborn babe

observe me in the beauty of the earth
where the blossoms bloom.
Hear me in the strains of music
sweet and compelling.
View my love in gold imprinted on graveyard stones.
Witness my peace
on the face of those who die in loving faith
see the glow accepted on them who follow.
Unconsciousness of my tearful pain
in life's blooded battleground
where man forgoes each other's misplaced affection
in acts cruel and hollow.
Oh, foolish man, I offered a gift in Eden's Paradise.
Free will!

Herr Lang's eyes momentarily surveyed the wretched scene before him; stagnant bodies contorted in death, the air lingering with the stench of humanity. "Oh God, tell me, is this the answer to man's free will?"

You took then abused the given love
a second chance I gave on Golgotha's hill.
Throughout my people cry
Crucify with blood-stained hands they cried
this to me a great concern
Will man never ever learn?
All this and more experienced in my love
You ask where is God?
do not question, but pursue.
You have the means to find the answer true!
In thoughts in mind in eyes and ears.
Seek diligently as wise men in years of old
if so, you shall find salvation's pot of gold.
If not remember omega tryst
which spells the beginning?
A tragic end for man's creation and progression.
For without God's love within the heart

all will wither then surely die
with Earth's lands in recession.
If your intellect does not perceive
the answer you wish to receive
then in unfounded faith
ponder upon the crucial words.
Resist me not, with weeds of evil heart
listen to a shrewd remark.
Be still and know I am truly God
for the good book tells us so
a trusted word of long ago.

Her Lang's brain drifted to unconsciousness on the day they carried Herr Lang on a stretcher out of realms of horror, to live and to fight again in another war. Same countries, same enemies, "Will man ever learn?

Scientific discoveries even more sinister have changed the whole spectrum of slaughter for those who defended their territory. Science with technology works hand-in-hand to slaughter the masses. This is man's achievement in a fight for victory. Over the centuries has Christianity failed, or is it man's inability to hold on to the truth, for man, is easily swayed to evil, relinquishing God's gift paid on a hill two thousand years ago? These were his sporadic thoughts as he stood to deliver a message of an act of war in another land far from home. With feelings of yesteryear suddenly banished from his mind, he now was attuned to the words he would deliver. Hopefully, those words would bring the understanding that his conversation came from his heart, which over the years had subjected his mind to pain, as he was secretly tormented by Germany's New Order injected into a mass hysteria by those seeking a New Reich. Herr Lang was an understanding man whose sensitivity had suffered much by man's brutality at the time of the Final Solution, a régime of true horror, kept as an undisclosed secret from the rest of the free world

Speaking slowly in English with a clipped German accent, his blue eyes gazed, searching from one to another then focusing on Rachel. His presence induced her to release the bond of her mother's enfolded arms. Rachel had seen Herr Lang in the course of his duties in St Peter Port, his white hair a feature of his mature handsome face. Hans had remarked on occasion that Herr Lang was a man of honour who had a sense of fairness to those under his command, and this honour extended to the Islanders when complaining of any injustice that was perpetrated by the occupation forces. Stretching out his arm his warm hand clasped Rachel's hand feeling the damped handkerchief clutched in her clammy fist. Her action was her desire to squeeze the moisture of grief back into her body, only to be replenished in further anguish, having no yearning to waste spent tears. This show of heartache was the only time she could weep openly for Hans in the tears she shed, showing as an outward evidence of grief for Eustace. Those tears that ran down her ashen face were for the two men who changed her life in different directions. Firstly, one who planted life within her body, the other who relinquished her of the sin of fornication. Eustace, taking the unborn child as his own, turning her from a truthful person into a liar, a lie that would haunt her as dishonourable for the rest of her life.

Herr Lang's warm hand matched the words he spoke. "It is a sad time for us all. Tragically your life has been robbed of this very special occasion. It is also a sad day for me having to bring the news of your intended husband's injury and also the death of a fellow human, a prisoner of war, in this case, a slave worker. Forgive me naming him as such. Conflict between nations leads to so much needless sorrow. War is the desolation and destruction of mans' understanding towards each other, leaving lives in ruins as we clash on the battlefield, each side thinking they are fighting for a better world, only to be disillusioned when peace is declared, There can be no harmony while men feed on greed. Today I do not come as your enemy, but as one who has also suffered the futility of war. Strange as it may seem, I come in Christian faith. Sometimes it is difficult to understand why God allows wars. What I do understand is that Jesus asks us to forgive those who wrong us. I ask you, as hard as it may be, to forgive the soldier who mis-aimed his rifle bringing despondency to your family. Realising what he had done, in the space of a few minutes, he acted as quickly as possible to transport the wounded man to hospital endeavouring to save his life. Please accept my heartfelt condolences. Praying to the same God who listens to our prayers, regardless of colour or creed, I ask for your future husband's recovery. I've taken the liberty of placing a car at your disposal to convey you to the emergency hospital."

Rachel spoke in a transient voice, the words near but far away, while her ears desired to cut out conversation reminding her of any incidence of this lost day. She thanked Herr Lang as he clicked his heels saluting the unwed bride. The Nazi salute offered as a token of respect. Herr Lang turned towards the opened door which had remained ajar during his visit, muttering as he left, "May peace dwell within these walls," leaving those within to be accompanied with continued sadness that will never lift in hearts of sorrow on this clouded day in June until the sun arises in the hearts of those who mourn.

Turning with one last look at La Petit Close, whose stones over generations housed happiness mingled with the inevitable sadness, he left.

Chapter 27
Herr Lang's Thoughts

His mind returned to the home of his happy childhood mired in his mind childish games; playing with his siblings and friends amid wildflowers growing in green fields, fishing in the nearby river whose soothing balm refreshed your sweating pores, swimming in the clear unpolluted water. The reflection of his parents was seen on his intellect's mirror, yet untouched by disintegrating mould eating the silvered backing of its picture, untarnished - no spots and specks directing you in irritation from the profiles you loved, long since gone! Oh, joyous and sublime times!

On this return journey to his headquarters, in the Grange in St Peter Port the mirror had cracked within, his saddened mind now flawed. His images were replaced by images of Seig Heil goose-stepping minions saluting banners on which a figure of one who would destroy, conquer, then own the world's soil once again with filtered blood which he prophesized in Mein Kemp. Seig Heil! Seig Heil! To rid the world of the Jew bastard or otherwise rampant homosexuals, leaving only those who abided in untouchable hierarchy of government to follow their desires and slaughtering those who did not fit into the place of high rank of a dictator's maddened dream, incubated by crowd hysteria, aspiring to conquer freedom and democracy in its process with a transfusion of blood from a sane philosophy to an ideology built on evil. This drawing of blood caused by a malicious incision injected to followers of the Nazi régime controlled by a once-Corporal, Adolf Hitler. So many things went through Herr Lang's mind.

Loosening the collar of a uniform not designed for hotter temperatures, his eyes glanced at the famous Guernsey breed of cows grazing in the fields, the animals oblivious to the turmoil of the fast-changing world while munching the cud of the good earth, a ritual since time began.

The Germany he knew and loved would go up in flames, including the city of Bonn, his birthplace and Beethoven's. Landmarks of history wiped out at the touch of a button. High in the sky, the aimer uncertain where the tightly-packed explosives would descend unknown to the recipient, receiving the parcel of death by one pledging his duty to king and country, or was this a myth, each brainwashed with belief that those below hated his guts. The shoe on the other foot matching the size of destruction, each side guilty of murder under another name under the guise of war! War destroys the semblance of freedom to release the chains that bind terrorism or unjustness. Once released mortals find alternative grounds to repeat the cycle. The interminable war is part of man's human nature. Is there no other way to proclaim peace in man's heart?

The warm breeze fanned his face from the heat he was experiencing, not because of the hot temperatures the Island was encountering during 1941, but through fear and humiliation that his allegiance was withdrawn from the country he fought for in 1914-1918, a secret he kept within his heart, disclosed not even to the younger generation of his family, who were, like so many youths, indoctrinated that Germany would be the greatest supremacy on earth regardless of the cost. He thanked God he was placed on this ideal Island, far from the battle scene of the Continent. Here it's people law-abiding to the occupation laws with small pockets of resistance.

Little did Herr Lang know what was going on below the surface, these Islands remaining loyal to the British king whose blood was intermingled with German ancestry. This bond was broken by the murder of an Archduke at Sarajevo lighting the flame of war to slaughter men by the thousands in a so-called 'War to end all Wars'. The 1939-45 war not only killed in the battlefields, blood flowed simultaneously in the family unit, technology finding its way to consume man's safe haven, his humble home, to a mass of rubble scattered over injured and dead bodies, thus turning his castle into a cemetery.

Herr Lang's heart was heavy that day remembering a picture of Rachel descending into grief witnessed only by those who had travelled the same road. Herr Lang detected on the tear-stained face the gathering storm that would only be exposed to others as Rachel's dream was shattered from disbelief to reality. Shattered dreams had been a constant companion to Herr Fritz Lang.

As he journeyed along the hot Island roads, unconscious of any speed limit, his only concern was to reach his headquarters in St Peter Port with its old age charm, a mixture of a bygone French and English eloquence with granite houses, shops whose bay windows had bottle-glass inserts attracting would-be buyers to purchase goods now in short supply. He loved the granite chiseled steps which could elevate those who chose a breathless climb to view the quaintness of the town from above, or to wander along cobbled streets set long ago by a mason devoid of modern cutting tools, a worker relying on the sharpness of his chisel to cut and fashion, creating a work of art for generations to tread and admire, not understanding why, in future days, this skill long lost would be buried in bitumen by modern insensitivity. Herr Lang respected the Island with its mixture of Anglo-French heritage.

Early St Peter Port

The older he grew an anxiety within caused deep concern, that these Isles and lands far from its shores would be dominated, controlled and raped of human rights by those whose behaviour was tinged with madness, co-opted with evil living. These restless thoughts prevailed far into the night hours of darkness, which should have produced balm for a troubled mind. He was ever thankful to be posted to these Pearls of the Sea, away from the bloodshed of fighting in foreign domains. In numerous ways he felt guilty that he was away and not close to his family and home which was subjected to air attacks. He prayed to God, for he was an advocate of the Almighty, praying his loved ones would survive, his sons to return from the theatre of war safe and unscathed. Is this too much to hope that his continued prayers be approved? What makes his family so special when millions die at the pulling of a trigger or by the blast of our modern killing machines? Thus were his thoughts on the day that Rachel Sarre exchanged her white bridal gown for the crisp white sheets of the hospital bed where the groom lay, his tongue silent from unsent messages of a mind tangled in confusion.

As Herr Lang drove along the coastal road his thoughts were interrupted by those working on the cliffside, the slaves of Operation Todd building a tower that would destroy enemies from taking back the lands they had once belonged to. Slaves worked and lived in pitiful conditions. If one of their number escaped, his payback was death, shot by a sentry's bullet that halted his flight for freedom. Liberty comes at a price. This man, in his departure from bondage, instigated the exchange of threadbare clothes devoid of hygiene for crisp white sheets that covered the living and the dead.

A cyclist rode past, destination Petit Close, the house of tears, cycling certainly no joy if your tyre had been replaced by one made from a garden hose. Catching Herr Lang's eye, the rider's carrier held three bouquets of flowers tied with coloured ribbon. Tears streamed down Herr Lang's face, tears of grief for the cancelled wedding. Yes, he cried, for the so-called enemy all have a right to wed whether friend or foe. These thoughts mingled with thoughts of yesteryear, the day of happiness for himself and a young bride, both full of expectation asking that life's journey may be sweetly perfumed as the roses that Greta carried down the aisle of delight. Dear sweet Greta, whose love had never faltered, even during the unsettled political times of Nazi Germany, when showing allegiance to a régime which he knew would pronounce an ending to the land in which his forefathers had lived and died. This was a time in Germany where life was given only to those who supported Hitler and his insane craving to rule the world after the purification of those who opposed him, his determination to create a world free from Jewish influence. Madness incarnate. To protest would denote suffering ending in death for his beloved family including all he cherished. On that day as he journeyed towards headquarters, he knew within himself where his allegiance lay, to ally himself to those whose fight was for freedom against terrorism, allowing men, women and children to live in a world free from terror regardless of race or colour and religious belief.

Chapter 28
Flowers

Pierre Sebire did not understand what had happened to the intending bridegroom at a suggestion by the florist that a heartbreak situation had occurred at Petit Close involving Eustace. Pierre wondered what calamity had befallen his friend, Mon Ami, since schooldays. He was reprimanded from asking questions, and to be on his way, to cycle post-haste to deliver the choice bouquets, even though, on the Island under Nazi rule, flowers and nature still waved the banner of freedom unconditionally for all occasions for either friend or foe. What Pierre expected to find on that sunny morning in a household that awakened on a supposed joyous morning was far from his imagination. He sensed as he entered the aged portal of Petit Close that wretchedness had enveloped the occupants. He placed the flowers on the polished oak table which had served many past generations of Sarres'. There, in the kitchen with the green bed and gorse oven, a rack hanging from the ceiling on which lay sides of salted pork to be consumed at a later date, was Rachel nestled in her mother's arms as a babe seeking comfort from the misery of what had transpired. It only took a few seconds for Pierre to feel the revulsion of what had happened with tears and misbelief that this could occur on what should have been Rachel's special day. Looking to Eunice he asked the full details what had exactly caused Eustace to be lying injured in Emergency hospital.

Eunice gently stroked Rachel's hair and the action released her from the dream state which had taken over her life, causing her to sit upright, gazing from one to another, expecting to see the bridegroom-to-be. In her disappointment, she focused her eyes on Pierre and whispered, "Is it true that Eustace is dead?' Sobbing eradicated any further conversation.

Eunice wiped the tears from her eyes. "No, my darling, he is injured in hospital. We must go at once - Herr Lang has kindly sent a car at our disposal."

"So he bloody-well should, those Ger…………" Whatever he was about to say, cut short by Eunice.

"War brings terrible distress. There is good and bad in all people including us Islanders. You have the rashness of youth like so many today. I pray Pierre, growing older. you'll understand that hate nurtures hate, producing negative feelings. Meantime, we have to live with our enemies. Remember, sometimes it does not take a war to hate. Hate is a word we use flippantly not understanding its true meaning. A terrible word. Unfortunately, there is very little that can be said regarding your friend. "Hopefully we will learn more at the hospital. In the meantime, we must dress for the transport that will arrive shortly that Herr Lang has kindly put at our convenience. Thank you, Pierre, for your concern and thank Jim Falla for making the beautiful bouquets. Sadly they will rest in the hospital ward."

Chapter 29
En-route to Hospital

True to his word, a car from Herr Lang drew up to await passengers. Still in the throes of dressing, the arrival of the car caused concern as the family hurriedly dressed the intended bride into clothes far from the beautiful white lace gown set aside for a day ringed with happiness. Rachel, on entering the vehicle was still in a state of disbelief, her father fulfilling a role far from of his expectations of escorting a daughter to the threshold of married life. Alas, this was not a journey of a bridal party on its way to the flower-decorated church in which Eunice had taken such pride. This journey replaced happiness clouded by tragic circumstances.

The car which had been put at their disposal was commandeered early in the occupation having served Lieutenant Governors during their time of service on Guernsey. Most of the Island cars had been impounded. Only those Islanders who serviced the Island such as doctors and ambulance drivers and those in administration for the welfare of the civilian population were allocated petrol. While Nickolas Sarre received a small ration of petrol to use his tractor for farm work, the family car remained in one of the farm sheds throughout the occupation. Many farmers had to rely on their farm horse to do the heavy work during the occupation. Mechanical machines relied upon in normal times became short or non-existent due to the rationing of petrol or diesel. Eunice often remarked, "What you do not have you never miss making do with what is at hand. Look what the good Lord did with loaves and the fishes. It a lesson to us all."

Eunice was brought up by parents who never envied their neighbors, and was a hard worker on the farm that her family inherited from John De Garis, uncle of the Sarres and Lihous', who had sadly died childless, making Eunice the next of kin, stipulating that the farm was not to be sold, passing only to her heirs after she died. By his will, John De Garis was foreseeing that Petit Close would remain in their family for generations. John De Garis was a man who stood by the Methodist church principles, seeing in Eunice one who also followed the teaching of John Wesley, a faith that Nickolas and Eunice instilled in Rachel.

Guernsey had a following in traditional worship: Roman Catholic, Anglican, Plymouth Brethren, Presbyterian and Methodist as well as Christian Science etc. The Island souls were well cared for in spiritual food. Prior to the war church attendance was on the agenda. During the occupation, many went to pray for deliverance from the enemy including those who only visited in a time of trouble.

The car advanced along the narrow lanes of the parish of the Forest at a slow speed due to military vehicles taking up space, leaving very little room for passing traffic. The German chauffeur allotted to the Sarres' apologised for the slow speed. Sid assured him they understood the reason.

Eunice eyed the soldier, a fresh-faced young blond boy, eyes as blue as the sea. His age reminded her of her nephew Harold, now in the army. Did this boy have a mother who worried about their welfare as she did? Yes, of course, he did. Mothers the world over shared the same love for family whether friend or foe. In the silence of the car, a mute prayer within her heart was said in Christian love for all mothers whose families were separated in their troubles. Eunice's thoughts went out to all who suffered by war.

Glancing towards Rachel a cold shudder went through her body thinking of the horror that had befallen the family. Eustace may have been wrong in helping this unfortunate slave. No, she must not condemn the poor lad. She did not know the circumstances, perhaps never will. No, he was not wrong, the good book says we must love and help each other. Eustace is a good boy. He did what he thought was right helping a poor starved slave miles away from his own family. Eustace must live; he is on the threshold of life with darling Rachel, her ashen face making her appear to be in another world. Eunice took hold of Rachel still clutching the tear dampened handkerchief whispering, "Have faith my darling, things may not be as bad as it seems. Eustace is young, a strong lad, he will fight his injuries."

Rachel at that moment realised the full impact of what had transpired. Her eyes opened to the surroundings around her. "Yes Mum, he is going to live, he must not die." In the poor girl's mind so much depended on Eustace living. The horror of him dying must be wiped from her selfish thoughts. Of course, he would live to claim the name of darling Hans's baby. Rachel shuddered at such thoughts. May God forgive her this mixture of thoughts, leaving her unprepared for what lay before at the Emergency hospital in the Catel parish which, in the future when peace arrived, would become the Island's mental home.

Chapter 30
Eustace at Hospital

The car drew up at the entrance to this somber granite building, its beauty unheeded by those who eyed it, and yet, within it walls over decades, joy and sadness had played a part hand-in-hand. It was a place of hope, a place where life suffering ended or became a refuge for some to restore to good health.

As Rachel and her family entered its portals they anticipated the worst. The smell of antiseptic permeated the building, its very essence welcoming the visitors in unspoken words, "You are now cleansed." This cleansing remained for hours after, attached to clothes, nostrils and mind, a memento of what was observed in the beds of suffering. The hospital porter greeted the family with a smile, ushered Rachel and family in haste along a hideous green and brown painted corridor to the ward where Eustace lay under snow-white sheets. Their guide intimated to Rachel as they proceeded along, "Your husband will survive his terrible injuries." If these words were said to bring comfort they fell on deaf ears bringing a flood of sobbing to the receiver whose only thoughts was to be near her intended. Eustace was not her husband, a position withheld by a quirk of fate. Perhaps he never will be! Those words filled her with fear and guilt. She was half afraid of entering the room occupied by a single bed in which lay Eustace, his head and face half-covered with bandages, a saline drip attached to his arm, an oxygen mask placed over his nose that protruded through the bandage. Rachel drew a deep breath, released her mother's hand and took courage in seeking Eustace's hand above the sheet; its coldness brought further fear to her mind. Was this icy-cold hand the symbol of death?

Nurse Beryl Lucas, who had stood by to see the patient's needs, saw the look of fright in Rachel's face guessing her thoughts. Don't be alarmed, his pulse is steady. Dr Gibson has every hope he will recover. It is still early days to see a great change; also a German doctor who practised in Berlin before the war confirmed the seriousness of his injuries. He is in good hands, both doctors making sure he receives the best possible care through this difficult time. Thankfully he is alive."

At these words Rachel nodded, a forced smile appeared. Yes, we have a lot to be thankful for, unknowing at the time what lay ahead. In the quietness of the room, the family gathered around the iron bed, quietly whispering their love in hushed tones, to a body incapable of movement or speech.

"Matron Rabey asked if you would join her in her office at your convenience." Sid took it upon himself to thank Beryl for her attention, his voice hardly audible to the rest. Sid, a man of tough Guernsey stock had weathered many a storm in his fifty-two years. The news he received today broke the hardness that other saw in his character, He wept, "War Bloody War!"

Turning to Eunice she put her arms around him. Tears also streamed down her pale cheeks. "Courage Sid. In these times we must show courage."

Eunice encouraged Molly Gaudion to accompany the sad, bewildered family in the knowledge she would support Rachel in uncertain times, a true loving friend since childhood. Molly was unaware of her friend's secret. Rachel did not wish to break their bond of friendship, for deep down she felt the pangs of guilt of what had occurred out of wedlock. An even deeper pain within was why she was using Eustace to cover her misdeed of fornication with Hans whose love will rate far above which Rachel could bestow on Eustace in marriage.

Matron Rabey's office still had the chill of an early morning; the contents of paper and tinder in the small grate had not yet been lighted. Matron apologised for the lack of warmth. The office was a small but a well-organised administrative centre. "I am afraid we are short-staffed, relying on volunteers, which do an excellent job in the circumstances, due to three unexpected people succumbing to dysentery. It is no wonder with irregular diets, plus the arrival of Mr Eustace Tostivin in the early hours of the morning, the poor man surviving some terrible injuries. The bullet wound was bad enough but he sustained further serious damage to his body due to the fall. At the mention of a fall, Eunice inquired the nature of it, being ill-informed of the character of his injuries. Matron apologised saying, "The staff understood you were aware of the extent of the damage to his body. Apparently, when the shot penetrated his skull it caused him to fall backwards sliding over the edge of the cliff into hard jagged rock fifteen to twenty feet below. He is extremely fortunate to have survived due to the soldier by not leaving him to die, which he certainly would have done."

A knock on the door interrupted any further conversation as John Ozanne apologised on seeing the visitors, "Sorry Matron, I came to light the fire."

Matron continued, "By the diligence of the soldier who caused the shooting, and raised the alarm for an ambulance, this prompt action saved his life. Thank you, John, come back when it's convenient." Matron went on to explain that John Ozanne lived further up the road at a farm at Benauderie run by his parents, Jack and Rose, a hard-working couple who always guaranteed a welcome to whoever called. A large hot kettle permanently singing on a Martin Range assured the visitor or tradesmen that Rosie would produce a hot cuppa, together with a slice or two of her delicious Guernsey Gache or a helping of mouthwatering blackberries picked from bushes that hugged the wall of this aged farm. The recipients received the fruit topped with golden Guernsey cream, its flavour long remaining on the taste buds. The Gache was made those days under difficulties due to the shortage of ingredients.

Gache

One thing you could be sure of in Rosie's spotless Guernsey farmhouse, with the hens coming and going through the ever-open door, eyeing Rose and encouraging her to throw some scraps in their continued search for tidbits, was her hospitality. Even in dire times, it was such that she found time to help those in need. Many a slave worker was offered sustenance and clothing to replace well-tattered smelly rags that adorned these poor unfortunate wretches, forced into labor by the commands of the Third Reich to build the Atlantic Wall – a defensive wall that stretched thousands of miles throughout Europe and Scandinavia to protect German coastal submarine bases, thus allowing them to chase and sink Allied shipping. The losses of shipping caused Winston Churchill unease; he pulled out all stops to defend the convoy's lifeline that brought essential supplies to Britain and elsewhere. The loss of ships was not his only concern; it was also the loss of gallant sailors.

Rachel noticed as John Ozanne walked out of the matron's office that he dragged his left leg. She wondered if he may have received an injury through a German bullet. This was not the case, John, as a twelve-year-old full of life in prewar Guernsey, on his way to school and full of adventure, peddled top speed down steep Catel hill, hands free of the handlebars, hit a gravel patch, missed a marmalade cat who snarled in return, as John somersaulted over the handlebars, sending the feline interloper up a tree, with the cycle landing on top of his leg causing a deep wound. Its existence stayed with him for many years in the form of T.B. in the bone which necessitated dressing twice daily. Little did Rachel know that John Ozanne would play an important part in her life, together with the occupants of Benauderie.

Rachel's thoughts were suddenly interrupted as she sat in the office on a day that should have been one of her happiest, by the wail of the siren which heralded the British pilots on a mission, either reconnaissance or bombing a German target, a sound that was all too familiar at various times.

Matron Rabey ushered them to the door that led to the cellar, informing them that she would return later after seeing to patients, saying, "You'll be safe here. I don't expect the raid will last long.

Our boys are after ships in the harbour or the airport, they will not drop bombs in this area." No sooner had matron left, the sound of an explosion in the distance filled their ears, a reverberation that would be heard at intervals during the occupation on an Island that had kept its freedom for a thousand years.

Matron returned as the All Clear echoed that the danger had passed. "You are welcome to stay as long as you wish on the understanding that the nurses and doctors will be in attendance, which will necessitate you leaving the ward for a short while." Turning to Rachel she said, "If you will kindly come to the office so that we can return what we found in Eustace's pocket: a set of keys, a marking pen, a man's handkerchief on which was scribbled S T E K C O R. E. R. F. R E. W. N .E .T E .K A. R. T I.B B .A.R. Matron handed the handkerchief to Rachel and suggested that Eustace might have been doing a crossword. Rachel took the grubby material, surveyed it, then returned it to Matron Rabey saying, "I've no idea what it means or why he wrote those letters. Perhaps you are right, he may have been doing a crossword. Eustace was quite good answering the clues."

Rachel felt a shudder go through her body as her eyes caught sight of a dark red stain which she assumed was blood. This was no assumption, it was blood, the very blood that had oozed from Eustace through receiving a bullet that would change both of their lives forever. Her unstable imagination took over at this time when everything had seemingly been taken from her, the loss of her wedding day, joined with a partial love in her heart for the man she was to marry. Yes, a love, but one not befitting a wife to give to her bridegroom. A love that hid a deeper tenderness in the recess of her heart, a love that she had given Hans in a hay loft, sealing it forever unconditionally as her virginal womb received his sperm. Whatever the outcome, they did not plan a future on that thoughtless day; it was those precious moments that counted. This was the reckoning time for an outlawed love. 'Seeds you sow are the harvest you will reap.' Life desires payment in cash or kind, irrespective of creed or person. Her sobs became the laundry to obliterate the erroneous stains she had wrought to Hans, to Eustace, to the lies that would lay hidden in her forever. Sobs cannot wash away the pain in a heart or brain. So Rachel in her anguish, distressfully cried out, "Darling Eustace, please forgive us." In her mind was it Hans and herself who asked for forgiveness from Eustace. "I do love you. Stay alive. I would never cause you hurt! Oh, Eustace, you accepted me as I am. Please stay we need you."

Whether those words reached his ears lying in a stark hospital bed, Rachel will never know, for the time had come for Eustace Le Poidvin to exit this life, peacefully, with no outward struggle, just a few deep guttural sounds heralding death, together with a fixed stare through a slotted eye-blooded bandage covering a shattered traumatized head, a final gaze at Rachel which the silent group interpreted as 'I Love you'. Eustace Tostivin, whose impediment of speech had received unkind taunts since childhood and his sexuality which had become a thorn in his flesh, was now banished, bringing a reconciliation. No more would he have to hide his sexuality; in Heaven all men are equal. Does not the Good Book say so!

At that moment Rachel felt far away from the Good Book, regarding its teaching. The Good Book also says fornication is a sin. Was this God's retribution for sin committed on the afternoon when love knew no bounds? "Oh Hans, what have we done? Our transgressions have caused Eustace's death." Such were the irrational thoughts in her mind on that fateful day.

As the evening shadows fell she sat holding his hand, a cold hand which she dare not leave, for it was a link with the condemned future. The hand was now in the process of rigor mortis, the very hand that would have placed a ring on the third finger of her left hand, a symbol of a bond that she was his 'Till death do us part.' Death had won.

After taking the small triple-diamond engagement ring from her finger, with a gentle touch, she transferred Eustace's token of love to his third finger left hand with silent words spoken from within her heart. "I thank you my dearest friend for the sacrifice you made in asking me to be your wife, knowing that it was impossible for me to be a true wife." A marriage of convenience so often described in romantic novels. Dearest friend keep this engagement ring forever upon your eternal finger in the grave. I am not worthy of your love. I make a solemn vow on this dreadful day that I shall not marry, thus bearing the shame of unmarried mother. May God be my helper." This declaration was uttered amid the silence of the green-painted ward of hygienic odours which proclaimed the room as germ-free.

Chapter 31
Corporal Rudolf Schmitt

Rachel's thoughts were interrupted. Her eyes strayed from the lifeless bridegroom's bed, an altar earned for the sacrifice he gave to an escaping wretch. Her eyes focused on a nurse's outstretched hands to guide her to the safety of her family, her mind sterilised by the happenings on a day of wedlock, unable to hear phantom bells of joy that no longer existed for Rachel. They would remain ever silent, together with later tears: mistaken by the undertaker when Eustace was buried as grief. Her torn heart knew the suffering of a forbidden love. Rachel watched as if an unearthly spectre was within the body of the nurse's white uniform, the image far away from reality. This was a product of her clouded mind and yet she knew that the two must be united. She advanced towards this eerie white figure whose sanitised caring hands took Rachel gently away from one whose life was extinguished, propelling Rachel from the bedside of death.

Surprisingly, in her grief, she was transported to veracity, the sensation of new life not her own. The babe quickened within her. It was a moment she could not enjoy, for her soul contained negative thoughts, all senses eyed through a mist. A German soldier stood standing by the bedside. Unnoticed, he nodded to the nurse who in reply said, "Would you kindly wait." No words passed his lips, just a shake of his head; he recognised this was no time for conversation. Rachel turned her head to the waiting soldier then and as if awakened from a dream asked, "Are you the one who called the ambulance? Are you the one who Sh…" No more was uttered, the dream world returned to the bride that never was.

"No Madame, I am not." No more was said.

Rachel drifted to the hands of the caring nurse and they slowly left the room.

The soldier had surveyed the room during the drama between nurse and patient. This person was not there for commiseration. He furtively scanned the ward and after one more look making sure he was alone, he shut the door to intruders and proceeded to the business in hand. First, he looked to the contents of the bedside table whose drawers proved empty. Another inspection of the meagre furnishing of the room, then he cautiously opened the unpainted pinewood cupboard, a makeshift wardrobe, then his hands rummaged among every inch of Eustace's bloodstained clothing. In a sealed brown paper bag was a pair of shoes together with a watch and a pencil, all waiting collection by the grieving family. He resealed the object of his curiosity and then a knocking on the door stalled any further search.

John Ozanne stood at the now opened door, somewhat taken back at the sight of a member of the Wehrmacht, whom young Johnny in the exuberance of youth just tolerated, his memory prompted by the remembrance of three of his uncles and his mother's first husband killed in 1914-1918 conflict, a war of slaughter and murder. "What are you doing here? This room is private! Have you no respect for one killed by your kind whose only crime was trying help one unfortunate from escaping the unjust treatment of slave workers by the likes of you. This hospital is run by us civilised Guernsey people, not by German Huns. Go! Go about your business. Matron Rabey is in her office."

The soldier shut the cupboard. "Brave words from one so young, dangerous if directed to the wrong people. I did not know this man, his eyes turned to the bed pointing at Eustace. I am in no way connected with his death nor do I partake in unfair treatment of slave workers. Remember this is war; war is ugly, very ugly. In future it might be wise to hold your tongue or the consequences may cause you and your family to hear words you will regret. The war is not over. Until then you are under German command. If you Islanders obey our rules then you have nothing to fear. Adolf Hitler is no ordinary man; he is a proclaimed God who will set the world free from capitalistic governments and Jewish scum. Heil Hitler."

With a click of his heels, he left the room leaving Johnny muttering in Guernsey French. Very little notice had been taken of the words spoken by the misinformed German victor. Luckily for Johnny, his words said in the Island patios were not understood by the departing soldier whose mind was in a state of confusion. His mission unsuccessful, not finding what he hopefully undertook to retrieve - a scrap of paper bearing vital information.

Matron Rabey, pre-warned by Johnny, proceeded from her office to be confronted by the nameless soldier who immediately saluted, thus embracing his semi-god, Adolf Hitler. Matron Rabey, somewhat taken aback said, "It will be more convenient and manners if you made an appointment."

"I have no wish to intrude fraulein. Corporal Rudolf Schmitt at your service madam. I only require a few minutes of your time."

"Very well, but next time make an appointment so as not to waste my time and yours."

Sitting in matron's office Herr Schmitt related what brought about his visit enquiring, "Did you find any letters on the shot man or scraps of paper on which something was scribbled?"

Matron held back her answer, then untruthfully said, "No, I did not. If that be all, I will get back to my duties."

"Thank you, madam. If you remember any conversation with the wounded man, please telephone."

"Did you not notice when you entered the room marked 'Staff Only' that the poor man was incapable of speech? Good day. Nurse will show you out."

Chapter 32
Losing a Mind

Rachel, her hands still locked tightly in the nurse's caring hands, caught sight of her mother.

"Hello, darling." Eunice stretched out her hands to her daughter but to no avail.

Rachel stopped, shook her head, "I want mummy."

"Yes Darling, mummy's here."

A far away expression took the place of apprehension upon her daughter's face. "No, mummy is not here, No, I've lost mummy. My mummy would have come lifting me up into her arms, cuddling me in her warm breast. I would snuggle while she stroked my hair as she did when I was so sad, softly whispering in my ear. 'Don't cry darling, Tinker has gone to live with Jesus, with gentle Jesus who cares and loves us all even our pets, especially Tinker the beautiful pussycat.' We all go to Jesus if we are good, mummy said so. I believed mummy but I don't anymore. Gentle Jesus took Hans and Eustace and now mummy is gone. It's all because of what I did. They must never know. I will hide in a cave forever." A wave of exhaustion came over her as her legs lost the support of her body. No more was said.

Rachel lay unconscious on the hard cold paving stones, with Eunice thoughtful over Rachel's words. Dr Rose was summoned to the pitiable demented Rachel. He gave strict instructions that his poor trauma patient be transferred to a bed and a nurse to sit with her till she regained consciousness with no interference, especially from German command. Dr Rose had remained on the Island, disregarding the warning the Island might be invaded, with thoughts that if the worst came to the worst, the Island population that remained under German rule would need medical care by someone they knew and trusted.

Eunice remained at the hospital on that fateful day. The rest of the Sarre family returned to the farm; work had to be done, milking etc. Farms are never silent even at night and when the cattle and sheep are in labour they need care. Who would have thought that this day, promising to be a time of joy, was altered in a few seconds, turning to grief with the death of the bridegroom, then a manic bride loosing reason of the situation? Also, there was an air of mystery surrounding the coming of a German soldier intent on searching the hospital room. Eunice at this moment was at loss in mind and body at what had transpired in less than twenty-eight hours, praying in the silence of her heart, 'Poor Eustace, my poor soul, find peace in Heaven. No more can be done, only the healing tears of grief. Rachel whose life promised joy and a life full of hope for the future reduced to a demented state. God knows how long this will last.' Eunice drew a breath, thinking thoughts she wished banished, that her loving daughter may not come out of the state she is in, perhaps would need psychiatric treatment. "Thank god there are no children." Eunice felt a comfort in those words, having not the slightest inkling that her world was on the brink of change. Yes, she must be positive; Dear Rachel will survive with the help of the family. All these thoughts and more went through her mind as she sat in vigil at Rachel's bedside.

The hours ticked by with Rachel in a state of calm except at intervals crying out but not returning to consciousness.

Chapter 33
German Headquarters

Away from the hospital, at the headquarters of the German intelligence, Corporal Rudolf Schmitt stood in front of his superior and was questioned regarding his search at the hospital. "You say nothing was found in the room and clothes of the dead man?"

"Yes, Mein Herr, nothing."

A grimace overtook the superior's face. He was a man who required results at any cost saying, "Try harder. This time Schmitt, my informant assures me the dead man was handed a paper with vital information. Go and find it. This time I will not have no for answer. Go, and remember if this information got into the wrong hands, it will change the course of the war costing Germany the victors crown. If required take help with you. Go to those in command. Expect results. Make sure you get them."

Rudolf Schmitt left with foreboding in mind and heart with the knowledge his superior was a hard man and that if he failed he would more than likely be sent to the battlefields far from his homeland.

Chapter 34
Rachel's Condition

Meanwhile, back at the hospital, Dr Rose called to check on Rachel. Then turning to Eunice he said, "No change as yet with your daughter. She may take some time to come around. I advise you to get some sleep. A nurse will sit with her. Matron Rabey I am sure will find you a bed, waking you if any change. In these cases, you do not know how the tide will turn. No more sedation until further notice. We must get the full picture there, the baby to consider at this stage, no wish to terminate or have her miscarry."

Eunice was thrown by the doctor's words. "Excuse me, doctor, Rachel is not pregnant."

"Sorry Mrs Sarre, we understood that you knew. Rachel is nearly four months in carrying the little one, even though her state is not yet noticeable. Oh dear, please accept our apologies. So sad to be without a father! What a dreadful day this has been for you, and now learning of your daughter's condition."

If Eunice wanted a shock to beat the day's takings, this was it. Rachel pregnant! Oh my God, and Eustace the father dead. Oh God. A thousand thoughts and questions were in Eunice's mind, but these would have to lay dormant until Rachel recovered. The question of sleep was far from Eunice's mind. The doctor must be mistaken; Rachel would never allow this to happen, she was brought up a Christian, so was Eustace. No, it must be a mistake on the doctor's part. Yet, they did push the wedding forward. I do not understand, we have always been so close, sharing each other's problems as friends, in a relationship that Eunice thought was secure and secret-free. Sometimes you can relate troubles without embarrassment. This was what Eunice understood and now maybe she had got it wrong. A wave of thoughts mingled with the idea of rejection on the part of Rachel that she as a mother failed in bonding with her precious daughter. These thoughts were banished at the realisation that her father would have to be told. Poor Nick, she was the apple of his eye; a loving man who abided by his Christian principles. This development will be a testing time for forgiveness. Then there is the pastor, a strict Methodist. Who lived by the bible? They shall not commit adultery or fornicate. "Dear Jesus forgive my daughter and Eustace." This prayer within her mind and heart on this set wedding day.

Suddenly a telephone sounded in a nearby room interrupting Eunice's thoughts. The nurse who had sat with Eustace appeared. "Excuse me. Matron has arranged a bed in this room for you to stay the night and your husband is on the phone in the office."

"Thank you, nurse. What is your name?"

"Enid Sebire," she replied. My father is Walter Sebire from the La Fregard. I believe you went to the same school."

"Oh yes Enid, we did. In some ways, after what has happened today, I wish I was back in those happy days with my parents at St Andrews when troubles seemed so minor."

In the office, Eunice picked up the phone to speak to her husband, his voice firm but troubled. "How are things? Herr Lang phoned to hear the latest. He seems a good man. Of course he has a family in Germany. All the world over people worry about family. I am so worried not hearing."

"Nick there have been developments here that I cannot say over the phone. At the moment she is sleeping, no change. I'll keep in touch. All we can do is pray not to lose our faith. Please let your mother know, and the others, they will be so worried. It is worse waiting at home. It is bad enough here, but at least I can speak to Dr Rose and the staff are so kind. Dr Rose suggested I lie down and try to sleep. Matron is putting a bed for me near Rachel; matron is so understanding. What with the occupation Nick, how do people manage in these situations, telephone, cable, cut off from England? What if Rachel needed a specialist?"

The very thought of isolation loomed in a mind traumatised by the day's happenings and set Eunice to lose her control emotionally. Her tears flowed, subdued, but soon held back for the sake of Nick, offering an excuse, "I must go, matron wants to use the phone. Goodbye."

She replaced the receiver to stop any further outbursts of the emotions that dwelt within. Closing the door she returned to Rachel's, room to find Rudolf Schmitt standing beside the bed. No nurse was in attendance and the bed had the appearance of being disturbed by someone making a quick search. Its ruffled state caused Eunice to ask, "Where is the nurse?"

Schmitt answered with a tone that betrayed no apprehension, "No cause for alarm madam, the nurse has gone with my companion. I've just come from the office. There was no sign of matron or your companion."

"Why has someone ruffled the bed? What are doing to my daughter?"

Rudolf Schmitt looked threateningly into the eyes of his questioner then leant forward with an ugly intonation in his voice "Do you question my answer? I trust not, life can be very difficult if you do."

Eunice's uneasy feeling stopped her from further questions at that moment. Schmitt's companion returned accompanied by Nurse Sebire.

"Matron was not in her office. I shall try in the other wards."

Schmitt turned to Eunice, "You see madam, Herr Schmitt does not lie, it would be well if you remember. Good day Madam Sarre, let us hope we meet in happier circumstances. Come," he beckoned to the unnamed soldier. "We will teach the Guernsey pigs not to question our words. Heil Hitler." For the moment he was gone out of Eunice Sarre's life.

Eunice straightened the bed covers. The regulation blackout curtains had been drawn earlier shutting out the darkness that covered the land. So it was with Eunice Sarre, the happiness of a promised day gone by a single shot. Consumed, forever. "I have the joy of wedded bliss but it is never to ring in the heart of Rachel and the lifeless form of Eustace, silent forever. Oh, what will happen?" was the cry of a mother bereft of her children.

After the chimes are silent will they ever ring again in the lives of the Sarres and Tostivins? In the silence of the room where Rachel lay, Eunice prayed for the healing balm of Lebon in mind and body for all who suffered; that day her tears and prayers were not only for her family, she included all the mothers over the world, innocent mothers of all creeds and faith. Affected by the scourge of war, her thoughts turned to the biblical slaughter of the innocents of old. Will man ever learn? Men and women sent to their deaths through the political ravings of governments, this one termed as The Final Solution by a man whose legacy was death.

As she prayed, a makeshift bed was placed next to Rachel so she may sleep. This was certainly a day to remember. Rachel slept oblivious of what was happening, a respite from the turmoil. As Eunice lay down, a clouded, colourless kaleidoscope of unhappy thoughts quelled any sign of sleep.

Chapter 35
Petit Close Farm

Back at Petit Close people came and went. Some had not heard of what had transpired over the last twenty-four hours. To say the least, all were in shock. Nick attended to farm work as best as he could, the cows milked with the aid of a friend. Eunice remained at the hospital. Nick engrossed himself in the mundane things about the farm believing that doing so took the mind off worries. As he fed the pigs an army truck drew alongside the pigsties. Herr Schmitt alighted with the unknown henchman, saluted Nick, then proceeded to question him regarding a note that Eustace supposedly had in his possession - of which Nick was ignorant. "I know nothing of any note or letter. If there had been I am sure Matron Rabey would have handed it to his father or my daughter." Since neither had seen any note or papers, then it did not exist.

Herr Schmitt did not accept the answer lightly, his face glowered as his downturned mouth went into a scowl. "I repeat, you all would be wise not to withhold any information. We know that a piece of paper was passed to your son-in-law."

Nick was quick to correct the threatening Schmitt. "Unfortunately, due to one of your soldier's actions, my daughter was deprived of a husband on her wedding day, so that and the accusation of giving false information regarding the whereabouts of a missing note is entirely wrong."

Herr Schmitt had no intention of correcting his mistake. He saluted, clicked his heels, said, "Heil Hitler," then left, leaving Nick with a sense of satisfaction.

Nick muttered to the waiting pigs, "You have more manners than that German pig." As he continued to feed and clean the sty, a job far removed from being father of the bride this day- an occasion that would have brought him joy as he had no fears that Rachel would be unhappy with her choice. They had grown up together, a childhood bond that grew into love. Such were his thoughts on a day that should have been a wedding celebration. Life must go on. This duty had to be done, and he splashed the bucket of swill into the wooden trough, his brain far removed from the task at hand, consciously knowing he must keep occupied in an effort to take his mind away from what had happened. As his thoughts weaved from one situation to another a nagging contemplation wrestled within. "Is this part of the curse that has followed the Lihous and Sarre for generations?" An unexplained phenomenon accruing at various times which never had been laid to rest, even though devout men of God had endeavoured to exorcise the spirit's unrest, all to no avail. Guernsey folk over generations believe in such happenings, saying that if you are skeptical of such occurrences of these ghostly figures they become manifold so that the sceptic will believe.

Nick remembered the tale of his great-grandmother whose long wavy brown hair turned white overnight. She was an unbeliever until an incident caused her to rethink. Unfortunately it was not only her hair that changed. Her mind also suffered. The poor soul was never the same; in life she gained no rest. Worse still, after her death, in the pale moonlight when the moon was high, this restless soul appeared walking the farm fields with an empty milk bucket in hand, searching in vain for cattle fast asleep in the hay. This disconsolate psyche of a woman searched, casting spine-chilling shadows on granite walls. On the stroke of midnight, each chime became starkly vivid in the ears, tantalising the brain to think of the supernatural. The locals warned sceptics to believe, if not accept their fate. Many carried a crucifix as an antidote against evil. Strange and mysterious things happened in Guernsey and Sark and the rest of the Channel Islands, as related by Edith Carey and Sybil Hathaway in their books of folklore. Nick, after what had occurred, could not reject the Lihou and Sarres curse.

Chapter 36
Mollie Gaudion

Mollie Gaudion appeared as Nick finished feeding the pigs. How she got there from the hospital Nick did not know or care, but at least it was a comfort for someone to be with him during this terrible time.

"Can I help," the first word that Nick heard from this young bridesmaid-to-be who, like the rest of the family were suffering shock over what had transpired during the day. A day that dawned with expectation only to be severed with grief and repeatable unhappiness.

"I would appreciate a cup of tea. Afraid its bramble tea, no more Lipton, still it will be better than nothing at this time. God knows when we get good old Lipton tea again unless it is on the barter or worse still the black market. What will Eunice do with the food that people generously gave for the reception?" Nick optimistically posed, as did Mollie. The guests would still come bringing condolences; maybe food will be eaten or perhaps will be wasted in their sorrow. What a day it has been.

These words stuck in his throat. At the very thought of the cancelled wedding it reduced this resilient man to sobs, tears which he tried to evade but could not. The Guernsey men, like Australian Bushmen, are battlers. Nick, a man of the land, knew that spring had died on this day replaced by a bitter winter. Nick's thoughts turned as so many do when faced with undeserved tragedy. Why, oh why? Unspoken words on his lips which turned him to the tasks.

Mollie turned as she walked away to the kitchen. Stopped, then with no embarrassment ran back to take hold of Nick in her arms, reading his thoughts, "Yes, why? There are some questions in life which we can only assume an answer Mr Sarre. Later, in hindsight, perhaps we may find life could not be any other way. Poor Eustace should not be the other way!"

Nick gently held Mollie's hand, saying, as uncontrolled tears ran down his cheeks ingrained by the sweat of his toil marked by the dust of the farm, "You are a good girl Mollie. You're part of the family, a good friend to Rachel. Oh, she will need your friendship more than ever." Little did he know how true those words would be in the days ahead.

Mollie nodded as she departed to make the bramble tea substitute replacing the unobtainable universal brands which had disappeared from the shelves of local shops due to the occupation. This period in the life of the Islanders led to a change of culinary delights. Dried and roasted bramble leaves became the traditional cup of tea; parsnips and carrots were also roasted to make a beverage. Sugar beet was boiled to produce a sweetener. Seawater left to dehydrate produced salt. The occupation caused the Islanders to find alternatives for food shortages and tools of trade for everyday living. Carrageen seaweed, blanched and dried was used to replace gelatin. Potatoes, a replacement for flour, their skins roasted for chips. The hay box was given life to continue cooking a meal, thus saving fuel.

The final years of the occupation were beginning to show its rigours. As supplies grew worse, it was not only the Islanders who suffered from the lack of food as well as the sorrowful inconvenient restrictions on the use of gas or electricity, which finally became non-existent, but also the captors. Cabbage soup made without essential stock or body, found its way into the meagre diet of the hungry population during the closing year of the war, regrettably bringing on frequent trots to the toilet. Islanders also retired to an early bed, a practice to keep warm, also reducing the use of candles, which in some cases were the only means of illumination. The occupation forces and slave workers were in some cases forced to eat cat meat, slaughtering stolen feline pets from the Islanders. The Islanders countered this despicable deed by locking up their cats and rabbits in the hope that this would stop the thieving, then if unsuccessful, reported the thieves to the Feildkammandantur 515, who would punish the perpetrators if caught. The Germans on the Islands found the situation harder, whereas the Islander, throughout the occupation, had been deprived of many foods, which primed them for the slow transition to starvation." Occupation forces lived on the fat of the land in the early years of occupation, so when starvation faced them their stomachs were unprepared to cope, plus, they were further depressed by the fact that the English Channel was no longer under their control. Consequently, German boats containing food and supplies so needed in the starving Islands were intercepted and sunk by the allies. The German U-boats were one of the greatest concerns to Winston Churchill regarding Allied shipping losses in the past. Fortunately, due to a turn in the war, they were now pursued more effectively, thus allowing ships to get through to England. The Royal Navy and Allies now had a grip on the English Channel, thus cutting off supplies reaching the Channel Islands in an attempt to starve the German occupation force, but in doing so it affected the Islanders. In the past, food and various supplies needed on the Island were imported from France due to a much-valued committee set up by a prominent Islander Raymond Falla and others, and with the cooperation of the German authorities they crossed the dangerous heavily-mined Channel to France. This was stopped later due to the advancement of the Allied forces.

One redeeming feature for the suffering Channel Islanders was a fine organisation, the International Red Cross, who through neutral Switzerland, arranged for chartered Swedish ships including the Vega to bring food parcels. This operation was sponsored by the Red Cross of Canada and America with Australia lending a hand. The parcels included dehydrated essential food, e.g. milk and egg, for fighting the starvation, a saving factor to the undernourished and weak who were on the point of death. The Islanders and prisoners of war everywhere owe an unpaid debt to the Red Cross who rally whenever a catastrophe arises throughout the four corners of the world regardless of creed or colour. This was yet to happen in the future of the Islands.

Mollie returned tea in hand, complete with a few sandwiches quickly made to induce Nick to eat and perhaps relax him from the work which now he had no real desire to continue. Two cups and saucers were laid out on a floral tray, a gift on their own special day. It was well used and brought back memories of happier times. Such a happy day a day he had wished for his beloved only child and Eustace. Nick's trembling hand concerned Mollie as he reached to pour milk into a Willow-decorated teacup. Nick's tears bleared his vision of the patterned story of young couple glazed in blue and white on the china tea set, fleeing in haste from a father who had forbidden their marriage. They, unlike Rachel and Eustace were granted happiness and magically transformed into two lovebirds as they flew away into marriage. He feared Rachel would never cease to remember this tragic day. As the cup smashed to the ground, he recalled an interrupted telephone conversation from Eunice regarding a baby.

"Yes Eunice, I can hear you. What baby? There is no baby here. Speak up, these Germans are messing with the lines again. What do you mean, Rachel pregnant? No, not our Rachel, she was brought up with Christian principals. In the Methodist faith, sex before marriage is a sin in the eyes of God."

Any further conversation ended as Mollie gathered up the broken pieces, in doing so making sure Nick was unharmed as he sat dazed on a convenient log near the pigsty. Mollie hastened to say, "Don't upset yourself, the tea was hot. Are you sure you are not burnt?

Nick shook his head. Unbeknown to Mollie this family man had more to think about than a broken cup. The words re-entered his fragile understanding of the past events. Rachel pregnant! No, Eunice has it wrong she miss-heard what the doctor said. Please God, let this day end." If ever a prayer was in Nick's heart, this was it.

The day certainly had not gone well. His thoughts turned to Eustace's parents. As Eunice mentioned the doctor said, doctors do make mistakes. His mind turned to unfortunate Phyllis Ogier when the doctor announced his prognosis, pregnant, causing her and family a great distress which lasted until the doctor renounced the word and said it was only wind caused by insufficient diet. The gossips had a field day preferring to remember that poor Phyllis was in the family way. This news remained on their lips until they spied a juicer item. Therefore, what hopes will Rachel have from their vicious tongues, her being a Methodist and a choir member, a disgrace to Charles and John Wesley, true preachers of God's message upholding Methodism?

"Is everything alright Mr Sarre?" asked Mollie, noticing a look of deep concern on Nick's face.

"No, my dear it is not." He felt here was a girl he could trust with what Eunice had imparted. Hesitatingly he continued, "I pray what Mrs Sarre told me is not true."

Mollie had no wish to pry but felt Mr Sarre needed to unburden his mind, so she gently asked, "It is none of my business, but is there any way I can help?"

"Mollie I know you are a good girl, a friend of both of us. Has Rachel ever confided in you with any secrets that she could not tell her parents?

Mollie was somewhat taken back by Nick's question which caused her to ask, "In what way Mr Sarre? Rachel has always been open and not one to hide secrets."

Nick stumbled for words. "Any trouble with her health, or why they wanted to get married so soon? They seemed to rush the arrangements, especially Eustace? Mrs Sarre would have preferred them to wait in these unsettled times, but Rachel went along with Eustace and his desire for an early marriage, saying, "In this occupation time every second counts." On uttering those words the anguish within was too much to continue. He lifted his hands to cover his face, letting the full vent of his feelings dissolve in the wretchedness of his grief. "Poor Eustace dead! Time has run out for the happiness he wanted to share with Rachel. Mollie, do you think that Rachel was pregnant? In addition, Eustace was the cause?"

Oh no, Mr Sarre, no, not Eustace! He and Rachel would not do such a thing. Both are good Methodists, not yielding to temptation. The conversation stopped. No more would be said as some intended wedding guests arrived, many with dampened handkerchiefs, some supported by a friend or partner. Many of the older generation dazed in disbelief. This was indeed a sad day for the Lihous and the Sarres, which has brought the Tostivins into this terrible tragedy. A time like this was hard to comprehend.

Any further conversation was withheld due to the rattling of a car which gave evidence that this deafening mechanical horse was not a Rolls Royce; you almost expected it to give up the ghost at any second as it spat out dense fumes. Sid Tostivin with wife Marion emerged from the car. Both decided no more could be achieved or done for their son as he lay in the mortuary awaiting a probable inquest which did not have a set date.

Eunice had given instructions to Marion to take charge of any further proceedings that may arise at La Petit Close. After asking Mollie if she could help, the bridesmaid-to-be organised food for those invited guests and any others who decided to call for the latest news or offering to help in any way. Eunice was still keeping vigil at Rachel's bedside. Rachel still lay in a state of unconsciousness. Dr Rose called once again before going off duty; his mind was relieved that she was laying peacefully. He left instructions to the staff he would re-visit again in the morning, or if necessary they could phone him if her condition should change during the night.

The families of the Sarre and Lihous did not know of the plans being organised at Military Intelligence in London that would throw both families into further confusion if they were carried out.

Part 3

Chapter 37
Nifty

The winter of 1942 on the Island of Guernsey under German occupation proved a trail to the Islanders with shortages of food and fuel. This state of affairs could not be described as an undue hardship at the time, as the Islanders survived this issue using their incentive to make do with substitutes. True privation and starvation were yet to be as the war progressed.

This tiny Isle of twenty-five square miles had for a thousand years had Independent rule but was now enslaved by a foreign conqueror. In hearts and minds like the rest of the Channel Islands, they remained true to the British Crown. They were awaiting the time when *God Save the King*, together with the Guernsey National Anthem, *Sarnia Cherie*, would be sung freely without the fear of the jackboot tyranny.

Deep underground, in a cellar on the outskirts of London, plans were being made for two fellow Islanders to return to the Island of their birth, one of which was a cousin to the fore-mentioned Rachel Sarre. He was to arrive on the Island during her wedding day unknown to either party in the drama that would follow. Lt Harold Lihou was in the company of another Islander, Corporal Peter Wormsby. Much is to be said for the rise of Harold Lihou (Hal to his mates) to the rank of a Lieutenant in British Intelligence M.I.5, especially since his headmaster's school report stated he showed no promise! After reading these comments from one of the seats of learning his father uttered, "God help us. Thank God for the British Army!"

The plan devised by the British Intelligence in their never-ending wisdom, was to secure information of the whereabouts of the latest secret weapon stationed somewhere on the Island of Guernsey. According to the German high command, this newborn instrument of slaughter would gain and secure a glorious German victory. Seig Heil.

What is the history of this wonder weapon? Plus how would it secure a certain victory for the glorious fatherland? Information received from M.I.5 stated this unique device, a destructor before its time, is constructed in such way that when a so-called bomb hits the ground there is no explosion, but seconds later it will set off a mechanical movement which sets in motion a highly powered drill which will trace its way to the underground targets such as railways or any major industries as programmed by the sender. Once the prey was located and being loaded with explosives it would create untold mayhem below the surface. This project code named Niffty was the brainchild of a mastermind physicist Sigmund Niffty-Von-Hoofer (hence the code name.) He was born an Austrian Jew who, through the command of fanatical Adolf Hitler destroyed all traces of Niffty-Von-Hoofer's Jewish ancestry, allowing this invaluable scientist to be untouchable regarding the Holocaust, Hitler's Final Solution, thus saving Niff-Von-Hoofer total annihilation.

On the appointed day in 1942, the two Islanders, Lihou and Wormsby, though difficult, were to be transported by submarine to the area of Le Joannet Bay which lay off the coast of Guernsey, then rowed ashore in a portable rubber dingy, and after initial landing were to be contacted by a secret agent disguised as a slave worker.

Chapter 38
Plans of Mice and Men

It is said all good and bad things come in threes, or so say those who consider they have wisdom. True or false, it is left to the recipient of this age-old superstition to decide.

Final briefing was given to the two brave Islanders who were about to risk their lives on the Island of their birth; both were set for an adventure among the enemy.

What man proposes, God disposes, or so the Good Book says. This day ranked as important, will certainly go down in the annuals of the Lihou and Sarre family memoirs. A day, which some say, is the doing of the Lihou's and Sarre's curse, so they say. Others say it is the will of God. Those with no belief intimate it was just bad luck. To the everyday non-professional it was a case of being in the wrong place at the wrong time! Fate can serve a dirty score in life. So be it.

On the appointed day in the hours of darkness, Lihou and Corporal Wormsby left the shores of England with the moon silhouetted high in the sky. The pale trickle of moonlight could prove helpful or deadly for the two lads as they boarded a submarine secluded near a rocky inlet on the Cornish coast.

Cornwell was chosen as a training ground, with its steep treacherous rock formation stretching from shore to cliff top because of its similarity to the cost of Guernsey. The initial training was hard going, leaving very little time to enjoy the desserts of life. Included in the schooling, a course of action in the simple and quick way to dispose of anyone or anything that stood in their way.

The instructor said, "Remember this simple rule:
Quick, Silent, Clean.
Your life depends on this uncomplicated rule. Q.S.C
Ah!

146

Quickness = Rapidity
Silence = No Murmurs
Cleanness = Efficiency
Neatness = No Blood
A Crack of the Neck =
No mess = No talebearers.

Good luck Lads.
Under the code name Nifty this operation may save the British Crown.

Long live the King."

The lads in question were certainly not thinking of saving Good King George during those moments as the sub dived into the icy cold waters. Their thoughts consisted of how to save good old Harold Lihou and Peter Wormsby - words that took preference in the minds of two perchance heroes in transit.

The last few days were spent in Penance filled with highlights for the two lads who were about to embark on a mission that could cost their lives. These insular Islanders were quickly learning that there was more in life than Guernsey milk; were becoming men of the world enjoying a drinking session at the local pub, although sensibly remembering what may lay before them both, they restrained from over indulgence in fear of letting a slip of the tongue escape their lips to the plans ahead, remembering the instructions from higher command: "This is wartime. Even the walls have ears. Espionage will flourish in England if talk is careless, so the order of the day is button your lips, careless talk costs lives."

Button their lips were to be adhered to. These soldiers of the King did not receive instructions to button their trousers, which both left well and truly unguarded during the last forty-eight hours. These sensuous young men were, sad to say, to become a relaxed Methodist and Roman Catholic respectively. Men must have a breather before going possibly to a predestined death! Who in time of war can be blamed for casting the first stone that brings either the best or worst in humanity?

The submarine slowly made its way along the English Channel to rendezvous with the secret agent at Le Joannet Bay. In the enclosed confined space of the sub, both Lihou and Wormsby found the whole environment claustrophobic. Lt Lihou passed the remark to Wormsby, "How the hell did we get into this situation?"

Wormsby replied with a touch of humor, "Maybe you wanted to see Mollie Gaudion, she who gives you the hots! Better not tell her of Penance or you are a goner."

Harold's mind immediately turned to the young girl who became a friend of his sister at the Forest school. Both were in the same class with young skinny Mollie spending most of her spare time at La Gree. At first, young Harold considered this giggling girl with fair hair and rosy cheeks as a time waster whose games consisted of playing nurses or shops, getting him to come and buy. The worst game of the lot, Mummies and Daddies, where he was expected to nurse and feed a baby doll. To him these were kids' games. Rounders and football were more his style. She never joined in the games, not like his cousin Rachel, who joined in all the rough and tumbles, climbing cliffs and diving off the high rocks and she could certainly handle the farm animals.

Rachel had a friend Eustace, a nice enough lad, but secretly Harold thought of as a pansy. Of course, his stammer didn't help, especially if he thought the other kids were making fun of him. As time went by and Eustace grew older, Harold found one of the reasons he did not take to Eustace was that he did not understand his conversation with his stammer. This held back the friendship. In due course they became friends when Hal gained patience much to Rachel's joy. Harold felt Rachel was the cat's whiskers who could do no wrong - tops in his estimation. The same with Mollie as she left her skinniness behind and developed into what Harold called 'a bit of all right'. Mollie had him smitten. Harold took pride in taking her to the Gaumont Cinema on a Saturday night complete with a bag of popcorn washed down with Guppy's Cream Soda, gulped down in fact in between a kiss and cuddle while sitting in the back row, while Mollie's heart-throb Robert Taylor passionately kissed Greta Garbo, causing Harold to puff on a Woodbine to ease the tension which somewhat annoyed Mollie, as the rising smokescreen blocked her view of the irresistible Robert Taylor. She often threatened young Harold with an alternative, her or a Woodbine, leaving Harold to cool it for a time. Then the war came and the advance of the enemy to the Channel Islands. Harold joined the army in England. Mollie to follow later but Mollie and family were never trapped in Guernsey. Deep in the briny, his thoughts turned to Mollie. Two years had passed since he'd left the Island with his mates to join the army. It was not so much loyalty that made him offer his services to King and country, but more a sense of adventure, so he went along with the rest of the crowd never thinking he'd end up as a Lieutenant in the Intelligence Corp. Which was quite a joke! He often wondered what his headmaster would say. Harold enjoyed the thrill of his job which seemed to open up his lazy brain, for lazy he certainly had been at the Intermediate school. This was no time to think of past deeds. After contact with the agent, his next move would be to contact Harry Caper, a wireless enthusiast, who would have a shortwave transmitter at his disposal to contact his English counterpart.

As the sub meandered towards its goal, Corporal Wormsby cast his thoughts to the pre-war days when the sun seemed to always shine. Peter was brought up in a middle-class home. Mr Wormsby, his father, a Bank manager at Westminster Bank in the High Street, St Peter Port. Mother was a teacher, who had retired to bring up a family of four consisting of identical twin boys, of which Peter was one, the other being David, plus two school-age girls, Elizabeth and Penny. The two pupils studied at the Ladies College, now commandeered under the guidance of Mr Peter Giraud, the Occupation headmaster at the Intermediate School, this taken over due to the college evacuating to England, leaving some college girls without a school. Peter, as did Harold Lihou, enjoyed a good family life residing at Village du Putron on the outskirts of St Peter Port. Peter at present had no romantic commitments.

He had left Guernsey on one of the last boats prior to the Islands being occupied, his brother and the rest of the family remained under German rule partly through family commitments, his father remaining because of his responsible position in the bank.

High above the ocean, Lancaster planes loaded with explosives were on their way to bomb Berlin and Bonn the home town of Herr Lang!

St Peter Port

Chapter 39
Le Joannet Bay

The journey to Le Joannet Bay took several hours, encountering some near misses through two depth charges nearly putting an end to the Nifty mission. The captain faked damage to the sub by letting oil out, thus putting off the hunter - a smart move by the captain who was determined to deliver the lads to the given spot. Victory depended on it his proud motto 'Britannia rules the waves - No bloody German going to sink this ship.' Winston Churchill had great concern when German subs and air bombardment had sunk many Allied boats. This ship at this time was the lifeline of food supplies and war materials coming from America.

Providence played a part after the sub surfaced, the moon hidden by the clouds making the darkness even deeper. This allowed the two men to depart for the shore in an inflatable dingy. So now the two were in home waters heading for Le Joannet Bay due to a slight wind which encouraged their journey on an adventure that could end in death.

Firstly the steep rocky terrain of cliff, booby trapped with mines had to be encountered. M.I.5 had provided a map, roughly drawn by one of their agents, describing a safe path through the minefields. Both lads prayed this sketch was correct as the author of this information was now safely in England having nothing to lose if the two brave lads went off with a bang.

Suddenly above them on the cliff top, a beam of light appeared and focused on two figures, one dressed in slave-ragged clothes, the other in typical farm gear. This unexpected commotion caused the lads to crouch low in their dingy, thinking any moment their adventure had ended before it began, especially when two rifle shots were fired in quick succession. Lihou peered over the top of the dingy to witness that both men had been shot, one of which had fallen backwards over the edge of the cliff onto a narrow path below thus saving him hurtling to the beach hundreds of feet below. The two lads remained speechless as the cliff top became a blaze of light together with the guttural Germans shouting orders. All this seemed to happen in a few minutes. The fate of the dingy plus those aboard remained in limbo; any movement would spell instant death. Both knew they were moderately safe behind the shelter of this large rock providing no one descended to the beach or the searchlights beamed on the Bay. This was unlikely, for at the moment the commotion above needed all the attention that could be given.

A car and a lorry appeared out of nowhere. This was a big problem for our two lads who guessed that the one raggedly dressed had seemed to receive fatal wounds and was the M.I.5 agent. Hal Lihou motioned thumbs down to Wormsby, indicating to stay low in the dingy. Hal was one not touched by adversity with a plan of retreat fully planted in his mind. Single handed he steered the little craft away from the shelter of the rock. This was a case of sink or swim, a determination characteristic often displayed by those labelled Guernsey donkeys. Lt Lihou knew exactly where he was, steering the dingy to a place he loved since childhood, none other than La Gree, the home of his ancestor. Steering away from the vision of those on the cliff top mayhem, Hal confided to his bewildered companion in a joyous whisper. "La Gree, here we come. God save Sarnia Cherie."

At that moment the hidden moon retreated from the clouds lighting the way to La Gree and its hideaway. Harold Lihou remained silent as he steadfastly paddled the dingy to nature's secret hidden cave that led to the smuggler's tunnel at La Gree. Harold was not going to be thwarted by those Germans who seemed well and truly occupied on the cliff top. Whispering in Wormsby ear he said, "We are going home to the place of my birth at La Gree. I hope my mother can stand the shock!"

Peter, with a look of surprise, remarked in lower tones, "How in name of hell are we going do that. The cliffs will be mined, not like the ones at Le Joannet which were left unprotected in certain areas so the Islanders could cut gorse furze for fuel. Surely the other cliffs would be mined?"

"Just wait and see, old son," jested Harold. "Providing we can scramble over the rocks we will be safe and not blown to kingdom come. Remember I am a country boy, not a town lubber - with all due respects."

As the dingy paddled out of earshot of those engaged above, a lone figure dressed in black civilian clothes complete with an old fashion spy glass stood on the cliff's edge surveying the adventurous lads below, watching until the little vessel disappeared around the rocky headland, both lads oblivious of the watching figure.

One cannot but praise the seamanship of young Lihou as he guided the little craft through an area of the rocks in the Bay that hid the entrance to the smuggler's cave. Feeling apprehensive but inwardly happy that they had made it that far without a hitch, Peter awaited Hal's instructions as to his next move fearing that he may put a foot in the wrong direction, which would herald goodbye Guernsey! In an undertone, Hal turned and pointed to a large rock and issued an order, "Jump to the rock and pray to God no one sees you."

Entrance to cave

153

Taking hold of the offered rope, Peter leapt to land on the sharp crusted boulder causing a wound on his a right leg. A trickle of blood ran into his sock as he pulled the dingy towards Hal who now stood in three feet of water. Grabbing the twisted rope he made his way to a series of larger rocks which shielded a narrow entrance. Beyond was a pool of fresh water devoid of movement, being fed by an irregular stream of crystal sparkling water jutting from the cliffside.

Suddenly the sound of a helicopter greeted their ears as it made its way to the action on the cliff side top. Luckily, both lads were out of sight as the plane circled and viewed the activity caused by the earlier shooting. After gathering further interest it turned flying low over the beach - and switched on a small searchlight to scan the area. After circling it flew back to the cliff top then returned for a further inspection of the Bay. The pilot and companion satisfied that nothing more could be achieved, flew in the direction of St Peter Port.

The aforementioned man in black watched with interest the comings and goings of the helicopter from a position unseen by others. The question arises, is he friend or foe?

Inside the cave, Lihou and Wormsby, though safe for the time being, had no idea of the ill-fated drama on the cliff top and what it meant. Its outcome would come as a great surprise to Lt Lihou and his counterpart. The news, when divulged, would cause great concern. Hal sat on a rock near the pool. Both felt exhausted but revived after sampling the crystal flowing water. Now, out earshot, they could talk freely. This was the first chance Peter had to ask questions regarding their plight. Hal had already deflated the dingy much to Peter's surprise.

Hal, seeing the look on his companion's face, uttered, "This is going to be our home for a few hours. Welcome to La Gree. I trust you will enjoy your stay. Feel free to enjoy its hospitality. Sorry about the lack of home comforts."

Peter smiled at Hal's invitation but desired to know what was ahead of them and asked, "Why is the dingy concealed between two rocks, surely it is needed to escape from this provisional safety area?"

Peter turned to his superior; rank had been dispensed with during this mission. "Did I not say we are going home to La Gree? Well, we are here; this is a sort of reception area which my ancestors used." Hal laughed as he said, "A reception area for their evil deeds. This cove is connected to a tunnel in the hallway in the main house. So old chum, we are home!' God only knows what my mother will say when we knock on the trapdoor."

Peter looked aghast at the information he heard. "Your forefathers actually tunneled from the house to the Bay, were they smugglers?"

"Yes, but we prefer to say salespeople, selling goods, tax-free. Of course, we did have pirates and the occasional murderer along the line. So you see I am well equipped to deal with the Jerrys. You're in good company old son! In the meantime, we have to find our way to the house. I hope the exit has not been blocked since I last ventured into the tunnel. I hope you are not afraid of ghosts. It's haunted by the past deeds of those terrible Sarres and Lihous. Remember if we are caught and shot, we will go down in history, us with the notaries Lihou and Sarre."

The very notion of being shot set off a nervous tingling sensation throughout Peter Wormsby.

Both lads struggled through the narrow cleft in the huge granite rocks. Thankfully neither were robust in stature. Once inside both produced watertight torches illuminating a cave sculptured since the beginning of time, uneven sharp pinnacled stalactites together with dripping water. They focused as diamond clusters made by the enlightening torches lit these medians hanging from above as if guarding its domain, perhaps awaiting the return of Neptune, the king of the sea. The chilled salty breeze enveloped the chamber in suffocating silence, a requiem for those who had traversed and stained in blood in ages past. Green variegated moss decorated the chiseled wall as if wallpapered to add interest to uninvited. Upon the floor billions upon billions of multicoloured pebbles, their shape unacquainted with size, created a solace melody to the feet of those who dared to enter, enticing a vision of those who walked with death so long ago, it's repetitive refrain played out in the silence of this tomb forever and a day. That spectre of yesteryear would appear to them initiated in such beliefs; for others whose attitudes fluctuate this would be a place of nature's wonder.

Harold Lihou stood as his whole body trembled, not with coldness, but a sensitivity of bondage to a place he had known and visited long before his birth. His eyes glimpsed the roughly chiseled crucifix etched and indented upon stonework formed a million years before the validation of one who died upon its symbol. Maybe the artist was seeking redemption from his evil acts.

Hal's thoughts were brought back to earth by Peter's intervention, "What a beautiful grotto. Did you come here often as a child?"

"No, unlike you, I felt a sadness and fear knowing the history of this place. Rachel, my cousin, felt the same; not a place to linger. But I hope it will serve our needs.

Many hours had passed since the drama of the Le Joannet Bay shooting.

Chapter 40
Rachel Awakens

Rachel regained consciousness. Dr Rose called to make sure she had not suffered a miscarriage and checked her mental state. At the moment no cause for alarm; she now seemed quite composed. Doctor Rose informed Eunice that Rachel could return to La Petit Close providing she was kept in the quietness of her bedroom. Eunice was worried that the full impact of the situation would return, thus sending Rachel into a further trauma when back in home surroundings. Dr Rose pointed out this could be expected due to the wretched state of affairs that the poor girl faced leaving her whole world shattered with no husband to uphold her, adding that with the support of her family she would face this grieving with fortitude and love. "You have my telephone number. Do not hesitate to ring me if the circumstances need my assistance." Then, as an afterthought, he mentioned to Eunice that he would probably converse with the retired specialist in Sark regarding the change of Rachel's personality towards people after hearing the upsetting news. This would have to have the permission of the German authorities. There would no problem from the Dame of Sark who seemed to know how to handle the Germans.

"Thank you, doctor, I will try not to worry you, we all have our troubles, even doctors."

"Poor Eustace's parents losing their son on his wedding day, my prayers go out to them." Nodding his head the good doctor left to continue his never-ending rounds.

Eunice returned to the ward preparing her daughter for the journey home where in the near future a lot of explaining would have to be done on Rachel's part.

The official German car, the one that Herr Lang had allowed the family to use at any given time during the tragic crisis, was made available again. Rachel walked slowly to the car supported by her mother then turned hesitantly to thank Matron Rabey for the care given under difficult circumstances. She felt as if her whole being was in the world yet out of it. Eunice acknowledged the care given. Matron passed (unnoticed by Rachel) the scribbled note found in Eustace's pocket that had evaded the hands of German searchers and the intimidating Herr Schmitt. Rachel sat thankfully in the rear seat of the car which took her and her mother back to La Petit Close.

Nick welcomed Rachel as tears flowed freely on both sides, her father holding her so close, saying, "We love you my darling. Don't worry, we will take care of you and the baby," saying no more as he glimpsed at the expression of disproval on Eunice's face. The look told him he had said too much. Eunice, like most women, needed no words to convey to her husband that he had said or done the wrong thing. Nick was always vigilant of those warning looks.

Rachel appeared not hear the words that Nick uttered, saying to her mother, "If you don't mind I shall go to my room."

Eunice nodded, and taking her daughter's arm, made their way up the stone stairway leading to Rachel's bedroom. Approaching the door Eunice remembered what lay beyond. Eunice fumbled for words to distract their entry. Unfortunately, those words came too late to stop Rachel opening the door to scan the room that had been hers since childhood, a place once filled with happiness until this Spring day in May.

A mahogany wardrobe faced the entrance, one of this room's treasured memories. Regrettably, its open doors revealed within, hanging neatly, a white bridal gown in company with a blue bridesmaid's dress; upon its floor a pair of white satin shoes embroidered with a blue dove of love and peace, "Which," her grandmother had lovingly said, "in those shoes you will dance over the rainbow to happiness."

Suddenly as she gazed with unwavering attention her eyes filled with ethereal mist from which there was no escape, focusing on the beautiful gown, now discoloured, replaced by a black torn dress, the matching shoes now black; gone was the bird of rapture and in its place a motif of a dead creature. Slowly, in apprehension, her hand instinctively felt her hair which was now ruffled and tangled, unkempt, completely lifeless; in her hand, the tightened handkerchief that had squeezed the tears now appeared as a twisted rope. The bedroom suddenly lost the warmth of love, welcoming the coldness of the tunnel surrounding her metamorphoses that wrought change. Rachel at that moment became the distraught bride who lived in the smuggler's warren. This was too much. She hurriedly slammed the offensive wardrobe door shut, as she did so caching sight of the linen Cobo Alice doll made by Alice Guille years ago, a present Eustace had given her on a birthday long ago when happiness was a companion. No more happiness. No more Eustace, No more Rainbow. Yes, this was her life re-lived; she had seen it in the tunnel. Oh, precious baby, what have we done? No answer came, Hans was no more. As she fought this nightmare a voice within shouted, 'He is Dead! Dead! Dead'.

Eunice beheld her daughter who gradually slid to the floor. Perhaps this unconscious state would eradicate the nightmare from her mind giving a modicum of peace, or will the curse of the Sarres and Lihous still live on? Will the bloodstains of the past claim absolution for today's heirs?

Chapter 41
In the Tunnel

Back in the smuggler's tunnel Lihou and Wormsby made their way to the trapdoor not knowing what lay before them. The light of their torches beamed faintly on the way ahead. Hal's only hope was that these trustworthy guides in the unknown darkness did not diminish as replacements batteries were not on the agenda. During these expeditions, you were only provided with the bare essentials. The whole atmosphere was humid, dank and foreboding, the dampness clinging to the roughly-hewn walls which had not seen ventilation for some time, for this was a place rarely visited as it reeked of past misdeeds.

Peter Wormsby remarked, "This is not the place to bring Mollie Gaudion for a kiss and a cuddle."

Hal jokingly replied, "If you are desperate, any port in a storm will do."

As they advanced towards the trapdoor Peter felt the clammy coldness in the whole of his body which tempted him to ask, "How was the curse placed? What happened to bring about this evil?"

Harold turned to Peter as he answered the question, "It's a long sorrowful tale according to legend of long ago which cannot be told in a short time, but I will give you a few facts that will help you understand the wretchedness of the situation. Apparently, one of my relatives way back kidnapped a Negro girl as she was about to be married to the chief elder of the tribe. The island which my pirate relies on, at the time was ruled by voodoo and black magic; so the chieftain cast spells on those born in the lines of the Sarres and Lihous. A curse due to malevolence would at various occasions meet with tragic circumstances. This curse would last for twelve generations, or until one male or female found true love in a partner from a foreign land. Stating that this would be an illicit love affair, the male or female Lihous and Sarres up to now have married

160

Guernsey spouses. No one yet has found a love from another land so the curse stays."

Peter wanted to hear more, to continue with that saga of the Lihou family, for the conversation helped to take his mind off the serious situation they were placed in, but Hal ended his exciting tale to Peter's disappointment.

Hal stopped the tale with the words, "We must press on or maybe the batteries will run out before reaching the trapdoor."

The trudge to the trapdoor exiting to surroundings Hal knew took some time due to the slippery pebbles underfoot combined with rotting vegetation, so extra care was taken in fear of breaking a limb. Hal heralded a cry of delight as he spied the rotten wooden ladder that led to the door to so-called freedom from this malevolence place.

Peter was quick to inspect the unstable broken rungs in the hope they would bear weight as each climbed to the stout iron rusty door. "We will be lucky if we don't break our bloody necks," he said.

Hal shook the age-old relic saying, "With any luck, one of us will make it to bang on the door. After my family gets over the shock, hopefully, they will pass down another ladder, that is if they don't die at the sight of two imaginary ancestors who summoned them from the deep."

"Up you go. Knock hard on the door. With a bit of luck, they won't shoot you."

"Thanks for volunteering," was Hal's sense of humour.

Peter played along, "I never volunteered."

"Oh yes, you did. I took the step of voting for you by proxy just in case you changed your mind. Anyway, you're lighter than me; I could not chance the ladder breaking. What would you do without me? Good luck, remember you are doing this for Sarnia Cherie."

Peter grinned as he mounted the precarious ladder, "May your ancestors hang and quarter you Harold." No sooner had he uttered the words than both torches ceased to work, the rung on which he was standing broke sending him to the hard pebbles in total darkness. Try as they might, no light returned. Peter groaned as Hal fumbled to help his mate.

If Harold Lihou and Peter Wormsby thought they had a problem then they would be in for a shock soon.

M.I.5 received word through the grapevine that the slave agent whom Peter had to make contact was shot dead on the cliff top. There was no difficulty in the future in getting the two lads off the Island after the Niffty mission completed. True to M.I.5 tradition, what mattered most was receiving the information regarding the secret weapon. The plight of the two lads unable to return to England if suitable escape routes were not possible became a negative priority as far as the Department was concerned. There were always others to fill their empty shoes. War has its casualties!

Chapter 42
Doctor's Orders

Eunice called to Mollie who was at that moment engaged in household chores. She hurriedly appeared helping with the lifting of Rachel onto her bed. Rachel stirred at the movement asking, "What has happened?" - with no apparent recollection of what had transpired previously at the sight of the wedding ensembles.

Eunice quickly answered, "You fainted darling. Just stay still then you will feel better. Doctor's orders. Lay quietly. Mollie and I will go and help Aunt Rita downstairs with the guests. Everyone has come over from the La Gree house which is empty. Little did she know who lay in the tunnel.

Rachel asked no more questions resigning to lay in her room. So she laid down, her muddled mind fed by shock recalling half-truths. Yes, today was her wedding day. Oh, what a beautiful day. No, it's a dark day, no sunshine, no wedding bells, the bells are silent. No wedding day. Why? Something was happening in the recesses of this troubled mind. What is it? Why is everything so difficult? Where are Eustace and Hans? Why aren't they here? The mist is lifted as she struggled to keep the pictures from her mind. No, no. Go away! Tears flow as the swirling mist disappeared revealing Eustace and Hans both lying dead. She covers her ears to cut out the tolling of the phantom death bell. No, not Hans, he is alive! As her hands soothe her stomach the picture is clear. Yes, Hans is alive, he moves within my belly! Shush, Shush. No one must know, it's a secret. Shush.

Rachel slept as she pictured Eustace as a proud father. Shush, it is a lie! Shush, it's Rachel's secret. Shush, Rock-a-bye-baby.

Rock-a-bye baby, thy cradle is green
Father's a nobleman, mother a Queen
And Rachel's a lady and wears a gold dove

Hans is a soldier who waits for his love
Shush, Shush.

In this state of semi-consciousness, Rachel travelled without purpose from reality to fantasy.

Chapter 43
The Rescuer

Harold meanwhile searched in his jacket for his cigarette lighter as his eyes became accustomed to the gloom. Once found the abject thing would not produce a flame which is sometimes the case in an emergency. "Bugger," was the word that came to his lips, after all, he was only human.

A converted non-smoker, Peter could do nothing to alleviate the situation suggesting more in jest, "Perhaps we could rub two sticks together and produce a fire; we learnt that at boys scouts and it worked. "I'll try and find two sticks."

Hal could not see the humour of the suggestion, the place being saturated in dampness with little chance of finding dry wood.

So in the bleak darkness, they had to stay until Harold could think out a plan to rid them of this desolate place. Retreat not on the agenda, someone must open the trapdoor. Perhaps shouting, someone may hear!

There was certainly too much activity at La Petit Close for anyone to return to La Gree at this moment.

The two lads huddled together for warmth in the hope an inspiration would arrive in either mind to get them out of this situation, however, they must be patient!

Sometime during the early hours of the morning a scraping sound was detected as they lay half asleep, rusty droppings descending on them as they lay. Now fully awake, the cranking of rusty hinges alerted them to stand. A beam of light penetrated the darkness of their makeshift jail, for that is what it was to the two adventurers.

"Is that you Aunty Rita?" uttered Hal for want of better words.

No one spoke till a male voice with an educated accent said, "I see your ladder is of no use. I shall endeavour to find another."

"Who are you?" asked Harold Lihou.

"Never mind who I am. At the moment the most important operation is to get you at of the tunnel before the Germans shoot you as spies, which I presume you are."

Ding-dong bell, Pussy's in the well
Who'll get them out!?
Little Tommy Sprout
Ding dong bell.

Both lads felt a sigh of relief at the appearance of this stranger. At least by all accounts, he was not the enemy, or so it seemed. Their rescuer disappeared without further conversation returning with a ladder that hopefully would reach the ground of the self-inflicted prison. Luck was with them so they hastily climbed into the hallway of La Gree, the birthplace of Harold Lihou.

"Oh, it's good to be home," he said, turning to the man who made this possible. "Thank you, may I have the pleasure of your name?"

Unbeknown to the two lads, there stood the man in the black coat who had spied the dingy as they paddled to the entrance of the cave. He forwarded his hand in a handshake saying, "Stafford Jones. No need for introductions on your part as I am well equipped with both of your credentials. I was born on this Island, my forbearers living in Guernsey for generations. My profession as a diplomat caused me to live the greater part of my life overseas. Germany became a second home while I was making many friends in high places in that troubled land, Hitler included."

He continued his story, "Just prior to the occupation, I returned to the Island with the blessings of the British government to act as a double agent if the Island fell to Germany. So I know why you are here. I shall endeavour to help you, but expect no favours, making it clear that if the Germans suspect I am involved in any way, then I have no alternative but to turn you in. My position with the M.I.5 and Germany cannot be jeopardised by any connection with you. If the cover means eliminating you both then so be it! No hard feelings I trust. Remember this is war and you are in the fighting line, so there is every chance you may be killed one way or another. Good luck. I shall be in communication you when it suits. Please remember, no matter what happens do not try to contact me. In the meantime, make acquaintance with Harry Capper, a wireless whiz who will supply a transmitter for you to get in touch with London. I am afraid you will have to wait here until someone returns. All are congregated at Le Petit Close due to the circumstances that changed Rachel's Sarre's wedding day. The curse of the Lihous and Sarres took a hand, leaving the bridegroom, Eustace Tostivin, shot while helping our agent who died while trying to escape. Tostivin was seriously wounded but unfortunately died in hospital later. I trust this information will help you understand why you could not land at Le Joannet. This has made things difficult for you but hopefully, you will receive further instructions and details from M.I.5. They can be very irritating at times. Go carefully and good luck."

With these words the black-coated man departed with, "Do not contact me!" leaving Harold Lihou in a state of shock with Peter Wormsby not far behind.

Chapter 44
À la Prochaine

Poor Eunice and Rita, with Mollie's untiring help, were kept busy with wedding guests calling to find out all the details of the heartaches, all desiring to know the true facts as many had a distorted story of the situation. Rita took turns to go to Rachel's room to see if she was sleeping peacefully. A decision was made that she would not return to La Gree tonight in case Rachel awoke in terror needing Eunice or herself to sit and comfort the poor girl. Rita had no idea that her niece was pregnant. Eunice simply could not find a time or place to explain the delicate situation. A pregnancy of an unwedded girl, especially one of the family, needed a lot of thought and understanding, for this was a time when a bastard child was discussed in whispers. Yes, a child without a father was deemed a bastard and certainly a sin in the eyes of God. This fact remained, even though she and Eustace, the recognised father, were about to be married. Devoid of the marriage license the child would remain illegitimate, or more cruelly a 'bastard'. Maybe in time the lawgivers would be more liberal of God's laws, only time will tell. Whatever the outcome of Rachel's child, one true fact remains; the baby was conceived in love.

Before Eunice confided with rest of the family regarding Rachel's condition, she must find out the full facts; some sort of explanation must come from the poor soul. Eunice was at a loss why Rachel did not seem fit to unburden her heart to the family. Now she understood why the wedding plans were hurried at one of the busiest times on the farm.

Eustace certainly pushed the dates forward, saying the times due to the occupation were uncertain. The poor boy must have had a presentiment of trouble ahead, certainly never thinking that his life would terminate on his wedding day. Eustace surmised that his father, an elder at the church, would find it hard to forgive his son regarding Rachel's condition, as his father always reiterated, "God ordained marriage for the proliferation of a family, a sin in the Lord's eye if not conceived in marriage." As Christians, the Tostivin family stuck to the bible teaching in life, bringing up their children acknowledging God's law and following in Jesus' footsteps. Unfortunately, many families had lost sight of the footprints to follow their lord and master. Eunice reflected on words her mother had once said, 'People lose sight of the footprints because the wind of evilness covers the footprints with self-centered indulgence.'

Poor Sid and Marion, good, God-fearing people, and yet this terrible thing has happened to them. I sometimes wonder why it always seems that trouble comes to those who put God first, not deserving the agonies of life, while others who care not for others sail along. The wicked shall reign for a season.

Chapter 45
Hickory Dickory Dock

Having got over the shock of the rescue by Stafford Jones, the two lads felt thankful that they had arrived without too much incidence, apart from the nasty reception at Le Joannet Bay.

Harold found matches on the kitchen stove and lit a cigarette, sitting on a kitchen chair to enjoy the obtrusive noxious weed, beckoning Peter to sit, knowing that his mate would not partake in this social grace (a wise man as later years proved).

A welcome cup of tea was next on the list. Ash fell from Hal's dangling ciggy into the Royal Jubilee souvenir tea caddy into a mixture of bramble tea, his nasty falling ash unnoticed or uncared for by the son of the house. "It's good to be home. It looks as the place hasn't changed, at least in the kitchen. I'm staying put until my parents arrive. I can imagine the look on my mother's face when she sees her long-lost son."

Peter nodded his head saying, "It may be a long wait.

Hickory dickory dock
The hands of time go around the clock.

Both lads waited listening to every sound with diligence as Hal puffed on a ciggy. One false movement could cost them their lives.

Silence is Golden.

Chapter 46
The Pot of Soup

The two lads dared not venture out as strictly instructed by Stafford Jones. The only thing to do was waiting with patience for the return of the Lihou family. Harold searched the cupboards trusting to find some edible food to stop the pangs of hunger that was now descending in both of these adventurers' stomachs which had not seen food for several hours. Hal felt a sense of guilt rummaging in La Gree kitchen, even though this was his parents' home. He had not lived in this abode for nearly three years. In addition, the Islands were on strict rations. He did not know the situation regarding bread and butter to feed two extra mouths. Searching the cupboards reminded him of Old Mother Hubbard's bare cupboards becoming the Lihou's bare cupboard. Later during conversation, his mother explained he did not look in the right places; in these uncertain times, starving slave workers burgled premises for fodder to sustain their lives so anything edible was hidden in places you'd least expect to find your valuable vitals.

However, luck was on their side when Hal discovered while sitting on an unlit stove a large iron saucepan which retained heat after cooking. This utensil was considered by Hal to be a relic from a past era. Electricity, gas and paraffin was rationed or in short supply so Islanders discovered ways to conserve heat and the old-fashioned hay box became a necessary essential in the kitchen, using this inexpensive way to finish and keep hot cooked meals. Occupation living required making use of whatever saved heating or lighting as Rita informed her son later, consuming food un-thought of in pre-war days.

The contents of the iron relic contained a healthy amount of vegetable soup made prior to the wedding day, a standby for while busy with wedding arrangements. Hal surmised this was a self-pronounced gourmet made from his grandmother Mary's recipe that had been handed down over the years. Legend has it, she made a soup made to quell the appetites of the smugglers before they went on their evil deeds. A soup Harold prided himself in eating three bowls at a sitting in days gone past. Some used the expression, 'making a pig of him.' Peter suggested soup would fit their requirements then set about finding matches to light the primus stove. Yet again none could be found. Cold soup topped the menu. He remarked, "Fit for the Ritz," so for the next few hours they enjoyed the cuisine of the Ritz, not knowing what lay at the bottom of the pot of this delicious entree.

The old grandfather clock was crafted by one of the Island's clockmakers, a noted craftsman of his day. Outstanding workmanship and art is always sought after in the Island. The pendulum of this treasured timepiece swung to and fro over the hours, its melodious chimes unheard by these two who, after their fill of grandma's soup, succumbed to the sweet peace of sleep in the safety of La Gree.

Rita's screams went unheard by the two sleeping beauties when two frightened women spied the two figures prone on the kitchen floor, unrecognised in the semi-darkness. She called to an unconcerned husband who was feeling the effects of a cider brew, drunk not in a festive mood but consumed to drown memories of this sad day. "Help," Rita cried, her imagination working overtime. "Ernie, we have two slave burglars. Ernie, do something, don't just stand there or I will be murdered. Oh, I think they are dead, murdered in our kitchen!"

The adventurous lads slept oblivious of Rita's plight.

"Oh, what will happen next? First poor Eustace and now two slave workers killed in our kitchen. Oh, Ernie, what shall we do? So inconsiderate of them to be murdered in our kitchen. We will go to prison Ernie."

Ernie appeared unconcerned for his brain was incapable of making any suggestion. He mumbled, "Go to bed and see to things in the morning. The Germans will not miss two slaves, you'll be safe Rita."

"Ernie get the police," she pushed Ernie into action.

Luckily Harold heard his mother's voice and returned to the land of the living saying, "Don't worry Mum. Mum, it's Harold, your son Harold Lihou."

Rita let out a scream that could revive the dead and bent down to examine the person who posed as her son and she let out yet another shriek. Seeing this prone human being was just too much, her shaking legs took leave of control and cascaded full force to land on top her unidentified son in an unmentionable place, which son struggled to free himself of this painful shock and caused him to utter, "Mum, Mum. I'm Harold your eldest child, Harold Clarence Lihou.

However, on hearing this statement the poor demented mother let out another piercing yell. "Ernie, it's Hal our son. Harold has come back as a ghost returning home, killed in battle." Saying irrationally, "Oh God, this is the curse of the Sarres and Lihous. May the good Lord save us. Oh dear, oh dear." Tears streamed down her haggard face. Placing her left hand on the brow of the said departed son her right hand clutched his arm in fear in case he would escape. "Ernie, he is still warm."

A bewildered Ernie stood scratching his head saying, "What's all the trouble, Rita?" as he managed to make his way to a chair to sit because he did not trust his unsteady legs, as his cider brew had gone to his head. His slurred voice addressed dazed Rita who had still had not come to terms with the situation; life for her that moment was just too much for this Guernsey farmer.

"What a few days this has been. Dear Eustace shot and now dear Harold returned as a ghost and our daughter away to a foreign land. What else can happen? Ernie for goodness sake do something." Rita was always prone to dramatic outbursts.

"Come on Rita, what are you doing down there? Who are those two?"

This conversation was too much for Hal who now endeavoured to extract himself from his bereft mother's clutches struggling to regain freedom in desperation saying, "I am no bloody ghost. I'm Harold Lihou, your son and this is Peter

Wormsby who you have woken by your screams. If you stop this nonsense I will explain."

Rita, hearing Harold's statement, turned to Ernie saying, "Oh Ernie, he is not dead, it is Harold." This revelation caused sobbing with hysterical laughter. "You're my son!"

"Yes mother, I am very much alive, so calm yourself. I know it's been a shock. Please listen and I will explain. In the meantime, how about a cup of tea or something stronger."

Rita, still dazed said, "Is it really you Harold, not a ghost?"

"Yes mother, it's your darling boy, Harold Clarence Lihou, complete with a tattoo." Hal proceed to unroll his shirt sleeve to display a red heart encircled in red roses with an insignia of the word Mollie, a piecing feathered arrow put the finishing touches to the adoring art that Harold would carry to his grave giving allegiance to a certain Mollie Gaudion. Now what about that cuppa?"

The sight of this memorable motif left no doubt that this was her darling boy who left to serve in the King's army bringing glory to his Island. As her tears subdued, Rita asked, "Bramble or English breakfast? I saved some real stuff for the Liberation when it arrives," intimated Rita who seemed to have recovered from the said 'Curse of the Sarre's and Lihou's.' Rita busied herself with the tea-making asking, "Would you prefer some of your grandmother's soup?"

"No thank you, I am afraid we already made a pig of ourselves."

"Did you heat up the soup?" asked Rita in anticipation of her son's answer.

"No, Mrs Lihou, we could not find the matches," answered Peter who had at last been introduced to the Lihous. "It is a very tasty soup. Congratulations, it must be difficult in these times."

"Thank goodness you did not find the matches. We have to hide our valuables and food in fear that the slave workers will steal them. They are in a far worse state than we Islanders. Poor things, we try to help them with scraps of food but we don't have much to spare, I sometimes think of what our Lord did on the mountain, bless him. Your father says if I expected a miracle, the poor buggers would starve. I told him you must have faith Ernie." This information was imparted as Rita made her way to the iron saucepan.

Much to the amazement of the two lads, she produced from the bottom of the vessel a watertight package saying, "This is our illegal radio. Radios were confiscated. If the Germans found you still had one you were in trouble so our radio was given in. This little crystal set was made in secret by a man who risked imprisonment if caught. This brave man is Harry Capper. These little sets are our only means of knowing how the war is going on and that's why we keep it in a hideaway." Hearing the name of Harry Capper, both lads turned to each other having the idea of thinking this man must be the same one to contact for the transmitter.

During conversation Rita offered more tea while still in a daze over what had transpired on her return from La Pettit Close, asking why they returned to Guernsey on a day so full of sadness. She explained the shooting of dear Eustace on his wedding day. "Harold, dear poor Rachel is in hospital demented, just as I would be if I lost your father."

Harold and Peter imparted briefly why they were on the Island, instructing Rita never to divulge to anyone what was said or heard for if she did, it could mean death for her son and friend and she and Ernie could be shot for harbouring the two boys.

Ernie retired to bed to rest his cider head. He had yet to be informed of his son's escapade. However in the meantime plans were being laid by the two adventurers, a strategy that would transform Rachel's way of life forever.

Chapter 47
Sussing a Hideout

Safford Jones made contact with the agents. He informed them that an old handbag factory in Charrroterie in St Peter Port was the suspected place where clandestine experiments were being carried out regarding the Nifty weapon. Both lads knew of the building but were at a loss of how to enter or survey what was happening inside this gaunt, early Victorian stone workplace. Peter suggested the factory was in a direct line with the Trinity Sunday school complex from which they could scrutinise the comings and goings of the building that drew M.I.5 attention. But how to obtain the key to this abode of Biblical learning?

Peter was attuned to his Christian parents' belief who deemed it important to instill the teaching of gentle Jesus as vented by the God-fearing Miss Steadman, an unmarried lady who had devoted her life to the saving of lost souls. She could be observed at various times giving sustenance to the poor and needy in the parish of St Peter Port, activating her mission in life to nurture the under-privileged. This remarkable spinster lady never walked on the fashion gangway though fashions changed. Her mode of dress remained static, proclaiming a bygone era going back to early Edwardian. Nevertheless, her love for the omnipotent came to the fore, a romantic interlude came to a conclusion after the man in whom she found consolation was killed on the bloody battlefield in the 'War to end all wars.' This horrific slaughter between nations robbed thousands of virgins, male or female, the joy of wedded bliss. A decision was made that Peter could not risk going to ask for the key in the fear of being recognised. It was then suggested by Harold that David, Peter's twin brother, should sort out the key as he was a friend of the caretaker's son. Some excuse would be offered so as not to arouse suspicion; every move regarded as top secret. Only the immediate family knew why they were on the

Island. Both Peter and Harold had made contact with the Wormsbys, visiting them at Village du Putron, their home overlooking the spectacular Fermain Bay. Dealing with a sort of cloak and dagger situation, the parents were concerned at their appearance. Information was down to a minimum owing to placing both families in jeopardy.

First, they questioned their decision to stay under cover at La Gree and making this their headquarters in the safety of the tunnel. This was a plan gained encouragement from Hal's parents. However, after much mind-searching, the lads concluded it would be best to seek accommodation away from either home, concealed in a place not directly connected with family or friends. If caught, the families could plead ignorance of knowledge of their sons' sojourn on the Island as any involvement with potential spies carried a death sentence or deportation to Germany.

Peter, yet again, came up with the idea regarding the Elizabeth College that had been evacuated with the Intermediate school, together with Islanders wishing to escape the oncoming opponent. They had escaped, travelling on the Batavia, a smelly Dutch cargo boat destined for Weymouth, a port in south-west England. Peter suggested the games shed situated in the playing fields in Rue a'Lor off Kings Road would probably be vacant and, if so, this could be the ideal place to hide out. Peter remembered the caretaker, Mr Allen usually held the key and may still possess it, as he did not evacuate with the school, and anyway it was worth a try. Perhaps David could suggest a way of obtaining entrance to the shed plus the key of Trinity Sunday School if the usual channels failed. However, If Mr Allen is approached, Harold intimated they will have to tread carefully in getting this caretaker involved and he must not be incriminated in any way. The less who knew of his participation the better so not to endanger his wife and relatives. This also applied to anyone drawn into this web.

Harold decided he alone will make his way to the playing field to observe if the plan of going undercover in the deserted shed was feasible. If so, he would approach Mr Allen, leaving David to obtain the Trinity Sunday School key. Peter would stay to await news of the transmitter.

Peter suggested he himself should go and sort out the land saying if seen, onlookers would think it was David his twin, hopefully with no cause for alarm or inkling of danger. Harold argued that in no way was David going to be directly involved in this particular case. But he would be allowed, if he chose to spy out the handbag factory. In no way would Peter be allowed to go to the field.

First the question of the transmitter-receiver. Harry Capper would be contacted in his Victoria Road shop. Stafford Jones suggested not to visit the shop, but to discreetly phone Capper arranging delivery at some given place. Any conversation must start in a coded conversation. "Any chance of firewood Harry?"

To which he would reply, "Logs or chippings?"

Replying, "I'll take chippings, Harry."

Harry Capper will then give you instructions for the pickup. Or he may respond saying, "Chippings out of stock, saw not working" - a clue that it is dangerous to talk. If OK, you shall receive further directions as to the time and safe place to pick up the order. Time, in this instance, is a game of patiently waiting, learning not to rush, or it may cost yours and others their lives.

Luck was on Harold's side as he spied out the playing field shed before curfew. The area was rather overgrown with weeds. He made his way through the unlocked iron gate placing his cycle nearby, having cycled from La Gree without incidence. Harold, beforehand, took the precaution of arming himself with a football to give the impression to any onlooker that here was a young fellow having recreation. As he dribbled the ball he spied on the perimeter of the field Mr Allen kneeling and pulling overgrown turf. Hal instantly recognised him, then slowly but deliberately made his way to the gardener kicking the football.

Mr Allen spoke before Harold could introduce himself, "How can I help you young Lihou? I remember you when you played in your school team against the college. Centre forward you were a proper tiger in peacetime, good enough for Tottenham Hotspur. You would have been snapped up if the bloody Germans hadn't come. Why are you here?"

Hal, rightly or wrongly, took a chance explaining the situation to him asking for the key. Mr Allen, with no love for the Occupation forces, agreed on one condition. he would leave the key under a placed stone to be collected and replaced. This way neither the college nor him were directly involved and as far as he was concerned someone had stolen the key if asked. Hal was agreeably surprised that there was no complication regarding finding a hideout. Unfortunately, he underestimated the 'best-laid plans of mice and men'.

Hal made his way back to La Gree farm and on arrival found Peter had the key for Trinity School; after David had found dear Miss Steadman otherwise engaged with a nasty bout of bronchitis leaving the poor soul bereft of her duties, thus leaving with an unspecified lingering in her bed. David eyed a note pinned on her Mansell St, flat door, 'No Visitors' in bold red letters complete with instructions regarding the school keys now lying dormant in the safety of the Despre's shop next to Trinity School to be collected if required by those using the hall. David retrieved it without fuss as he was well known to the Despre's family. He also took it upon himself to have a second set cut, returning the originals saving any questions that may be asked.

"Well done, David," was Harold's remark.

With Miss Steadman out of the way, the stage was now set to spy out Professor Nifty's handbag factory. Securing the plans, the two lads settled temporarily at La Gree for the night, with David returning to Fermain. On the morrow, their headquarters would be Elizabeth College's playing field hut.

Chapter 48
The Wardrobe

Loud ringing on the front door cow bell at La Gree sent the two would-be heroes into an over-large wardrobe cupboard intermingling with an array of assorted contents. Herr Schmitt entered the hallway at this inopportune moment. Rita was attired only in an overlarge fleecy lined nightgown reaching way past her toes. Schmitt saluted Heil Hitler for Rita's benefit. She demanded "Why such a late call? It is past midnight. Away with you. Come back in the morning if you must! Better still, stay away, you were never invited to this Island."

Schmitt answered, "I offer no apologies Frau. This is wartime; I have my duties no matter the time. I come to ask if Frau Sarre has handed you a piece of written paper or told you of its existence, a paper we know your nephew, Eustace Tostivin, received before he was shot. If you do not co-operate you will find yourself and your husband under our control in a situation not to your liking after we have searched your house.

The look on Schmitt's face told disturbed Rita he meant business. Impulsive Rita, as usual, presented an element of surprise after a rush of blood in her confused head looking for an acceptable answer to this fearful Schmitt, a response she hoped would get him out of this house away from the two in a suffocating wardrobe. Rita replied with a forced sweetness, "Oh the paper, you must mean the one poor Eustace gave the day before his wedding."

Ernie appeared to incorporate substance to her story. "Yes now I remember when poor dear Eustace gave me the measurements for alterations to his trouser leg a day before his wedding."

"Are you sure he gave it the day before his wedding?" asked Schmitt.

A wave of tears issued as she replied, "He could hardly give it to me the on his wedding day, the poor darling shot by your soldier dying in hospital."

"Hmm," replied Schmitt who was still unconvinced. "Please give me this note with his measurements. Quickly, I've no time to waste."

"Sorry I can't Herr Schmitt, I gave it to my husband to burn which he did. Eh, Ernie, you burnt it. No use now he is dead, it will only bring back sad memories."

Ernie confused replied, "Yes Rita, I put a match to it but I kept the trousers."

This information came as a shock to Rita as the note was her fabrication, with the trousers non-existent in the La Gree household.

"I see," replied the interrogator. "Where are these trousers now?"

"In the wardrobe," replied Ernie. "I shall fetch them."

Schmitt. quick to answer being impatient for an ending to this fiasco said, "No, we will all fetch them."

Another flush of blood rushed to Rita's head as she spoke. "Ernie, they are not in the wardrobe. You have forgotten, with all the excitement you returned them to Eunice. He is so forgetful these days. It's because of the food shortage through you Germans."

"Do not blame our glorious Germany; it is you British who sink our ships coming to your islands. Heil Hitler to the Further who will make you British swine obedient to his new order. Heil Hitler" a fanatical Schmitt said. "Quickly the trousers."

"No Rita, I remember leaving them in the wardrobe after you gave them to me."

Herr Schmitt turned to the couple saying, "There seems to be a misunderstanding as to the whereabouts of the trousers, or as you say in English, a balls-up. The wardrobe please!"

At that precise moment, Rita Lihou could have killed Ernest her husband, herself and Herr Schmitt as well as they made way upstairs to the bedroom where the much-discussed wardrobe was concealing her son and companion. As Rita confided later if she was a Roman Catholic this was the time for three Hail Mary's but she did not owe allegiance to the Pope. A Methodist prayer would have to suffice to perform a miracle to survive what Schmitt will see when the wardrobe door was opened. Distraught Rita stood in front of her would-be execution chamber feeling the cold clammy prison cell or worse still the wrought iron gates of the concentration camp miles away from Sarnia Cherie. The poor, now almost demented soul, let out one, last plea to Ernie. "You gave them back to Eunice."

"No Rita, see!" As he opened the door, the wardrobe was empty except for one pair of black trousers which would fit Eustace for he took the same measurements as their son Harold. Rita turned to Herr Schmitt and then to Ernie with a murderous look in her eyes that blinked love. When this was over she would have a lot to say to her spouse.

Schmitt with a satisfied look received the trousers and felt in the pockets. Disgruntled that no note was hidden within, in anger he threw them back into the wardrobe as the air-raid sirens sounded bringing this fiasco to a close.

"Those British pigs. Heil Hitler "You will hear from me again," he said as he hurried down the stairs to stumble into the darkness on his way back to headquarters.

Rita kissed Ernie saying, "I am usually the one who gives surprises. How did you do it, Ernie?"

He replied, "Someday I may tell you."

Chapter 49
Professor Nifty

Plans were in hand for our two adventurers to sort out what was going on in the handbag factory. M I.5 had underground information of a supposed secret weapon being constructed under the guidance of Professor Nifty, a weapon, according to Adolf Hitler, which would change the course of the world. Harold Lihou and Peter Wormsby both lay in waiting in the Trinity schoolroom for the arrival of the darkness of night, when, on the stroke of ten, two extra-large empty garbage bins would arrive replacing two filled ones with unwanted waste. These were situated inside the storeroom entrance of this clandestine building. On this particular pick up, the local bin driver was a born and bred Guernsey Islander, a man known to the occupants in this undercover building. On such excursions of this nature, the driver would make a stop at the entrance of Trinity Sunday School, collecting and replacing smaller bins. As soon as this happened Hal and Peter were to secrete themselves in the larger bins while the driver hopefully seeks refreshment in Madam Despre's grocery shop which is thankfully established conveniently next to the school. The plan should go accordingly, for the driver is well known having carried out this duty each day without incidence. Once inside the factory garbage storeroom, the lads would disembark, and then hide behind whatever gives them cover until it was safe to photograph the desired plans on microfilm. Oh, yet again, the plans of mice and men.

Four days had passed since their arrival in Sarnia Cherie, four days of planning to arrive with a mode of attack to obtain what exactly is going on in that building. The aforementioned transmitter had yet to arrive into the hands of Harold. No word from Harry

Capper at this point of time, so no contact with M.I.5. Or for that matter, none from Stafford Jones

The idea of staying at the college playing field was terminated after Hal found two soldiers installing a large metal construction of some sort, probably housing a searchlight. Evidence of activity would make it too risky to use the shed, the tunnel at La Gree would suffice until a further hideaway was found or an escape route established. Harold also refrained from making contact with his cousin Rachel or Mollie, as understandably they had enough worry to contend with. Unfortunately both lad's abode was now the La Gree tunnel, the comfort of home above stairs considered too risky, especially after the unexpected visit of Herr Schmitt who could return at any moment.

As darkness approached, Harold set his mind to carrying out this do or die operation. Failure was not on the agenda; being shot or arrested would bring suspicion to both families with the inevitable outcome a term in prison, or even death. Both lads had the necessary false identity tags in their possession so as not to be connected with their families if caught. Nevertheless, this bogus idea would be certainly squashed by the Heinrich Himmler Gestapo secret intelligence organization, or more likely Herr Schmitt; for him failure must not be the order of the day!

The slow dragging tractor engine could be heard to their attuned ears as the vehicle drew closer to the Trinity School. Both Hal's and Peter's blood pressures had risen to an excitement level as they waited on the ready for the next part of their adventure. What happened next produced a breath-stopping surprise when the driver stopped at the entrance then advanced to the door saying, "Quickly you two, into the bins." To say Peter was shocked is an understatement, for the driver, believe it or not was his brother David Wormsby! "No time for explanations. Get into the bloody bins." Both lads jumped as David opened the lids revealing a space that was certainly not Ritz accommodation; knees crouched and head bent almost touching their feet, a kind of foetal position, a perfect situation to induce cramp which quickly took over all parts of the muscles.

The tractor slowly made its way to the back entrance of the once-handbag factory, its door guarded by a sentry smoking a cigarette which David recognized by its odour, a Galois. It must be noted that this pillar of the German army, at this moment of time was more interested in the inhalation of the French noxious weed and was virtually oblivious to the stopped tractor as he continued puffing. Needless to say, its arrival was a daily occurrence, so he opened the door for the vehicle to chug through the entrance, This inattentive sentry failed to notice the driver's new identity. If he had, it might have saved him a heap of trouble. Many classed this man as being of a happy-go-lucky disposition, leaving the world to go by, a status he achieved with a Galois in his sucking lips. Poor Edie would say, 'Here's one for a chimney.'

Let us hope his luck will stay with him in the drama that follows. Suddenly the Galois left his lips, as Herr Schmitt made an unexpected appearance. Combined with his usual assertive aggressiveness nature he said, "You do not smoke while on duty. The Fuehrer forbids such uncontrolled behaviour. Heil Hitler." Schmitt was one for protocol. "I will show you discipline," he said, as he lifted the well-worn truncheon in a threatening action. "What are in those bins? Show me, you Guernsey pig," he demanded, pointing to David as he spoke.

"Excuse me," answered David, "I am a stubborn Guernsey donkey, certainly not one of your kind. "Open the lids yourself."

In fury Schmitt advanced to the bin with truncheon in hand lifted the lid and spied crumpled Hal. Schmitt cried, "Actung" as Hal grabbed this despicable Herr Schmitt around the neck and David took control of the truncheon and knocked Schmitt on the head sending him to the land of make believe. This was unnoticed by the undisciplined sentry while he was searching for another Galois and in actual fact laying down his rifle to light the devil's weed, which proves as stated earlier, he was a happy-go-lucky fellow. He leaned over the bin at the inverted Schmitt, and with due respect saluted, "Heil Hitler," then sat to enjoy the Galois.

Suddenly the inner door opened with Professor Nifty standing as if glued to the mosaic floor, gun in hand pointed to the trio within. A nasty smirk appeared on his ageing face; his eyes penetrated the amazing scene within his brilliant mind. One selfish thought came to the fore, "What will become of me! Shall I shoot them or join them." Yes, Professor Nifty was an opportunist, investing and speculating on which side will serve him best. After seeing Herr Schmitt head-first in the bin, his Jewish intuition told this eminent Scientist which way to go. If this Jewish German professor was a Christian, Judas would be a suitable label.

Schmitt's legs were wriggling in the hope someone would extract him from this uncompromising position, uttering words if translated, would come under the agenda of foul language. On seeing the deplorable Schmitt (for sorrowfully he is not of a likeable nature) it caused Professor Nifty to utter, "Thanks are to our gracious Judah. The Lord giveth and the Lord takes away." He asked, "Are we liberated?"

Peter, now out of his bin, retrieved the gun from Professor Nifty's quivering hand saying, "No, we are not liberated but you will be if you give trouble." He lifted his bin lid pointing to the vessel and commanded the Fuhrer's scientist to share its company. "Heil Hitler," uttered the amused Peter as the now demoted Professor Nifty slivered into his new residence.

The bin lids were closed then positioned on the back of the tractor. The Galois-smoking sentry was forced to sit by the driver with his rifle at hand. He showed contentment in his new position, providing Galois were in supply, for he was a happy go lucky person and a backer of which side was winning, and at this precise moment, Schmitt was a loser.

Harold issued orders as the overloaded tractor slowly made its way in the darkness oblivious of what it would encounter on this perilous journey with hazardous interruptions. "La Gree, here we come. May God help us." Hal wondered what his mother would say with two uninvited guests in the tunnel.

Harold and Peter were covered by a tarpaulin while David steered the tractor through country lanes surrounded in darkness. Luckily most of the Island's inhabitants were asleep, or so they thought, when suddenly air-raid sirens sounded, causing Hal to use some well-known profane expletives saying, "Our lads will not bomb the Island, their planes will concentrate on the shipping in the sea or harbour; hopefully the Jerries will go post-haste to St Peter Port. If luck is with us, we will make it to La Gree."

Schmitt and Nifty started banging inside the bins as the sirens blared. The obedient sentry searched for another Galois, unconcerned at the plight of past comrades around him banging on the bins. He tried to quieten the captives to little avail. It took very little to pacify this soldier of the Fuhrer, for it is a known fact when seeking the fair sex, his offering rate was considered reasonable. Ten marks and a bunch of grapes was his paying price for his indulgence with the ladies of the night. For he believed in moderation.

David suggested they take the back lanes to La Gree which would skirt the airport boundary. No sooner had he uttered the words than a lorry with blazing headlights appeared, then darkness as the tooting sound of a rather over-loud horn and the waving arms of a co-driver shouted to clear the road, all coinciding with the sound of exploding bombs and repeated gunfire as tracer bullets filled the sky, which the lads assumed came from the harbour which was some miles away. The lorry passed unconcerned much to the lads' satisfaction.

Hal remarked, "Thank God for the British air force. Let's hope the bombs will keep the Jerries occupied till we get to La Gree."

On they travelled, meandering through back lanes almost at a snail's pace. In the distance a searchlight lit the sky, the intense light catching sight of a British plane. The gunners below scored a direct hit and the meandering beam of the light traced a parachuted airman descending in the night sky, his whereabouts uncertain in his escape from death. He probably landed in the ocean, hopefully close to the Island. The burning damaged plane hurtled into the cold waters of the English Channel. The three lads were thankful the pilot escaped from the burning plane, and hoped he would be rescued from the sea. Another lorry approached at a reckless speed, whizzing past with the indication by its arm-waving occupants to get out of the way, which suited our lads. The lorry sped on to St Peter Port undisturbed by the tractor.

Once again Hal remarked, "Thank God for the R.A F, or we would be guests at St James Street clink.

Schmitt, with captive Professor Nifty continued to seek attention by banging and an issue of persistent verbal abuse echoed from within the bins. The Galois sentry, who now appreciated his new found position, kicked the bin, shouting in German to 'Shut up or be shot, Heil Hitler.' With a smile he continued with his favourite pastime.

Peter remarked, "Galois has seemly left his allegiance for the glorious Fatherland," as he gave a mock Heil Hitler salute.

On an on travelled the captive tractor till finally La Gree was reached without incidence, coming to a stop outside the cottage that Hans once occupied. This residence was now given over to a senior official who thankfully at this moment was on official business in Sark with the Dame of Sark who was seeking justice for an Islander who was accused of a small misdemeanour. Mrs Hathaway was a champion for justice on her island.

Suddenly, the exterior lights disregarded the blackout, as Stafford Jones stood in full glare and shouted in agitation, "Get in here bloody quick I said. Quick David, get rid of the tractor as far away as possible then return here to stay the night; too risky to go home." After tipping out Schmitt and Nifty from the bins, Hal and Peter ushered the three captives, Galois included, into La Gree.

"Needless to say, this was certainly the curse's doings," said a dazed Rita.

Once inside, Stafford Jones congratulated the lads on their efforts saying, "This is not what we expected; we now have extra cargo to take back to dear old Blighty. A sub is waiting at your convenience at Moulin Huet complete with a dingy. Sorry Harold, Mollie Gaudion is out the question this visit. By the way, the Russians will be blamed for this shemozzle and kidnap, so that no blame is accredited to the Islanders. Her Lang will co-operate."

Harold embraced his weeping parents. "Love to Rachel and Mollie!"

Peter gave a push of encouragement to Schmitt and Nifty to descend the ladder, Galois handed over his rifle unconcerned as he entered the tunnel enjoying that his sentry duties were over, leaving the whiff of Galois for the occupants to enjoy or reject. The R A F were briefed to keep reconnaissance till the sub got away.

Twenty-four hours later, our Lads enjoyed an ale of old England as they smiled at the newspaper headlines,

RUSSIANS KIDNAP GERMAN SCIENTIST AND GESTAPO AGENT

The entire operation, unbeknown to loyal Islanders etc., Churchill praises Russia, It is understood through Reuters that a further male is involved as a hostage with a fetish for Galois cigarettes. Our reporter understands from an unknown source that this may be an advertising gimmick to boost sales; so far this is unconfirmed. Winton Churchill cannot be reached. It is a fact that his choice is not Galois, showing a preference for an old fashioned Havana Cigar as he puffs with his fingers in a vee sign. One Australian reporter suggests this symbol interprets Good old Australian vernacular 'Up you mate.' Australians say peculiar things in peace and war.

The two lads, after whetting their appetites, left the Old Bull and Crown to seek further appetites with the fair sex of Plymouth, for now Peter considered himself a man; Harold Lihou, though conscious of Mollie Gaudion in faraway Guernsey decided, 'Life is for Living' - or so they say.

To quote Poor Edie's Mother, 'Gather the nuts of May before winter's chill destroys their flavour.'

Part 4

Chapter 50
The Gruber Visit

Rachel rose early on that day in June 1950. The day promised to be fine and sunny, but of late the weather unpredictable.

Her eight-year-old son, John, was quite excited at the prospect of an overseas visitor. Asking would there be a boy of his age, and if so, perhaps he could show him the farm and maybe offer him a ride on his pony Toby, one of the birthday presents from grandpa Tostivin and Sarre for his eighth birthday. Toby, a beloved animal, became his close companion, together with Rover, a scamp of a dog. The Tostivins were prone to spoil young John, their only grandchild. This was understandable due to the loss of a dear son Eustace in tragic circumstances.

Rachel, between milking and preparing breakfast thought of the hundred and one things yet to attend to before she played host to her Aunt Rita and the Lihou family at La Gree, as well as Rita's overseas friends. Rachel had no idea who the travelers were. Aunt Rita intimated it was someone who knew the war history of the Channel Islands, the only British soil which succumbed to occupation forces during the war. Rita never said too much regarding these surprises she imposed upon people, so Rachel assumed it was probably one of the Occupation soldiers returning to see Guernsey in a different light, not as an enemy, but probably someone who had perhaps made a friendship with an Islander. Not all Germans were bad, she thought, bringing to mind a saying grandma often repeated, 'There is good and bad in everyone.' However, at this point, she was completely unaware of who or what would be sitting at the lunch table. The unexpected is always a challenge. Throughout life she adapted herself to most situations, learning to take things in her stride.

Today's meal was prepared in advance by Poor Edie consisting of an old traditional Guernsey recipe: Conger eel soup made from the head and tail of the eel - very tasty; Guernsey mackerel and crab cutlets, or a choice of curried beef served with fresh farm vegetables. True to form, a Guernsey dessert consisting of apples D' la Gache Melee, followed possibly with a glass of cider that the Catholic brothers (ordained priests of Les Vauxbelets) produced at their seminary in the parish of St Andrews. All this followed by local cheeses with either tea or coffee or whatever.

Aunt Rita did not disclose one inch of what she called 'a very special occasion.' How special? Rita may, unfortunately, live to regret those words! Rita's secrecy could be exasperating. Secretive until the last moment, trusting her motive to bring an element of surprise and enjoyment to those around her. In the past she succeeded. This time, Rachel remarked to her grandmother, Mary, that she had bad vibes regarding the visit. She also understood Mary did not know of Rita's arrangements. "I wish they would decide to cancel their trip to the Island and La Gree. I feel something is wrong granny. Oh Granny, why am I feeling this way? I feel silly. I don't even know them, or understand the reason why they are coming here."

Grandma took Rachel's hand firmly as she smilingly reminded her of the stress that her granddaughter had experienced of late. "Car brakes failing. Burst water tank. Then the ancient barn roof caught up in the high winds sending it smashing the new greenhouse windows - all in the space of one week. "Is it any wonder you fear any new development. I am sure your aunt Rita is acting in the best interests; things will work out. John tells me he is quite excited, wanting to be the man of the house, showing people around the farm, perhaps taking them to the German gun-emplacement and the place where his father was sadly shot. John considers him a hero. He is a good lad. Eustace would have been proud of his son, such a tragedy," continued Grandma Mary. "It is a pity John has got an extreme dislike towards the Occupation soldiers. I pray he will grow out of these feelings."

Rachel drew a breath at those words, as an ache clouded her mind, and then turned from grandma's eyes when distracted by hearing a car stopping in the driveway lane. Hesitating, she replied,

"Yes, he would." Then, as an oversight, "Yes, of course Eustace would." She did not wish to continue the conversation regarding John's relationship with a father he did not know. Whatever information he gleaned from her on this subject was based on a lie, a lie that had lived in her mind and voice and which had escalated over eight years. At this time she had no wish for the truth to be exposed or rectified, in fact, the deceit ceased to be an untruth, for as time went by it seemingly became reality in her everyday thoughts. It was only when questions pointed to John's father that the falsehood surfaced with guilt. Fortunately, both her parents and the intended in-laws, the Tostivins, including the extended families, inadvertently supported her charade of John's conception. Yes, they accepted John was born out of wedlock. Many knew of this; Guernsey had its bush telegraph. Furthermore, his so-called father, Eustace, had died a hero helping a slave worker escape, therefore Eustace's sacrifice of his life found posthumous integrity and forgiveness by society. If the poor lad had survived, he would possibly have been branded for committing fornication, a pre-marriage sin in the eyes of these church-going people. However, the very fact he was killed on his wedding day brought a wave of sympathy, with clemency to the couple involved, enabling Rachel's later cover up of the true fatherhood of her son.

Rita's appearance alleviated some of the tension which Rachel was experiencing from the question her grandmother had asked. Her smiling aunt announced, "They have arrived!" Everyone in the room awaited the supposed surprise that Rita was about to unfold.

Poor Rachel prayed the very mention of John's parenthood, especially concerning his father with its inexplicable secret entombed, would not enter into the conversation by those about to call. Her secret, trapped in her mind caused a claustrophobic situation verging into fear. The subject that lay hidden in her heart over an agonising period, the deception incubated in her womb, a fabrication concocted to save her face as a whore; an untruth to exonerate herself and the one she loved. This consequential lie would live flourishing throughout her life gathering momentum, buried only when she had the courage and honesty to dispose of its duplicity. The cruelest lies are often told in silence. All this and more terrorised her as Rita's visitors appeared.

Rita was today dressed in her Sunday best, clothes that became visible only at church on the Sabbath, or funerals. This was an important occasion, farm clothes were left aside for a workaday. You have no idea of the excitement it caused to hear from Herr Gruber who had unfortunately written in sadness about his son's health.

"Rachel dear, you remember Hans, such a nice boy. You may recall that at some stage during the occupation Hans was billeted in the farm cottage. One of the reasons Herr and Frau Gruber are here today is a sort of thanksgiving to Islanders who recognised violent opposition would have caused untold damage to this small Island - but I must admit we had devious ways of resistance. Hans enjoyed his time on the Island from what I gather. Sadly though, it was in a time of war when Hans was classed the enemy, though we never looked at him as such. Rachel dear, you remember the cottage which was his home? You painted a lovely watercolour after the war, a sort of remembrance of those Occupation days. You are very gifted dear, that painting speaks of your talent. The good book says we must forgive our enemies and rightly so. Surely, Herr Gruber feels the same."

Smiling she turned to Otto Gruber as he slowly entered saying, "Now that sadness of war is over, its aftermath has left the Gruber family personal mourning. The death of a daughter with their grandchildren as well and the tragic life of their son Hans after serving his country. Whatever words her aunt said after those fatal words, 'Gruber and Hans' were lost in silence. In Rachel, a feeling of isolation from body and mind came over her, her heart fibulating in uncertain beats. In her face the usual freshness was now gone, a nightmare pallor resided instead.

Slowly Rita's voice became attuned to her niece's ears. "Herr Gruber had come to Guernsey on a sad mission with his wife, Maria, and their dear son Hans"

"His son? His son? - not his son! –Certainly not his son! Oh no, this a dreadful mistake. Oh." Rachel, drawn with idle curiosity to those words was quickly placed under their hypnotic spell, believing it or rejecting it, as her eyes focused on the trio entering the portals of La Gree. Herr Gruber, a person of medium height in his middle seventies, projecting an unforced smile upon his lined face, a face of character, a man who had weathered many a storm who was now accompanied by his wife Maria, coming to this Isle on a mission to fulfil a wish of their beloved son who accompanied them in a wheelchair guided by Frau Gruber.

Following the trio was young John Tostivin fresh from playing in the garden, his shirt displaying a semblance of mud. What had occurred in the room he had no idea of, or cared, as his eyes searched for a playmate; but none had come from overseas only the Grubers.

Frau Gruber was a short stocky woman of undecided age, at a guess a few years younger than her husband. She was dressed in a mauve dress complemented by a white and black lace-trimmed hat, giving maybe the impression to the observer she was perhaps dressed in mourning garb, portraying the character to those onlookers of a kind gentle woman whose face contained a wisp of sorrow. It was through her genes that probably Hans had inherited his looks, his blue eyes offset by his blond hair, the facial appearance that had first attracted Rachel. She wore a diamond brooch sparkling on the smooth lapel of a black coat tailored with style to match her lace-trimmed hat. She steadily walked into La Gree as warm sunrays illuminated the diamond earrings which sat neatly upon her ear lobes. Completing her love of diamonds, resident on her marriage finger a cluster of 'a girl's best friend,' offset by a black sapphire which emphasised the status of a platinum wedding ring, which had been lovingly placed many years ago. Those with animosity towards past enemies might wonder how they were acquired, legal or plundered. Such is men's inane, mindless thinking. The past is past; let it rest undisturbed; let the future be built on love and understanding.

"Oh, this is not my Hans, my tall, blond, handsome lover with blue eyes setting off a tender face, with a smile captivating the onlooker. No this horrendous crumpled scarred body is not Hans Gruber the one who lay on a Winter's day in the sweet-smelling hay loft so long ago. This is an image, an imposter. Beloved Hans, killed in battle, had I not mourned his death in silence, alone with no one to share my grief. What is before my eyes is a repetition of ghosts, the curse that invades the Lihous and Sarre. I, Rachel Sarre, have witnessed them in the tunnel here at La Gree, feeling the harsh, sharp grit, those unsympathetic piercing splinters offspring of embedded rocks, undisturbed, since ancestors trod into acts of murder." Tears flowed down Rachel's cheeks on this day. Oh the bitterness of remembrances. Oh, the inane cruelty of those vile ghosts, whose very appearance destroyed the happiness of the living and focus on death."

If she had any misgivings of the scene before her, disbelief quickly dispelled as Herr Gruber spoke. "Maria and I are indebted to you all granting our request regarding our dear son Hans. I now believe your family was unaware that he was alive after his brutal brain injuries occurring with much suffering on the battlefield. These horrible injuries caused his return home from the war zone with untold agony, living at our house damaged in the fires of hell that reigned from the sky in worn-torn Berlin. Martha, our daughter, whose husband was a major political figure in Hitler's Reich, arranged for us to take Hans to a leading neurologist in neutral Switzerland after his discharge from active service as unfit to serve or live a normal life, an arrangement in which we are indebted. The three of us journeyed to Geneva where we remained thankfully during the conflict; we had no yearning to be part of Hitler's mad war. I witnessed so much bloodshed on both sides in the 1914-18 Great War, a murderous inconsistency horrifically known throughout history as a blood-bath.

Rachel felt a cold numbness creep through her body with what Herr Gruber revealed, trying to restrain honest tears in her demented soul. Motionless, awaiting the return from a dream world bordering on a nightmare, from which she would hopefully awaken. To her, there was a falsehood in Herr Gruber's conversation.

Otto Gruber continued his inventive story (for this is what she believed and heard or was it a hallucination in her imagination). Yet, as she perceived through her haze, the rest of the occupants appeared to be flesh and blood alive and living. Only the Grubers were ethereal ghosts. Is this another performance in the Lihou and Sarre's turbulent curse? For Rachel Sarre, all that had transpired caused her deep denial of the conversations.

Otto Gruber continued, his words unheard in Rachel's ears, her eyes now transfixed on this man who seemed bent on destroying her world with disbelief that this person named Hans by others is not the man whom she loved who fathered her son. Both had pledged their devotion to each other remaining true forever; to her, in truth, this is certainly not the man. Is this act of deception played before her eyes the finality of their love? God's punishment? No, God is a God of love, the bible tells us so, had she not learnt that in Sunday school; but she sinned. Has God forsaken her, a fornicator?

Otto continued, "The Geneva specialist's prognosis was bleak; in fact, the doctors are surprised that the end had not come sooner for this pitiful sight, our dear son is now having constant care."

Rachel gazed at the figure before her, questioning in her mind why they are here?

Otto Gruber's words returned to her ears. Otto continued, "Hans asked in a letter written when stationed in Guernsey, that if and when he died could he possibly be buried on your beautiful Island. Little did we think that this day would come? Parents should not have the trauma of living longer than their children. Our daughter our only daughter...." Tears welled within as he spoke. Maria reached over to comfort his shaking hand, hopefully instilling strength to continue. "Our daughter was a good child but caught up with the ravings of a lunatic doctrine. So many youngsters forced to join Hitler Youth, only wanting the best for Germany who was suffering and paying what was set down at the Treaty of Versailles. Martha's allegiance to the new order led her to marry a staunch supporter of the Third Reich, a devious man who seemed to have hypnotic power over her as well as their young children. His ill-formed beliefs led them to perish in the Berlin Bunker with the evil man's followers. May God rest their souls." Those last few words were too much. "Please forgive this emotion," he said, wiping the tears from his reddened eyes and

198

bursting into pitiful sobs. We both loved her in spite of all her faults. Children can break your heart!"

Rita came forward consoling Herr Gruber. Maria whispered in her husband's ear that she would continue if he so desired. Otto nodded in agreement. They both knew that he was on the point of collapse due to the strain of the last forty-eight hours, as the journey began to take its toll. Otto clasped Hans's hand, pitifully receiving no recognition from a body whose voice was incapable of offering thanks or emotion towards any who sought to ease his suffering.

The specialist gave Maria and Otto a prognosis that did not prove favourable for recovery. Both knew his wish to be buried in Guernsey must be granted. Hans appeared to be living in a vacuum that held him prisoner in mind and body, all exit hatches locked and barred with no exit. Consequently, it was just a matter of time when Hans would leave behind his suffering when allowed, passing through the final exit, gaining freedom from his earthly suffering. Maria apologised for not continuing with all the facts -perhaps a little later when both had rested. Hans sat immobile, awaiting impossible movement from his static situation, unable to accept compassion from others or accept the offer of ordained death if and when it arrived, or the generosity of euthanasia from one who rules our destiny. Until then, Hans had to wait and linger in the brutality caused by man; he had no choice.

Rachel sat on a chair near her grandmother Mary, who likewise was taken aback by what she saw and heard from Herr Gruber. The only one who perhaps had an idea of what was happening was Rita. She saved whatever information she gleaned regarding the Gruber's visit, accumulated for what she called an element of surprise. Judging by the looks on people's faces in the room, she had achieved what she set out to do - and more!

Suddenly, a young voice shouted breaking the silence. I hate Germans, they killed my father. A ripple was sent throughout the room as Mary ushered young John out of the area, leaving her embarrassment behind her in the room of humiliation with the Grubber's head bowed as if in prayer.

Rachel rose slowly from the chair, trance-wise, her inattentive feet almost incapable of making her way to this person, wrongly named Hans, sitting immobile in his wheelchair, who, to all onlookers appeared as a carved grey concrete statue. In Rachel's eyes, Hans was a moulded, faceless, sub-human being without expression or the power of recognition, as if his mind and body were frozen in time for all to see the nemesis of war. Mysterious, unseen puppet-like strings seemed to control Rachel's movements, strings tightened to drag her clammy hand to stroke his face and half-shut eyes, which did not flicker at the necrophilia caress to induce life. She too, at that instant, became a moulded statue, when, at that moment, on touching a hard face, her shaking hands revealed the bitter truth, for around his shattered neck lay the locket, the pledge of love, the token given as lovers parted. Clutching this emblem she slithered to the floor into oblivion.

The silence was broken as cries of alarm were uttered by those within the room.

At this moment young John re-entered from the garden having escaped from Mary. On seeing his mother on the floor at the feet of Hans he said, "Who is this horrible man? What has he done to mummy?"

The Grubers looked on.

Maria bent forward and her hands tenderly encircled the child's face saying in an inaudible whisper,

"Don't cry beloved Hans, mummy is here." Her tears slowly trickled onto the blond hair of the child known as John Tostivin. Maria's tears evaporated as a tender smile appeared.

Rachel awoke in a room at La Gree devoid of light. Heavy curtains were drawn to assure Rachel that it was nightfall and inducing her to sleep if possible, gaining a sense of recovery to return to a place where all unpleasant thoughts of everyday perplexity were attuned to happiness. Unfortunately, that world does not exist. She desired a spot that cut all contact with life, both pleasant and otherwise, to be in a position where she could travel a pathway of her own choosing, a preference denied as an alien voice of either Eunice, or was it Rita, interrupted her awakening, a voice to her at that moment was hard to define.

"Rachel, do you feel better?" asked Rita, tenderly raising her niece's head to the comfort of the floral printed pillow case on which she had slept in her curious state.

Hopefully, Rachel could now feel the coziness of the head support but she responded with the unkindly response, "Go away. I do not want any of you" with an intonation of venom unaccustomed to Rachel's way of conversation, causing a perplexed look on their faces during this outburst.

Rita spoke quietly to Eunice, "What has happened? This morning at breakfast she seemed quite cheerful, except maybe worried over the visitors, not knowing who they were. I blame myself. Perhaps I should have confided. Eunice, please understand, I hoped it would be a surprise for everyone. Poor Rachel, I take the blame for the outcome of my surprise, I acted foolishly."

Eunice held Rachel's hand as she faced Rita and quietly commented, "Don't blame yourself. This behaviour has happened before. Doctor Rose indicated her mental state has been in severe shock due to past events. Apparently, she rejects the present, reverting to a zone where the present with its unpleasantness is no longer an issue. This may be true. If only we could visit a specialist, but at the present none are available in Guernsey. According to Dr Rose, the retired specialist who deals with this sort of problem lives in Sark. He may be able to help, that is if she agrees. The trouble is, she remembers nothing of her outbursts, saying she is perfectly well." Rita spoke in almost a whisper as if frightened that the words she uttered had to be avoided by Rachel's ears. "Eunice, perhaps her condition is through the Lihou and Sarres wretched curse, which has dammed the family neigh on two hundred years? Such a dreadful affliction, this blight specified for sinful actions, an irritation perpetrated, to unsavoury ancestors."

Rita turned to her sister-in-law saying, "Christians should not believe in such things."

Eunice nodded. "I know, but strange, unbelievable happenings have occurred."

Rita continued, "Causing the old people to say, 'those who do not believe will be bewitched sending families of the Lihous and Sarres to perish in the fires of hell. Their blood line will die'. Look what happened to Peter Sarre, an unbeliever. His cows died of a strange illness, his well water turned sour, the wheat fields unripe all had to be cut down. Finally, so the onlookers say, 'Ghostly figures chanting in the house for three whole days, then a fire as if from hell, rendered him and the house to a cinder.' Our ancestors swear this is true. Esther Lihou prayed outside Peter's house with bible in hand, praying for his salvation. Lo and behold, in doing so, the good book caught fire leaving a page with drops of blood smeared upon the smouldering page with vaporous writing in bold letters. 'Lucifer Reigns.' Those who witnessed this terrible advent say what more proof do you want? Believe or perish. Rachel's behaviour could be due to the curse; such bizarre things happened in Guernsey. The folklore states: 'All witches fly at night, working their spells with the poltergeists joining force. Together they roam in the darkness of the earth accomplishing frightful deeds when you least expect them.' Such strange unexplained activities occur. Surely Eunice, you remember the carryon at La Houget, the home of our distant cousin Paul De Garis. After a sleepless night, he and his family of four came down to breakfast only to find the table laid for five people. The strange thing was, Eunice, the electric kettle was switched on ready to boil. Furthermore, the toaster was filled with bread for morning toasts. Eunice, do listen. Upon the stove four eggs lay beside the pan half-filled with cold water ready to be poached, another egg in an eggcup to be boiled or fried. Eunice, are you listening? How did the poltergeist know the de Garis only eat poached eggs? Strange, very strange, to leave an uncooked egg for a fifth person."

Eunice nodded in agreement.

"The table was set for five people." Listen, Eunice, there were only four persons in the Paul De Garis family then. As they sat half in fright and wonderment half way through breakfast an impatient knocking came on the front door which echoes percolated through the house. Eli de Garis said she never heard such knocking, very upsetting.

Eunice, are you listening? Paul De Garis opened the door and there stood his unexpected cousin from the jungles of South America. No one knew he was arriving. This is the sad part, when Mrs De Garis senior heard of the carryon she took a turn and is now buried in the Forest cemetery. The cousin was full of remorse, said he should have sent a telegram as it might have saved his cousin, Mrs Harriet De Garis senior the inconvenience of being buried. Tragic it was, as she was in good health, but as Paul De Garis remarked, you can't go against a poltergeist. When you come to think about the weird happenings those poltergeists do, it is no laughing matter. Funny things happen in the dark of the night."

"I must admit it takes a lot of believing Rita."

"Oh Eunice, what about that time at Mrs Du Jardin's funeral. Surely what happened to you will take away any disbelief you may have had. I can see it now; Eunice, you were pushed into that grave."

"Rita, enough of this nonsense. I slipped as I threw a rose on the coffin of dearly beloved Mrs. du Jardin. I felt so embarrassed."

"Oh no, Eunice, you were pushed. Madam Baudin vouched it was a mighty wind that blew on you, a wind sent from the unknown to cause annoyance on a very a sad day. Shameful, a poltergeist has no respect for the dead or the living. She knew it was a wind because it whistled up her skirt much to her humiliation as you can imagine. No Eunice. Please believe me, you were surely pushed. What about the voice of Mrs du Jardin crying out from the depth of the grave, a lament because her eternal rest was disturbed."

"Rita, it was me crying out. My foot jammed between the coffin lid with my shoe stuck by the muddy soil. Everyone ignored my request for help with a look of horror on their faces."

"Yes, Eunice. Well, it might be after hearing the voice of upset Mrs Du Jardin. Very strange, that voice Eunice. Mr Clarrie Le Tocq, the undertaker, was not convinced or impressed that the poor soul was at rest. He wanted to unscrew the coffin lid making sure he had not made a mistake burying her alive and this he would have done; only the minister insisted it would be irreverent to disturb the poor soul after such a lovely service and her being a

Roman Catholic. Clarrie would have ignored the minister only he left his screwdriver in the vestry toilet. Such mortification, what was he doing in the toilet with a screwdriver?"

"Rita, never mind the screwdriver or Mrs Du Jardin. What about my indignity stuck between a coffin and people throwing roses?"

Chapter 51
The Intervening Years

Rachel stirred as she lay, her in mind in confusion after the appearance of the lifeless statue of Hans Gruber. Is this a hallucination or a dream or part truth? In her life, there were so many half-truths. The optical illusion changes on seeing the old pendulum clock in the hallway of her beloved La Pettit Close. As her vision changes, she struggles to see the time on the small clock on the bedside table. Why is everything so muddled? Her glance catches sight of the Calendar; 1942 displayed in bold letters. Oh, the pains playing tricks with her eyes, for now she is back in the Occupation. The pendulum of time swung to and fro, never requiring to be rewound at La Pettit Close, or for that matter at La Gree, as seconds turned to minutes, then to hours, then weeks, months, when days were swallowed in everyday living. To Rachel one day seemed a frenzied week before the awaited nine months arrived ending her unsettled pregnancy due to minor complications, for confinement had not been easy. On one occasion, an issue of blood trickled on to the bed clothes, during spasms of violent pain. This subjected Rachel to panic, plagued by the implication she could lose her precious baby. Fortunately for both concerned, Doctor Rose, after an emergency visit, stated, 'No cause for alarm.' However, in or Rachel Sarre's mind alarm bells had issues in her mentality in a place where truth and a silent lie lurked, destroying the background scenario known only to her.

The inescapable happened during a late dark Occupation winter's night in 1942 when all was quiet at Le Pettit Close, except for nature's unpredictable weather, for a ferocious wind approaching gale force echoed around La Pettit Close, its strength would deny a would-be traveler safety, urging those within to venture not far from fireplace or bed. Nevertheless, on this night of all nights, its memory will be etched in awareness of a night to remember, the picture is so vivid. The pendulum stopped to recreate a now bygone occasion of eight years past. Rachel left the comfort of the snug blanket with her hand searching beneath the bed for the Robespierre chamber pot, the same one that lay dormant for many years as an heirloom of the historical era. Tonight it would still be an unused empty vessel. As she searched, anguish overtook her weary body, a prelude to birth Rachel's waters broke, the splashed water received unto the plain thirsty carpet. Rachel's scream summoned Eunice followed closely by Poor Edie, both rushing to the expectant mother's room, wakened by her cry, fearing it may be another false alarm or even worse. Birth has uncertainties either good or bad and with the Guernsey Occupation, it was no exception.

"Why do troubles happen in the middle of night during curfew hours? Please God, comfort my daughter if it be your will and save her baby; she has suffered enough after Eustace's death. It's alright darling, I phoned Dr Rose. Don't be too alarmed. These incontinences happen, sometimes brought on by stress. I know a few women who have experienced what you are and having it never affected the baby. Dr Rose will explain it better than I can."

Eunice's conversation altered seeing the residue on the carpet, intuitively knowing Rachel's time of waiting had arrived. Her arms once again encircled her daughter like she always did in times of distress, gently saying, "Darling, be brave until doctor arrives; we are all here." Turning to Nick as he appeared after hearing the commotion, "Nick dear, please phone the doctor and just say Rachel requires his attention as she is in labour, he will understand" said Eunice, not prone to panic.

Nick hurried to the phone but in the confusion he could not bring the number to mind after winding the telephone winder for connection to an operator who answered in a typical Guernsey accented voice, "Number please." "Nick Sarre here. Yes, Nick Sarre." Please get me Doctor Rose quickly, Rachel having a baby. Hurry, she is in a bad way.

Nickolas Sarre was in a state of distress after the reply he received from Grace Bichard, "Sorry Nick, doctor is in Sark unable to get back. It's the weather, bad time of the year, unreliable." Don't worry; go have a hot drink, tea is always a saver in emergency. Hope Eunice has some good old Lipton English Breakfast, not occupation bramble. I'll phone around and see if I can find a midwife, or the German doctor, Now Nick, stop worrying, in an hour or two, you will have your grandchild in your arms. Tell Eunice and Rachel not to worry, if all fails the ambulance will take poor Rachel. Perhaps they might refuse without a doctor's signature, not like the old days. Now Nick, get off the line so I can phone around seeing if we can find help."

Nick returned to the bedroom to see Eunice sitting on the bed comforting Rachel who's spasm of pain accelerated rapidly as the of harsh sound of labour progressed. Nick blurted inadvertently, "The doctor is in Sark, held up by the weather. Grace Bichard says not to worry; she will phone us as soon she finds a midwife or a German doctor to help with the confinement. Don't worry Rachel darling, help will arrive.

At these words Poor Edie, who had remained silent, spoke in her usual tone as Rachel let out scream, jarring Poor Edie to say, "You can tell Grace Bichard she is a fool. Does she know it's your daughter not a cow having a baby? Get back on the phone and tell her so, then fetch me four large bath towels. Large ones! Make sure the kettle has plenty hot water. Also scissors, and in the kitchen drawer you will find some new cat gut. Don't stand there go! We got to be ready for whoever the foolish Grace sends. In the cupboard you will find old newspapers bring six.

Nick stood in amazement at what he heard; realizing Poor Edie was once again in command, this time not in her kitchen. As always, you do no argue with Poor Edie!

Eunice embraced Rachel who again experienced the security of a mother. Over time no help arrived with any news from Grace Bichard. Nick fulfilled the duties requested by Poor Edie keeping the kettle ready with hot water. Rachel's labour pains were now continuous. Perspiration dripped from her face as she tried to hold back till help arrived.

By instinct Poor Edie sensed time was running out, causing her to make a pronouncement and taking command, "Nick, out the room. Now Rachel, down to business my mother always said, 'When a Woman receives a bite from man's apple a price has to be paid! You now pay the price!' Eunice, you can stay and help. Out Nick, keep the kettle boiling. You Rachel push and push again." She issued this directive for an half hour until Poor Edie, who was branded to serve fellow men, now lived her finest hour.

On this night she will link the past with the future when Rachel Sarre, a cousin twice removed, her mistress, gave birth to the said John Tostivin. Love and pride appeared on the face of Poor Edie as she handed the new-born to his exulted mother. A new life crying at the joy of being out of bondage, to breathe God's air.

As Rachel received her son, silently within her mind uttered, 'Your son Hans.'

Her thoughts were interrupted due to a knocking on the bedroom door. Nick, a proud grandfather, entered with the German doctor who had come at Grace Bichard's bidding, arriving too late for it was Poor Edie, a first time midwife, doing the necessary duties, her unpracticed knowledge learnt by watching her mother delivering family babies. She, of little education, arose to the occasion to serve the Sarres and Lihous. Not bad for one who found the three Rs beyond her learning.

Needless to say, much frivolity was heard on that early morning at La Pettit Close as Rachel rested with her precious son. The German doctor praised Poor Edie for her skill, the foe and enemy united, then produced a bottle of French Champagne giving a toast to the new-born and family saying, "Whatever our differences, may we obtain peace without the brutalities of war. To Rachel and son." That same son was now nestled in his mother's arms sleeping as the wind without subsided. Dawn slowly appeared heralding a new day and life. On the housetops, hedges and tree boughs the birds proclaimed a dawn chorus, a thanksgiving from deliverance from the storm.

Over the years young John brought much happiness to the families of Sarre and Lihou, Rachel never revealing the secret of his father's love close in her heart as he grew during those occupation years.

The sound of Eunice entering the room brought Rachel back from that day in 1942 when her child was born to the time of the Gruber's visit. How quickly the years go! Otto Maria Gruber had stayed a few days at La Gree as the guest of Rita with an arrangement that their son, Hans, would be cared for by a district nurse with all expenses paid by them, strangely stipulating that the said Rachel Sarre would act as Hans's next of kin, a request leaving a few wondering. Why Rachel? Perceptive Otto with discerning thoughts, knew his son would be in the safe loving hands of Rachel with her seeing to his every need in the cottage at La Gree.

Hans lived a few years in a vacuum. Upsetting as it was to Rachel, she gained comfort with the satisfaction that her Hans would live through the presence of his son.

Part 5

Chapter 52
Rachel and Edgar

Rachel only recalled Edgar Heaume when they were both young children before the time his parents left the Island of their birth in the early 1930s taking up residence in England until his father, Elias, was posted as a lawyer with Lloyds of London which focused Elias's family elsewhere. Due to the nature of his work, the residence could change at a drop of a hat, sending the family to any part of the globe, which actually suited young Edgar, new schools, new friends, and of course new girls.

Elias was educated firstly at Elizabeth College then Caen University in Normandy, France. This further study was necessary if one desired to practice Law in Guernsey as it was mandatory to study at Caen for the necessary qualifications. Elias, in the course of his studies, met attractive young ladies who he dated, each for a short time, until he met the love of his life. Yes, the love of his life, the beautiful Marie Naftel, the daughter of a prominent Island lawyer. Both youngsters were studying International Law and after a whirlwind romance they returned to Guernsey to marry, bringing joy to the family. A second blessing came to the household when Edgar was born, a Honeymoon baby, so say some, a great delight in having a son to carry on the name of Heaume. Joy at times was overcast with sadness when it was discovered Marie was unable to carry more children due to an infection of the womb which nearly cost her life after the birth, an event making Edgar a very precious child.

At irregular intervals, Elias and his family returned for holidays staying with either parents, the Naftel's or the Heaume's [Senior] only terminating on the deaths of Marie's parents during the late 1950s in a tragic plane crash off the coast of Majorca. Within a short time, Mr Heaume Senior also departed this earth after an illness. It was then the Elias family, after much thought, decided to return at a future date to the Island of their birth.

During this period Edgar was introduced to Rachel, due to a situation regarding his car, which he just purchased from the Bourgourd Brothers garage at Les Banque on the outskirts of St Peter Port. The wretched vehicle decided at an inopportune moment to have two punctures. Fortunately for Edgar it happened within walking distance of La Petit Close; maybe fate had decided the time and place. He knocked on a stout wooden door complete with an unusual brass knocker cast in jest, portraying as an angel apparently to keep away evil spirits. This one replaced a skull that some ancestor intimated that this sign represented the Sarres and Lihous ongoing curse. "Whoever made and placed this original skull object on this stout portal door of La Pettit Close remains a mystery; some say it depicted death through the curse!" Eunice, Rachel's mother, urged her husband Nick to replace this unwelcome symbol with a figure of an angel which, in due course, he did.

Edgar, when passing the house previously had noticed the angel knocker cast in shinning brass, gleaming as only Poor Edie could achieve; He often wondered what was behind its grained portals. Until now Edgar had never entered this intriguing La Petit Close but the house became familiar for he often passed the frontage on his way to the Heaume residence. From its exterior this aged house had an interesting air to the onlooker; how interesting he would soon find out.

Edgars knocking ended abruptly when answered by Poor Edie. She was still in grief due to the loss of her mother several years earlier, a grief that unfortunately would last until the griever reached eternity; such is Edie's manner of dealing with a situation affecting her lifestyle. Poor Edie was a third cousin removed but was now a truly established housekeeper at La Petit Close, a position that would last many years. She quoted, 'La Petit Close was her home until the good Lord seems fit to take her to a land without dusters.'

"Excuse me, my car has a puncture, two in fact. "May I use your phone if that is possible?" asked Edgar politely.

Poor Edie did not take well when interruptions knocked at the door. She commanded him abruptly to wait until she fetched Miss Rachel Sarre, then, without any more ado, shut the door in his face and subsequently hurried to fetch Miss Sarre. After a brief wait the door was re-opened by Rachel, who had a look of surprise on her face, surprised to see such a handsome mature man standing in her doorway.

"Forgive my housekeeper for not inviting you in, she is wary of strangers. Please come in" You certainly may use the telephone. Oh by the way, I am Miss Rachel Sarre."

Edgar shook her hand saying, "Edgar Heaume at your service. You may not have heard of our family as we very recently returned to Guernsey after an absence of many years; even so I consider myself an Islander. Guernsey is a special place. Its heritage blood runs in our veins." Then smiling he said "You have such lovely flowers blooming on your Island," he shyly said to the still attractive person who stretched her hand in welcome. "Sorry, our Island. We should have arrived earlier Miss Sarre."

If Edgar could have read Rachel's judgment of his words he would have seen, 'Watch this one' as Rachel had a perceptive nature when introduced at a first meeting. Edgar entered the stone hallway, the same passageway with a winding granite stairway with its wooden settle adjacent to the front door, on which Rachel's father had proposed to her mother many years ago. He walked past the chair where Rachel had sat within her mother's embrace on that dark day Herr Lang brought news of Eustace's death. In this same hallway she was crying with unspoken grief in mourning for the death of her intended husband, Eustace. She also grieved silently for Hans Gruber, her invalidated husband in the eyes of the church, but consummated with child within a unsanctified womb, a sanctuary yet unblessed by church ritual. Memories unconsumed by time, repetitive daily. This portal hallway knows bereavement; its grieving stains remain encrusted within the granite walls, with a duo of sadness at times transported with a fleeting transit of joy embedded over generations. Those who are of a Fey nature will feel this entrance has a sad story injecting a momentary coldness to those who enter; only to be warmed by the presence of love, preordained by those who reside within, for the act of love banishes the unpleasant with its soothing balm. It is a true fact; a house retains its warmth from past and present of those in residence. The mother of the infant of forbidden love became a living memory within these walls, until savage cancerous consuming war robbed her life of truth, pointing her to a different direction. It is here in this passageway that a lie was born - only on lips - but true in heart. If the present two characters in this hallway could foresee the future, the lives of Rachel Sarre and Edgar Heaume would also enter on different pathways.

"You shall find the telephone in the small recess at the end of the hall." Please excuse me for a few minutes; my house keeper seems to be having trouble with a vacuum cleaner. Machines never seem to work at a time you need them most, and to be without a cleaner is a tragedy for my efficient housekeeper Edie! I often wonder how our grandparents managed without the mechanical aids which seem to govern our lives. But I must not complain, Edie usually has everything under control in the running of La Petit

Close. Home help is difficult to obtain since the war. Girls today want more out of life than scrubbing floors, considering it one of life's drudges. Wars change so many things, not only our everyday lives, but also elusive precious moments we hold dear, many never to be regained!" She spoke those words in a whisper, as if frightened for others to hear. "Perhaps after you have telephoned you will care to join me for some refreshment?" She left, pointing to a recess housing the phone.

In the distance, Edgar heard the agitated voice of Poor Edie saying, "Some people think we have all day to see to their needs; this is a house is not a telephone box."

Edgar smiled as he phoned the Royal Automobile Club and asked for assistance. When he replaced the phone he heard Rachel replying, "It's all right Edie, cars can be troublesome, we must help if we can."

"Yes but that does not get the work done," mumbled Poor Edie.

The whirl of the vacuum informed Edgar Poor Edie would soon put this house in order, the unwelcome dust sucked into eternity.

Rachel returned smiling, "I am apprehensive, Mr. Heaume, when mundane appliances are not working; it takes very little to throw Edie into a situation where she is not in control. Luckily, today it was only a loose connection in the plug top, so now Edie is occupied in what she enjoys. Let's have coffee or something stronger. Is it too early for a sherry or perhaps a beer or brandy maybe? May I suggest one of Edie's homemade delicious shortbreads, which I can entirely recommend Mr Heaume?"

"Edgar is the name my mother unfortunately gave me at birth, meaning rich. Woefully I'll never be. I answer to Ned, which my friends insist on using, so please feel free to use either - but only on one condition, that I dispense with Miss Sarre and call you Rachel, which I believe means a symbol of innocence. As we say in court, innocent or guilty? Please excuse my weird sense of humour. Coffee will be excellent. I feel your recommendation of the shortbread is a must, thank you."

Rachel replied with a laugh, "I am neither guilty nor innocent. Yes, you may call me Rachel please. Not Rach as so many do. I rather like the name Edgar and Edgar you will be."

Edgar bowed his head offered his hand saying, "We now know who we are."

"Do we ever know who we are?" replied Rachel in thought.

"What a charming room overlooking a delightful garden; you must have green fingers judging by such an array of flowers. Forgive me saying this. It is magical seeing flowers at this time of the year in late January. How do you work this magic?"

I am no magician my mother had a glass roof covering that part of the flower garden which you cannot notice from here. Most of the flowers are nursed in the side conservatory of the house in the warmth of pots, and then transplanted as you see them, a sort of an illusion to the onlooker. I am just a Guernsey farm girl from a long line of Guernsey stock; it was my mother who came up with the idea of a glass roof. I am proud of my Island heritage, are you Edgar? In this fast changing world we must hold on to our past legacy. I am all for our history with our patois being learned on the school curriculum. The future of these islands depends on youngsters not losing their identity.

"I am truly glad that the car stopped by this interesting house. I would have missed such charming hospitality with such wisdom. Yes, it is important for the young to hold on to tradition as they travel to the future. The 1960s present a problem. It is not only the schools who have to uphold this but also their parents must be integrated into the structure. Edgar smiled. "Together we will change the world. Speaking in praise, Your garden is enchanted," saying as he continued, "With a beautiful hostess."

Poor Edie entered, complete with a silver tray holding the coffee and shortbreads and without a smile or words, placed the tray on an occasional table, surveyed the room, and then hurried out oblivious of the occupants denying Rachel the opportunity to thank her.

"Edgar, you see what a treasure she is. I had not yet ordered anything; thankfully you did not chose beer or you would have been landed with coffee. Re-ordering would have meant tears from Edie."

"Do you garden yourself, or employ a gardener?"

"No, Edgar, I potter, trying to keep it as my mother did. She and my Aunt Rita spent many hours cherishing their gardens. We have good soil here as my mother often remarked, 'We are blessed with good earth at La Petit Close; we must use God's gift rightly,' which she did, and judging by the results as you can see Edgar, when I was a child in magical thought, as sometimes children do, these gardens of La Petit Close and La Gree were to me the real Gardens of Eden. Secret gardens, their beauty seen only by those who understood the reason why they were planted in love just as the original Eden was. In life Edgar, we sometimes do things not fully understanding its full effect on others."

Rachel quickly changed the conversation in fear she may have said too much. "Mother still has a lovely garden where she and father retired to after leaving the farm due to father's ill health. My father had a bypass. He hated not having the farm but his doctor advised retirement due to his attack. I suspect he has never forgiven the doctor. We nearly lost him at one stage but poor dad did not take retirement lightly even though his heart was in a bad state. Thankfully he devotes time to volunteer work at his church and for the retirement village. Of course he visits La Pettit Close making sure I am doing the right things by his cows, after all they were his life's work. Mother too had enough; farms are not playgrounds. Away from the farm dad enjoys good health but of course with the heart you have to take care. Mother tries to keep him on the straight and narrow. I run the farm now and after I am gone, my son. At that moment the phone rang ending the conversation regarding her son. Excuse me I must answer the phone. Edie won't while she has her pride and joy the cleaner operating.

When Rachel returned she said no more on the subject of, who would run the farm after her death. "Sorry wrong number. As I was saying, mother does very little to the Retirement garden, but her instruction to the paid gardener is enough to make sure it up to her usual standard, saying, "God planted trees and flowers and before us, so we must take care of them." Grandmother, who had a sense of humour, often replied, "You are right Eunice, all living things in earth are antiques, precious, going back to the beginning so we must keep them safe. Old people included."

"Rachel, I've yet to sample the perfumes of your enchanted garden. I see it with love. Hmm, you are quite right; these shortbreads are the real thing. I shall name them Edie's delicious highland shortbreads. My mother never had success with Scotland's favourite; the taste would make her quite envious of Edie's achievement. By the way, mother's name is Maria and Dad is Elias. Forgive me, but would it be presumptuous if I brought my mother to visit to see the garden, and to ask Edie her secret regarding shortbreads. Our family have been away so long, associates move on and mother has to make new friendships. I am sure both of you will get on like a house on fire. Mother is a sociable, good-natured lady, still attractive for her age. I know you lead a busy life, I'd understand if a visit is not possible."

"How I could I refuse her after your glowing report. You must bring both your parents for dinner to do justice to Edie's cooking."

Any further conversation halted at the sound of the R.A.C services van summonsing Edgar to get the punctures mended.

After thanking, Rachel for her hospitality, Edgar left La Petit Close to face whatever the R.A.C. mechanic had to say. One thing Edgar Heaume was sure of, this was not his last visit to Miss Rachel Sarre! Rachel returned to the house after bidding her unexpected visitor a safe journey. Edgar waved goodbye with a blown kiss as he drove off, wishing the serviceman had taken longer to fix the punctures.

Rachel pondered what this charming man had in mind, in some ways wanting him to return as she desired companionship, a desire she very rarely felt. These thoughts lingered as she made her way to where Hans's ashes lay and she glanced at the memorial of the man she loved and always would. "Darling, no one will take your place." Her hands closed in silent prayer as she knelt on the patch where he rested. A soft breeze floated through the meadow bringing the long expected rain. Rachel wept. Weeping perhaps, with thought of how she had denied nature for male companionship of the intimate relationship, of bearing children, closing her body to maintain a solemn promise made to Hans, regarding the custody of her cove, a forbidden territory, a place only he had transgressed in love, a location no one else will ever enter.

After returning to the house, Rachel busied herself in the daily chores. The visit of Edgar Heaume had taken her thoughts to other things. This rather unsettled her. She usually brushed uneasy feelings away, but today they seemed to remain. It was not so much what he said; it was his very presence that brought havoc feelings that had laid dormant over the years. Why they should appear at this particular time? She began searching for an answer, gaining no positive explanation after analyzing, then discovering what could become a major issue if not put to rest. Why it should, she could not comprehend. This was an annoyance to a person who always wanted an answer, never dwelling in the negative.

The ringing of the telephone stopped any further search on the topic. Edie appeared saying, "It's that man with the puncture wishing to speak to you. I told him you were busy, told him to ring back, but he said he would wait. You have to be firm with him or he'll be ringing every five minutes. Some people take advantage of good nature."

"Thank you Edie; that will be enough."

Edie departed muttering, "Some people have no thought."

Rachel picked up the phone to hear Edgar's voice. "Mother invited you to dinner. Can we fix a date?"

Rachel was somewhat taken aback by so quick an invite to the Heaume's house. "Thank your mother, but I think you all should dine here first, leaving her time to settle into the new house. Moving is tiresome so they say but I have never had that experience after living at La Petit Close since I was born. I intend to invite my parents also so you can get to know us!

"Yes that's very thoughtful of you; it's ideal. Our house is topsy-turvy, but still, you tend to think you know where things are.

At the best of times, house and car keys are elusive. Anyway, I want to get to know you and your parents."

Rachel smiled answering, "I'll look at the calendar; hold on for a moment," as she advanced to the small table where a flowered calendar lay. Her finger searched for a suitable date. "What about Saturday week, the 23rd January?"

"Yes that sounds good to me. I am sure mother will have no prior engagements on that day, but if so she will have to cancel them."

"Edgar, no, only if she is free on that date, if not I will arrange another time. Thank your mother. It was so kind of her to offer an invite. I trust she won't be offended at my suggesting you dine here first."

"Of course not, my mother is not like that. You'll love her, she's a sweetie; her only fault is spoiling me to the hilt. I hope she spoils you one day."

Rachel made a quick retreat from the conversation which she regarded was now on dangerous grounds. "On the 23rd January then. I must go. Goodbye Edgar."

"Goodbye Miss Rachel Sarre, my new friend."

Edie appeared saying, "Not another puncture?" then turning to her mistress remarked, "You're not getting a fever are you? You're looking very flushed."

Rachel hurried from the room wishing Edgar Heaume had knocked on someone else's door - Or did she? "Oh, why do I feel like this? Is this the curse of the Sarres and Lihous creating mischief?"

In due course the evitable happened. Edgar was smitten with Rachel. His curiosity desired to know more of this attractive woman who he guessed was around his own age. Many questions went through his mind while pondering his next move of getting to know this Miss Rachel Sarre - as she termed herself when they first met. The question in Edgar's mind was, is she divorced or separated or perhaps never married; an attractive woman as she would have been and still can draw a look from an interested male; she surely had offers. Did she have children? Perhaps she had received proposals it would be interesting to know. Why the 'Miss,' was she ever married, is there some dark secret? No, in his estimation she is a lady who would be open regarding her past. He dismissed any further questions in his mind with an idiom as they say in Australia, 'No Worries Mate.' Australia, a land where he had a tragic romantic interlude during his employment as a qualified lawyer in Melbourne. His fondness for Australia was jarred through a courtship leading to a proposed marriage, thwarted by an instance that should have never happened so he was now proceeding with caution in any further relationship. Once bitten twice shy. In this reflective mood, his thoughts returned to Australia.

Australia was still lingering in his blood, a country for which he felt infinity. He had a desire to reside there again, with its attraction of the wide open spaces, the extent of the vast bush, its flora and fauna, the beauty of yellow wattles, its persistent scent, tea-trees, the refreshment of flowered eucalyptus gums, the surfer riding on foaming booming waves proclaiming victory over those who fail to complete their mission on Neptune's, bubbling horses. Snow covered mountains, lakes and rivers, minerals in glittering shades, still a virgin land unfrocked awaiting many future cultures to advance Australia fair. Fun times, the barbeque in the back yard, complete with sizzling sausages compelling onions, tomato sauce or a whatnot concoction squeezed between a bun, its taste to be remembered; vulture flies ready to descend to share or infect the feast, the swill of cool, cool tinny of Forster's beer downing a throat that is ever calling for the balm of hops, transporting temporary relief in a gullet parched by sweltering unforgiving heat. However, he had now exchanged all this to live in the land of his birth. Will he be claustrophobically choked in this twenty-five square miles of Island? Will its smallness devour his intellect to a mundane level after giving up the broader infrastructure of Down Under? He will require learning Australia is Australia, Guernsey is Guernsey, each with a different interesting chapter during his journey in life, accepting the realization that 'Never the twain shall meet' while pleasantly enjoying individually what each has to offer!

If Rachel could have tuned in to Edgar's thoughts at that moment, she would agree with him on the same descriptive Australian wavelength, as James Corbin, her far distant cousin, had explained to her in the spring of 1938.

Australia loomed again within Edgar's consciousness as he dismissed the joys of Down Under, as past tragic circumstances brought to mind Natalie. Natalie, a nice enough person. He enjoyed her company, she was certainly sexually attractive to the eye, clever in her profession, a law court stenographer, both in a relationship where he understood she loved him and he returned this love with the suggestion of a permanent relationship. Until she implied she was considering an abortion for a child not of his making, then the truth came out. Oh, the caustic bitterness when this shocking news came out while he was working on a sad case of child abduction in Sydney. Apparently, she attended a staff party in Melbourne where she was reduced to a drunken stupor and entered into a sexual one-night-stand, regrettably leading to pregnancy. This woman, who he had every intention of marrying, dropped this bombshell, having two-timed him with her boss's married son who stated he had no wish to divorce his wife and as far as he was concerned it was end of story for him and he suggested Edgar took the blame for the pregnancy or she should have an abortion. He said he was a happily married man and in no way would he be contributing or supporting to end a life of one he helped to create. Tragedy then struck. Natalie, by all accounts, threw herself under an express train. Verdict suicide. However, Edgar had other thoughts. He though she was murdered! Perhaps this nagging thought was guilt. The matter required proof which he did not have. Always the question remained with a sense of remorse that perhaps he did not help the unfortunate girl in her trouble. Guilt eats deep into the soul. Understandably, he was so sickened by her deceit, he had no wish to get involved, and so he did nothing. Now he was trying to live with himself. Edgar Heaume also had a guilty secret!

Chapter 53
The night of the dinner

The day of the get together of the Sarres and the family Heaume had dawned with anticipation on Poor Edie's part, not that she was incapable of arrangements for a successful dinner party. Nor the choice of food worried her; she, with Rachel, had made a sensible menu to satisfy all tastes. She was concerned that guests would leave remnants of a meal untouched on the sacred gold-ringed dinner plate, an inheritance of great-grandma Sarre. Edie, a perfectionist, could not abide waste in the past. Not a morsel of the meal must be returned to the kitchen; if any scraps did find its way to the garbage bin, then, to Poor Edie the meal was not a success. Not until the cheese platter and coffee cups were safely in what Rachel named Edie's private domain, hand-washed then stacked in the places which Poor Edie had ordained, could this angel of domesticity relax. She often reminded her mistress that this dinner service had survived three generations. "I don't want it broken by a mechanical robot! My mother, bless her soul, often said 'God gave us hands to use. Lazy hands who stay asleep will never find love.'

Over the years, Rachel learned to distant herself from Edie's idiosyncrasy, knowing, in spite of Edie's outbursts, she was a treasure of a housekeeper when she was in control of her duties; dinner to be served on time after pre-dinner canapés with selected refreshments. But lo and behold if the guests arrived late, the wrath of Hades was fervently uttered from Edie's indignant lips, directed to the culprit saying, "If Miss Sarre is good enough to invite them to eat a meal we prepared, they must understand 'Time is Time.' Meals are served hot, not cold at La Petit Close and at La Gree, or anywhere else if I'm cooking."

Rachel, always alert on these occasions, made sure Edie was out of earshot of her guests while she herself was endeavouring to be decorous. Today was different, most guests knew of Edie's outbursts, thus taking her harsh words in their stride, for it is known Poor Edie has a heart of gold yet a tongue of fire.

By all accounts, the Heaume family are nice people and this is their first visit. Edie, as usual, had preparations under control because this was an evening when Rachel wanted the Heaumes's visit to be a welcome back to the Island. She checked herself and oversaw all the arrangements that both she and Edie had prepared, generally leaving all functions to Edie, but this occasion was different so why this uneasiness? Is it because of Edgar? There is something about his company that affects her. Edgar's presence was certainly not an issue that she considered unpleasant; however, he stirred something within. Is she frightened that he will be asking questions? She is perhaps afraid the topic of John's father will arise and how Eustace Tostivin died, and being queried on the reason why she still used the name of Sarre, not Tostivin if he was John's father, then the most dreaded frightening question, "Who is this Hans Gruber? Why has this so-called German enemy named Hans Gruber had his ashes buried on her land? What hold did he have on the Sarre family? What brought these thoughts to her mind? Is it the curse of the Lihous and Sarres set to bring Edgar Heaume into her life? Is this a form of punishment for the lie uttered ever-after, told on the day Eustace died, accepted with reassurance? It is now, on this day, she will remember the words of Edie's mother, as quoted by Poor Edie who did not have the intelligence to learn the three R,s at school, yet will come out with wisdom when you least expect it? 'Often a lie is squeezed by truth, so that the deceiver, or others, knows not the truth because it became a strangled truth.' A strangled truth united between her Hans Gruber and dear Eustace who was blighted in homosexuality. All have covered the truth with a lie. Over time, these unsettled thoughts surfaced to taunt her. She had learned one lie is a breeding ground for others.

The pendulum of the Paul Naftel grandfather clock swayed to six fifteen, while Poor Edie sat waiting for their guests' arrival on time, six-thirty for the intended visitors. Edie always allowed herself a sitting period before answering the expected door knocks announcing an arrival, for it was not in her nature to rush, believing the often-quoted words of her mother. As a child, Poor Edie rushed at every opportunity. She remembered words told after a reprimand, 'Rushing addles the brain, causing confusion.' Suddenly, awakened from her momentary thoughts, a gentle knocking came on the front door, announcing the arrival of the awaited guests. When eying the clock, hands stated six-thirty. She walked slowly to answer the door after straitening her apron, glancing in the gilt-framed hall mirror, seeing if her now greying hair was not ruffled from domestic duties. Poor Edie took pride in her appearance. She opened the door that could perhaps tell many tales if gifted with speech, and there in the arched porch stood the invited Mr and Mrs Elias Heaume.

"Good evening," greeted Mrs Marie Heaume as she and Elias entered the warmed hallway. It is a cold evening at this time of the year." A tortoise-shell headband adorned her blue-rinsed grey hair, coloured jewels of no value implanted around the hair band, focusing the onlooker to the characteristic features of Marie Heaume, a kindly woman by nature who was dressed in a long, silver lame dress, interspersed with scattered sequins, accompanied by a white fur shoulder stole, much needed in winter. Guernsey could have its fair share of cold weather in January.

Edie nodded, her eyes fixed on the dress, noticing a diamond brooch with impressive sparkle due to the light in the hall. Edie stepped aside for both to enter. Then, with severity on her face, after looking from left to right, she asked in a manner that matched her countenance, "Where is the one who had the punctures?"

Marie Heaume turned to Elias for support as she spoke. "I am afraid Edgar is delayed on an overseas telephone call, apparently from the law firm he worked for in Australia."

Elias nodded as she continued, "Please accept his apologies." Elias, turned to Edie saying in a gentle manner, for he is a man of equable nature, "Edgar, I am sure, will be as quick as possible; these law firms have a habit of ringing at awkward moments. So sorry."

"It is not me he has to say sorry to, it's Miss Sarre. I only hope the dinner is not spoilt. He should have told them to phone back." This lecture to the Heaumes's was their first introduction to

La Petit Close, receiving a taste of Poor Edie's mannerisms which she used if things did not go to plan. Any further conversation regarding the situation was saved as Rachel came to the rescue, dressed in a delicate blue lace full-length gown bought exclusively from haute couture, Mary Tom's, dress premises in St Peter Port's State Arcade. The dress was loose-fitting covering Rachel's mature figure which was devoid of excess fat or plumpness. Her trim body belied her age. In her hair was a small red rose picked earlier from the small garden greenhouse which supplied a variety of flowers during the winter months. Upon her shoulder sat a matching stole on which rested embroidery of small clusters of purple violets. Around her neck hung a locket, the one given many years past, retrieved from its owner who, through the ravage of conflict, had wiped all memories of its existence. Such was the condition of his brain. This precious locket that once encased the photo of herself now held the image of a very special mortal to the now owner. This adornment in silver represented an irreplaceable tryst given in war time, a token of their love, a symbol that never or rarely left the owner's neck, its history secretly stored in the wearer's mind.

"Welcome. So nice of you to venture out in the cold after the heat of Australia. Apparently, Edgar has been delayed? I gathered this after overhearing Edie's rather somewhat unnecessary remarks; I trust you will not take offence!" Rachel spoke stretching out her hand in welcome.

Marie and Elias returned the handshakes, Marie smiling as she spoke. "Most certainly not. Edgar did intimate that your very capable housekeeper on occasions speaks her mind; we perfectly understand. It is a pleasure to be here. By the way, we do have cold days with unsettled weather Down Under!"

Rachel ushered Elias and Marie past the dining room on the way to the lounge, catching sight of the table superbly set for six persons; mixed roses arranged in three blue and white Wedgewood rose-bowls placed in spaces opposite the guests to enjoy their delicate scent. Upon the white tablecloth, the often-admired gold-ringed dinner service, waiting patiently to receive the cook's prepared portions of sheer delight. There were wine glasses along with sparkling, crystal water tumblers with two matching water jugs, ready to receive refreshment of fruit juice, wine, or water. Resting on each end of the oak table was a red three-armed Venetian glass candlestick, each with three lighted candles. Placemats showed old Guernsey scenes, on which was laid silver cutlery for each up-coming course. Also displayed was the infamous silver cruet complete with condiments, scattered amid the table sprays of winter greenery complemented with pink camellias. This whole setting was meticulously positioned with thought by the one and only Poor Edie, who always insisted on white starched napkins. According to her, "Paper ones no earthly use; unhealthy, and crumbled during the meal with a habit of falling to the floor." To which at times Rachel disagreed, not due to the laundering of linen napkins though, her thoughts were for Edie, serviettes other than linen would save time.

Edie would not have a bar of it saying, "Your mother and grandmother always remarked, 'No napkins are better than paper ones!' So, white linen napkins always graced the Sarre's table.

Rachel escorted Marie and Elias to the lounge where Eunice and Nickolas sat to enjoy a pre-dinner martini. As their daughter introduced her parents to the Heaumes, they also accepted the martini offered by Edie.

On the two small walnut occasional tables, carefully displayed on silver platters, was mixed finger-food ready to be sampled pre-dinner; selected with appreciation, eaten randomly by the guests. Edie prided her finger-food often saying, "They whet your appetite. Getting pleasure from whatever comes after."

Eunice was also in formal dress; a pale mint-green taffeta skirt with a black top interspersed with polka dots of a colour to match the skirt. Her hair was held in place by a diamante hair slide which ornamentation featured eight rhinestones catching the light of the fixed electric wall brackets and flickering candles. In no way would they oppose the sparkling of Marie Heaume's diamond brooch displayed on her dress. Both Nickolas and Elias dressed in black evening suits with a red rose pinned on the coat lapel. Each sported a white hankie tucked in the upper coat pocket, a place deemed to hold such article.

Poor Edie interrupted any further conversation, much to Rachel's embarrassment, saying, "He is here, the one with the punctures." Such was her way of speaking!

To which Rachel replied, "Are you referring to Mr Edgar Heaume?"

"Yes, him who had the puncture," replied Edie, unaware of Rachel's correction.

Edgar Heaume entered, also in a black evening suit, and joined the rest of the guests as Poor Edie retreated to the kitchen in preparation of serving dinner after offering him a martini.

"Good evening. Please accept my apologies for arriving late; an important call all the way from Melbourne, Australia. I believe the Sarres have relatives in that great country."

"Yes, but far distant cousins on my father's side, four times removed so they say, whatever that means," answered Rachel. "Due to the war, we have lost touch. The Sarre's history go back a long way in Australia," Rachel laughed as she whispered, "The poor souls travelling in a convict ship, leaving the curse of the Sarres and Lihous behind, a curse which is active to this very day! War does change things with peoples' lives disappearing in different directions." A fleeting memory of the war years occupied her mind as she continued. "Yes, in a different direction. There is no need for apologies Edgar, you are here that is all that matters. I am sure Edie is on tip toes waiting to start. If each of you will kindly link arms with the other's partner we will go into the dining room to sit and to enjoy Edie's efforts."

Edgar smiled as he linked his arm with the host of the evening. Rachel wished she had not suggested the change of partners, for within her mind that uncertain feeling she experienced after Edgar phoned to summon the Royal Automobile Club., an unsettled sensitivity came again to interrupt her thoughts. Oh, she thought, how foolish I am, a grown woman, not an adolescent school girl!

Edgar had no qualms as they linked arms together feeling how lucky he was to be close to this beautiful woman. These thoughts and deeper ones lightened his mind as Edie sounded the brass dinner gong with gusto for in her estimation the dinner would be spoilt due to that man with the puncture.

Chapter 54
The Dinner Party

Rachel linked on Edgar's arm who guided the rest of the guests to their allotted chairs in the warm, cozy dining room. A log fire burned cheerfully, brightly inviting all to banish the January chills. As Edgar later remarked, the weather here in Guernsey was so very different from the heat of Melbourne at this time of year. Taking his place next to Rachel who was at the head of the table, his thoughts returned to the telephone call, wondering why there was such an imperative call from the Australian office. Very little information was given, with instructions to phone the following day. A flight had apparently been booked for Melbourne via Singapore with a short stay in Sydney. He only gleaned the urgency was for details regarding Natalie's tragic death. He also wished to ask further questions. However, at that moment, the Australian caller replaced the phone, much to Edgar's irritation not having been given a return phone number; in a case like this, he hated being left hanging in the dark.

Edgar's mind returned to where he was when he noticed the front of each place card with the name of those who occupied the seat. They were attractive cards with a symbol of Australia's wattle tree and were designed by Rachel. Certainly a woman of initiative. This very thoughtful gesture to welcome them back from a land of unimaginable size, its vastness not comprehended by a Guernsey farm girl. Over the years Rachel had hosted many celebrations here at La Petit Close and at her aunt's place, La Gree. Tonight's dinner was special, but if asked why, she was now at loss to give a true answer. Was the notion of dining at La Petit Close a tormented whim of the curse of the Sarre and Lihou, perhaps to cause a mischief between her and Edgar? 'Oh no, it's just a welcome back invitation,' she thought, banishing the puzzling idea out of her mind. 'Yes, a welcome back, the Heaumes' having left the Islands when Edgar was still a baby.'

Edgar found delight in sitting next to Rachel with the thought that perhaps she may have ideas to further the relationship. He established himself comfortably at the table in a room tastefully furnished, its walls with many photos of the past and present, each positioned chronologically upon the matching neutral-design wallpaper with a cream background. On the far left, noticeably away from the others, was a watercolour of a cottage at La Gree, one of the three buildings on the Lihou's farm. Only Rachel Sarre knew the true reason why, after the occupation, it took time to preserve this delightful cottage in a delicate painting. When the viewer gazed at its innate magnetism, a tinge of sadness clouded the eye, the artist capturing its beauty with a strange spiritual representation of desolation within its portals. If the gifted artist was asked why this was depicted, the answer would be integrated into a lie; her secret must be kept.

Rachel announced the pleasure of having the company of the Heaumes' and that her beloved parents and Aunt Rita and uncle Earnest would join a little later for coffee.

Poor Edie appeared with a chosen red, and a sweet white wine, and proceeded to pour each to the guest's own taste. Edgar noticed Rachel chose a sweet white. A burgundy was his choice. Rachel had previously asked if he would propose the toast and he had stated he felt honoured to do so.

Edgar stood, and with a sense of humour befitting to the occasion, said "Ladies and gentlemen pray silence for the toast," as each raised their glass. "To Rachel Sarre, our beautiful host into whose home we have been warmly welcomed. I also toast Miss Edie, who I understand is the best cook and housekeeper this side of the English Channel. To Miss Edie. May she long stir the pots of good cheer. God bless this house and all who enter. Thank you for your attention." The clinking of glasses united all in spirit.

Edie, after hearing the special personal mention from Edgar bore satisfaction upon her face, maybe thinking, 'That puncture man is not so bad!' It took very little for her looks to change if things or conversation were not to her liking.

Edie served the first course, a soup made from turkey giblets and neck, and then to follow roasted turkey served with cranberry sauce, together with minted peas, baked crispy potatoes, parsnips and carrots, with a helping of Brussels sprouts which Rachel humorously hinted were "Not the sprouts in her grandmother's story of the curse cast by the Longfrie witch." The meal was completed with chestnut stuffing, rich gravy, complementing the yet unserved meal with vegies waiting piping hot in the gold-ringed tureens; there was no half measure with Edie.

As the delicious soup found its way to the guest's mouths Rachel spoke, "I….. No, Edie and I decided to serve a traditional Guernsey Christmas dinner, thinking perhaps our Island's hot roast Christmas festive meal is not cooked in Australia at that time of the year due to its temperature. So, tonight is a Christmas in January for our returning Islanders." Turning to Edgar she asked, "Do I have it wrong?"

Edgar smiled, "No, as we say Down Under, "Good on yer!" To Edgar Heaume at this precise moment Miss Rachel Sarre could do no wrong.

To the onlooker, Poor Edie appeared to be keeping watch over her flock as each one finished the soup with remarks such as 'Congratulations to the cook', giving Poor Edie a sense of pride, smiling to the one she designated the puncture man, offering him a generous selection of carved turkey, complete with cranberry sauce. It seemed Edgar Heaume was back in favour.

The meal progressed with healthy appetites enjoying the serves of Edie's open-handed portions which occupied their plates. Edie later remarked to Rachel when all had left, "I like the man who has his belly full."

To which Rachel smilingly replied, "You are referring to Mr Edgar Heaume?"

"Yes, that's right. Him that had the punctures. You can invite him again; I like a man who enjoys his food."

"Oh Edie, you are impossible." Then silently thought, 'Yes what harm can it do?'

She served the usual tasty, fruity Christmas pudding mixed and stirred with stout ale and a noggin of brandy. All these ingredients were needed to make Poor Edie's special pudding using a family recipe handed down over the years. Edie warned all to look out for the inserted sixpenny pieces that may appear, if lucky, in your portion. Legend has it, 'He or she who finds the first coin will fall in love before the buds of May appear.' The inevitable happened and the so-called lucky coin found its way on Rachel's plate. Edgar was the first to hear the tinkle when the uncovered coin dropped on the plate, for it was he himself who had in jest secretly placed the sixpence on her plate while her eyes were otherwise engaged, giving Edgar the opportunity to announce, "Rachel is the winner," much to everyone's amusement.

She asked as she faced Edgar whose smiles turned to laughter as he pointed to the lucky sixpence. "I wonder who this knight in armor will be. Is he a tall dark stranger who will carry the sixpenny winner away on a camel to a foreign land?" He added, "Whoever he is will surely love you."

For the first time in years, Rachel blushed.

Poor Edie joined the laughter of amused guests as they proceed to pull expensive decorative crackers complete with paper hats, each taking a turn to read riddle mottos, during which time she offered a second helping of what is to her 'Grandma's Christmas Pud' for as a child it was grandma's pudding she remembers.

Later, Elias took an interest in the photos, especially, the aged drawing of La Gree, probing into the history of this impressive watercolour of the cottage, intimating he would offer more information on the subject of La Gree later in the evening, stating, "and La Gree property is well worth the interest."

"Yes, it is a lovely old farmhouse with a dark beginning, as Aunt and uncle Lihou will surely tell you," answered Rachel. I expect they will arrive very shortly to meet and chat over cheese and coffee or be tempted by Edie's Christmas pudding! I invited them to join us for dinner, but unfortunately, they are both connected to a retirement village social committee, even though at the present it is not their residence until retirement. Regrettably, this evening is the home's fund-raising meeting discussing ways and means to swell much-needed funds. Aunt Rita, as President, feels obligated to attend and it is with disappointment they could not dine with us tonight. There will be other occasions when you can enjoy Aunt Rita's company, a born organiser" informed Rachel.

"I am sure both Marie and I will look forward to a further get-together. Thank you for such a superb meal. We envy Edie's cooking skills, yours included Rachel, for such an unexpected evening. I suggested earlier that I may have something interesting to tell your aunt and uncle regarding La Gree, something which happened to an ancestor of the Heaumes' many, many, years ago. Maria darling, I thanked Rachel on our behalf for a wonderful welcome back to Sarnia Cherie after so many years away. Edgar was a young boy when we last came for my father's funeral; life holds sadness when we lose loved ones." Tears welled as Elias spoke.

Rachel clasped his hand saying, "Life has always had a measure of sadness. It can also bring a deep joy after the clouds are lifted if we search with God's helping guidance giving us the right directions, for treasures on earth are not found without searching."

Maria and Elias, their arms outstretched, encircled Rachel. Elias said. "You are a good truthful woman. Our wish is for Edgar to marry a good wife, a person like you. Dear Rachel we both would love grandchildren, eh Maria, but we think it may be too late for such a blessing as he has suffered tragedy leaving him uncertain of direction."

Then she realised what a hypocrite she was. Before John's birth she told the truth, now that truthful woman became a liar. If Elias, a lawyer, had crossed examined her he would never find the truth, a lie had destroyed the truth. Truth, over years, reduced to non-existence regarding John's father.

Conversation ceased as Rachel heard the sound of knocking on the front door, thankful that Aunt Rita and Uncle Earnest had arrived, saving any more discussion with the Heaumes', regarding a suitable partner for Edgar.

Rita and Earnest entered the hall as Rachel bid them, "Welcome" as she opened the door. "Come in out of the cold. Just listen to the howling wind, the rain seems to be coming down in buckets. What a dreadful night to be out."

The late arrivals were not attired in evening dress but clad in suitable winter clothes. They shook their bodies to release any moisture on dampened, almost soaked coats, which they offered to Rachel to hang in the lobby as she enquired how the meeting went.

Rita answered, "As usual at such meetings, a lot of time was spent on unimportant matters, but I suppose as meetings go, good. One good point we did settle, who pays for the new drain, the Home or the States. The States, of course, are being held responsible for that useless alteration to the roadway when their digger caused damage to the drains. The question is can we get the money from them? It could cause a problem! You know the States where money is concerned! Ambrose Sherwill says there will be no holdup; let us hope he is right, money has to be obtained from somewhere. Fortunately, it is not the Home's problem. Anyway Rachel, how did your evening go? Edie on her best behaviour? Are we too early?"

"No, it seems everyone is in good spirits. Ah, here is Edgar.

Edgar, this is Aunt Rita Lihou and Uncle Earnest very special people."

Edgar extended his handshake to both, saying as he did so, "I trust mother will invite you both to our home so we can get to know your part of the family at La Gree. I believe my father has an interesting story to tell you regarding La Gree as you will see!"

Earnest, unspoken until now, said, "Pleased to meet you, Edgar. Let me say, any tale of La Gree would not surprise me - a very interesting property. I don't believe in ghosts but for one exception. I believe ghosts do haunt La Gree. Eh, Rachel, you and Edie have seen them.

Rachel nodded and Edgar laughed.

Suddenly a streak of lightning lit up the room through the heavy, drawn curtains. Such was its power that the electricity failed. Strangely, the two, three armed, Venetian candlesticks at each end of the table diminished without human aid. The air in the room was warm and calm without movement, so why no flames? Crockery rattled, the kettle whistled in the kitchen, the fireside hub howled as its temperature gained momentum.

Poor Edie let out a scream at the mention of ghosts and rushed through the darkened room to the safety of her kitchen domain but to no avail as darkness also reigned there. Peals of thunder roared reducing Poor Edie to sobbing. On such occasions as this, she remembered the tunnel incidence, her mind crossing over thirty years when, as a youngster on that fateful day, encountering what she saw at La Gree, the shock reducing her intelligence. It was after that she was referred as 'Poor Edie' which name would remain all her life. This sorrowful information was passed on to the Heaumes' later.

"Oh, the poor child. Thank God you care for her Rachel," declared Marie.

Meanwhile, the electricity restored itself and the candles were re-lit, this time by human hands.

The evening continued with wine and coffee with a handout of chocolates, a thoughtful gift to Rachel from Edgar. The traumatised Edie retired to bed on Rachel's instruction, Edie insisting the kitchen remained untouched until her return, a request Rachel agreed to, for this was the only way to restore Edie's piece of mind.

As the evening progressed, Rita was anxious to hear the promised tale, for she could tell many herself. Eunice would say, 'That one is best untold. Rita!" For such was her imagination, in some tales contents went unlaundered, Rita oblivious of the word risqué.

Rachel suggested that they all adjourn to the comfort of the lounge then Rita hinted to Elias to tell the tale of past history of La Gree that he had intimated earlier.

Elias Heaume, sitting apparently comfortable in a Queen Ann high-backed chair smoking a cigarette, began his story.

Rachel, a non-smoker, always kept a supply of mixed brands for guests until it became known a few years later of the dangers of nicotine.

Edie, in her inimitable manner unique only to her, often quoted her mother, "If God wanted us to smoke, the good Lord or his son would have attached a chimney to our heads." Oh, the true wisdom of Edie.

Elias began, "I hope this tale will not upset you. What I am about to say is true, or so I am told." As he spoke the Paul Naftel grandfather clock chimed eleven. "My goodness, eleven o'clock, it is way past our bedtime. Perhaps I should, as we say in court, adjourn my story till another time."

A chorus of no's reached his ears. It was then Elias told his tale.

Chapter 55
The Tale

"Over two hundred and fifty years ago, a young girl fresh in the flush of youth lived in the district of Petit Gree. Her father, who loved his only daughter, started to build her a house as a wedding gift for her and her intended husband who also loved her dearly. He was a young man of social standing, an Islander, a distant relative of mine over generations who, they say, worked in London employed in a ship chandler's business, which employment he would relinquish before returning to Guernsey. The bride-to-be had all the things a bride should have including her beautiful wedding dress. The wedding reception was to be held at the yet unfinished La Gree.

On the eve of his departure to his Island home while waiting at the docks in the port of London, there came unexpectedly out of the misty foggy darkness two men of a notorious press gang intent on kidnapping a crew member, one who had no wish to sail on the briny sea with all the rigours thrust upon a jack tar. He was grabbed from behind with a sharpened knife's cold blade drawn uninvitingly across his throat, a throat that in a second could be shedding flowing blood ending the life of a man upon the throes of marriage. If the uttered words of those who crept out of the misty shade were not obeyed, the poor unfortunate man would find the blade imbedded in the veins that give him life; furthermore, after cruelly kneeing him in the groin, they pushed and viciously dragged him to a ship heading for Australia. For this un-wed bridegroom, the nuptial bed cover will remain un-touched. In that fair land beyond the briny, his life would not be his own. The poor bride was left forsaken. It is whispered she haunts La Gree dressed in a white wedding dress, upon her head a flowing veil covering a contorted tear-stained face. In desolation that poor demented soul died broken-hearted.

Nothing more is heard of the bridegroom until after he died a few years later in a drunken stupor, in all probability due to his having no news of the fateful bride. He married into a loveless relationship to a relative of the Corbins, who it is said, have the Sarres as Guernsey relatives. It was noted on his death certificate that evil drink together with deep depression caused his downfall. It is noted he sired children, some dying at birth, others in childhood. I am afraid Edgar, Australia is founded on tragic beginnings."

Elias finished his tale saying what I have told is possibly only half of the story. "Do you know any further information Ernest, are the Corbin's related?"

Rachel listened intently as Elias continued, near to tears as she recalled the summer of 1938 and James Corbin, lovely James. "Oh, that wretched war!"

"Yes Elias, we are related." Silently Rachel remembered her truthful, sunny six months with dear James. Four years later her life changed and the sun faded as foreign footsteps trod her land, gone the Paradise she hoped to retain. "Yes Elias, that bride lives below in the tunnel at La Gree, silent to those above, where she has roamed since fate robbed her of love. Knowing her story, I realise she is a counterpart of me who found love inflamed and provoked, then lost it to the whims of men. That poor lost soul knew the anguish of a bride doomed by fate living in a space that knows no clock."

Marie Elias and Edgar Heaume sat amazed, drinking a refreshing wine as Rachel continued.

Tears formed in her eyes, eyes that had shed so many tears ever since Hans and Eustace died. "Is the complex answer to life that all of us are governed by fate? That phone call you had this evening Edgar, is it fated to what lies ahead? Will some person haunt you for the rest of your life, some past trivial mis-deeds or haunting memories, unseen or heard by those who know you best? Did life evolve or was it created? Are our lives evolved by circumstances? Or alternatively created within our heart and brains in partnership with good and evil? The ghosts that we see, are they a reality or a figment of our imagination? Did Edie and I see the ghosts of the past in the tunnel or did we see what we wanted to see? I leave it to you to decide. Is God a reality or created to control the masses? I once communed and sang to him. Oh, joyous time. Was it ordained that I lost his fellowship by a selfish action to cover a pride, a pride I could not afford to lose. Will I ever be able to sing to him in truth? Must I lose my pride before I can regain my lost fellowship?"

No sooner were the words were spoken than she knew she had said far too much. This was not the time or place for personal dramatics, mindfully asking herself why she had entertained these issues while she was not yet ready to disclose. One thing was certain, Rachel Sarre had created an audience.

Edgar was somewhat taken aback by what Rachel said. He could not help thinking the situation which appeared unexpectedly required analysis before accepting what was proposed. Edgar, as a lawyer, knew he must be in command of all the facts, which, at the moment were negative. He was expected to rush off on a far distant plane trip to Melbourne without fully understanding why the flight was booked for him. A wave of repetitive annoyance lingered regarding the fact that his past employers, without consideration or any knowledge of his now Island lifestyle, saw fit to arrange flights without the courtesy of asking if this would suit any prearranged plans. The whole thing was unjustified, as what more could he tell them since he had already made a statement at Neil's request? Turning his head, his eyes caught Rachel thanking Elias for the La Gree's most interesting account of a past relative. 'Yes Rachel Sarre, you are a bright cookie. You, my dear, are worth more of my attention.' Such were Edgar's thoughts.

The chiming of the hall clock brought to mind that the guests might have overstayed their welcome as Rachel rose at an early hour. They apologised for such a late departure, but received the reply, that on occasions such as this, the farm worker, Charlie Lenfesty, stepped in until Rachael arrived; farms demand commitment and holidays become second-place or non-existent and, luckily for her, her father, when in charge of the farm, passed on a routine which she had managed to adhere to.

Leaving the dying warmth of the log fire, each departed into the cold morning after a most satisfying evening, with a promise

241

that the Sarres together with the Lihous, including Edie, would dine in the near future at La Grande Mare, the Heaumes's residence. Likewise, this house had a history. Previous owners from the Arts and Film world had held all-night parties under the moonlight, naked of clothes or dignity, at times re-acting debaucheries of the Senate in Rome, all performed with strains of music that would turn Handel's hair white overnight. The reverent vicar of the parish complained to the jurists of the court of such goings on, only to discover some of the pillars of the court had joined in the festivities, saying it was only an enactment of the past, just like Shakespearian plays.

Rachel surveyed the rooms as she switched off the lights, making her way to the stairs, reflecting on the past evening; the outcome, good by all accounts, if a little bizarre to say the least.

The Heaumes' were certainly not fazed by the unnatural turn of events of an interlude beyond control, at the conclusion of which Poor Edie would declare, "Not a natural carry-on. The power of darkness had encircled the house and no good will come out of it."

Rachel lay in the warm bed, which Edie in her upset had not neglected to switch on the electric blanket. Her thoughts turned to Edgar, wondering 'what was the full explanation of the telephone call. How long will he be away?' She strangely thought, 'I will miss him. Oh rubbish, you hardly know him,' she thought as she drifted off to sleep.

Chapter 56
Edgar's Australian Journey

The following evening Edgar received the promised telephone call from Anglo Associates, a reputable law firm, whom Edgar had worked for while in Australia during the 1960s. Their main office was situated in Collins Street, Melbourne, a city he had grown to love, but he became disenchanted with officialdom after the death of Natalie and what was involved later regarding the tragedy. He kept his mind open, for he always tried to balance the whole story, like he did in this particular case, as he had done throughout his working life. Unfortunately for him, there seemed to be a cover-up of the facts. He suspected murder, not suicide, but he did not have any positive evidence to be able to point his finger at the culprit. Deep down he was living a life of guilt; if he had accepted the baby as his own she might be alive today.

He loved Natalie to the point of marriage and in some way, he still did love her. She was honest enough to say the pregnancy was implanted by another man, the son of her employers, which apparently happened on a drunken one-night-stand after a staff party in Melbourne when Edgar was stationed in Sydney. Edgar knew the expected baby could in no way be his, so did Natalie, as on the rare occasions he and Natalie gave way to passion, both knew he was fully protected. Edgar at that time was in Sydney briefing a case involving the kidnapping of a child, an upsetting case for Edgar. The prosecution suggested the crime's ransom was paid in traceable money which had been laundered in the offshore Channel Islands. The police's interest in pursuing the case was to produce an outcome to imprison the top dog of a very active crime syndicate. In the course of investigations, Natalie Wilson's name appeared in connection with the top dog, insinuating she knew of the syndicate's various unlawful dealings. If so, murder could not be ruled out with the method being a means for silence as dead women tell no tales. This was the vein of thinking in Edgar's mind knowing that Natalie insisted these claims were untrue.

Edgar's recall to Australia was to substantiate suggested clues in police hands. The police now believed that in some way Edgar could be involved through Natalie's yet unproved involvement. The summons stated that if he did not comply with returning to Australia, there was likelihood of extradition to Melbourne. This was the gravity of the information he received. Edgar was going to comply with what the Australian police required, as he had intended to return temporarily, having some unfinished property settlement to complete. A property he and Natalie had acquired to be their future home when married, which of course with her death would never happen. However, he would still keep the house as an investment having no desire to live in a house that had promised happiness and had turned to a place of grief. The four-bedroom house was in Toorak and was now on a tenant lease to a family who offered a good remuneration in the up-market suburb in fast growing Melbourne with its beautiful parks and spacious gardens - a tribute to the forefathers of early Victoria, leaving space open for all to enjoy a heritage in the future. The skyline over the years was slowly re-etched, as multi-story skyscrapers occupied vacant blocks and demolished older premises – a so-called advancement of the modern world in the liberated Swinging Sixties about to bloom in Australia.

The Heaumes' decided time had come for semi-retirement for Elias. In one way they were sorry to relinquish the open lifestyle of Australia for the Island's open-minded tranquility of their birth. Edgar had joined them on the return to Guernsey

Far above the clouds on his way to Sydney, his thoughts turned to Rachel, who had telephoned before he left, "God speed with a safe journey." He countered with if she is interested, he promised on his return asking her to accompany him on a visit to Sark. He had an uncle who lived on the Island; a bakery owner who, with his wife, had survived the German Occupation. He had holidayed there as a youngster with his parents, gathering enjoyment in the knowledge of this enchanted Island.

Sipping slowly to enjoy a liberal brandy-and-dry, a freebie by the courtesy of Qantas, he flew faraway with the snow-white clouds beneath as he relived his visits in Sark when a blonde curly-top boy. 'Oh how we change,' he thought. Relaxing in his seat, his mind's eye saw the boat from Guernsey approaching Sark, an excited boy who ran from side to side to glimpse the Sark lighthouse perched high on the cliff as foaming white waves brushed against the rocks while the boat proceeded to the harbour. The shrill hissing of the boat's horn announced to the Islanders that another load of holidaymakers would soon be on shore. Slowly, as the captain steered his craft, the harbour came into sight. He arrived at the small Creaux Harbour with the horses and carriages waiting for a hirer. When hired, the driver and passengers would pass through the solid rock tunnel carved through the cliff face many years ago. The clean, fresh breeze encircled their faces, the salt of the sea still lingering on lips. Screeching, scavenging gulls had followed all the way from Guernsey, demanding and circling in hopes of morsels, viciously fighting for who gets it first as they spot the scraps of fodder. Listening to the clip-clop of horses as they traversed the graveled, arduous hill, passing young and not so old who, with effort, were walking slowly to reach the summit which connects to The Avenue, Sark's commercial main street. Thirsty travelers would stop at the intersection eager to refresh throat and tongue in the cool surroundings of the hotel Avail Creaux on Harbour Hill.

Edgar smiles at the thought of Main Street in Australia which would be classified as a wide lane, his thoughts broken when the attractive air-hostess offered another refreshment, thoughts which returned after he declined.

On both sides of this tree-lined avenue were businesses and gift shops or otherwise. Displayed in one jeweler's boutique were rings and other adornments containing the famous Sark stone, purple amethyst. Handmade fine Sark silver and fairy glass jewelry was prudently positioned in the fancy see-through window, all for the purchaser to give as a gift or self-ornamentation. Exploring as you walk along the unspoilt avenue there is much to see for those on a visit. Cycles for hire catch the eye. Bikes are the favourite mode of travel for the locals and visitors to explore the Island, or they may wish to use Shanks's pony to see, as Edgar will verify, the magnificent scenery Sark offers. Cars are forbidden by law on the Island. Another law states, No female dogs allowed to live on the Island permanently, except those belonging to the Seigneur as head of Sarks's feudal Government. This position allows the feudal lord to be an allotted owner of a bitch. Motorised tractors and horse and carts are the only means of transport for heavy goods and chattels. These restrictions help to maintain the tranquilly and peace on an Island trying to preserve their way of life, history and tradition. Tucked between various shops who sell an assortment of daily needs and gifts, Edgar's aunt and uncle's premises came to the fore. When approaching this well-established business, an inviting aroma of newly-baked bread temps one to buy crusty bread and assorted cakes, all laced with a taste like no other. Oh, the joy of spreading the rich, yellow Sark butter on crispy toast!

If Rachel agrees to become his travelling companion, perhaps later a further relationship would develop if she so wishes. Any further thoughts on the subject were extinguished as the pilot announced the weather, altitude and whys and wherefores of the plane.

Chapter 57
Edgar's Australian Story

Back in Guernsey, Rachel busied herself with everyday commitments, expecting the promised phone call from Edgar. He had left London three days ago and by all accounts should have arrived in Sydney. The fourth day arrived without a call, strange. When no word came on the fifth day, she began to worry he may be ill so she decided to phone his parents. On reflection, with second thoughts she decided this may give the wrong impression, encouraging the Heaumes' of thinking of a closer relationship, which may not be the case if Edgar had that idea then forgot it. She has no intention of an intimate understanding. If he was seeking further than a friendship, then he must look in another direction. She will make that clear when he returns. In the meantime, she trusted nothing serious had befallen him.

She had brought up John who became an adored son under a cloud of ongoing lies regarding his fatherhood. He was now living in Switzerland in a property which was a mystery to many why this estate was left to him in a will by Otto Gruber and his wife. To Rachel it was no mystery, as all those years ago when the Grubers visited La Petit Close, Otto had a direct perception of the truth who was John's father, a secret Otto Gruber kept. She also beheld his awareness behind the liar's fold. John, at the moment, had no desire to live at his age-old heritage of La Petit Close, which he would eventually inherit on Rachel's death. John was happily engaged as a teacher at an exclusive co-ed school near Geneva, its remuneration far above what he would receive from La Petit Close. His departure from the Island caused Rachel concern but proud of his achievements as a PhD. Rachel never disclosed at any time who is his father was.

Over the years she had many admirers, some no doubt may have suggested marriage to her but this she ignored, it was Hans or nobody. Oddly, Edgar seemed to bring to the surface feelings forgotten by her. Here was a woman who muted a desire to be co-joined to a man who would want a sexual unity, a bed-fellow who would crave from a woman a natural simulation, a partner who would share intellectual understanding both in mind and body, a man whom she would endeavour to instill spiritual acceptance of her frigidness. Friendship was the only way if Edgar sought her company. Over the passage of time, she burnt her boats in self-illusion. If asked to explain this she could not. Here she was, a middle-aged woman who had wantonly denied sex, who chose remain as such till it became possible to marry the impossible, Hans Gruber. War had deprived her of the sanctity of marriage to the one she loved. This was perhaps a repetition of the ageing spinsters who had loved ones killed in the1914 slaughter of war; women who could never regain the loss of a generation of virile men. They lived on memories of what destiny ordained some considered necessary and cantered their loss by tasting the clove of bitterness, which spittle they spread to neighbours.

This though was not the case with Rachel. In Edgar's presence she felt a gentle warmth from deep down in the innermost brain that had stifled the essence of love to other would-be suitors. Today came the alarming urge to touch his lips with tenderness and consume his body, a prize yet unoffered. These feelings provoked by an un-received promised telephone call. All this reduced Rachel to a state where Poor Edie remarked, "Not getting a fever I hope - there is a lot of chickenpox about with children. Grownups get shingles, very nasty. I remember my poor mother had them all about her chest and face and was covered with calamine lotion; such a sight she looked. I was a child at the time and I got a fright when I saw her. Sure you haven't got a rash? Let me look."

"No Edie, I am alright, just busy, thank you all the same."

"You are not worrying about him with a puncture? Sorry, Mr Edgar I mean. I hope they give him good food in Australia, he has a good appetite. Funny he has not phoned. Poor mum used to say 'a way to a man's heart is through his stomach,' and you fed him well the other night. Edgar will phone in due course."

Edie, it was you who fed him two plates of the main course if you remember, not me!" Then, smiling as she spoke, "So watch out Edie, enough of this nonsense, I've work to do."

Rachel walked away into the garden, the creative garden which her mother had so loving made, a locality sought when unrested in mind and body, a healing spot, the balm of Lebanon. To Eunice, who stated 'each of us in this world when troubled must have a sanctuary to commune with their special God.' A God may be different to hers, hopefully, a god of love. A thin layer of overnight snow lay underfoot, her undisturbed prints quickly viewed by sparrows searching for morsels hidden now by the quickly fallen flakes. The crisp air upon her shoulders summoned for the left-behind cardigan, it's message causing her to make her way quickly to shelter in the small greenhouse, the one her father built prior to his marriage after hearing Eunice jokingly request, "A small greenhouse for my plants, if not, no bride for Nick." Needless to say, Nick started at once for such was his love throughout his marriage to Eunice and for Rachel. Both found a special place in his heart! Nick, a hard-working God-fearing man, who embraced a loving simple faith to the whole of his family. Nick never bigoted other people's faith and repeatedly remarked if drawn into religious conversation, "Other people may travel another road to find Jesus, so be it. However, for the Sarre family, Charles and John Wesley's path is good enough for me!" Once inside she felt the warmth of the controlled radiator installed to nurture delicate out-of-season flora chosen wisely over the years by Eunice, and overseen now by Rachel. These flowers were used solely within La Petite Close, a decor bringing personal charm to this Guernsey icon. As she moistened the roses, her finger pricked on a thorn. A minute trickle of blood matched the deep colour of the blooms, and she thought with Guernsey -inbred superstition, "What has happened? Is this a symbol of his blood, Edgar's blood?" The sky darkened and the snow fell heavily covering her footprints as she returned to the house. Sparrows fluttered away to the shelter of the barn leaving Rachel to return to the perpetual reassurance she had always known at La Petit Close. Thoughts came of long ago when a red insignia of blood lay upon the red-breasted robin that flew into the hay loft on that day, when she wept for the future, weeping again today at the sight of a bloodied finger. "Please God take care of him." This time she prayed not for her enemy whom she loved, this time she prayed for Edgar Heaume, a man she hardly knew. Oh, the curse of the Sarres and Lihous, or is it Cupid's bow?

As she entered the house, its arched portals, its wood-hewn from a tree grown on this land, her land, she eyed the heirlooms, settle and chair, bringing its memories of the Occupation and a tragic day when she vowed this house would never be relinquished for any other home or man.

Entering the hall, Edie's excited voice rang out calling to her mistress, "It's him, you know him with the punc..." on seeing Rachel stopped at "......ture. Mr Edgar!"

"Thank you, Edie," she replied as she hurried to the phone, whether it was hurrying out of the snow or the phone call causing breathlessness, she only knew he was alive and wanting to speak to her. Astonishingly, she was anxious to hear his voice, seeming as if a developing magnetic field was working to attract attraction to each other. This state of affairs Rachel had no yearning to seek, however, in this unexplainable situation she did not, funnily enough, want to relinquish it. "Yes, Rachel speaking," the first words she spoke to Edgar's question after regaining her breath, "how are you. We have been worried due to the fact that no call had been forthcoming. Our only assumption was that illness had kept you from phoning."   Edgar detected concern in her voice. "So sorry my dear, I can only apologise for others' inconsideration, a state of affairs beyond my control. All due to a requirement we were told when I arrived, 'Hush, Hush.' No one was allowed to have contact with the outer world until cleared to do so."

"Oh how terrible, are you sure you are alright. Where are you?" asked a concerned Rachel.

"Yes OK, but tired; only just come out of Customs, a beautiful sunny day here in Melbourne with the temperatures rising to thirty degrees Celsius, a vast difference to Guernsey weather. Enough from me at the moment. How are you and the family?"

asked Edgar. "I will never forget the marvelous evening spent at La Petit Close to welcome us back to the Island."

"It was a pleasure to do so; Edie started to like you. I think it was because you always accepted the second helping she offered." Smiling, she continued, "Since you left snow arrived; January is nearly always cold in sunny Guernsey. 'The north winds do blow and we shall have snow and what will poor robin do then?'" Suddenly, at the mention of a robin, her mind floated to the day she and Hans made love when a robin red-breast flew by. Her voice trembled as she spoke trying not to show emotion when finishing the sentence. "It's a little rhyme I learned when a child."

"Rachel, is everything alright?" asked Edgar as he noticed the change in her voice.

"Yes Edgar, all is well, childhood memories affect my emotions. Silly, here I am a grown woman affected by a child's story."

Edgar did not know that what he heard was a lie, an untruth that covered a greater lie.

"Edgar, I am rude, please forgive me." I interrupted you telling me of the dreadful time you experienced. Please continue."
"Rachel, darling friend, there is nothing to forgive. You can imagine the furore caused to over four hundred passengers including children and older people. All put through this agony because the British Prime Minister and his bodyguards were on the flight quite unknown to us. Only the flight crew knew the identity of the V I Ps, the rest of the passengers had no idea that the VIPs were secreted in the business section of the plane. Unbeknown to us, the Boeing was inadvertently directed to Bahrain by some upstart terrorist organisation."

"Oh Edgar, how worrying. Thank God no one was hurt through this stupidly. Things are certainly upsetting these days."

"In the end the whole thing was a fiasco or hoax, probably an autocratic blunder from an overzealous official in government security, which ending up having to accommodate a mixed bunch of four hundred irate passengers in hotels at the British government's expense with many travelers threatening to sue the British government. Rachel, I must t……."

251

At this point, he was interrupted by Rachel. "Edgar, this phone call is going to cost you a fortune!"

"No worries, I am using the hotel phone. Since they want me here they must pay all my expenses." I am staying at the Hotel Metro in Collins Street near where I worked. You will have no difficulty if you need to call my number (26389 extension 10). Please phone whenever you like. I miss you dear Rachel Sarre." There was no further conversation from Edgar as he replaced the receiver.

Rachel wished a goodbye, saying as she did, reciprocating his words, "I will miss you too!" She stood in the phone's private recess, echoing words that perhaps needed rephrasing as she questioned the sincerity of what she spoke. "I will miss you too. Please keep me informed." What compelled her to utter those words? Why should she miss him and he her? They hardly knew each other!

A loud intermittent crackling on the line offended her ears as she waited for Edgar to continue, then silence, as Melbourne and Guernsey became to each other faraway lands; sound waves neutered any further voiced affection, breaking a bond between two people who had found a new interest in one another!

Poor Edie could not restrain asking Rachel when she returned to the hallway, "He's alive then?"

"Yes Edie, he seems very much alive!"

On Edie's countenance was a broad smile as she nodded her head. She noticed Rachel had a flushed face, causing her to say, "He's given you a fever."

"Yes, maybe he has, Edie - and over the telephone," answered a bemused Rachel as she remembered the fun day spent in his company at the gymkhana before he went away.

Chapter 58
Rachel's and Edgar's Conversation

"Dear Rachel I've grown very fond of your companionship. I sincerely hope it may blossom further," announced Edgar as they sat in Edgar's car returning to La Pettit Close. They had been to the annual horse show in St Peter's parish, an event which took place in a farm paddock of Edgar's cousin, Francoise who, though not a blood relative, obtained this status by Edgar's grandparents' friendship with Francoise's past relatives. This afternoon had come as a surprise to Rachel as Edgar suggested a get-together before the party as he was impatient to see Rachel away from La Pettit Close.

Edgar and Rachel had spent a very pleasant day at the gymkhana in the company of Francoise who introduce them both to his French relatives who had arrived earlier from St Malo. As they journeyed to La Pettit Close, Edgar related tales or legends of Francoise's ancestors, much to Rachel's amusement. Francoise, like the Heaumes,' had only recently returned to the Island. Unbeknown to Edgar at the time, Francoise had, in the past, a certain yearning to marry Rachel, but she had quickly curtailed his enthusiastic impromptu desires. Rachel herself had no romantic interest either in Francoise or Edgar, or ever would. The outcome of this one-sided infatuation led Francoise to leave Guernsey to curb his broken heart full of disappointment. This lead to a spontaneous whim of marrying a high-class French courtesan with a fetish for expensive fashion shoes. However, to coin a phrase, 'Marry in haste, repent at leisure.' This was, unfortunately, the case with poor Francoise; no sooner had the honeymoon bed cooled she, the little hussy, was up and away with a high couture shoemaker who swept this newly-wed bride off her shod feet and into his bed, leaving poor demented Francoise once again with a shattered heart. This broken heart was only repaired when Mother Luck spun the wheels of fortune and made the saddened Francoise a millionaire - a fortune not bequeathed but unbelievably through rearing thoroughbred horses. He was known to quip, "Horses are more dependable than women. At least you can have a good ride on a horse." Such was his sense of humour.

Edgar had warned Rachel that Francoise had some peculiar sayings entwined with vernacular, however, his heart was in the right place. A generous heart of gold, which was vaguely looking for someone with experience to fill the nuptial bed, with the added inducement of sharing his wealth. Maybe in the near future Mother Luck would spin the wheel of love in his direction. In the meantime he was content with his four-footed thoroughbreds while awaiting a two-legged companionship that is not prone to high-class footwear.

The day went well, with both Edgar and Rachel enjoyed seeing the gymkhana performed by Grahame Frome's talented young riders followed by a superb lunch cooked and served French cuisine style by inimitable Francoise. His great-great-great-grandmother, Leonine, had the odious honour of cooking the last meal for those who were executed by guillotine, nothing fancy, but substantial and tasty. Her cooking skills added charm to the French Revolution as she often repeated, "Christ offered a last meal before he went on his way." She likewise was following his footsteps, trying to be a good humane woman with compassion filling their bellies for the final journey. Unbeknown to Citizen Robespierre, a mean man, she included a noggin of cognac as a farewell toast. "I am sure it takes away their feeling of loss, if you know what I mean. It must be awful losing your head and never getting it back. I often wonder how they are recognized in Heaven." Leonine, while in the service of Robespierre, a devious man who nevertheless allowed her a resident apartment in the Bastille, the chamber of horrors, complete with what was considered then a modern kitchen which at times provided certain amenities - fat juicy rats.

Rachel said, "Oh how awful," as Edgar continued.

"Poor Leonine used at times whatever was at hand for a tasty soup. Francs had to be saved for the rebellion and the departure noggins. Many of her recipes were handed down to relatives, which Francoise still used to fit the occasion - minus the rats of course. The story goes that when the influx of work at the Bastille quietened down, and shortage of funds with not enough heads rolling, Leonie thrust the blame on a certain gentleman, The Scarlet Pimpernel. She, ever a resourceful woman then entered a nunnery, but things did not go too well due to nondescript meals lacking in creativity due regrettably to the choice of the appropriate meat at hand. Mother superior sternly but nicely asked if the menu could be more understanding, to which Leonine took umbrage stating, 'What was good for the poor souls exiting this world for the realms of Paradise was good enough for the frustrated souls within these walls.' Hmm.

Needless to say, those words uttered by Leonine did not fare well with Mother Contracepta, who then asked for Leonie's resignation. In spite Leonie married Father Purvis (French by descent meaning provider) who provided the staples at the nunnery. This stopped after his illegal marriage to Leonie, much to the wroth of Mother Contracepta. With his beloved Leonie he sired fourteen children. What more could he or she ask for? When queried about bringing up children, Leonine would say, "I give them the same le petit dejeuner as I served those poor souls on the way to the guillotine, a good healthy soup plus an escargot entree to keep them regular." Luckily for Francoise, his ancestors survived the rigors of her cooking; if not perhaps Françoise would not be here today."

Rachel laughed as she remarked, "Poor Francoise, it is a miracle that he is here with Leonie's menu! Is the story true Edgar?"

"So the story goes," answered Edgar who continued with the saga. "After his marriage Father Purvis was replaced at the convent by aged Father Neroli (Meaning orange blossom). He was nicknamed Butterfly Blossom, as quoted by the secret Rainbow fraternity to which he belonged, a true relative of Aunt Dorothy. According to Mother Contracepta, things were never quite the same since dear Father Purvis left, she admitted saying, "Withdrawing his provisions was a mistake. Only withered blossom now in the nunnery." So, what's in a name?

In respect to Father Neroli, it must be noted that apart from his inadequacies in the nunnery, he was welcomed in the cloisters of the Brothers. 'Meat to one man is poison to another.' Poor Father Neroli was deported for some unwarranted misdeeds, shipped to Devil's Island with strict instructions from the Pope, Not to meddle with sacred parts of the anatomy! However, he succumbed again to the sins of the flesh on that God-forsaken Island, causing the venerable Pope gross dismay so he had the wayward Father Neroli whisked to the Vatican hoping the said Father's indulgences would evaporate in the safety of the Cardinals. Needless to say, this story repeated itself. Dear Father Neroli lived to a ripe old age enjoying what he liked most in life - yes, a tasty soup!

Dear Rachel I've no idea why I told you this nonsense. It simply has nothing to do with my love for you; said perhaps to cool my nervousness."

Rachel smiled as she touched his hand, "My dear Edgar, a delightful story. Thank you. Don't let us spoil the day with your nervousness. Darkness is almost upon us and these country lanes will be unfamiliar to you, my dear friend. La Pettit Close will welcome us with a meal from Edie. I trust not one of Leonie's. (Within her heart she had no wish to hear of his love at this point of time.)

"Rachel Sarre, I love your sense of humour. I also L.....".

"Edgar first turning to the right, La Pettit Close is the next turning on the left. " At this point in time, Rachel Sarre had no idea which turns in life she would take. La Pettit Close's significant house lights came into sight, its warmth beckoned her to a safe haven. She left Edgar Heaume in limbo regarding his unfinished word, awaiting his last word at the dinner party.

Chapter 59
Edgar in Melbourne

Two days passed before Edgar got over jet lag, together with the annoying combination of being unable to contact the outside world. In actual fact, what happened was the British Prime Minster was on his way to avert another Suez crisis which the government believed was about to recur. It was mooted in certain circles that the Prime Minister was in for the chop with a load of accompanying passengers as Edgar later quoted to Rachel, "Yours truly included." Consequently, as it happened, a false direction was given in this serious situation, there was no danger to anyone in this misguided plane. The Prime Minister included.

Edgar walked to police headquarters in Russell Street, where a seemingly unhelpful officer informed him, "You are Mr Edgar Heaume of Guernsey? I see a notice for Mr Edgar Heaume to attend a 3.30 interview this afternoon."

Edgar, when asking for further information regarding his return to Melbourne, was briskly told he would learn why and the seriousness at the forthcoming interview. "Did Sir not have any inkling why, after travelling halfway around the world?"

Before a reply from Edgar could be said, the phone rang and the officer nodded with an impatient finger and pointed to the exit saying, "Good morning Sir! 3.30 pm." End of conversation as far as the law was concerned which left Edgar in a brittle mood.

Edgar proceeded from Russell Street, and made his way to the picturesque French quarter in nearby Collins Street where his ex-firm, Anglo Associates, was situated. He still held a few gold-edge shares, which were floated some years earlier to allow growth in overseas property. This reputable firm where he had practised as a Barrister dealt with many aspects of the law with diverse clients. Anglo Associates prided itself that, as a firm, it was not involved in a personal scandal of any type past or present. The Firm, the name used by staff here and overseas, was started by the present owner's grandfather, a retired judge, long since passed on to an international court way above the bright blue sky. Over the years The Firm continued to make its mark under the leadership of the founder's family. Neil Timpson, his grandson, was the present-day owner with his married son, Cameron, holding the reigns here in Australia and overseas.

When Neil heard of Heaume's intended to return to Guernsey he suggested Edgar open up an offshore subsidiary in the Channel Islands to ease heavy income tax and death duties of the wealthy who resided in England, a beneficial direction of funds and a perfectly legal transaction on these off shore Islands. The idea pleased Edgar and he was considering taking up the option, delaying further commitment until Natalie's sad enquiry was laid to rest. In the past, Edgar had no qualms regarding Anglo Associates, but today he was uneasy regarding any future commitment. If asked why at that moment he would be unable to give an answer. Maybe it was only a gut-feeling through the unsettling experiences that happened during his journey to Australia.

He arrived at the office. The previous receptionist, Pattie, had given her notice due to harassment, or so she said, but this was denied by The Firm, leaving an undercurrent of suspicion. In Edgar's mind, Cameron, the second-in-command, whom Edgar did not particularly like, was the one causing Pattie to be accused of lying, giving the poor girl no option but to resign, the same Cameron who had allegedly impregnated Natalie.

However, when the police took an interest in Natalie's untimely suicide, it was Cameron who threw the innuendo that Edgar knew more, and perhaps was concealing all the facts and that conceivably the girl was murdered. The innuendoes he dispersed gave the police the notion to review the case which originally seemed a straightforward suicide. The question remained, what had caused him to do this, obviously trying to divert enquiries away from himself, since he is the undisclosed father of Natalie's unborn child, a fact only known to Edgar. Natalie had not yet publicly disclosed this fact except to Edgar in her confession of her affair, trusting Edgar with the complete issues. Issues, which up to now he never divulged, acting according to her wishes when she impressed Edgar she did not want to implicate Cameron further, and she would take her part of the blame for what happened on that guilty night. Natalie, this extraordinary woman, believed if she went public this would cause a split in the Timpson's close-knit family, stating also she did not want Edgar to accept the responsibility of a child not of his making. After much thought of what was best for her and the unborn child, she had decided to face the future as a single mother. This was never to be.

If Edgar had offered marriage in her condition, possibly a rift would develop over time regarding the child's parentage. At that moment he was not in a frame of mind for such an agreement, nor was she. This was understood by both parties. Edgar was shocked at the turn of events, with a deep hurt that only time would heal. He now inwardly had a loss of direction regarding his future; perhaps returning to Guernsey with retiring parents would be a balm to a troubled mind! Fate had other ideas.

Cameron Timpson was to play a devious part in this drama, which could save his skin if trouble loomed time would tell.

The new receptionist, Jill, had a fresh complexion which radiated upon her teenage face. Edgar guessed her age between eighteen or nineteen. She seemed to know the running of the office without difficulty, when, after glancing at the appointment pad, she suggested Edgar take a seat as Neil was in a conference with a prior client and that hopefully there would not be a long delay. Would Edgar like tea or coffee while waiting?

Yes, he would, milk plus two sugars please, which Jill produced in record time, complete with a shortbread cookie made by her mother, an excellent cook as far as cakes go. Mother and her second husband, a European and not Jill's father, owned a pastry shop in one of those busy alleyways off Bourke Street. Jill was not shy in making conversation and in the short time of five minutes made sure he had learnt more of Melbourne's unique alleyways than a guided conducted excursion. However, at the conclusion of the whys and wherefores of Melbourne's famous alleyways, she produced a business card proclaiming 'La Petit-Beurre, suppliers of sweet and butter delights to suit exclusive taste!' In her exuberance, she demanded Edgar pay a visit. Life has a peculiar way of directing you to pathways least expected, La Petit-Beurre being no exception.

For Edgar, sitting waiting for Neil to appear, time slowly ticked away as he enjoyed the cookie and over-sweetened coffee, thinking, 'Why do people over-do the sugar?' Silence reigned as Jill conscientiously typed away on legal documentation. Edgar had no inkling of what he would learn in the little shop situated in the busy Alexandra alleyway near Block Place in central Melbourne, a city which in future years would be classed as one of the great cities of the world.

Edgar began to become impatient at Neil's delay and his thoughts turned to Natalie as he sat. It was here in this office he first met her when she came to seek legal advice which he was able to offer in this well-groomed office even if a little clinical in appearance. Gone is the phlegmatic, dispassionate. dark-grained wood panels of a bygone era, preaching that this was a place of law not one of entertainment. This was the site of the beginning of a two-year relationship which bloomed with a prospect of marriage; the unattained goal ending in tragedy. As he sat he suddenly felt a pit of loneliness, a pit that John Bunyan aptly said was a 'slough of despondency.' 'Oh Natalie, why, darling Natalie, Why, Why, Why' etched into his brain as beads of perspiration formed and dripped onto his light summer coat. He rose to escape this hellhole of thoughts, though escape he could not.

Reality brought him back to the present as Jill announced Neil's entrance.

"Good morning Edgar, thanks for coming to throw some light on such a tragic subject."

Neil advanced into his office, followed by Edgar who then sat in what was always alluded as 'The seat of justice,' for on that seat sat clients who either offered truth, lies or fiction to a lawyer who was willing to defend that so-called innocence. Today's client would utter the truth which would be either accepted or rejected. Edgar felt uneasiness as he faced Neil although he had nothing to hide.

"I am afraid I am at loss to know why I have been summoned back to Australia, a situation which I may say was inconvenient both in time and financially."

"Yes I agree, but certain developments have made your presence needed," said Neil in a voice and face denoting a tone of gravity. "Apparently Edgar, you were heard arguing with Natalie with threats being made to her. I am sure such words were only said in the heat of the moment, but the police have to follow up on such information from a reliable witness."

This news came as a shock to Edgar having no recollection of such a threat. "Who has accused me of this?" asked Edgar.

Neil replied, "I am afraid I am not at liberty to divulge that. In the meantime, you are assured that Anglo Assurance will do all in their power to help."

'All in their power to help.' Edgar could not bring himself to comprehend what Neil had implied. What help did he an innocent man need? What other maligned suggestion would be inflicted upon him? Perspiration gave away to a cold clamminess, his blood chilled by thoughts of this place where he had found love, which had now become an execution chamber, a place where his accepted credibility would be challenged. Moist sticky hands searched for a handkerchief unseen, unfound, yet imperative.

The inquisitor Neil passed a few soft dry tissues of colourful design, soon to be clutched, squeezed, impregnated by moisture that anticipated the anguish of fear. Edgar's eyes caught Neil's as he almost snatched the tissues. Neil stood but not alone, as with him was his son, Cameron, who was standing, but then seated himself to enjoy the proceedings that would follow. Cameron came not as a friend, but a bearer of past malicious reflections. Both sat, the lion and his cub waiting to pounce on Edgar's answers and questions, for Edgar is now in 'No Man's Land,' It's soil may consist of lies or truth. An earth without substance with a longing for fertilisation. He alone must survive.

The air became suffocating as he heard what Cameron said, "Please Edgar, this is not a personal wish to implicate you with the police. They asked me about your relationship with Natalie. I could not withhold the conversation which I overheard from my office unknown by you. Unfortunately, that conversation held threats. The police chose to believe you meant harm to the girl you wished to marry. Why harm? I am at loss! You both seemed very much in love. The police discovered that Natalie was pregnant and they suggested that perhaps you wished to rid her of the baby. After further enquiries suspicion was laid that both you and Natalie were connected with the Mafia through money laundering here and overseas, a suggestion which both my father and I find ridiculous."

Neil nodded in agreement saying, "I am sure the police have misinterpreted the situation. Please forgive Cameron if he has caused embarrassment. I am sure there has been a hideous mistake. He only told what he overheard and no more."

"Neil, the whole affair is disgusting" exploded Edgar. "Cameron, what you just said is completely untrue. I have never threatened Natalie, nor is the baby mine as you know perfectly well. How can you imply such a notion? That conversation never took place as such so why say so? Natalie confided in me telling me the whole story of what happened between you both on that night I was in Sydney. And I forgave her. What you have said regarding Natalie and me is libel. If needs be, I shall take it to court. Anglo Associates will have their dirty washing hung in public for all to see."

"Edgar, are you doubting my son's word?" asked Neil.

"No Neil, I am not doubting his word. I go further; he is lying to cover his own failings. Have the decency Cameron to tell your father; it may be better to hear what really happened from you than the police."

Neil stood dazed as Edgar swept past him with no recognition, swung open the door leading into the reception area where Jill was typing. She was about to speak to Edgar as he exited into busy Collins Street, knocking into a second client who was entering, causing Edgar to thump the man off balance with a look of shocked dismay. Edgar continued on his way without apology to the taken-aback would-be client. Such was his haste for escape and ridding himself of the unjust accusations. Once in Collins Street, his eyes glimpsed the building as he turned. He remembered that it was in that office he learnt the bitter truth; honesty will survive.

Natalie told him how much she loved him, how she mistreated his love, revealing to him the exactness of her story, recalling how she had fallen foul of Cameron's advances while he fueled her to a drunken stupor where he sought to validate his illegal passions, giving no thought to the consequences despite Natalie's state of mind. Her non-consent to his behaviour in a court of Law would be classed as rape, with the tragic outcome discovering two months later she was pregnant. She was told or advised, unwisely by Cameron, to have an abortion, or better still, keep her mouth shut and blame Edgar, saying, if he is a gentleman as Edgar is supposed to be, he would marry you! Within Cameron's mind he had scripted the scenario of Edgar's downfall as follows, 'Edgar Heaume will exit from his world of civility to a state where basic instincts ruled jealously. His anger, his refusal to pardon or exonerate her failing, his envy, his bitterness with his uncontrollable words, said to the point of cruelty, murderous words. Yes, murderous words! Edgar's Heaume who loved her now sent her from a state of reason to - in theory - a grave, an act generated by his unforgiving mind in unison with a tongue used which he programmed to destroy her.'

All this was cannily orchestrated by Cameron, a ploy hidden unsurfaced in a mind that denied the truth of his own actions. Truth and lies took on a horrific legitimacy, even authenticity, while he, Cameron Timpson sat in Anglo Associates office to face Edgar and his father. By destroying Edgar's reputation it would bring absolution to his guilty psyche, his sin would be washed, cleaned. Unfortunately, lies, when woven with evil intent cannot be eradicated; the spinner's weave will leave shattered broken threads.

Edgar wept as he trudged towards La Petit Beurre. Perhaps the refreshment would restore his confusion, a disproof of mind that had been associated with a negative response by those who afflicted such. A meandering crowd of pre-teen schoolboys impeded his way to Alexandra Alleyway, where hopefully, the environment of the bakery cafe would lead to a de-classification of the mental state he had been thrust into by a would-be an enemy bent on destroying his creditability. He was yet to face the police at 3.30 pm.

Chapter 60
Appointment in Russell Street

As 3.30pm approached, Edgar stood outside Russell Street police headquarters, a gaunt building somewhat out of character with its neighbours. Nevertheless, it catered for the guilty or innocent who entered the threshold of this well-visited establishment, a place you left on your own accord or were escorted to a section where liberty is denied until resurrected by a magistrate who deemed it fit to issue bail or remand.

Edgar mounted the stairs to the appointment room, a domain he had encountered many times in the course of his work. In that particular area his emotions remained static, but today was different insomuch whatever the relevance of this interview, its outcome would make mockery of the whole affair. The very idea that Natalie worked in company with a top dog syndicate, utter rubbish. In the pit of his stomach resided anger with intermittent apprehension, for he was not fighting justice for himself, but exclusively for Natalie Wilson.

Entering the room, Edgar came face to face with the Chief Superintendent, Cyril Wilson, (unrelated to Natalie), a tall grey-headed six footer. His appearance bore the pallor of a heavy smoker, but maybe Edgar got it wrong. The paleness of his face brought out the deep dark-encircled shadows of his eyes, which features could be the trophy of tragic encounters through his work policing. Poor Edie would remark more wisdom from her dear departed mother. 'Your face and eyes tell the story of your life imprinted with joy or evil.' Cyril Wilson introduced himself shaking Edgar's hand, not a clasp grip but firm.

"Good afternoon Mr Heaume, I do apologize for any inconvenience caused. I can assure you the top brass insisted you travelled back to Australia. As you are probably unaware, this case is classed as top priority; in fact, it has been taken to Federal level insomuch as involving your past lover, Natalie Wilson. The word lover was flippantly said and angered Edgar to the point of saying, "Natalie Wilson was not my lover. Correction please, she was my fiancée. We were on the verge of marriage. My intended wife's character has been smeared with innuendoes of theft and cohorting with underworld criminals. This is why I am here today, not to vindicate myself but to clear Natalie's name of all hints of wrong doing."

Cyril Wilson saw that he had over-stepped his mark in using the word lover, which led him to say, "My apologies for my choice of words. I am afraid by the time this case is brought to justice, many people will be upset. Mr Heaume you are bound by ASIO not to mention any remarks surrounding Miss Wilson's death. They stipulate that as far as you are concerned, she rightly or wrongly in your mind committed suicide. ASIO also states that on no account is the idea of murder to be talked about in any conversation. Do you understand Mr Heaume? Have you got it in your mind that Miss Natalie Wilson died by her own hand. This line of thinking will remain until the criminals in this case are safely in prison. Remember, this is an international crisis so much is at stake. My advice is to go back to Guernsey until you are recalled in the future, which I am sure you will be. They also stated that you must repair the misunderstanding you had yesterday with Anglo Associates. In some way, you must make sure those people know you have had a change of heart regarding Miss Wilson's death and that you consider it was not murder. I understand this is upsetting, but it is imperative for Australia that you follow this course of action. Please excuse my bluntness. If you continue to take the line she was murdered, you too could be a target for elimination. These people will stop at nothing for their own ends. The stakes are high, so go back to the safety of Guernsey. When you have a conversation with Miss Rachel Sarre - yes we know of your friendship," said Cyril Wilson when he noticed the look of surprise on Edgar's face, "you must make up some story that will not upset ASIO. Good luck and good bye. There is nothing else to say on my part or yours.

He quickly hurried Edgar into the rush-hour of busy Russell Street. Confused, dazed, certainly perplexed with life with and amazement at his silence. As a lawyer, he had so much to say yet remained wordless. Yet again he had done nothing for Natalie, remaining unspoken. In his mind the law is bent on injustice at Natalie's expense.

Edgar, much to his better judgement, visited Anglo Associates before he returned to Australia, informing Neil that due to his conversation at Russell Street police station, he now had a different understanding of the situation. He then apologised for his outburst on his former visit. Anglo Associates accepted his change of heart which set him right with ASIO. However, to Edgar Heaume, the imparted words were not his true thoughts. He would still fight for justice for wronged Natalie regardless of ASIO.

Melbourne Tram

Chapter 61
La Petit Beurre

Edgar juggled through the crowded pavement with a mind on things he wished to forget but which surfaced to annoy him. Why, at this time of the year, were there so many people about? The reason eluded him until he noticed a collection of Asian males dressed in their traditional garb carrying multi-coloured banners with painted symbols, images of Chinese culture reflecting China's dynasty. The brightness of the colours transmitted his thoughts to a happy day in Melbourne two years ago when he and Natalie joined the Swanson Street tightly-packed pavement of adults with flag-waving children, amid a mixed bunch of fast-growing cultures, to enjoy the celebration procession The Chinese New Year denoted the year of the Rabbit. He looked and noticed this year had the symbol of the snake, as the seemingly never-ending man-made dragon, serpent-like ambled along Melbourne's thoroughfare with music befitting of the occasion as only the Chinese can produce. Oh, that happy day, never to be repeated, after lust and alcohol evaded his forthcoming happiness to the unhappy position which he was at today. Natalie dead, and him suspected either of murder or Mafia involvement. 'At times the gift of memory is terrifying only to be sweetened by transient optimism.'

The hot summer day at the end of January did not help his frame of mind added to the fact that he was attired in a suit and tie, the latter discarded. No one on a day with temperatures reaching forty degrees would be foolish enough to be dressed as he. However, he had decided on formal dress due to the appointment at Anglo-Associates. Lawyers have a strict regime regarding dress.

As a tram approached he decided to hitch a ride to Block Place which connects to Alexandra Alleyway; the heat was oppressive. He remembered when, as a boy on a visit to Guernsey, his father took him for a ride on the upper deck of a red tram admiring the sea view and Castle Cornet as it proceeded to Bosque Lane where his father visited an old school friend. At that moment he remembered the luscious pears that grew in the friend's garden, pears he never had seen the likes of, or never will again. The memory was brought back vividly after glancing at a sidewalk fruit stall selling their wares to passers-by. It was shortly after the holidays; the tram company closed, signaling no more Guernsey trams much to his disappointment. No more pears. Their holiday visits ended with the death of Grandfather Heaume. The memory of the pears would always remain as a childhood treasure.

In some ways coming back to Australia was a sort of homecoming, as he remembered residing here with the family for ten years, making Melbourne, their home port, a significant life-changing situation which, at the moment, seemed to be happening to him over the last three years. Alexandra Alleyway came in sight and he was thankful to get out of the fast-raising heat. A cool spasmodic circle of air breezed through the alleyway due to electric fans placed at critical places. These modern aides were no match for the unruly heat of the day. Minion slave-workers toiled in a constant war to satisfy man's comfort, a war where these aides need more ferocity to gain relief to those who sat in the alleyway.

Edgar had no difficulty in finding La Petit Beurre due to Jill's instructions. Its window display enticed all and sundry with an assortment of Danish pastries, plain, fruit, and cream cakes, assorted sandwiches, and tucked away in the recess of the window the much sought after shortbreads, their popularity assured - they did not need to be at the fore. Edgar sorted out a table near the entrance and, as luck would have it, above him was a whirling ceiling fan revolving at top speed sending down semi-warm air which was better than the oppressive heat he received on his way to the domain of the shortbreads. He no sooner sat when a young pre-teen school girl inquired of his order, accompanied with a smile that reminded him of Jill. 'Could be a sister?' No, as it turned out she was a cousin. He placed his requirements for a Danish pastry and a coffee latté and the much sought-after shortbreads.

"I was told to order La Petit Beurre shortbreads by a young lady who may be a relative of yours who works in an office in Collins Street."

"You mean my cousin Jill. People say we look alike but I don't think so, she is pretty. My name is Kate. Plain Kate and no nonsense. My friends call me Katy and I don't mind because I love the story and film, *What Katy Did*. Do you know Jill sent a tin of her favourites to the Beatles who replied with a record of their new album? My aunt has a picture of them eating the shortbreads. If you turn around you will see aunt's picture gallery of all those stars who have eaten at La Petit Beurre. I work here school holidays for Aunt Myrtle and Uncle Kurt, a German; a nice uncle, all his family was killed during the war before he met my aunt Myrtle. Aunt has had a sad life too, her first husband was killed in London during the German blitz, and then after the war, she married Uncle Kurt. As my mother says, 'You must let bygones be bygones.'"

"Kate your mother is right; one cannot go through life hating people. You will have to forgive those who wrong you, but sometimes forgiveness is hard," replied Edgar. At that moment he was at loss of how he could forgive Cameron. "I am Edgar Heaume, so nice to meet you and having you cheer me up despite the heat." As he spoke he thought it's not only the heat that I will have to forgive.

"I love my aunt because she says, eat what you like. On one condition: don't be sick, which was silly really. How could I be sick on her yum-yum cakes and homemade chocolates," she laughed as she repeated the order. "I talk too much, or so says my father. I don't take after him, he is very shy. I expect it is due to when as a baby he was kidnapped by a blind lady. She said it was a mistake saying, 'his pram was the same colour as her friend's pram.' How would she know if she was blind? Luckily for me, they got him back or he would not have been my father, would he?"

"I expect not. Sometimes things have a habit of working out right," answered Edgar as Kate went away to fetch the order.

Kurt Muller, the part-owner appeared, his hand outstretched in welcome, and smiling as he announced his name with a slight Teutonic intonation with guttural phrasing which almost gave away the land of his birth, Saxony, eastern Germany. "Please excuse my niece if she has overpowered you in conversation, she sometimes gets carried away."

"No she is delightful, in fact, she is the best thing that has happened to me in days. I've just returned to Australia on sad business, after a terrible journey from my present home in Guernsey in the Channel Islands. Do you know of the Isle of my birth? Edgar Heaume is an old Island name and I answer to it."

As he spoke a look of surprise entered on Kurt's mature, once-handsome face which now carried lines of past anguish, perhaps caused by some great distress in the past encouraged by mother nicotine, a desire of tobacco to ease a mind caught up in the killing of war, the craving long since gone but lingering in the lines of his features. In life we are bonded to the past traumas, Kurt was no exception. Kurt Muller is a good man: husband, stepfather and business man!

"Oh yes, Guernsey is no stranger to me. It was occupied by my birth country during the war. I spent three years on that beautiful Island. The people were peace-loving but loyal to their government, playing a part in resistance which occurred in minor ways, unlike the major sabotage in Europe. The Island was too small for operations of that kind. We knew it was happening to show us that we had trespassed on a land that was independent for over a thousand years. The Islanders had a stubborn nature, to the point of battling to survive with very few amenities. There is a Guernsey saying, 'You can lead a horse to water but you cannot make him drink.' So it was in the Channel Islands during that period."

Now the surprise was on the other foot when Edgar received this reply and stated, "What a small world. I just arrived in Australia and one of the first people I meet has knowledge of Sarnia Cherie. Have you revisited since the war?"

A look of sadness seemed to cloud Kurt Muller's face as Edgar waited for an answer. "My wife wishes to go but I shall not; if she decided to visit it would be without me. I do not wish to relive a terrible happening in my life and see the person who I caused suffering to, even though I did not meet her all those years ago. I fought to forget the time on a cliff top when I shot two men, one a slave worker who was an unknown spy at the time, the other an Islander who only helped the poor man to escape from the terrible conditions these slave workers endured. It was war and killing is a part of a horrifying waste of lives. I was on guard by a gun post when the two appeared. The Islander knew the safe way through the cliff minefield as he was in charge with a permit to collect furze bracken for Island house fuel. Because of this, he helped the slave worker to get to the beach for escape on a fisherman's boat. The young man who I thought was another slave worker turned out to be an Islander who was to be married later that morning and the bride they say was expecting a baby. I was posted to Jersey a few days later so I did not know the outcome. War does terrible things to people. I live with the silent thought every day of my life. I never met the young bride who suffered at my hands."

Edgar noticed Kurt Muller wiped away a tear as he spoke.

"I shall never forget the misery I must have inflicted on Rachel Sarre. I sincerely hope she found forgiveness for me."

It was Edgar's turn to stand by the table in surprise, saying as he did so, "Did you say Rachel Sarre?"

Kurt Muller nodded. "Do you know her?"

Edgar was certainly taken aback by such information, which caused him to say in the heat of the moment, "Yes I do know Rachel," then, with hesitation, "I am going to marry her," adding a rider, "if she will have me." The prospect of marriage was never discussed with Rachel, who at this time accepted a friendship with Edgar which Rachel would probably class as platonic. Perhaps sometime in the future it would grow into a married relationship, but devoid of sex was her thinking. However, unbeknown to her, Edgar desired more; hopefully if would happen after the Natalie issue had been settled, and he was exonerated of all uncertainties leading to her death.

Kurt Muller smiled which momentarily seemed to lessen the anguish lines, saying, "Congratulations. I had to wait a long time before I found a person I could marry. I was only eighteen when I went to war and many friends and the family were killed in the bombing raids. Returning dejected to the house, the family house was now a heap of rubble, no place to live. My country was defeated through the mad ideologue of Hitler, a leader whom could have resurrected Germany as a great fatherland. But no, instead he sent barbaric armies to capture and kill. When I returned, the time I spent in the army left me in guilt, a period when I had no wish to live, uncertain of the future, taking a few years to come out of the fogginess to settle and find a partner. There is no glorification in war or its end product, leaving sores that can erupt and do, leaving scars that hurt at any given time. I know I've been there. I came to Australia and met Jill's mother and some of the sadness faded into the background, but memories of the day I shot Rachel Sarre's intended husband lives on. May she find joy with you at her side. When you talk please do not mention Kurt Muller, the man who changed her life and that of her child!"

Little did Kurt know that it was another of his countrymen, Hans Gruber, who brought about the change.

Edgar said, "Rachel Sarre is a remarkable woman running La Pettit Close farm with the help of a Mr Lenfesty after her father retired. I will be proud but humbled if she accepts to marry me. I am sure she bears you no malice."

Kate came to Edgar's table as Kurt moved to serve another customer to ask if he required more coffee or shortbreads. He refused saying, "Thank you, Katy, your shortbreads are tip top. I will certainly be in for more to be served by a bubbling young lady, Miss Katy, who on this hot day blew my cobwebs away."

Katy laughed, saying as she waved her hands, "Away with your cobwebs! I love the story of a sweet pretty spider and her web. Have you read *Charlotte's Web*," asked Katy. I read a lot, my father calls me a bookworm, however, after reading the story, I do not now eat bacon sandwiches out of respect for the poor pig's feelings. When on holiday once, I saw a black baby pig which the lady kept as a pet because of her children's allergy to dog and cat hair, telling me how domestic pigs are when trained. Pigs are very intelligent animals. Maybe I'II be a vet when I leave school!

School is O K, but I'll miss my friends when I leave. It is sad, sometimes you never see them again."

"I think a nice girl like Katy will never lose her friends," Edgar replied.

"Do you have a pet? Pets are friends especially a dog," Katy smiled as she spoke. I have two white mice! My mother is afraid of mice and frightened that my brother will let them out as he is always up to tricks. My Gran says he is an Australian larrikin. You would like my grandmother, she has arthritis but keeps cheerful. Some old people are grumpy but not Gran, always laughing even though she has a lot of pain. She often says, 'A laugh and an apple a day keeps the doctor away.'

"Both are very good for you," replied Edgar. "Sorry I must go, Katy. I shall come again. Make sure you are on duty, we may visit the zoo since you like animals. I've never seen Melbourne zoo, but only if your mother says it is O K."

"Oh thank you, I am sure she won't mind. I'll tell her you're my friend and a nice man."

"Katy, you saying to your mother that I am a nice man is not enough before she allows you into my company. I will arrange to meet her."

The time Edgar spent with young, energetic Kate gave him new found refreshment of spirit. Unfortunately, he knew he would have to leave La Petit Beurre or Katy would continue to chatter away till after closing time. Much to his regret, he bid a goodbye to La Petit Beurre, an oasis to his concerned mind.

Myrtle and Kurt wished him a happy stay in Australia, but due to customers coming in he did not have a chance to have a conversation with Myrtle. He informed them that his departure was on an unknown date. "Certainly I will return to enjoy coffee and shortbreads."

Kate blew him a kiss as she took an order from an over-fussy, independent, unrepentant elderly lady who insisted she would not sit under the whirling fan as fans induced asthma - which she did not have - nevertheless, at her age she was taking no chances of catching it.

Edgar left the establishment that had taken his mind off, but regrettably not eliminating, his worries ahead. Glancing at his watch he saw that he had several hours before his appointment with the arm of the law. He decided that Myers could be the place to find mementoes of his visit for Rachel and his family on his return journey, if he is not jailed on false, unproved evidence. Perhaps jewelry would be an answer; not a ring that would maybe be jumping the gun. He had noticed a tarnished silver chain around Rachel's neck. What was attached to it, hidden beneath the neckline of her dress he could not observe? This demanded thought; possibly she would welcome a replacement. But no, maybe the stained chain has a significant place in her life with no wish to lay it dormant in a dressing-table drawer that collects once-prized bric-a-brac. He did not know that with her, this refined element of the ground held a pledged vow vowed thirty years past; a replacement would be an act of assault to her, flawing a friendship in the making.

With the facts of the enquiry presented to him, he felt a relief that he was now in command of the answers he would present at his inquisitions. As a Barrister, this innocent man knew the loopholes that he would face and to produce before the court if necessary.

In the forthcoming hours, he planned to visit his property in Toorak making sure all was well, checking if the repairs were carried out on a broken armchair in the dining room. His house was leased furnished and he wanted all his furnishings kept in tip top order. So many owners, as well as tenants, do not seem to bother as long they are usable. But Edgar was not of that category. He guessed knowing Poor Edie would quote from her mother's many proverbs, 'If a thing is worth using, then it must be righted, for a broken article is akin to a broken mind and heart. To be of use it must be healed and restored.'

He purchased a gift for Rachel. Time had flown and been flittered away due to a period of searching for the right keepsake while he did not having the slightest idea what the recipient would enjoy. In desperation, he choose a silk scarf woven in traditional aboriginal colours, a complete turnabout of what he originally thought regarding jewelry. This gift represented heritage and land of a people older than civilisation, a subject matter close to Rachel's heart, and a woman of the land and proud of her heritage and having been inspired by Australian culture since James Corbin's visit when she was in the spring of her life. What Kurt had imparted regarding Rachel left Edgar with an open mind of the whys and wherefores of her existence.

The family gift decision he left till later, allowing himself space to brunch at Pellegrini's in Burke Street, an unpretentious established Espresso bar, serving true Italian cuisine. One could sit at the stooled long bar, or on varnished raw wood forms placed at the undressed wooden kitchen table while waiting. In the rear of the restaurant all is prepared by young Rosa, an effervescent Italian. For appreciative customers, this shop is known worldwide by locals, interstate travelers, stars and cast from nearby theatres. In fact, all the world and his mate dines here at some point, for this restaurant is a Melbourne icon, a venue Edgar will miss when living in Guernsey.

Rosa and Rocco

This was a place dimmed in sadness for him, but today he would enjoy three of his favourites: minestrone soup followed by apple strudel, then an icy, flavoured watermelon granite, hopefully cooling him from the fast escalating temperatures. On entering, a cheer went up from the surprised staff who had remembered he had recently gone overseas so they did not expect to see him back so soon. The welcoming cheers caused the rest of the clientele to turn to observe the commotion, joining in the mood of good spirits, an action showing the ongoing friendliness at Pellegrini's! This friendliness was not only for those who choose repeatedly to sup and dine but to all. The bar wall facing the service counter represented a museum of memories, incorporating knick-knacks of the present pinned with a fastener. Interesting photos were displayed on the adjacent counter's wall. Customers may wonder why three varying unexplained, possibly lost, bank notes are displayed with the collection. Perhaps waiting for someone to claim them from this honest enterprise. The atmosphere of the whole place induces you to understand why this popular restaurant has survived over the years.

Sisio and Rocco

The comings and goings of regulars caused him to remember the times he had there with Natalie after a late night at the office, a period when shadows cast no darkness on what appeared to be Halcyon days of courtship, to be later bludgeoned by an act intertwined with lies and man's primitive, lustful instinct. It was here she poured out the essence of evil perpetrated by one who took advantage of her stupidity of alcohol, ending in tragic circumstances that will encase Edgar's mind forever, a stigma of guilt which he should cast off but cannot, as it was held fast by Natalie's death.

On that hot sunny day he completed his business regarding the repair of the broken chair at the leased house. Thankfully, he will not be required to traverse to the so called Golgotha in Russel Street police station again to be crucified or vindicated of his innocence navigating for justice for Natalie. Also he will now be able to return to Guernsey to face the prospect of marriage.

Chapter 62
Conversation Regarding Marriage

It was on a cold winter's night when Edgar phoned Rachel to ask if he may call that evening, explaining he had something important to ask her so vital that a delay was out of the question.

Rachel said, "By all means do feel free to call; I shall be glad of the company."

"Are you sure Rachel?" answered Edgar. "I have no wish to impose on your time."

Rachel continued, "Edie is away for a few days in Bath sightseeing with my father's cousin, who also is somehow related to my mother. Please do not ask me how; Guernsey people have funny family connections especially with cousins. You may like to join me in a cold duck salad with a red wine; a friend presented me with two bottles from La Loire Valley which I enjoy, loving the subtle bouquet within its taste. I believe Australian wine has caught on in the English market."

"Sounds great," replied Edgar, see you in a half-an-hour, dear Rachel."

As he replaced the phone she was about to ask why the visit was so urgent but the click of the phone told her Edgar was no more on the copper wire to receive her questions. Rachel was anxious to see Edgar after his return to Guernsey. He had briefly phoned from the airport two days before to say he had arrived but with no word of the results of his visit to Australia. Edgar's visit to that far country had caused her concern so the very fact he was back in Guernsey was a relief. The Melbourne trip seemed finalized, then, on second thoughts, perhaps not, since he needed to see her urgently so he may have to return. These mixed thoughts caused her to be on tenterhooks with regard of knowing the best or worse of his Melbourne encounter. In the meantime she busied herself preparing a duck salad in which she would use a special dressing which had become a favourite for such occasions. It was originally one of Edie's exclusive gems even though she was too shy to pass on her recipes remembering what her mother quoted. 'Beware of those who meddle the taste for self-gratification.'

Edgar arrived poste-haste. He knocked on the guardian angel knocker, a knocker he would use innumerable times if tonight's conversation does not go well. He proceeded to open the door and entered announcing he had arrived.

Rachel eyed the clock with surprise seeing he made the journey from his house in just twenty minutes and wondered why the speed when a telephone call would have sufficed? However, she was glad an effort had been made to see her at short notice; strangely she had missed his absence over his weeks away, even though they had spoken over the phone while in Australia. She was now bemused as he had taken the liberty over time to address her as 'Darling Rachel' with tonight as no exception.

"Darling, may I come in?"

Rachel replied as he leaned forward to embrace her kissing her right cheek when she appeared from the kitchen, "Of course Edgar, you do not have to ask or knock, you are always welcome. Do join me in the kitchen massacring the duck which I cooked this morning! My only hope, is it tender? Ducks require slow cooking according to Edie who has great success with ducks topped with her piquant orange sauce. I trust duck is on your menu Edgar, if not the Forest Hotel will be the port of call, from what I've heard an a-la–carte, tiptop menu. Edie is superb at producing juicy meat; ducks can be very dry if not cooked slowly but I am afraid I rather rushed this poor thing seeing I also had a doctor's appointment."

The mention of the word doctor shocked Edgar when he appeared in the kitchen. "Darling Rachel, if you are unwell I would not have bothered you. What did the doctor say? Nothing serious I trust. What can I do to help?" Taking the knife he preceded to complete the pre-massacre of the duck, for such was his concern for Rachel's health.

Rachel smiled, "No Edgar, the well bucket got caught on the side of the well as I tried to release the wretched thing, the result being I slipped slightly, spraining my ankle. A stupid thing to do. The doctor suggested painkillers which I loathe to take, but will. It is nothing serious, Edgar dear, only a nuisance. I will survive and Leale's workman will fix it before I break an arm. Now tell me what is so important when you should be resting to get over jet lag?"

Edgar started to fuss over the duck without knowing where to start until Rachel stated, "Please Edgar, I am perfectly capable of seeing to the duck. I'll pop it into the fridge. Sit and have a wine while telling me your news. I see you have brought a bottle of Champagne so this must be a special occasion."

Edgar replied smiling, "Well darling it all depends on your answer to what I ask." If yes, then I'll be the happiest man in Guernsey, no in the Channel Islands! However, before I explain the drama, here is a souvenir of a lonely trip Down Under; I was at a loss what to buy until I spied it in Myers, an iconic store in Melbourne. I knew you are a lady of the land whose interest in the culture of our beautiful Australia, which interest I believe started with the cousin whom you held dear, James Corbin." He could tell he had made the right choice by the look in her eyes as she unwrapped the neatly-packed gift.

"Oh thank you, it is beautiful, I shall treasure it displaying it with your love, kissing him in an embrace, an embrace he wished would last forever! She said again, "Thank you Edgar," as she wondered in her mind if the unsaid question was what she feared, marriage. Rachel had stifled any thoughts that invaded her mind over the period of their friendship regarding this subject. Her intuition told her a proposal would be eventually asked, but inwardly she knew she would have to give a negative response. Unfortunately, her answer for Edgar will not be yes, as their fate had been sealed many years ago. In no way did she want to hurt this good man's feelings. She knew in her heart, in different circumstances maybe it could have a positive outcome for she had a muted love for Edgar Heaume, a love she could only express in words of companionship, a love as with James Corbin and Eustace which could only be displayed in sisterly friendship. A negative outcome to his question could be classed as one of the many tragic states of affairs of war, seemingly as in the 1914-1918 bloodbath when unmarried spinsters could not replace a love of the one lost in battle. These virginal ladies ended up carrying a torch for the rest of their lives as no suitor was found, or wanted them. Many of them became embittered in character for life.

Edgar turned as he asked for an bottle opener. After receiving one from Rachel who was still admiring her gift, he asked, "May I sample this recommended red from La Loire?"

"Be my guest. Let's find a comfy chair in the other room. In her mind, troubled heartfelt thoughts had returned. "You will find the glasses in the top left-hand kitchen cupboard. No dear, the top left-hand shelves," repeated Rachel.

"Sorry darling, replied Edgar. Have you noticed men seem to have trouble defining left and right when in other people's houses? I do!"

To which Rachel replied, "Aunt Rita always states, men do not listen, concentrating on other things when they should be listening to their wives. Uncle Ernie replies, "Yes Rita, but just look in history, the trouble in the world through men listening to their wives."

Edgar took Rachel's arm as they proceeded to the dining room, both smiling as they left the kitchen complete with wine and glasses, exonerating for the moment the duck salad in the safety of the fridge to be consumed after Edgar's important news. The smile on Rachel's face covered the anxiety in her mind as they sat drinking the flavours of the La Loire valley.

"Dear Rachel, I suppose you are wondering why the haste to see you tonight at such short notice - so here goes, I shan't bore you with all the details. Firstly, I desired your company; the absence was more than I want to admit. Never shall I travel again without the woman I love, a person who has borne fortitude over the years, including her intended husband's death on their wedding day, a stamina shown all her life Darling Rachel Sarre, please excuse this un-romantic proclamation of love. Rachel dear, I am asking you to become my wife. If you can find a way in your heart to accept, you will make me a man who has been blessed with a countless love, more than all the stars in the sky. Forgive me if I sound a romantic teenager who has unforgivably arrived at your door without even a bouquet of red roses which I understand is the traditional custom of one in love. Nevertheless, I give you the loving roses from my heart. I could not possibly postpone the question another hour. Over time, my affection in friendship for a straightforward candid lady has turned to love.

Hearing the sincerely spoken words of his love, she inwardly recalled the night of the dinner party when she sensed the outcome of their friendship would be marriage and knew this evening would end up upsetting for dear Edgar. Why is it that every male friendship she ever had ends in a negative sphere, its bubble breaking in shattered irrepairable pieces leaving desolate hurt? She knew the answer but turned away to dwell in the negative. She had made a vow which could not reside in the light of love for another suitor. Once again, is this the dreaded curse of the Sarres and Lihous? Does this mean this friendship is disguised in a semblance of love which was unreciprocated on her part? It was nevertheless sincere, and dwelt in an alleyway of lingering twilight friendship. Her love for a would-be suitor shall never arise to glow as the one she had for Hans Gruber! Will the words she will offer mean an end to friendship?

In Edgar's present state concerning the idea of marriage this must be voidable, annulled, stopped, ended, then steering clear of any further heartbreak, two lives lodging in shadow land, of disappointment with very little hope of a sunlight resurrection, both lives destined to loneliness unless a magical transformation happens

The departure of Natalie from life with the indented word suicide a recurring subject matter which would never be removed from the recess of Edgars mind Edgar's only hope is finding a healing love that will absolve the guilt. However this love will not be granted from one who also has the stain of guilt within, namely herself.

Rachel sipped the wine as she sat in anticipation on the red cushion sofa, her thoughts elsewhere of how she will reply when asked the presumed question of marriage. In her mind she had no wish to comply with his request, or causing unhappiness. His worth certainly deserves a wife who will give him more than she is capable of, a wife with no hang ups from the past.

"Dear Rachel, I know this may come as a shocking surprise to you as we are both beyond teenagers. However, I know my love is not fickle, it is not a crucible heated for a moment then cooled. It is a love from the heart for a person who, with dignity, has weathered many storms in life. One such causing you anguish on your wedding day. This information I unintentionally gleaned while in Melbourne from a person who believed he wiped away your happiness on the day he shot your loved one during the course of duty, a soldier in this Occupied beautiful Island. Kurt, a baker by trade, by all accounts a good man caught up in war on this Island, the act of shooting two men in Guernsey while on sentry duty leaving him with a guilt complex, a consciousness of that night remaining with him for the rest of his life, or until he seeks your forgiveness. Rachel Darling, wars leave a septic scarred mind, outwardly seemingly healed, but festered, gangrenous, hidden or secreted in the recess of a soul which is only too ready to erupt unpleasant memories, as one dwells in a well of loneliness, an infected well destroying human credibility, poisoning the desire to continue or communicate on life's journey, an extraordinary enduring action regardless of race or colour."

Edgar had certainly stirred her emotions co-joined with fear, a fear going deeper on what he had learned in Melbourne, dreading what will be unwrapped in Guernsey tonight. These thoughts glimpsed in her mind as she sipped the flavours of La Loire: has her secret been betrayed by some unknown in Melbourne, perhaps by this un-known Kurt? She spoke in a voice upsetting to Edgar ears, "I feel honoured at your proposal of marriage, also humbled that you chose me to fulfil the place in your heart which Natalie filled, a person and place you hold dear which cannot be allotted to others. This location belongs to one whom you deeply loved, a saintly area held in memory for all time, an independent region given only once. I also hold such a place which cannot be given to another, even if I so wished. My life took a different turning than yours, holding complications that I cannot disclose. I lived in fear, in fear of truth and its consequences. I, Rachel Sarre, raised in a

Christian home with loving parents, denounced my faith by sinning in the eyes of God. I gave my body to a man who deeply loved me and I him; bore his child, my son, born of a fornicator in the principles of Christianity. On the day my intended husband Eustace died, I lived a lie. Lying to my mother, to my father. I lied of my son's birthright, I lied to dear Eustace's family regarding John as their grandson, lied to carry on the name of Tostivin for my son. After the first untruth I uttered, said to save humiliation, it gathered more and more issues as time went by, until in the end I believed them; the original lie turned a truthful women into a compulsive liar.

So you see Edgar Heaume, I weathered the storm with lies, nothing dignified in that. You would not want a woman such as me as a wife, even if I agreed. However, there is more to the story of Rachel Sarre. I am a woman perhaps cursed by the curse of the Sarres and Lihous. One day, maybe I'll have the courage to tell the truth of what happened over twenty years ago. Until then my dear friend, keep what I've told you in your heart, it is for you alone. I pledged my love long go to a man who also loved me. He died but my vow lived on never to be broken. We were to be married in life after the war but this was not to be. I had learned, when reading as a young girl, that in a faraway country, women who lost their husband in death smeared their body with his ashes, a ritual from a pagan country to bond them forever in life and death. This I did also in secrecy. Dear Edgar, you now see what kind of woman you asked to marry. In this life, I cannot share a bed or enjoy the pleasure of a man. I have become a self-inflicted frigid woman. Dear Eustace accepted the situation that both of us had secrets to be hidden."

As she continued tears fell from her eyes, tears that Edgar wished he could absolve. He also was overcome by the words Rachel had spoken. He gently said, "Please Darling, no more. You are too distressed to continue. I know what heartaches are, to lose your loved one especially on your wedding day. Kurt told me some details and that you were expecting an unborn baby; a terrible thing to happen on such a day. Kurt seeks your forgiveness. Poor Eustace, never given time to hold his son in his arms, never to see the first steps that his child would take. The poor man missed so much, and you my dear Rachel, having to accept a great deal during the occupation with so little in return. So tragic. You deserve happiness; let me give it to you."

Please forgive me Edgar, this is the first time I have opened my heart to anyone. All the emotions of the past flooded back assertively, waiting in the background for the opportunity to be exposed, deviously shredding the guilt that has encircled my life instead of facing the wrongs I inflected over years. My dear Edgar, only half the story has reached your ears, the rest may be told at a future time."

The repetitive ringing of the telephone ended any further conversation. As Rachel answered Edgar heard her voice saying, "Yes, Rachel Sarre speaking. Yes, Edgar has mentioned you; unfortunately, we never met at the time! Yes, I understand why you are phoning all the way from Australia. Yes, Kurt Edgar told me of your guilt. No of course not. Yes, it was war time and it was not your fault you doing your duty! Yes Kurt, war is horrible, causing us to think and do things contrary to our nature. I do appreciate what you felt. I sympathize with what you experienced. Yes, at the time I knew hate. Circumstances changed my way of thinking. I hopefully learned how to forgive, forgetting the hurt. Yes, Kurt it is hard."

Suddenly the phone died interrupting the call. Kurt's voice melted into the oblivion absorbed in silence.

Rachel waited; no return call arrived that evening leaving Kurt's guilt unresolved awaiting absolution.

Edgar ventured into the telephone recess as Rachel replaced the receiver. She wept as Edgar's arms outstretched to hold her tightly in an embrace. He wanted to stay forever.

On that evening nothing was resolved; the duck remained in the fridge mutilated, awaiting the salad trimmings as two people bared their souls. Perchance in different circumstances, Rachel Sarre would have relinquished the past, but La Petitt Close held the reins tighter than ever.

During the coming years many changes were wrought in Rachel's life. Edgar unwisely pursued justice for Natalie, but as always, evil reigns to swallow the innocent.

Chapter 63
Letter to Rachel.

La Gree Close, Switzerland
June 10th 1974

Dearest Mother,

This letter, as you will see, is sent from a repentant son who should have confided earlier the genuine sincere reason why I left our beloved Island to live in Switzerland. Please note the address of my house; the original name was changed to a combination of the two farms in Guernsey which brought me much happiness although sometimes tinged with indelible sadness through your sorrow. I say repentant because, over time I did not share your anguish of the past. I suppose you could say in reflection my head was in deep sand for what was going on in your life. At this time I offer no excuses for all that. I have been going through a phase battling with mixed emotions, which, as a child, I did not fully comprehend; the outcome of irrational thinking instilling hate over the loss of my father. I now realise that this feeling should not have surfaced. In using the word 'hate' flippantly people must fully understand the meaning and the consequences of such a word before it leaves their tongue. Valid hate relinquished growth in my mind bent on vengeance for the loss of my said father, Eustace Tostivin. A child needs a mother and father. I used to hate because unlike other kids I myself was denied the father who was alive and caring. Because of this loss, someone had to be blamed. My way was hatred.

You my darling mother bore burdens which you never disclosed, living an existence where you dreaded any conversation when the questions could turn to our immediate family when seeking information surrounding my birth; fortunately those close to you accepted what you told them. During those previous years you kept the secret of your love for a man not at that particular moment eligible for marriage.

War has a habit of dividing people in numerous ways which, in your case happened, bringing a tense chapter into your life when your empathy began a shedding of the tears of guilt on a daily basis, when constantly in the fear of a slip of the tongue exposing a very private era of your life, a period which in some ways you should have shared the burden; the involvement of partaking of the sorrow with someone else may have shared the load you carried. However if you had disclosed who my father is, then Grandma and grandpa Tostivin and Sarres would not have a grandson to carry on their name. God bless them my beloved grandparents. This undisclosed secret you chose to conceal bestowed such joy in this belief that Eustace Tostivin was and is my father.

As I've already written it was during my young years as you will probably remember I hated Germans with the notion that one of their soldiers killed my father. I now understand it is not only German soldiers who shoot a father, our soldiers too deny some child of their father in the brutal act of war. What Eustace, a brave man, chose to give you in friendship and marriage these generous actions proving him capable of an obvious and unselfish love; he loved you so much. Dear mother. I would certainly have been proud to know him, accepting him as my natural father. My hatred flared even more when Herr and Frau Gruber brought their son Hans, unknown to me as my father at that time to die in Guernsey. This brought a loathing burning with ignorance to the fore against Germans. After I witnessed your untiring and loving care given to whom I now know, this scarred unhealed person has his blood running in my veins, a period in time when I did not realise I am part of him. It was not until Edgar mentioned his chance meeting with Kurt in Australia, plus the inscription on Hans's grave at La Pettit Close, Hans Gruber 1958. The Chimes of our love will never cease. Rachel. Combined with the Gruber inheritance I fitted the final piece of the jigsaw.

Time cooled my critical way of thinking, diminishing my irrational detestation of hate, seeing the broken body of a human being unable to move or talk and relying on you for survival, devoid of all communication in every sense of the word. I then comprehended the pure unselfish love you offered to a soul who had nothing to give in return or, was it a case of him being there was that enough gratitude and thanks? Only you can answer.

Understanding came after realisation that we all are capable of killing someone's father, son or husband etc. in the brutal act of war. After the conflict, each side must wash away the blood stains showing no bitterness, for during hostilities terrible things happen; it is in mans' nature and it will be until man shows universal love. A love that understands mans' foibles, his weakness and quirks, forgiving without animosity. Each culture has to find its way into an accepted love devoid of all brutality and greed. I carried my acrimony for too long, my attitude brought silent despondency in your already troubled existence, through my obtuse behaviour when a child.

Dearest mother, in truth I now understand I am Hans Gruber's son, so I must return to the land of his birth claiming my father's inheritance, an act I do in respect of Otto Gruber, his father and his mother Maria, she who cradled my head as a child in her belief I was Hans's son.

In doing this, I am leaving my beloved Sofia, your treasured grandchild, to claim La Pettit Close when the time arrives, for I am not the rightful heir. I am the grandson of the Grubers', the son of Hans Gruber, the posthumous husband in word of Rachel Sarre, my dearest unselfish mother. Please my darling take care of your health you are so precious.

May God bless you in his forgiveness, for each one of us is capable of falling by the wayside.

Your ever loving son, John Gruber-Tostivin. XXX

Rachel Sarre never received this letter which was delivered after her death; discarded, lost, misplaced or stolen. She never knew if her son John knew the real truth regarding the circumstances of his birth. Maybe the delayed letter was postponed through a curse of the Sarres and Lihous. Who knows? Funny things happen in Guernsey.

Chapter 64
Who Knows?

With the book launch of After The Chimes Are Silent over, a happy but tired Rachel took it upon herself to visit where Hans lay. It was her custom to visit his grave at some time during the day. The grave was situated underneath the boughs of a matured English Oak planted many years ago. Nearby stood a wooden garden seat which she purchased at Leale's after deciding his would be an ideal sanctuary for private thoughts when she visited the memorial stone of Hans, a place to commune in prayer and spiritual conversation. As she sat on this bench on this special day, suddenly she felt a sharp pain in her arm and chest, causing her to say, "Don't worry Hans, it's been a busy day; I tend to forget my age; pains come and go. She smiled as she leaned over to touch the white stone on which is engraved: 'Hans Gruber 1958. The chimes of our love will never die.'

Over the past, these pains subsided quickly but unfortunately today they lingered, however, she was determined not to worry on such a beautiful day. "Yes, darling, I've put to rest those lies I uttered after dear Eustace died. Now our love story can be told in our dear granddaughter's book. Yes, Hans, Sofia is your granddaughter too! Yes, darling, our love story is revealed after so many years. I can now breathe the free air of absolution. Our son John will read that Hans is his father. Yes darling, your son, our son! Forgive me dear, I never told him and he never asked because he accepted Eustace as his father. Oh, I was so wrong. He is a good son living far away in your home. Excuse me dear, I am having a little trouble breathing but it will pass. These annoyances will go, there's work to be done, even though my share of the work on the farm is now meagre."

During the warm quietness of the evening as she sat, a pure white dove alighted upon the white marble memorial stone, unusual, for normally it is red-breasted robins that nest in the matured oak tree, at intervals taking the liberty to peck at this precious headstone. Rachel stretched out her hand to caress this seemingly tame creature. Its cooing broke the silence and it appeared to be without fear. They say white doves are the symbol of peace. Rachel received the peace. She was aware that the past guilt she carried was a corrosive wounding, scarring her heart and mind. Now, tranquility dwelt within, perhaps through instinct, feeling that each day the clock of life was ticking rapidly away. A gentle breeze rustled the grass at her feet. As she listened, her imagination gave the impression that the collection of meadow bluebells was echoing chimes playing a bell-like ringing which seemed to match those of the town church. When a child, she sat with grandma Mary in happiness to listen to those bells. Oh, such wonderful days.

Turning to where Hans lay in the solemnity of the grave she softly whispered, "Those chimes will never be silent in our heart when we lay together my darling." The dove cooed as the sun disappeared, replaced by a leisurely silvery moon enthroned with a galaxy of twinkling stars which ascended to light the twilight darkness. Rachel sat there, feeling once again a sharp pain in her chest causing her to draw uneven breaths. She said, "Hans, don't leave me, stay near my darling."

As the seconds ticked away, to Rachel Sarre earth was no more for she now continued her journey to immortality devoid of fear; her face showed a contented smile. As the swelling mist cleared, her searching eyes found Hans Gruber waiting, the same Hans she first knew at La Gree, his arms impatiently waiting to enfold his Rachel. As she walked towards him, a white dove flew by. She then knew it was Spring again bringing a message of love with a peace that passed all understanding. For in God's mercy all is forgiven; she received pardon by the telling of her story for she had read in God's good book. 'By admitting your sins you will receive the grace of God and dwell in his house forever!' For both, this would be a new chapter, for on this evening she now truly belonged to Hans and him to her. Time had now caught up for them. The pure white dove cooed as it flew away, leaving the peace it bestowed, for God is no man's debtor.

Chapter 65
The Way Ahead

For those who have taken an interesting pathway at La Pettit Close which leads through the part owned by the National Trust, there is a meadow which is a diverted shortcut to La Gouffe. This land was given as a gift from the bequest of the estate of Rachel Sarre, for it was her wish that this meadow be held in trust for all time. In Spring the meadow is fringed by hundreds of bluebells. As you walk, you come upon the aged oak, one that is favoured by red-breasted robins to build their nests. Under its spreading boughs, you'll notice a carved wooden seat which has a story, for it was on this hallowed seat Sofia embraced her grandmother in death. No Sofia, not death, for it is upon this place of rest Rachel found life! You will perceive the white marble memorial stone, a replacement one of many years. Engraved upon its surface in simple gold lettering are the words:

'Hans Gruber deceased 1958. Rachel Sarre deceased 2010, posthumous beloved wife of Hans Gruber and treasured mother of John Gruber Tostivin.

The chimes of our love will never cease.

Treasured memories of Edgar Heaume deceased, devoted friend of Rachel Sarre, unjustifiably killed by persons unknown as he sought justice.'

James Corbin Australian relative killed in active service1945!

The above earned a special place in Rachel Sarre heart.

Sofia had included Edgar Heaume's name on the stone for he deserved a mention. Sofia knew if things had been different her grandmother would have become, Rachel Heaume.

Eustace Tostivin is buried in the family vault at the Forest cemetery with the inscription: 'Beloved bridegroom to be of Rachel Sarre. Father of John his posthumous son.

Dear Eustace, may you find peace as you dwell in God's house, Rachel.'

If you believe in folklore you will hear the chiming of bells, perhaps wedding bells pronouncing someone is getting married in Heaven, or so they say. On occasion, a robin red-breast can often be seen perched on this special memorial denoting it is Spring again. Those who know Rachel's and Hans's story will surely believe that 'Marriages are made in Heaven.' For tradition has it, all love stories must have a happy ending - or so they say.

THE END

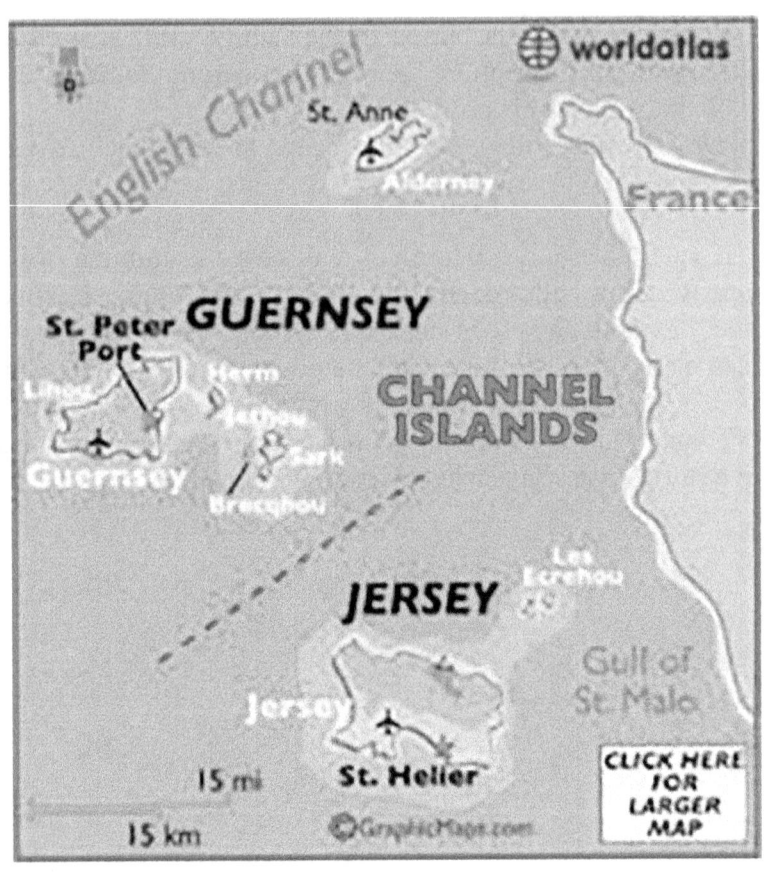

POOR EDIE'S RECIPES
WHICH SHE HAS KINDLY SHARED

These were originally passed on by her grandmother who wished those who came after her to carry on their ancestor's eating habits in her memory. Listed are favourites at both residences, La Pettit Close and La Gree.

She has a set of rules:

Rule 1   Don't skimp, a good cook never goes for cheapness.
Rule 2   Keep to her instructions, shortcuts spell disaster.
Rule 3   Cooking is a love marriage from cook to eater! An act of marriage which can easily be divorced by an inattentive cook so stay alert for perfect bliss.

Make sure the way to their hearts is through their taste buds not their stomach!
Oh the wisdom of Poor Edie.

It is a custom to place a sliver coin into the mixture before boiling; a coin to bring luck to whomever finds the coin in their portion of this yummy pudding.

Serve pudding with brandy sauce or homemade custard sauce or Poor Edie's special Orange and lemon delight.

Conger Eel Soup

1kilo of head and tail of Conger eel cleaned and washed
1litre water
1 pig's trotter
3 leaks -green top can be included
2 cups of green minted peas fresh (if unavailable frozen)
1bunch of fresh asparagus

2 small bunches of chopped chives
Half a cup parsley and thyme
2 bay leaves
1 cup of cumin
1 crushed red spicy pepper with a Bouquet Garnie in a small muslin
bag
1 litre of milk
1 tub of sour cream
1 litre of water

In a large pan add pig's trotter and chopped conger.
Add herbs with salt and pepper.
Cover and simmer for 1 hour, then strain through a course strainer.
Return liquid to pan with chopped leaks, peas and asparagus
Bring to boil and simmer for 30minutes, stirring occasionally.

Add milk and bring to the boil.
Add cornflour to thicken if desired.
Serve with chopped celery leaves with sprinkled Parmesan cheese.
Save fish for homemade patties.

Conger Patties

Put 4 cups of saved eel in basin
Add 1 tablespoon of malt vinegar, salt and pepper
2 cups of rolled oats
1 teaspoon of mixed herbs
1 dessert spoon chopped parsley
1 finely grated carrot
1 clove of garlic

Mix all together and bind with two well-beaten eggs
Shape into patties
Cover in breadcrumbs
And deep fry 'till golden brown.

Guernsey soused Mackerel with crab cutlets.

This recipe it is said was a favourite of Victor Hugo.

Choose six fresh mackerel cleaned, gutted and filleted, heads included.
Place in oven dish
Add 2 tablespoons of olive oil
Add salt and pepper.

Place in oven temperature set at 180 Celsius
Par-cook for 6 minutes turning over twice.
Remove from oven
Cover with malt vinegar to which has been added a grated lemon, a pinch of paprika, and 2 bay leaves
Cover and marinate for 2 hrs. while preparing crab cutlets.

Crab cutlets

Shell two Chancre crabs saving claws
Transfer crab meat to a medium sized basin
Pepper and salt to taste
Add half a teaspoon of mixed fresh herbs finely chopped
Rind of a grated lemon
Squeeze lemon juice after grating
1 dessert spoon of homemade mayonnaise or a top grade from exclusive delicatessen
(Only top ingredients in Poor Edie's recipes)
Two fresh eggs well hand-beaten. (Note Poor Edie states hand beaten.)
Liberal amount of finely chopped parsley with a tablespoon of fresh mint

Half a basin of homemade bread crumbs buttered and lightly fried in best Guernsey butter if possible
Three large firmly- mashed potatoes. (Poor Edie preferred the red variety - fresh not stored.)
Mash potatoes with cream and Guernsey butter to a firm consistently

All ingredients are folded slowly into crab meat except crumbs, and then transferred into a shallow buttered baking dish.
Top with the prepared buttered crumbs
Place in an oven at 180 degrees.
Cook 15 minutes or until crumbs are golden brown and crispy.
Serve on a platter with crab claws, asparagus, green peas, carrots, lemon slices to garnish on a separate platter, or if required a mixed salad.
Both dishes can be served with french-fried chips.

Gache Melee

¾ lb. plain flour
One and a half lbs. of Granny Smith apples, peeled, cored, and sliced
1 grated lemon rind
1 teaspoon nutmeg
1 teaspoon cinnamon
250 grams Guernsey butter
350 grams Demerara sugar. Save a little to sprinkle
4 fresh eggs.

Chop the moist apples slowly into the flour
Add lemon rind with its juice and spices
Mix together and set aside for three and a half hours. This allows flour to soak up the juices.
Cream butter and sugar
Slowly fold in beaten eggs
Combine all ingredients.

Grease square baking tin
Spread mixture with a little nutmeg over top with Demerara sugar
Heat oven to 170 C
Bake for one and a half hours till top is golden and crisp.
Cut in squares when cooked and serve with thickened cream.

Guernsey Bean Jar

500 grams dried haricot beans
1 pig's trotter
1 meaty marrow bone
500 grads chopped topside steak or eye fillet
400 grams butter beans
200 grams Lima beans
1 chopped onion
2 carrots in small pieces
4 teaspoons thyme
3 sprigs rosemary
1 beef stock cube
Salt and pepper to taste - not to be added until last hour of cooking.

Soak beans covered in water for 24 hours.
Cook in earthenware casserole dish in oven or a slow cooker for
twenty-four hours.
Make sure the contents do not run dry.
Remove bones after cooking making sure beans are cooked.

Poor Edie remarks, "Rushing the cooking is a waste of heat and
time, leaving the taste to linger in the pot never to be enjoyed.

Poor Edie's Grandmother's Christmas Pudding

240 grams self-raising flour (not plain).
1 teaspoon of mixed spice
Rind of a grated lemon, save juice of lemon

1 tablespoon orange marmalade
1 teaspoon mixed spice
3 cooking apples very finely grated to be rubbed into flour till mixture becomes as one.
Leave to stand for three hours with 2 teaspoons of brewer's yeast and 12ounces of finely shredded suet.
Make sure bowl is placed in warm area
After which you add fruit that had been soaked in brandy overnight:
12 pitted prunes in brandy
4 cup currants
4 cups sultanas
4 cups raisins
1 cup mixed peel
2 cups chopped glace cherries.

When fruit is well-mixed, stir in 3 large cups of fresh white breadcrumbs with 1 cup of chopped blanched almonds
Add 2 well-beaten fresh eggs
Then slowly add Guinness to make the mixture a thick dropping consistency.
Poor Edie quotes, "Always use a wooden spoon to stir mixture."
Add lemon juice
Add more flour if mixture too thin
Keep stirring until mixture is well combined.

Make a wish as you stir. Poor Edie adds, "A wish does no harm, but expect disappointment if a young girl expects marriage for she must first stir the heart of the man of her interest."

Transfer mixture to greased pudding bowls
Cover with greaseproof paper
Tie tightly with string.
Place in a roomy saucepan to allow you to lift out basin after cooking.

Half fill with hot water making sure the level is only half way up on the pudding basin so as not to allow water to enter uncooked pudding.

Bring to the boil
Cook for five hours or longer according to the size.
Every so often top up water. Pudding must be kept boiling.
Poor Edie says, "Extra boiling does no harm as long as the water level is maintained."
She also says she does not accept the blame if the cookery is not up to standard, the fault is not in the recipe; blame rests with the cook's lack of love in preparation.
Poor Edie also states, "Patience is required if you are worth your salt as a cook.

Orange and lemon delight.

1 jar orange marmalade (Seville oranges)
1 jar lemon curd.
(Both homemade if possible).
Half a cup of slivered almonds finely chopped
1 small wine glass of Tia-Maria
1 sherry glass of Mascot
Mix marmalade and curd, Tia Maria and Muscat, in a blender till smooth. Add more spirits if necessary
Heat on stove
Serve hot over pudding with almonds.

Poor Edie states this sauce is suitable for any boiled sweet pudding.
Poor Edie's tip for those who believe in folklore, "Don't stir or make the pudding on a Friday night for that's the time the lady on the broomstick casts spells, so beware you don't chance a spell to spoil your efforts.

Happy cooking

Sequel to

Islands of Sunshine and Shadow – 2013

www.ingramcontent.com/pod-product-compliance
Lightning Source LLC
Chambersburg PA
CBHW071853020726
47502CB00003B/732